D1006785

a field guide for

heartbreakers

a novel by
KRISTEN TRACY

HYPERION
New York

First Edition
1 3 5 7 9 10 8 6 4 2
V567-9638-5 060 2010
Printed in the United States of America

This book is set in 11.5-point Palatino.
Designed by Joann Hill

Library of Congress Cataloging-in-Publication Data

Tracy, Kristen, 1972–
    A field guide for heartbreakers / Kristen Tracy. — 1st ed.
        p. cm.
    Summary: When seventeen-year-old high school students Veronica and
Dessy go to Prague to attend a summer writer's program for college students,
they experience romance, conflicts, and, ultimately, the strengthening of their
friendship.
    ISBN-13: 978-1-4231-2718-5
    ISBN-10: 1-4231-2718-8
[1. Dating (Social customs)—Fiction. 2. Friendship—Fiction. 3. Roommates—
Fiction. 4. Prague (Czech Republic)—Fiction.] I. Title.
    PZ7.T68295Fi 2010
    [Fic]—dc22
                        2009040378

Reinforced binding
Visit www.hyperionteens.com

SUSTAINABLE FORESTRY INITIATIVE

Certified Fiber
Sourcing
www.sfiprogram.org

THIS LABEL APPLIES TO TEXT STOCK

For Al Young and Stuart Dybek —
my Prague mentors

Chapter One

"*Is that dust?*" Veronica asked, reaching inside my giant duffel bag and running her finger along its flat bottom. She removed her hand and stared at her index finger's powdery white tip.

I turned back to my notebook and my story. My protagonist had just entered a truck stop bathroom, and I was searching for the perfect adjective to describe the wash basin: *graffitied.* "My mom used it to carry supplies to her master baking class," I said. "It's probably flour."

Veronica picked the bag up, hoisted it above her head, and then threw it onto my bedroom floor. A white cloud escaped from the bag in one giant puff.

"You'll look like a drug mule," she said. "Let's go to the mall. You're going to want something with wheels, trust me."

And I did.

We were leaving for Prague in six days. And it wasn't going to be a small stay. We'd be gone a month, attending a writing workshop led by Veronica's famous literary mom, for school credit. Unlike Veronica, who'd spent much of last summer in Rome, I rarely voyaged anywhere. A senior in high school, I still hadn't managed to leave the Midwest.

As soon as we were strapped in, Veronica threw her

car in reverse and peeled out onto the road. Lakeland Parkway spread its uninspiring gray mass out in front of us, and we rolled along on top of it. Small swatches of greenery stuck to its asphalt borders, while a sad plastic grocery bag blew like a tumbleweed across the scene.

"What are you thinking about?" Veronica asked.

"Fulmars," I said.

"Is that a fruit?"

"No. They're seabirds. They mistake plastic bags for food and they eat them and die."

"Gross. Near the mall?"

I shook my head. "Mainly on beaches in the Netherlands."

Veronica pulled to a stop at a red light and exhaled a frustrated breath. "You're not lying to your inner self right now, are you?"

She adjusted her rearview mirror with one hand and reclined her seat back a few inches with the other.

"I don't think so," I said. But that wasn't entirely true. It had been almost a month since the dumping. And even though I tried hard not to think about him, when darkness came, or long periods of silence, I became consumed by memories of my first love. Hamilton Stacks.

"It's pretty common in the early stages of heartbreak for the dumpee to fixate on the dumper, and concoct all these crazy scenarios about how the two of you are going to reunite. Under streetlamps. On park benches. Riding bareback on the beach."

"Do you mean on horses?" I asked.

The light turned green and Veronica slammed on the gas. Then she steered the car off the road into a bank parking lot. "Listen, Dessy." She turned to me stiffly, as if she were going to deliver the worst news of my life. "Normally I don't interfere with people and their heartbreak process, but I feel like I'm being asked to deliver an important message to you."

"From Hamilton?" I asked.

"No, that creep is dead to me. Mess with my friends and it's over." She spit on her fingertips and wiped them on her jeans, I guess to communicate her "overness." "This message is being sent from an entirely different power." She scooped my hands up into hers. Then she dragged them onto her lap. "I know that you love Hamilton. You went through a lot of important milestones with each other. You picked buckshot out of that owl together. And his was the first man-stick you ever saw—"

I pulled my hands back and held them up, making the universal sign for "stop."

"I never saw Hamilton's man-stick," I said. "I've never seen anybody's man-stick."

"Are you serious? My god, you dated for a year. I swear you said you'd touched it the night of the big power outage!"

"No. It was too dark to see anything clearly, Veronica. I touched it through his jeans. How is this related to the message?"

"Yeah, okay, listen. I know that you love Hamilton. And his was the first man-stick you ever touched *through his jeans*, but there's no way on God's green earth that he's ever going to change his mind about this."

"Maybe you're right," I said.

Veronica exhaled dramatically and ran her fingers through her thick brown hair over and over, until the gesture released crackles of static electricity.

"Hamilton is on his way to college. He's entering a whole new league."

I didn't say anything. I didn't like to think of Hamilton leaving the state of Ohio without me. It made our future (which, even though I refused to admit it publicly, I still held out considerable hope for) seem kaput.

"Seriously, Dessy. You know me. I'm a total optimist, but Hamilton is very decisive. He wears that stupid T-shirt that says 'UNWAVERING.' And he's the only person I know who's declared himself a vegan and then stayed one. Not even cheese or bacon pulled him to his senses. And those two foods generally doom any vegan. He's made up his mind on this one."

I hated it when Veronica latched on to something with total certainty. She pulled back onto the road.

"I don't think his T-shirt is *stupid*," I said. I crossed my legs at my ankles and looked out the passenger window at the fast-moving, blurry scenery. So far it had been a rainy summer. The fields were as green as a crayon. And it was hot. According to Veronica's mom, the weather in Prague would be warm and sunny. She said that during the peak of the day, some women carried small umbrellas to shield themselves from the sun's damaging rays. I wanted to see that. In fact, I wanted to buy an umbrella and try walking down the streets like one of those women. The person I planned to be in Prague wasn't the person I was in Ohio.

Seagulls squawked overhead, and I closed my eyes. Fowl always drove my mind right to Hamilton. It was, in fact, Hamilton's personal essay on his lifelong interest in the woodland duck that had helped land him an acceptance to Dartmouth *and* a scholarship.

"You're still thinking about him, aren't you?" Veronica said as she shifted into a faster gear.

"Maybe," I said.

Veronica turned on the radio, and an old Madonna song pumped loudly through the speakers, electrifying the fine blond hairs on my thighs.

"He's gone, Dessy. It's like a wise, psychotic woman once said on Fox News: The only way to secure a man permanently is to lock him up in a trunk in your basement."

"Don't be stupid," I said. "You're not taking any of this seriously. We're talking about my heart, Veronica. *My heart.*"

Veronica sped around a slow-moving Focus, honking as she passed, and ignoring my comment altogether.

"Sometimes I feel like I'm going a completely different speed than the rest of the planet," she said. "Like me and cheetahs are the only ones who are moving fast enough to enjoy anything." She rolled down her window and flung her arm into the wind. Damp summer air raced around me.

"You're nothing like a cheetah," I said.

"Of course I am," she said. "Look at my hair. It's wild!"

She shook her brown locks from side to side. They swam around her thin shoulders and smacked against the low roof. The car swerved right.

"Jealous?" she asked, looking at me.

I was, and she knew it. I flicked her two times on the thigh. My hair was too fine and too blond to amount to the seductive mass I longed for. Fate and genetics had determined I'd have short, barely shoulder-length hair.

"Watch the road," I said.

Veronica flipped her head straight. "I might have even been a cheetah in a past life."

"I doubt it. Veronica, you're nothing like a cheetah," I repeated.

"Look at you," Veronica said. "You take one lousy course in zoology and you think you're an animal genius."

"It was two courses. I took a year."

When Veronica hijacked the conversation, which was often, I tried not to take it personally. Her attention span wasn't all that stellar.

"So how am I unlike a cheetah?"

"I'm really supposed to answer that?" I asked.

"Well, don't bother with anatomical differences. I know I don't have a tail."

"Okay. You're not like a cheetah, because it's a vulnerable species. Out of all the big cats, it is the least able to adapt to new environments."

"Sometimes new environments suck," she said.

"Also, cheetahs are difficult to breed in captivity."

"So? I probably wouldn't be so good at breeding in captivity either. Having to do it on a cement floor with all those zookeepers gawking at me." Veronica laughed and honked the horn for no reason. Then she roared like a lion.

"Well, unlike other big cats, the cheetah can purr as it inhales, but it can't roar," I said.

"Okay. You got me. That's one way I'm not like a cheetah. But I was watching a show on Animal Planet and it said that female cheetahs in the Serengeti are sexually promiscuous and often have cubs with lots of different males."

"You've been dating Boz for two years," I said. "And you've never cheated."

Veronica may have been a zealous flirt, but we both knew that Boz was her anchor.

"I know. I know. But I've got that potential."

"To be a cheater?"

"To roam." At a stoplight, Veronica uncapped her lip gloss and smeared on such a generous coat that it made her mouth look wet. "Dessy"—she squeezed my thigh hard, clamping down on my femur with tourniquet-like pressure—"any molecule of time you spend thinking about Hamilton Stacks is a total waste of your life that you'll never get back." She released her grip. Her hand left bright red finger marks on my skin.

"Time isn't measured in molecules," I said.

"Fine. My point is that his molecules have divorced themselves from your molecules, and you need to build a whole new future with another man's molecules."

I swallowed three times until the lump went down. "When did you start referring to our dating pool as men? We're seventeen. They're guys," I said.

"Oh, Dessy, we're not going to waste our time on *guys* in Prague," Veronica said. "We're looking for *men*."

The moment she said this, I knew that finding a man wasn't the solution. It's like suggesting to somebody who just lost her beloved tabby that she should go out and track down a Siberian tiger.

"The downside is that, unlike male cheetahs, female cheetahs are solitary and tend to avoid each other."

"Veronica, you're nothing like a cheetah. We've been friends since seventh grade. That's not exactly living alone."

"You're the only *real* female friend I have."

I mulled this over. "Cheetahs can be taught to fetch," I said.

"I could fetch."

"Yeah, but you wouldn't like it."

"Who's to say?"

"You're insane."

"I don't think I'm insane. Look at me. I have every-thing. You. Boz. Great hair. Wicked-strong fingernails." She tapped her index finger energetically against the dashboard. "And my Audi. I've got it all. I'm totally thrilled to be alive." She punched me in the arm.

"I'm happy too," I said. "Sort of."

"Dessy, you need a man."

"Whatever."

Veronica jerked her car into a parking stall, sloppily taking up two spots. "Dessy Gherkin, unbuckle your seat belt. It's time to recycle your heart."

Chapter Two

"This looks like a keeper," I said, tilting a practical-looking bag onto its rear wheels and giving it a pull.

"That looks like accountant luggage," Veronica said. She turned and walked deeper into the forest of multi-colored bags.

"So no black at all?" I examined a dark gray bag that I thought could pass for non-black.

Veronica lifted a yellow suitcase over her head and then set it on the floor.

"That looks like a flotation device," I said.

"I agree." And she moved on.

For this trip, Veronica had already purchased three new pairs of butt-lifting jeans, two short skirts, multiple tops spanning a wide range of decency, flip-flops for our dorm shower, walking sandals designed for uneven terrain, dancing sandals designed for guy-populated terrain, and a reversible tote for carrying water and other essentials. But so far she hadn't shown any interest in the writing part of our trip.

"So have you even started writing your story?" I asked. "Veronica?"

She'd disappeared. I spoke louder. "We can't show up unprepared."

The fact that we had been accepted into the program

at all had been a minor miracle. It was affiliated with Northwestern University, and Veronica's mom had been asked to lead a workshop. This news had upset Veronica considerably because she had no intention of spending the month of July in Columbus with her grandparents. So she determined to go to Prague too. And take me with her. Behind my back she'd assembled two applications and sent them in one envelope on the day of the deadline. For a writing sample she'd submitted a collaborative essay we'd written during metal shop, about the myriad ways a girl could die in the class. "Metal Shop: Fifty-four Ways a Girl Could Go."

Taking shop had also been Veronica's idea. She liked the potential guy–girl ratio; neither of us had contemplated the reality of working with sheet metal, automotive parts, or metal inert gas welders. We wrote the essay as a way to tune out our industrial surroundings.

But then the acceptance letter from Northwestern arrived, and Veronica showed up at my house to break the good news: we'd each been awarded a spot in the competitive July Prague Writers' Conference.

There was one caveat. Veronica had applied for the nonfiction section taught by the celebrated American memoirist Amy Allen. Instead we'd been placed in her mother's class, Short Fiction. Veronica wrote a charming e-mail to the dean, but it was no use. Mrs. Knox received her roster two weeks later, and there we were.

While Mrs. Knox was quite impressed, she wasn't exactly thrilled. Neither was Veronica. But I didn't mind. I thought she could teach me a lot. And I was overjoyed when she agreed to let us go.

Veronica's mom wasn't like my mom. Tabitha Knox was famous. She'd been nominated for the National Book Award twice, and writing conferences often asked her to teach. Mainly she wrote short stories. I'd only read one, in her second collection, *Unlikely Dogs*. It involved a three-legged German shepherd that commits arson. His name was Twix.

I spotted Veronica crouching beside an upright purple suitcase.

"What are you doing?"

"Measuring. We need to be able to fit inside our bags."

I looked down at her, but she was completely focused on her measurements. Then I asked the obvious question: "Why?"

"Because I plan on having real fun!"

"Inside your suitcase?"

Veronica knocked over the suitcase and continued looking. "Listen, I don't intend to play by the rules," she said. "We're going to be the youngest people there. I can predict right now that there's going to be a ton of sneaking around. Therefore, we need to be able to fit inside our suitcases. Because that's the ultimate sneak. Trust me. It's how Boz sneaked me into his bedroom three times this spring."

Boz and Veronica had a very exciting relationship. It was what I would call tumultuous. Except mostly the tumult seemed like fun. Separate, those two were already fearless. But together they had no inhibitions whatsoever, like nobody had ever clued them in on the fact that they were mortal. You could see it in the way they danced. And swam. And assembled sandwiches. And downhill skied.

It was just like Veronica to think of something as crazy as sneaking around in luggage.

I rejoined her beside a mound of bright bags.

"So who'll be pulling us around?" I asked. "That could turn dangerous. Some crazy person could run off with us. We need to make sure we can unzip ourselves from the inside."

"How lame," Veronica said. "That totally deflates the thrill."

Veronica accused me of deflating the thrill on a fairly regular basis. But deep down, I suspected she appreciated my foot-dragging nature. It's as if I operated as her second conscience—the one that was fully functioning.

"I'm not magician's-assistant bendable, like you. I'm five foot seven." (Veronica was five foot three, which gave her a clear advantage in terms of making herself suitcase-size.) "I was thinking about something more like this." I pointed to a medium-size green case.

"Why do you want to limit our options before we even go? The world is our clam," she said.

"Oyster," I corrected.

Veronica licked her finger and stuck it in the air, to notify me that I'd scored a point. Then she continued her search. It reminded me of the way she shopped for bras. She firmly believed that there was a perfect bra out there somewhere, made specifically for her cup size, back shape, and skin sensitivity. She referred to it as her "soul bra." Those shopping expeditions always lasted for hours. I was starting to worry that Veronica believed there was such a thing as "soul luggage."

"Look! Look!" Veronica's voice was urgent but quiet.

Even though her personality showed signs of volatility, she was an extremely task-oriented person. I watched her energetically shove an orange suitcase off a gigantic red one.

"This one. This is my bag," she said.

It looked like you could fit three goats in it.

"And here's another one," she said, pointing to an even larger red suitcase. "We're set."

I walked over and took the second red bag by its handle.

"I know what you're thinking," Veronica said. "And

you're right. I'll climb in and give this baby a test run."

She unzipped her bag as normally as you would a pair of jeans. Then she tipped the bag on its back and climbed inside. I watched her thin, flexible body curl itself into the shape of the letter *U*. Then she tucked her head down. She fit. She even had room to flex her feet.

"Zip me," she said.

In the spirit of friendship, I leaned over and yanked the zipper around the bag's perimeter as fast as I could.

"Ouch! You got some of my hair," Veronica said. "In the future, you need to watch for that."

"I'm leaving two inches unzipped near your feet," I said. "So if something happens to me, you'll be able to force your way out. Do you have enough oxygen?"

"Plenty," came her muffled response.

As I hoisted the suitcase upright, extended the handle, and tugged Veronica into the fine jewelry section, I felt a certain excitement tumble through me. I liked having a friend who was so into risk-taking. Because without Veronica, I'm pretty sure I wouldn't have had nearly the amount of fun that I'd already had in life, especially over the last two years.

"Take me to hair care products," Veronica said.

I turned the corner and steered her through the dregs of the season's swimsuits. Pineapples near crotches. Papayas pasted right over boob areas. I only made it a few feet before I saw something incredibly disturbing.

"There's people from school here!" I said.

"Guys?" Veronica asked.

"No. Suzanne Mack, Raquel Cesar, and Gloria Fitz."

They were a trio of snobby, thin brunettes with asymmetrical haircuts. I might have expected to bump into them at the Ann Taylor store in Tower City Center, but crossing paths with them in this JC Penney took me by complete surprise.

I pulled the handle forward, tilting the bag into its roll position, and could feel the full weight of Veronica fall into my right hand. It made my forearm burn.

I felt like running. What if these three asked about Hamilton? It was too soon for me to discuss it. I was an open wound that hadn't begun to scab over yet. If they asked one question, I was certain I'd bleed all over them. So I shoved my pain into a deep pocket somewhere and forced myself to look happy. Maybe they didn't even know about me and Hamilton. How fast does breakup gossip spread in Parma during summer? Then again, how pathetic would I look if I pretended not to know about the demise of my own relationship?

I waved. "I'm buying a suitcase for Prague," I said.

Suzanne, Raquel, and Gloria all abandoned the rounders of cotton shirts they were fingering and walked toward me.

"It's big," Suzanne said. "Are you taking a lot of shoes?"

"Well, I'll be gone for a month!" I replied. "We leave in a week!"

"Prague sounds cool," Suzanne said. "Lots of supermodels come from there."

"I didn't know that," I said.

"They're very angular people," Raquel said.

"Yeah," said Gloria. "It's the bones that make the face." As she spoke, she tilted her head, making her earrings swim in the air. They looked like silver mallards. Even though I wasn't dating Hamilton anymore, I wanted to know where she'd gotten them. Because I knew he'd love them. They'd be the perfect jewelry to wear to our reconciliation dinner, if we ever had one.

"I love your earrings," I told her. "Where did you buy them?"

Gloria shrugged. "Online."

"What Web site?" I asked.

She shrugged again, a little annoyed. "I can't remember exactly. A duck one. Hey, where's Veronica?"

"She's around."

Gloria shook her head, making her razor-straight black hair and silver ducks shiver around her face. "I heard the police are looking for her. Will she even be allowed to travel internationally?"

"I heard that too," Suzanne said.

In a display of either judgment or hostility, all three of them folded their arms across their chests.

"You mean that whole warrant thing?" I asked.

The "warrant for Veronica's arrest" rumor had arisen in May regarding a traffic violation. I thought it had blown over.

"This isn't about her speeding tickets," Gloria said. She uncrossed her arms and walked closer to me. I continued to hold the suitcase at an angle. Veronica grew heavier as the seconds ticked by.

"She and Boz are in trouble," Gloria whispered.

I felt my stomach tighten. It appeared likely that whatever Gloria Fitz was about to tell me was true. Veronica and Boz had finally gone out and done something so disastrously stupid and illegal that they'd both be locked up in the big house and my trip to Prague would evaporate.

"What did they do?" I asked.

"They got caught last night removing construction materials from a building site," Gloria said. "Somebody wrote down Boz's license plate number. They're in big trouble. BIG."

Gloria's father was a judge. I didn't think she was lying.

"What kind of stuff?" I asked.

"Building supplies," Gloria said. "You know. Hammers. Saws. Sheetrock. Crap like that."

"Veronica stole Sheetrock?" I asked. This made no sense.

"That stuff is worth money," Raquel said.

"How do you know it was Boz and Veronica?" I asked. Maybe it was simply two people who looked like Boz and Veronica, who happened to be driving Boz's car.

"It was Boz in the car for sure. Maybe it wasn't Veronica who was with him," Raquel said, almost smiling. Her lipstick made her mouth look purple, like she had entered the early stages of hypothermia. I didn't have a chance to respond.

"You're lying!" Veronica yelled from inside the bag. "Get me out!"

The red suitcase leaped away from me and fell onto its back.

"She's in the suitcase," Gloria said. "It's Veronica Knox."

Veronica didn't wait for me to unzip her. She kicked against the bag's wall, until the top peeled away. Then, puffing and sweaty, she punched the lid off and crawled out.

"You're insane," Suzanne said. "You just wrecked that bag."

"Yeah, well, you three can't walk through the women's casual section of a store saying lies about people. That's slander. What's wrong with you?"

"What's wrong with us?" Raquel asked. *Us?*

"I wasn't lying," Gloria said. "It's the truth."

"No it's not. I wasn't even with Boz last night!"

"Well, Boz was with somebody. It's in the police report," Gloria said.

Veronica stood doe-eyed and stunned. Then her anger surfaced, and she focused her glare on Gloria.

"He's way too spastic anyway," Gloria said. "Kiss him good-bye and you'll be better off."

I knew that would send Veronica over the edge. Nobody insulted Boz to her face, even with valid criticisms. And nobody told her what to do.

"You have no soul," Veronica said.

"You're overreacting," Suzanne said.

"Guys are unpredictable," Gloria offered.

"I feel like making a death threat right now," Veronica said.

By this time a few shoppers had stopped culling through sales racks and were staring at us.

"Don't say the words 'death threat,'" I whispered. "We're in a mall."

"You're so hyper," Gloria said. "Dial it down."

"But this is your fault!" Veronica said, kicking the bag toward the trio.

"That almost hit my foot," Gloria said.

"We should go," I suggested, turning away from all of them.

"You are awful people," Veronica said. "And I'm not going to leave until I tell you all the ways you suck."

I stopped and turned around. This might take a few minutes. Veronica was a gifted orator.

"I know that you and your gang are lying about Boz. You are all liars! And spoilers. Always trying to ruin other people's lives. It's like all that the three of you know how to do is invade people's happiness and crap on it."

"We're not a gang," Gloria said.

"Yes you are. You're a gang of crappers! You follow each other like horses, one after the other, looking for happiness so you can crap all over it." Veronica took a big breath and kept going. "And Dessy and I are going to buy our suitcases for Prague and leave here and enjoy our freaking lives. And you, you three pathetic, gutless wannabe hipsters, you can watch our butts as we leave."

Veronica pivoted and walked toward the luggage

section. I followed her. I couldn't look at Suzanne. Or Raquel. Or Gloria. If they were laughing, I couldn't bear to see it.

Veronica picked out a new bag for herself and one for me. "I'll get them both."

"You don't have to do that," I said.

"I know. But I think I made you feel uncomfortable just now. And I didn't mean to. So, as an apology, I'd like to buy your bag for you."

I glanced at the price tag. It cost over a hundred dollars. I really didn't have the money to buy a new suitcase. I'd be traveling to Prague with roughly three hundred dollars that I'd scraped together in the last few months. With the new case, only two hundred.

"Okay," I said.

Veronica's face was a deep red, frustrated color. I could tell she regretted what had just happened. I'd never seen her flip out this badly before in public. It was a disconcerting development.

As Veronica and I rolled our suitcases across the parking lot, she surprised me again.

"I need to see Boz immediately."

"Aren't you going to drop me at home first?" I asked. I had no desire to witness one of their fights. Sometimes they threw stuff at each other. Like lamps. And shoes. And nectarines.

"I want you to come," she said.

"No. You two should work this out alone."

Veronica dropped into the driver's seat. She was still red. "Please," she said.

"No."

She leaned over me and popped open the glove box. She took out an oversize tube of glitter lotion and flipped up the cap. "I'm chafing!" she said. "Look at me."

"I don't think you're chafing," I said.

Veronica loved body glitter and utilized it as often as possible. Glistening like a decorated cupcake made her feel extra special, and that was something Veronica valued.

"Do you want any?" she asked.

"I don't," I said.

I watched her squeeze out a generous dollop and smear it on her arms until the cream vanished and left behind a layer of sparkles.

"I'm begging you to come to Boz's with me," she said.

I held firm. "No."

She threw the tube of lotion into the backseat with enough velocity to smack the rear window.

"Dessy, I need you." Her voice trembled with authentic dread. And that was an emotion I could relate to.

"Can I stay in the car?" I asked.

"Yes."

"Okay," I said, but I regretted my decision already.

"I'm really glad you're coming with me, Dessy. Because I'm so mad right now, I have no idea what I'm going to do."

Chapter Three

$\mathcal{W}$e pulled into Boz Tidwell's driveway, and Veronica slammed her car into park. Afternoon had shifted toward evening, and the temperature had fallen. Through a second-story window, I could see Boz at his computer. Backlit by a lamp, his head cast an exaggerated silhouette on the drapes. He looked like a giant, though in reality, even when he spiked his brown hair, he was only five feet six.

"Who do you think he was with?" Veronica asked me. She was breathing purposefully, releasing air out of her flaring nostrils at two-second intervals.

"Maybe he wasn't with anybody," I said.

"Gloria took way too much pleasure in telling me he was with somebody. That means it was the truth." She cracked open her door. I locked mine.

"Would you please come with me?" Veronica asked.

"You said I could stay in the car." I stretched my legs and leaned back in the seat.

"But I feel like I want to hit him in the head with an iron," she said, pounding her fist on the dash. I glanced at her. The driver's side section of the windshield was totally fogging up.

"Well, don't," I said.

"What if he was out stealing building supplies

with Celerie? He's not supposed to break the law with anybody but me. It's a couple thing. Don't you get that? Doesn't *he* get that? And Celerie Sandoval? I hate foreign exchange students. They have no concept of American fidelity!"

I wanted to point out that a few hours ago it was Veronica who was contemplating "roaming" like a cheetah. Maybe she needed to take a good look at her relationship. If she was already feeling the impulse to carouse at seventeen, her union with Boz probably wasn't all that fantastic. But I figured I'd try a safer response.

"You are so much more attractive then Celerie," I said. "And way more interesting."

"But she's from Honduras, and everybody knows that's an extremely liberal country. I think their government even encourages its citizens to do it on public buses." Veronica swung her legs out of the car and turned her back to me.

"I know a lot about Honduras, and I've never heard that. You're letting your imagination run wild."

I could tell Veronica was crying. She didn't cry often, only when something terrible was happening.

"Do you have your cell phone?" she asked me.

"Why?"

"Because if you hear screams or the sound of somebody's skull being split open, you should probably dial 911."

I wanted to hold her back. I was her best friend. Calming her down felt like my job.

"Veronica, I need a favor."

"You want a favor right now?"

"Yes. I want you to walk around the house five times before you ring the doorbell."

"No."

"I think you should. I mean, you don't look good.

Your face is blotchy. And you're making really tight fists. Boz's mom has never seen you like this. You might ruin her impression of you."

Veronica clucked her tongue. "Well, I'm not going to walk around his house five times. I'd look psycho. I'll walk around the block once. And then I'm going in."

"Fine," I said.

Veronica got out of the car and hung a hard left, setting off down the sidewalk at a good clip. I opened my door to get some fresh air. I knew Boz wasn't cheating on Veronica, but I was surprised that he would hang out with another girl. He knew that would unhinge Veronica. That's why he'd never done it. Until now.

She and Boz fought a lot. It seemed oddly necessary for them, like they had all this extra energy, and if they didn't erupt periodically at each other, they might overheat at night and explode in their separate beds.

Yes, there would be a fight. Yelling. Wild gesticulation of arms. Screaming. Tossing of random items from Veronica. Boz shielding himself from objects. Extreme cursing. Crying. Further gesticulation of arms, but less frenzied. Apologizing. Hugging. At which point Veronica would walk to where I was waiting and ask if I wanted to drive her car to my house, where she'd retrieve it later. "Things are fine now," she'd say, smiling, as she walked back to Boz. Yes. That's the note I was hoping they'd hit: *Things are fine now.*

When Veronica came back from her journey around the block, she looked more furious than when she'd left. She was blotchier. And her pink eyes were now filled with rage. She walked right to my door.

"What happened?" I asked.

"I thought I saw Celerie," she said. She was crying and biting her lip with such intensity that I worried she might draw blood.

"Was it Celerie?" I asked.

"No, it was some other anorexic-looking brunette wearing paisley pants." She wiped the tears from her eyes. "Paisley pants," she whimpered. "Nobody's worn those since the Depression. How could that out-of-date tramp turn his head?"

"Maybe you should walk around the block again," I said.

"My heart feels like it's breaking inside of me," she said. "Like it's being dissolved in battery acid."

"I know the feeling," I said. But really I thought she was overreacting.

Veronica shook her head, and a fat tear spattered onto the driveway.

"I know I joke about unloading Boz, but that's not what I want at all," she said.

"Go around the block two more times."

"But I don't want to see that slut who looks like Celerie again."

"Cut a bigger block and avoid her altogether. Here. I'll come with you."

"I don't want a babysitter," Veronica said. "You don't need to sit on top of me!" She ran across the street without looking for traffic and hurried down the sidewalk.

Watching these events unfold brought me back to my Hamilton tragedy. I squeezed my eyes shut. Fresh into my first broken heart, I didn't want to be this close to more heartache. I craved solitude. No. That's a lie. I craved what every dumpee craves. My dumper. I knew it was wrong to want this. Because what kind of guy breaks up with his girlfriend by reading her a typed (and laminated) list of her three worst flaws? Who thinks to make a list *and* has access to a laminating machine? He read me my flaws in the order of least offensive to most. It had felt like I was being stoned. First, by the sound of

Hamilton's voice as he uttered my shortcomings. Then, by the accuracy with which he landed his blows. *Thwack. Thwack. Thwack.*

I'd felt so bruised by the event that in the weeks since I'd received the list and hidden it in my underwear drawer, I hadn't told anyone about its existence. Even Veronica. Which wasn't *that* surprising. Because, as Hamilton pointed out in what he deemed my first and least significant flaw, *I had a habit of selectively withholding important information for the sake of creating a more pleasant reality.*

Boz's shadow stayed positioned behind his computer. What was he looking at? Couldn't he sense that his universe was about to blow up? He leaned back and stretched his arms over his head. Nothing about the image seemed to foreshadow disaster.

When Veronica returned she looked like she had a better handle on her emotions.

"I won't crack him over the head unless he tells me something devastating," she said.

"Veronica, please don't get violent."

She looked at me like she was surprised to hear that advice. "If he breaks up with me, I'll die," she said.

"But you might be getting worked up over nothing. You don't even know if those two were together at all. Maybe he's part of a carpool that just started."

"Boz is not part of a carpool!" Veronica said.

"Let's just go home and look at our suitcases. I'll let you zip me up in mine this time."

Veronica pushed my door open wide and crouched at my side. "That's not what I want," she said. "I need to save my relationship!"

She stood up, and I watched her trek across the lawn. Even when she wasn't furious she had a fierce and sizable stride. She rang the doorbell three times, but Boz stayed put. She pounded on the door with her fist. She kicked it with her shoe. His shadow didn't budge.

I opened my door. "I think he's listening to his iPod," I yelled.

Veronica looked at the window, then reached down and picked up a couple of rocks. They were big. I closed my eyes. But when I heard the bangs, I forced myself to peek. Boz parted his curtains, then stood up and opened his window. He ripped out his earbuds.

"You're nuts!" he yelled down. "You could have hit my window."

There were two healthy-sized dents in the white vinyl siding of his house.

"Don't worry. I've got excellent aim," Veronica said.

"What the hell are you doing?" he asked.

Good question. What was Veronica's *goal* in this situation? She bent down to pick up more rocks and walked closer to his window.

"Where were you last night?" she asked.

"Is this about Celerie?"

I tensed. Boz kept raking his hand through his hair, making it stick up in unattractive clumps. He seemed alarmed.

"What's the story?" Veronica asked. She raised one of her rock-armed hands.

"Calm down," Boz said.

Veronica lowered her arm, but even that gesture looked menacing. I decided that things were on the brink of going insanely bad, so I got out of the car and made my way to Veronica's furious and unstable side.

"I want to know everything," she called up.

"Just give us the highlights," I added.

I reached out and took hold of Veronica's right hand. It was still slick with lotion. I held on to it until the rock fell from her fingers.

"You damaged my house," Boz said. "When my parents see that, they're totally going to freak."

I was very relieved that his parents didn't seem to be home.

"That's beside the point. Why were you with Celerie?" Veronica asked.

"I'm helping her build a doghouse," he said.

"For what?" Veronica asked.

"Her dog," Boz said.

"What kind of exchange student buys a dog? She can't take it back to Honduras. You can't even take fruit into California! They make you throw it away at checkpoints before you can enter the state. Right?" she asked, looking at me.

"I think you're right," I said.

"And why couldn't you buy a doghouse that was already assembled?" she shouted.

I reached for her other hand, but she pulled it away.

"We thought building it would be more fun," Boz said.

"Why do you want to have fun with Celerie? Why are you two out stealing supplies?"

"That's basically a misunderstanding. I had permission to take what I took. Mostly," he said.

"They wrote up a police report. You're in trouble," Veronica told him.

"They did," I added. "Gloria informed us at the mall."

Boz nodded. "I'll get it straightened out. It's totally fine that I took that stuff."

"Totally fine?" Veronica asked. "Totally fine? I don't feel totally fine about any of this."

Boz disappeared, and Veronica buried her head in my shoulder. "Why is he doing this to me?"

"I don't understand the doghouse project at all," I

admitted. If Hamilton had taken up a project like that with another girl, it would have irritated me quite a bit too.

"Men suck," she said.

"I know how you feel."

She sniffled and wiped her nose with the back of her hand.

"It will work out," I said.

"I don't know."

"You two always end up okay." I patted her back and rubbed my hand along her bony spine.

"I need to do something," she said.

"I think you *are*."

"No. He needs to learn a lesson."

She lifted her head off my shoulder and smiled. Traces of glitter sparkled underneath her nose.

"Don't do anything stupid," I said.

Boz opened his front door and stepped out onto the porch. He looked up at the dents by his window and shook his head.

"Veronica," he called. "Come inside so we can talk."

"What makes you think I want to talk to you?" she asked.

"I'm your boyfriend."

"Are you?" she asked.

Boz took several steps toward us. "Of course I am."

"You sound so sure and cocky," she said.

"What's your point?" he asked. "Are you threatening to break up with me?"

Veronica took out her lip gloss and applied a fresh coat. "No," she said, slowly shaking her head.

"Then what?" asked Boz.

"I'm not threatening. I *am* breaking up with you."

I heard myself gasp. I looked at Boz, then Veronica, then back at Boz.

"You're joking," he said. "You love me. You can't dump me. We're perfect for each other."

"You're cheating on me."

"I'm not."

"It feels like you are."

"But you're wrong."

"But it feels like I'm right."

"That's because you're terrible at reasoning," he said.

Veronica took a deep breath and tossed her rock onto his porch. It skittered across the cement and landed in a holly bush. I hated the idea that a union between two people could end so suddenly.

"I'm out," she said.

"Do you want me to call you later?" Boz asked.

"Why would I want that?"

I thought about trying to force them to patch things up. But I just stood there and watched their two-year union disintegrate.

"You're breaking up with me in front of Dessy?" he asked.

"Yeah," she said. "Things haven't been working for me for quite some time. I mean, this relationship hasn't been firing on both engines for a while."

"Are you being serious?" he asked.

"As a heart attack. I'll have Dessy return any of your crap that's still in my possession before we fly to Prague. And you should do the same. No need to hang on to my crap any longer than you have to."

"Don't do this, Veronica," he pleaded. "Let's talk."

"Call Celerie. I'm sure she'll talk to you all night long."

She flipped around, and I watched her small-waisted shadow walk to her car.

"This is awkward," I told Boz.

"She's joking, right?"

"I don't think so."

"Whatever. She'll change her mind," he said. "I know Veronica."

Watching the reaction of a fellow dumpee made me realize how pathetic a dumpee looks.

He raised a fist over his head and shouted, "I'm not finished, Veronica. This isn't over until we both say it's over."

He was in total denial. And I could relate. Being in such close proximity to a second breakup, so near my own, stirred up all these feelings of helplessness and vulnerability. Hamilton Stacks didn't love me anymore. Given the choice between being with me and being alone, he'd chosen the latter. He preferred to be with *nothing*. It hit me hard. Even with three flaws, was I that bad? It was easy to feel doomed. Would my flaws always drive guys away?

I heard Veronica start her Audi. Then she honked. "I guess I'll see you later." I waved good-bye to Boz and walked over and got inside her car.

"I feel awful about this," I said. "It's like the apocalypse of relationships."

"I don't feel bad. Boz will be here when I get back."

"So you weren't even being serious?" I asked.

"Oh, I was being serious. I had to do this. I had to do something so big that he'd feel my absence like an elephant on his heart the entire time I'm gone. Plus, now I can go to Prague like the cheetah I really am and have some fun."

"You mean you did this so you can look for a guy in Prague?"

"No. A *man*, Dessy. Those college studs won't know what hit them. And neither will Boz; I plan on e-mailing him photos of all my conquests and adventures. By the time I get back, he'll be so crazy in love with me, I won't even know what to do with him."

"That seems risky," I said.

"I'm the walking definition of risk," Veronica said.

My skin goose pimpled. "What if you end up hurting him so badly that he can't forgive you?"

"That won't happen. Quit being such a wet sock." She punched me in the arm again, harder than her average slug. "We're going to have the time of our lives in Prague. You can count on it."

I thought about telling her that she meant wet *blanket* not *sock*. But I was tired. It had been a long and crazy day. I leaned my head against my window and let my mind drift to Hamilton. More than once we'd talked about backpacking through Europe. Just the two of us. I pictured him sitting with me on a park bench in France, kissing me under the soft glow of a Paris streetlamp. In my head he was still mine. And I let him trip around in there the entire way home. I missed him.

In the darkness I watched Ohio fly by. Bushes. Trees. Turnoffs. Mile markers. We drove in silence as cars on the other side of the freeway zoomed by, lighting up our faces in the white flash of their headlights.

Chapter Four

"I can't believe you're leaving the country," my mother said. She glanced at me in the rearview mirror, flashing me a nervous smile. Overhead, jet-liners soared into the bright blue day. In a few minutes we would arrive at Hopkins. I was about to become a bona fide international traveler. There was no turning back. My newly acquired passport would have a stamp in it. My life felt surreal.

"Prague is a great introduction to Europe," Mrs. Knox said. "Easy to get around. Safe. Fairly cheap. Great dumplings." She sat in the passenger seat, completely relaxed, looking out the window. Mrs. Knox looked like a cross between a mother and a politician. She was slim, serious, and wore a lot of blazers. Her hairstyle was the only thing that didn't fit this pattern. It strongly resembled Veronica's: lots of long, flowing brown layers.

"Rome wasn't a bad starter city either," Veronica said to me. "Did I tell you about all the gnocchi I ate?" She pinched my leg and released a low growl.

Even as we approached the airport I found myself poring over another definitive eyewitness travel guide.

"I want to visit the Church of Saint Nicholas," I said. "It says here it's the best example of High Baroque north of the Alps." I slid the book toward Veronica so she could see the picture.

"Cool pipe organ," she said.

I felt the car make an unexpected left turn as my mother pulled into the Rite Aid parking lot. "I thought of something Dessy might need," she said. She parked near the entrance and left the engine running. "I'll hurry." I watched my mother race out of the car and fly into the store.

"I should probably go in too," Mrs. Knox said. "After reading the first of the workshop stories, I've come to the realization that I'm going to need more red ink." She climbed out of the car and followed my mother.

"Considering my mom's age and the amount of bread she consumes, I think her butt looks pretty good," Veronica said. She leaned forward between the driver and passenger seat and flipped on the radio. "What station is this?"

"NPR," I said.

Veronica turned it to something loud that involved drums and guitars. Then she opened her bag, grabbed a handful of peanuts, and shoved them in her mouth. "What does this city have to offer in terms of nightlife?"

I hadn't researched that. "We're definitely not old enough to go to clubs," I said. "But there's this thing called Black Light Theater that looks fun. Originating in the 1960s, it says here that Black Light Theater uses black curtains and UV lighting and fluorescent costumes to make mystifying visual effects." I flipped to a page of two headless people wearing blue glowing unitards, bending to form the letter *K*.

Veronica threw a peanut at me. "I heard there's a ton of dance clubs and that they play awesome music. Techno. Trance. Jungle. Everything."

I had never heard the words *trance* or *jungle* used to describe music. I turned the page in my travel book, exited Prague, and entered Bavaria. A crazy castle with enormous spires sat atop a fog-crested green hill.

"Do you think there's a chance we might be able to make a weekend trip to Bavaria?" I asked.

"Bavaria? Dessy, nobody goes to Bavaria."

Our mothers returned at the same time, each carrying a small plastic bag.

"I bought you this, Dessy," my mother said, handing me her sack. I opened it up. It was an extra disposable camera. "I want you to be able to snap shots of everything you see." She glanced at me in the rearview mirror as she pulled into traffic. "Don't skimp. Shoot your heart out."

When we reached the airport, my mother waited by my side in maternal fashion until I took off my shoes and plunked them into a gray plastic bin. When my carry-on had passed through the metal detector, the airport worker made it clear that my mother couldn't go any farther.

"I love you," she said, rubbing my shoulder.

I held up my boarding pass, and walked through the metal detector without setting off the series of loud, accusatory beeps.

"Wash your hands a lot," my mother called. "You aren't used to European germs."

My gray bin rolled out of the machine and collided with another gray bin. I grabbed my shoes, dropped them on the floor, and tried to stuff my feet in them as quickly as possible. Another bin—Veronica's—smashed into mine. I grabbed my backpack and threw it over my shoulder. When I turned to wave good-bye, I saw my mother crying. Why was she crying? She shouldn't be crying.

"Call home!" she yelled.

"I will!" I said.

Veronica grabbed her shoes from her bin and made a gagging sound. I waited by her side until she had all her things in hand.

"Your mother is acting deranged," she said. She walked in her socks and didn't seem concerned about re-shoeing herself anytime soon. "Only crazy people yell *that* loudly in airports."

But I was glad she'd yelled. My mother's voice echoed in my head as we passed the hot dog cart, and pretzel shop, and coffee hut, and cinnamon roll stand, and fruit smoothie booth.

In the terminal, Veronica's mother sat down across from us and opened her writing satchel. As a closeted aspiring writer I'd always coveted her writing satchel. It looked leathery and sophisticated and literary. I watched her pull out a pile of papers.

"Are you working on a new story?" I asked.

"No," Veronica said. "She has writer's block. Bad."

Mrs. Knox sent Veronica a stern look. "How old are you? Twelve?" She turned to me. "They're stories from our workshop."

"When you criticize my maturity level in front of Dessy and random airport people—something Dad would never do—it only makes me want to regress more," Veronica interrupted.

This fight had been brewing for some time. And I hated being dragged into it.

Mrs. Knox gave Veronica her full attention. "Put your shoes on."

Veronica shook her head. "I've regressed to the point where I no longer require footwear."

"If you step on something sharp, then you're on your own," Mrs. Knox said.

"I've actually felt that way for a while. Come on, Dessy, let's go buy useful crap for the flight." She moved her backpack next to her mother's seat. "Do you mind watching this for me?"

"We board in fifteen minutes," Mrs. Knox said. "If

you miss the flight, prepare to live at your grandparents'
for a month. I won't rebook you."

"Fine," Veronica said.

We hurried toward an overlit magazine store. Glossy
covers, T-shirts, and bags of corn chips draped two of
the walls.

"When I went to Rome I didn't bring enough snacks.
It sucked."

"Are you going to fight with your mom like that the
whole time?"

"Not you too. Everybody needs to get off my back.
Hey, did you bring aspirin? Altitude changes can cause
severe headaches."

There was no way I could tame Veronica. I just had
to hope that she mellowed. "Didn't you pack a ton of
ibuprofen? Can I borrow some of that?" I asked.

"Sure." Veronica reached to the back of the cooler so
she could get the three coldest water bottles. She handed
them all to me.

I watched her buy a shot glass and an Ohio-shaped
oven mitt along with our snacks. "We need to hurry," I
said.

Veronica handed me the bag of stuff and then took
off in the wrong direction.

"Where are you going?" I asked.

"I want to buy one more thing."

"Why didn't you buy it here?"

"Because the stud at the pretzel counter is way hotter
than the dude at the magazine store."

"Well, I'm going back. I'm not going to miss the
flight!" I turned to leave.

"Thrill deflator."

I turned around. "Okay, I'll wait. But be fast." I backed
up to a wall and watched passengers flood by. There
were so many. Businesswomen with briefcases, men in

cowboy hats, six-year-olds with security blankets, girls in tank tops, dogs in portable kennels. And some of the dogs were wearing jackets.

"Got it," Veronica said.

"That was fast."

"He didn't do much for me. He had a weird tongue."

"He showed you his tongue?"

"If you look hard enough into people's mouths, you always see their tongues. Anyway, his looked spotted. He probably had a disease."

When we arrived at the gate, Mrs. Knox had already packed her things and was waiting in line to board.

"This is your first flight, isn't it?" she asked me.

"God, Mom. Don't make Dessy feel like a cave woman!"

"I'm trying to honor her moment," Mrs. Knox said.

I appreciated that.

"Do you want the window?" Veronica asked as we filed down the carpet-walled chute toward the plane. "Technically, it's my seat, but if you want to watch the engine and see if it sucks up any geese, you're totally welcome to do that."

"That's all right," I said.

"Whatever floats your rope."

"Boat," I corrected.

Takeoff wasn't bad at all. I felt incredibly alive as the plane left the runway. I was amazed by how tidy and orderly the world looked from several thousand feet in the air. For the first half hour, Veronica let me crane over her and stare down at the miniature scenery. But then she got bored and our flight became tense.

"How many days of workshop are we allowed to miss?" she asked, leaning over me to look at her mother.

Mrs. Knox didn't answer.

"If I suddenly become feverish, I'm allowed to take a week off, right? And if that happens, Dessy, my roommate and presumed caregiver, is allowed to take a week off too, right?"

Mrs. Knox clenched her jaw and kept reading the workshop story.

"And if my condition worsens, and I become freakishly feverish and phlegm-ridden, and I need to take a few more days off, that would be acceptable too, right?" Veronica asked.

"Veronica, you know where I stand on this. You attend everything. You got into the program without special consideration and you will participate in the program without special consideration. Unless you'd like to reimburse me for your airfare, that is the end of this discussion."

I looked at Veronica. She had taken out an enormous set of earphones. "Fine," she said.

"What are those?" I asked.

"They cancel out noise. My dad got them for me for my return trip from Rome."

She slid them on and continued to talk to me really loudly.

"I think I'm ready for our corn nuts!" she said.

Mrs. Knox reached over and snatched the headphones off her daughter. "Veronica, please do not embarrass me on this plane." She put the earphones on her own head.

Veronica didn't object. She pulled out her backpack from underneath the seat and tore open a bag of corn nuts. She popped them into her mouth one at a time.

"You can't eat these in front of guys," she told me.

"Why?" I asked.

"They're too crunchy." Veronica tossed another one into her mouth. "Guys like watching women's mouths when they eat. So mealtimes and snacks are crucial times to flirt."

I had never thought of that.

"You want to eat slowly. And avoid noisy vittles. You also want to put the food in your mouth one piece at a time. It's seductive and prolongs the meal."

"If you say so."

"Furthermore, ice cream is a top-choice, guy-getting food," Veronica said.

"Because it involves the tongue?" I asked.

"Exactly. Eat it slow. And don't let your tongue go wild. No need to behave like a dairy-addicted strumpet. Also, if it feels natural, make a couple of *mmm-mmm* sounds. Guys dig hearing *mmm-mmm* sounds. It's very affirming."

This felt like ridiculous advice. And I had never heard her use the word "strumpet" before. "Shouldn't we be eating healthy foods? Like, what if I'm eating celery?"

"You shouldn't eat that in front of a dude. If you really want to capture a guy's interest, eat a banana."

"You're insane," I said.

I reached under the seat in front of me and grabbed the first two workshop stories. They'd been e-mailed to us earlier in the week, but I hadn't finished reading them. I also pulled out my own story, which was still in progress.

"What are you doing?" Veronica asked.

"Working on my story," I said. "Veronica, have you still not started working on yours?"

Mrs. Knox had already e-mailed the class our workshop schedule. Our stories were due one session prior to our class critique. Veronica and I were two of the last to go, which gave us an extra week to compose and polish. But I didn't want her to procrastinate too much, then turn in something embarrassing.

Veronica didn't answer me.

"Do you want to hear about mine?" I volunteered. "It's about a girl and a guy who want to go to Guatemala together, but the girl is afraid of airplanes, and the guy is afraid of cars. So they're paralyzed. It's sort of like a metaphor for their love."

Veronica groaned.

"Don't make unflattering noises when I talk about my story," I said. "It makes me feel vulnerable."

"*I* make you feel vulnerable? Imagine how you're going to feel in the workshop. Everybody in there will be in college. They won't respect anything you write. They'll trash you."

That wasn't what I wanted to hear. Yes, we would be the only high school students in the class, but our acceptance letters had stated that we'd been selected based on our "strongly crafted image-based prose" and that our writing showed "exceptional promise" and the director was "honored to be accepting such fresh talent into the program." He'd even closed the letter by stating that discovering and encouraging students like us is what kept their program "vibrant, successful, and diverse." I wanted to focus on those claims rather than on what Veronica was saying.

"You're way too hung up on this. I mean, have you read the first two stories yet? They're trying way too hard to impress my mom. They're suck-ups. Seriously. I already know what I'm going to say. First story: *I liked the goat, but I had serious reservations about the other farm animals.* Second story: *Your protagonist didn't feel like she was living in Maine. Can you add more landmarks and additional lobsters?* We'll dish out a few comments and the rest of the time is ours. It's no big deal."

"Whatever," I said. I didn't like Veronica's attitude. I knew she was disappointed that we hadn't gotten into the nonfiction section. But she needed to get over it. We were still going to Prague. For a college-level program. And I, for one, was determined to make the most of it.

"Okay, okay," Veronica said, sensing my annoyance. "I plan on writing about a fox who gets his leg caught in a trap and a second fox comes along and they end up doing it. You know, a nature piece. As far as I'm concerned, they can take it or leave it."

"That actually sounds good," I said.

"It doesn't matter. They'll say it's slight and expository and derivative, and compare it to Kafka just to show off how much they love Kafka. Then Hemingway. Then Salinger. Then Steinbeck. Then Camus. Writers love to demonstrate that they've read more books than you have. They shoot off literary references as an ego defense. My mom does it too."

I glanced back at the sleeping Mrs. Knox. I'd been dutifully working on my Guatemala story every night. Adding concrete details. Rearranging clauses.

"I might turn out to be a writer," I said.

"I doubt it. You're not selfish enough. Trust me. I'm being raised by one." Veronica picked up her magazine. "In life, you're given three choices: making something, making fun of something, or making out. I choose the last two."

I barely recognized Veronica as she spoke. She'd never been this insensitive and horny before.

"Maybe I should have told you sooner, but the whole point of this trip is to meet guys. I've got a plan. Trust me, Dessy, Prague will never be the same."

I had no response to this. Outside our oval window I watched as the plane's wing cut into a bank of puffy clouds. "How much longer to Prague?" I asked. We had a layover in London, and I couldn't remember the time difference.

"Don't think about it," Veronica said. "We won't be in Prague for, like, a billion hours."

Chapter Five

A trillion hours later, we landed. We'd had a long delay at Heathrow, which gummed up the works for our connecting flight, and now it was nighttime. I wasn't sure of the date anymore. After our layover, and countless bags of mini pretzels washed down with Sprite, time felt muddy. The interior design of the Ruzyně International Airport was sleek and European and bright. Everything was glass or metal and curved. In the duty-free area, most of the signs were written in English, but the "price attack" discounts were written in a currency with which I was unfamiliar. And who buys Giorgio Armani at an airport? In a near comatose state, Mrs. Knox and I staggered through Terminal One toward the luggage carousel.

"It smells funny here, don't you think? And I feel totally different. I think my aura has changed. Do I still look pink? Can you see any blue?" Veronica hopped back and forth, from one foot to the other, in front of the conveyer belt. International travel had a unique effect on her; she acted like somebody who'd just eaten her own weight in Skittles.

Mrs. Knox sat down on the carousel's metal ledge and rubbed her eyes. "It's very important to force yourself to go to sleep as soon as we get to the dorms.

Otherwise, jet lag will hit you like a Mack truck." She clapped her hands together—hard. "Blammo!" she yelled.

Mrs. Knox looked tired, but beautiful, even without makeup. She had exceptional bones. I'd felt terrible when Mr. Knox left Mrs. Knox and fled to Rome.

I spotted my suitcase tumbling out of the chute. Veronica's followed. They were easy to tell apart because she'd decorated hers with an Australian flag.

"Americans are targets for pickpockets and scam artists," she'd told me the night before our flight, as she'd secured a small, cloth replica of the flag to her bag. I'd felt like telling her that unless she schlepped her suitcase with her through the city at all times, people wouldn't think she was Australian. But I let it pass.

Veronica, Mrs. Knox, and I dragged our suitcases across the glossy airport floor. An announcement in another language blared through the loudspeaker. It sounded vaguely like a warning, but the place was practically empty and nobody seemed alarmed. Flickering fluorescent lights overhead made me sneeze and sneeze.

"I know what this place smells like," Veronica said. "Ham!"

"Keep moving," Mrs. Knox said.

Veronica pressed her finger to her nose to imitate a snout and glanced back at me, snorting. Her nostrils looked dark and cavernous.

"Cut the porcine references," Mrs. Knox said. "This country has endured enough already."

Veronica rolled her eyes and ceased snorting.

I watched Mrs. Knox hustle over to an ATM. All around me, people chattered in different languages. My knowledge of languages wasn't at all refined, but I could pick out the cadence of Spanish somewhere behind me. And thanks to my two years of high school French, I was able to translate a four-year-old boy's remark that his endives had been acrid. I peeled my ears for Czech. I'd only memorized a few words for the trip. *Dobrý den*, which means *Hello. Pomoc!* which means *Help.* And *Kde je véce?* which translates to *Where is the toilet?* At the moment, nobody seemed to be uttering those phrases.

Mrs. Knox returned and led us toward the giant automatic doors. They parted, and we stepped into the damp Prague evening.

The terminal was bright but quiet. A handful of people were boarding a bus dozens of yards away, but we appeared to be the only travelers in line for a cab.

"This place is dead," Veronica said. "Where are the taxis?"

"It's the middle of the night," Mrs. Knox said. "Give it a minute."

Beyond our bubble of light, the Prague landscape was cloaked in darkness. A soft mist floated through the air at my knees. Without thinking, I reached down and trailed my hand through it.

"Did you drop something in the land-fog?" Veronica asked.

"No," I said. I watched the mist part like a curtain around me. A Czech candy bar wrapper fluttered by. Before I could try to read it, a white cab pulled up and crushed it beneath its front tire. An unsmiling blond man got out of the cab and brusquely hefted Veronica's suitcase into the trunk. Then Mrs. Knox's, then mine.

"Thakurova Forty-one Praha Six. Masarykova Kolej," Mrs. Knox told the driver.

We climbed inside and sped through puddles down a dark, broad street. We passed under streetlamps every few seconds, and I caught glimpses of houses, apartments, and trees. The scenery grew increasingly urban. We passed under what appeared to be a metro platform. My stomach flipped. I was dying to take the metro. I wanted to speed through this foreign city upright, like people did in movies, holding on to a pole.

We didn't pass a single McDonald's. Or Taco Bell. Or billboard. The urban scenery gave way to a stretch of grassy fields. The air rushing through my window felt heavy, like you could wear it. Ohio was chemical and fishy. But this place was sweet and metallic. It made me thirsty.

The driver pulled onto a major roadway, and suddenly, through the fog, I could see a dense cluster of lights dotting the horizon. In the mix of black-and-gray darkness I searched for Prague's famous skyline, its countless dramatic spires and steeples rising up in the distance.

"Look!" I said, nudging Veronica. We were in Prague!

"I will never remember any of these street signs," Veronica complained. "Italian is way easier."

I pulled my Czech dictionary out of my bag. "We're good. This has all the phrases we'll need."

"But look at that street sign!" Veronica said. "*U dejvichého rybničku.* Do you see all those letters and accent marks?" She leaned into me and whispered, "We'll never be able to get far on our own. We're screwed."

It was 2:07 a.m. when we got to the dorm. The building loomed in front of us like an enormous and boring block of cement with windows.

"This place is so square," Veronica said.

"It's supposed to be," Mrs. Knox said. "It was built by communists."

"Ugh," Veronica said. "The whole thing is pigeon-turd gray."

I wished the whole thing had been pigeon-turd gray. Inside, we encountered the dorm's two dominant colors. Dull white. And bright yellow.

"Whoever designed this place must worship the egg," Veronica said.

"Let's try to say as little as we can until we get a good night's rest," Mrs. Knox said.

A tired young woman with dark hair eyed us from the front desk. When Mrs. Knox introduced herself, the girl silently slid a fat envelope over the counter. Mrs. Knox tore it open and dumped out the contents.

"We're staying in separate wings," she said.

Veronica poked me and smiled.

"Let's get you to your rooms first," Mrs. Knox said.

But before she could guide us anywhere, a group of people burst through the front door. They were guys. Two brown-haired and one blond. I suspected they were drunk. They stumbled more than walked.

The first brown-haired guy doubled over in laughter. "Peat bog!" he said.

"Peat bog, man!" said the second brown-haired guy. His hair was considerably longer and better maintained than the first brown-haired guy's. It appeared extremely touchable.

They stood near the doorway and didn't make any movement toward the inside of the building. I thought maybe they were too inebriated to take more than five steps in a row.

"I'm wasted," groaned the third guy, the blond.

Mrs. Knox glowered at the threesome until they noticed her and lowered their voices.

"Sorry," said the second guy. "Hey, are you checking in? Do you need help with your bags?"

Veronica's smile was wide and freakish. "They're hot," she whispered. "It's time to launch the plan."

I shot her a nervous look. Because I didn't know the plan yet.

Veronica stepped closer to her mother. "These three

look like college students," she said. "I wonder if they're in your fiction workshop?"

All three guys straightened and attempted to look less inebriated.

"Are you Tabitha Knox?" the first brown-haired guy asked.

"I am," Mrs. Knox said.

"I'm in your workshop," he said. "I wrote the story about the goat."

Veronica batted her eyelashes and stepped forward. "I'm her daughter, Veronica. This is my friend Dessy. We're in the workshop too. We're from Ohio."

I waved. "Parma," I said. "It's near Cleveland."

"Cool," he said. "My name is Kite."

"Nice," Veronica answered.

"Well, Kite. We'd love help finding our rooms," Mrs. Knox said. She handed him a card with our room numbers on it.

"Very cool. Welcome to Masarykova Kolej," he said, grabbing the handle of Mrs. Knox's bag. "We checked in this morning. Have you been here before? This building was designed by the KGB. It's a total maze."

Mrs. Knox turned her head away from Kite's beer breath and nodded politely.

The second brown-haired guy reached for Veronica's bag. His cheeks were flushed, and a drop of sweat was sliding off his temple toward his ear. "I'm Waller," he said. "It's actually a nickname. It's short for 'Walnut.'" He wiped away the sweat bead and ran his hand through his long hair. "I have a talent."

"I've seen it, "Kite said.

Veronica surrendered her suitcase handle and giggled. I raised my eyebrows at this, because giggling was something I'd never seen Veronica do.

I figured the blond guy would take my bag, but he

didn't. I watched him teeter and fall face-first into a very large plant.

"Awesome," Veronica said.

"Is he okay?" I asked.

"It's Frank's first time in Europe," Waller explained, sweeping his long hair behind his ear.

I nodded and made a mental note. Even though I was a first-timer in Europe too, I promised myself I would not ingest any substance that would cause me to topple like a drunken fool into a ficus tree in a dorm lobby.

Mrs. Knox looked on with a pained expression. "We can't let Frank remain in the plant," she said.

Then, as if on cue, a fourth guy, taller than the others, walked through the door. I couldn't tell what color hair he had. He wore a baseball cap so low that it hid even his eyes and ears.

"Hey, Roger, can you get him?" Waller asked.

"Sure," Roger said, giving a stoic thumbs-up sign. "I'll drag him to the room."

I pulled my own suitcase as we followed Kite and Waller through a maze of white hallways. Kite may have made a few wrong turns, but these went unacknowledged. When we finally reached room 106, Mrs. Knox opened the door with a magnetic card. We stepped into a small galley kitchen equipped with an undersize stove and a minifridge that was way too mini. Adjacent to the kitchen was the bathroom. And beyond these rooms was a hallway that led to three more doors.

"It looks like you're sharing room B," Kite said. "Here's your keys for that door."

Veronica gasped. "We're sharing? I thought Dessy and I had our own room."

"You do," Mrs. Knox said. "But you have suitemates. Two girls in room A and one in room C."

"What if they have atrocious hygiene? Or are pathologically immature?" Veronica asked.

"You'll deal with it," Mrs. Knox said.

The guys backed into the hallway to wait for Mrs. Knox. I thought I heard them doing an impression of Frank.

"I'm hungry," Veronica said.

"I've got a protein bar in my bag," Mrs. Knox said.

"That sounds terrible," Veronica said.

"Here's some money for the vending machines," her mother replied. "Good night, girls."

In our small kitchen a large window opened up into the hallway. Through it, I watched Mrs. Knox follow Kite and Waller to an elevator.

Veronica threw her big suitcase onto a bed and began unzipping it. I rolled mine over to the corner and figured I'd hold off on unpacking until tomorrow. Everything I needed for a good night's sleep was in my overnight bag. Clean socks, a T-shirt, and boxer shorts.

"Are you really hungry?" I asked. "I've got crackers from the plane."

"No, I just wanted money. Do you want to go check out the vending machines?"

"I'd like some water." I reached toward my throat.

"I feel parched too. Let's go."

The hallway was silent.

"Those college guys were so cute," Veronica whispered. "I hadn't expected to run into them first thing like that." She peered over her shoulder, then turned to me. "So which one did you like the most? And you can't penalize the one who passed out in the tree."

"Why not?" I asked.

"Because that kind of crap happens to everybody at least once. For guys, usually a couple of times a year until they turn twenty-seven."

"It's not going to happen to me," I said.

"Don't get all judgmental. I'm trying to talk to you about men." Veronica giggled again. "It doesn't matter. I already know who you like."

"No you don't," I said.

"I sure do. You like Waller. He looks a lot like Hamilton, except Waller has better hair."

"That's not true," I whispered. I worried that our voices might carry through our neighbors' doors.

"You cannot be serious. Hamilton Stacks's hair looked like an eagle's nest. I'm surprised he didn't have a major large-bird-attempting-to-roost-on-his-head-every-other-day issue."

"Here's the vending machine," I said. "Where are you going?"

Veronica kept plodding down the hallway. "I'm going to check things out."

"We need to get to bed or jet lag will smack us like a truck. Remember?" I clapped my hands. "Whammo!"

"I believe the correct sound effect was 'Blammo,'" Veronica said.

"Either way, we don't want to get jet lag," I said.

"Yeah, I don't really care."

I watched Veronica turn a corner and disappear. As I stood in front of the vending machine, I realized that I didn't have any useful money. Why hadn't Mrs. Knox suggested that I pull out some money at the airport too? I thought about calling for Veronica, but I didn't want to wake anybody up. Nor did I want to chase after her.

"Do you need something?"

I turned and saw Waller standing next to me. Had he heard what Veronica said? The part about my possibly liking him? The part about Hamilton's wacked-out hair? This was terrible. Where had Waller come from? And why was he so sneaky? Why hadn't he made his presence known to me immediately? By clearing his throat. Or saying, "Hi, Dessy."

Luckily, I didn't have to admit that I was crownless and somewhat desperate. "I wanted water," I told him. "But the machine only has soda."

"You can drink the tap water here," Waller said. "It's totally safe."

"Really?"

"Yeah. Me and my friends have been drinking it for two days. If you're worried about diarrhea, you shouldn't be. It's fine."

My eyes widened. I couldn't believe that Waller was so comfortable using the word *diarrhea*.

"Thanks," I said.

"Not a problem."

Waller dropped some change into the machine and bought a bag of potato chips. He smiled at me and then walked off. I realized he did look a little bit like Hamilton. Same height. If they were wrestlers, they'd probably be in the same weight class. But he didn't seem self-conscious at all. I mean, he was walking around in a T-shirt with a stain on it, and flip-flops. He even had a little bit of BO. And it didn't seem to affect his interpersonal skills at all. It was like I'd just encountered a new species of guy.

Maybe Veronica was right. Maybe college men were the answer. I wandered back to the room, floating in a new, Waller-filled, optimistic, and marshmallowy place. But when I got there, the positive energy ended. The door was locked. I had our room key, but I'd forgotten the magnetic card.

Dizzy and exhausted, I sat down in the hallway. There was nothing I could do but wait. Orientation was tomorrow, and I wanted to show up to it well rested. When I didn't get enough sleep, sometimes my eyes grew dark, ugly bags. That's not the first impression I wanted to make. I was single now. I needed to look good. Cute.

Slowly I lowered myself into a horizontal position. The floor was hard and it smelled like wax. Carpet would have felt better, but I had what I had. I hoped Veronica would end her expedition soon. I needed a blanket. I needed a pillow. I needed a softer place to dream.

Chapter Six

$\mathcal{I}$ woke up facing a cinder block wall. *Ich liebe Anja* was scribbled into the paint with such intensity that the letters went all the way down to the cement. I reached out and touched her name, and the *j* flaked off onto my fingertip. I turned over and flicked the paint chip onto the brown-carpeted floor.

The light was on, and Veronica's bed was empty. I blinked a few times, then pulled my blanket over my head. One whiff of my overtraveled, undershowered condition made me throw the blanket off. At the same moment, Veronica, very damp, burst into the room, swinging her arms, sending small water drops down on me.

"That thing is a beast." She stood in a towel in front of me and ran a pick through her hair.

"Strong water pressure?" I asked.

"You'll see," she said. "And don't leave anything personal in there. Our suitemates could be degenerate thieves. By the way, the place is ours. They all left."

I grabbed my toiletries and towel and walked past the kitchen to our small bathroom. I noticed the problem right away. Up to this point in my life, every shower I'd entered had shared the same design. The nozzle was opposite a wall, so after you turned on the water, and it reached the desired temperature, you stepped into the shower's flow. But here, in the dorm, the nozzle was opposite the curtain. So when you turned on the shower, water shot out of the nozzle and flooded the entire bathroom. The only way to prevent drenching the place was to stand in front of the nozzle as you turned it on, thereby being assaulted with cold water. Veronica and I could not have been the only people to notice this.

When I came back to the room, Veronica was groomed and fully dressed. "Throw yourself together. Let's escape this edifice," she said.

I rushed to put on my jeans. While I did this, Veronica began cutting pieces of paper.

"What are you doing? Where did you get scissors?" I asked.

"I'm making a man-wall. I brought the scissors from home. Because without them, I knew I wouldn't be able to properly construct my man-wall."

"What's a man-wall?" I asked.

Veronica held up a cutout shaped like a paper doll. Sort of.

"This is the paper replica of a hot-dude. We met four hot-dudes last night, so I'm going to stick them on the wall. By the time I leave Prague, I aim to cover my entire wall area in hot-dudes."

"What?" I asked.

Veronica stopped cutting and looked up at me. "Let me start over. I'm constructing a man-wall out of hot-dudes. I'm making four hot-dudes right now. A Kite. A Waller. A Frank. And a Roger."

"Who's Roger?" I asked.

"The hot-dude in the ball cap who pulled superhot Frank out of the ficus tree."

"I can't believe that you remember all their names."

"Dessy, it's hard to conquer a man if you don't know his name."

Veronica put her head down and resumed cutting. I selected a T-shirt and decided to view building a man-wall as an occurrence as routine as flossing one's teeth. When she'd finished, Veronica taped the four paper guys to the wall and smiled. Then she labeled them and drew a big star on Frank's head.

"What's that for?" I asked.

"I plan to mark the extraspecial ones. I think Frank is double hot."

"The drunk one?" I asked.

"Oh yeah."

She flashed a big grin and then put her face right up to paper Frank and licked his starred face.

"That's so unsanitary," I said.

Veronica shrugged. "Come on," she said. She took a moment to study my outfit. "Good choice on the shirt. Guys always find buttons intriguing. But you can't wear your sneakers."

"But they're comfortable," I said, loosening the laces and inserting my foot.

Veronica's jaw dropped. "Dessy, we didn't travel to Prague to be comfortable. If that was our goal we would have packed tracksuits and togas. Seriously. Put on your sandals. You've got great toes."

Rather than object and create waves on our first morning, I took off my socks and rooted through my suitcase for my sandals.

"Let's hurry. We need to get out of here and scope a three-street radius so when orientation is over we have immediate destinations. Otherwise, we're behind."

"Why three streets?" I asked.

"Do you understand what scoping a street involves? No way do we have time for more than three."

Veronica looked very eager to leave, but I still had questions.

"Do you think we should bring anything?" I asked.

"Nothing beyond ourselves," Veronica said.

I sat down and held my bag on my lap. It contained three pens, a notebook, and—at my mother's insistence—a small packet of baby wipes.

"Are you going to tell me about the plan?" I asked.

"Here it is in a nutshell." She flipped her hair over her shoulder and stuck up her pointer finger. "One: We gain rudimentary knowledge of our surroundings and locate all potential hot-dudes within our scoped area. Guys have fragile egos. Also, some are territorial. We don't want them to know that we're playing with multiple hot-dudes. For example, if we strike up a connection with hot-dude A, who lives on Main Street but shines shoes on Grand Street, we can never forget that. Because if we parade down Main or Grand with hot-dude B on our arm, we stand to lose both hot-dudes."

"You want to date shoe-shine guys?"

Veronica frowned at me. "It was a hypothetical. And I spotted a few shoe-shine guys at Heathrow that weren't half bad. Don't judge my hot-dudes. I'll do that."

"Okay. Scoping is important. I get it."

"Good." She held up her middle finger and made rabbit ears. "Two: In order to isolate and interact with hot-dudes, we will need to create a map of hot-dude density. We have a month. We've got to focus our efforts in target-rich environments." She lifted another finger. "Three: We need to capitalize on male friendships." She pointed her three fingers back to the man-wall. "These writer guys are more than hot-dudes. They're skeleton keys. Because they're older, if we hang with them, we'll look older too. *Legal. A*nd this will be essential in gaining access to the more exclusive parts of Prague. Also, odds are one of them is bilingual and that will unlock an entire new world for us."

My head was swimming. "How long have you been mapping out this strategy? It's crazy."

Veronica waved me off. "Don't interrupt me. I'm only at three. Moving on. Four: We need to befriend the janitorial staff. If we're lucky, we can gain access to more than one hot-dude's private living area. And in addition to uncovering whether they prefer boxers to briefs, I anticipate finding boatloads of useful information."

She'd gone too far. "Whoa, this isn't so much a strategy as an unchecked impulse to stalk guys."

"So you're not ready to hear the fifth major component?" Veronica asked.

I looked out the window. Veronica made our excursion in Prague sound incredibly laborious.

"Don't you want to meet a guy? Wouldn't you feel better if you had *somebody*?" she asked.

I thought about my heart. Even though it was broken, I could feel it pumping away in my chest. I looked at Veronica and nodded.

"Listen. We're young and hot. Plus, we're smart."

"What if there are other girls in the program who are hotter? And smarter?" I asked.

"That's why I devised the seven major components!" Veronica said. She sat down next to me. "And it doesn't really matter, because our trump card is that my mom is basically a celebrity here. We will conquer the hot-dudes. I'm being serious, Dessy. We will rule them."

Veronica sounded almost combative, and I wasn't sure why. I decided not to interrupt as she continued to dish out her hot-dude plan.

"In addition to the major components, let me impart some useful hot-dude advice. We need to act mature and interesting. We need to laugh a lot at their lame jokes. And trust me, they will tell lame jokes. It's some weird genetic disadvantage that hot-dudes are born with."

"I guess."

"Dessy," Veronica said, reaching out and taking hold of my knee, "what I'm about to tell you next will be more valuable to you than CPR."

By the edge in her voice I believed her.

"We need to be good listeners. Hot-dudes love to talk about themselves. Athletic accomplishments. Academic pursuits. Hunting expeditions. Video game scores. Childhood encounters with squirrels. The biggest advantage we have over all the other girls here is that we're younger, so the guys will feel enlightened and knowledgeable around us. And we should never challenge that. We need to use that as a way to worm our way into their hot-dude hearts."

Even though vast amounts of what Veronica said were crazy, this advice made sense. But still . . .

"Guys aside, don't you worry about whether or not we'll make friends and be liked?" I asked.

"No," Veronica said. "Because there's always the *zoo strategy*. It's a surefire way to win people over quickly."

"What's the *zoo strategy*?" I asked.

"If you want to make instant friends, give them free food."

"That's dumb."

"No, it's effective." She shoved a cracker into her mouth. "You haven't called your mom yet. Didn't she want you to call her?"

I nodded. "I told her I'd call her on the second day."

"That's weird. Why not the first day?"

"I don't know. I guess I thought it would take me a day to find a phone and figure out how to use it."

Veronica picked up the receiver and studied both

ends of it like she'd stumbled across a never-before-seen species of fish.

"Don't make fun of me," I said. "I wasn't sure how easy it would be to access phones in Prague."

"What did you think Prague would be like?" Veronica asked. "Burundi?"

She was mocking me. I'd done a report on Burundi in Government last fall. I'd selected Burundi after learning that it was the poorest country on the planet and had the world's lowest gross domestic product. The report had turned into quite a downer, especially the page on deforestation and soil erosion. Veronica had given her report on the Netherlands. I still remember her opening paragraph: *The Netherlands are cool. It's legal to smoke pot there. You can buy it in coffee shops.*

"Why are you just sitting there?" Veronica asked me.

"I'm thinking about Burundi," I said.

"Let's go!"

I did as I was told. But sadly, before we could bolt, the phone began to ring. Veronica answered.

"We're coming," she said. I could hear Mrs. Knox's voice droning from the receiver.

"Fine." Veronica slammed the phone into the cradle. "I guess we scope later."

As I pulled our bedroom door closed, I noticed several hot-pink sticky notes fastened to it.

"They're from our suitemates," I said.

Veronica groaned. "Does this mean we have to leave *them* sticky notes?"

"Come on. We have to read them."

"Wow. Our sense of obligation is triggered by very different things," Veronica said.

I pulled the first note off the door. "This one is from Brenda Temple. It says that she's an early riser and from Maine and that she's staying in room C. She's already showered and we can eat some of her granola if we want. It's in the cupboard."

"All that fit on a sticky note?" Veronica asked.

"She writes small," I said.

"Is there anything else that's actually worth reading?"

"This one is from Annie Earl. She's from Florida and she's also in room C. She knits and she sleeps late. She welcomes us. And she says she brought extra blankets if we get cold."

"So we're living with old women?"

"Just because somebody knits and brings extra blankets doesn't mean that they're old. A young person can have poor circulation too. Okay. Here's the last note. It's from Corky."

"Corky?"

"Yeah. She says that Annie Earl and Brenda made her write this note because they want everybody to get along. But she's a loner. And we might not ever see her. Except in workshop. She wants to experience the counterculture of the city. She'll only be showering twice a week. Rock on."

"Did you say 'rock on' or did she?"

"She said it," I said.

"Nobody says 'rock on' and only showers twice a week except for people who use hard drugs. Let's avoid these wack jobs."

Had I been by myself, I would have written responses to Brenda, Annie Earl, and Corky. But considering Veronica's current emotional state, I let her pull me out of the suite.

A moment later we arrived at the double doors of the conference room on the ground floor.

"After I open this door, the mystery is over. We will see clearly who is here and available. Their level of hotness will be quantified. No more daydreams. No more pipe dreams."

Veronica opened the door, and a flood of chatter tumbled into the hallway. "Oh my god!" She leaned her head into the room, and I leaned my head into the room, and we both took it all in.

Dozens of college kids sat around tables eating pastries. And there appeared to be more guys than girls. Everybody looked young and athletic and happy.

"There are a ton of brunettes," I said. All my life I'd had a soft spot for guys with dark hair.

"I probably should have worn tighter jeans," Veronica said.

I glanced at her. She was staring into the room, nervously chewing on her bottom lip. "You look great," I said.

Veronica squinted and then sucked in a big breath. "I know."

I turned my attention back to the room. I spotted Mrs. Knox sitting at a table.

"There's your mom!" I said.

"Shh," Veronica said, bumping me. "Why are you looking for my mom? Look for guys, Dessy."

She was right. Why was I looking for Mrs. Knox when the room was crawling with cute guys?

"Hot-dude. Hot-dude. Hot-dude," Veronica said, pointing. "Look, even that grandpa-dude is sort of hot."

I saw the grandpa-dude, but I did not find him hot.

"This exceeds every expectation I had," Veronica said. She walked into the conference room beaming like the sun. "This will be the best month of our lives. Follow my lead."

Chapter Seven

$\mathcal{A}$ did exactly what Veronica did. I grabbed an unglazed pastry, stood against the wall, and applied some lip gloss. Mrs. Knox sat at the head of a table. A big placard in front of her listed her name and her genre.

TABITHA KNOX: SHORT FICTION

An older woman and an attractive college student were sitting with her, but Veronica held back.

"We stay on the periphery," she said.

There were five other tables with placards.

STEVIE BLOOM: POET
DINO WASHINGTON: PLAYWRIGHT
DORIS MOSES: THE NOVEL
SYD COVERT: EVERYTHING
AMY ALLEN: CREATIVE NONFICTION

Students continued to trickle in and join their workshop leaders. It looked like the program had about a hundred students. The nonfiction table was twice as crowded as the others. Veronica noted this.

"If we'd gotten into that class, we'd have double the dudes."

"Our table doesn't have any dudes," I said.

Veronica glanced around and bit her lip. "Our table has to have dudes. We've already met them." She leaned into me and whispered, "They're already on my wall."

"Right," I said.

I turned my attention to the faculty. I'd been researching them for weeks, and now here they were. I felt like I was glimpsing celebrities.

"There's the playwright," I said, pointing to the table where Dino Washington sat with fifteen eager students.

"That guy sucks," Veronica said. "He was rude to my mom at a conference in Tennessee."

"What did he do?" I asked.

"I don't remember," Veronica said. "Something involving a pineapple. It doesn't matter. He's a dramatist. Nobody respects those clowns." She kept looking around.

I think Veronica could pick up on my star-struck excitement, because she immediately tried to puncture my mood.

"Here's the deal: these people are not real celebrities and you shouldn't treat them any different than bus drivers," Veronica said. "My mom is the most respected writer here. After that, Amy Allen is the second-most respected."

I didn't say it, but Amy Allen was actually more famous than Mrs. Knox. I'd heard an interview with her on NPR about her memoir, which had recently been turned into an HBO movie, *Kicking Apart the Moon*. It was about her turbulent affair with a former astronaut who suffered from a neurobiological brain disorder.

"She looks so calm," I said. "I can't believe she held that astronaut hostage at that Taco Bell in Houston."

Veronica's eyes bugged out with enthusiasm. "I know. She's brilliant *and* insane."

"The poet guy is big too, right?" I asked.

Veronica made a gagging sound. "Poets are never big. They're basically miserable and poor and eat organic cows and avoid gluten and crap like that."

"There's Doris Moses," I said. "I heard an interview with her on NPR too. She's fluent in six languages and does humanitarian work in Bangladesh."

"Dessy, turn off NPR," Veronica told me. "That's a total geek station. Besides, Doris Moses is a one-hit wonder. She wrote a novel about an alligator that ate, like, nine people in Florida, and then she ended up on the *Today* show and her book hit the *New York Times* best-seller list. Her whole plot totally ripped off *Jaws*. She's been working on her second novel about a group of genetically mutated chickens for twelve years."

"That sounds interesting," I said.

"Dessy, don't grow up to be a writer. Because when you live too much in your own head, you neglect the people you love and become an insulated wack job."

I doubted this was totally true. Because I felt that to become that way you had to have a fair amount of wack-job impulses already.

"What about Syd Covert? He's the director, right? I heard he's a nice guy."

Veronica shuddered. "That guy offended my mom worse than the pineapple playwright dunce. Basically, we avoid him."

"Okay," I said. I had no idea that the literary landscape was such a political place. I felt like I'd been dropped into a field of well-read land mines.

"Let's move in," Veronica said.

I followed her as she briskly threaded herself through the room. She took a seat right next to her mom.

"What did you think of your first European pastry?" Mrs. Knox asked me.

"It was flaky," I said.

"We'll grab some groceries later. This climate always makes me crave quinces and crackers."

I stared at Mrs. Knox. I didn't know what a quince was.

"It feels muggy in here," Veronica said. "Can you ask somebody to crank up the AC?"

Mrs. Knox shook her head. "There is no AC. It's called natural ventilation."

I watched Syd Covert come up and tap Mrs. Knox on the shoulder. Veronica leaned in and whispered, "You're getting sweat marks near your pits. Try to lower your body temp."

"What?" I asked. "How?"

"I'll get you some water."

I didn't want Veronica to leave me alone at the table, producing grotesque sweat marks. "I'll come too."

We crossed the room again, and I glanced at my armpits. I was wearing a white shirt, and the fabric under my arms was saturated. "This is awful."

"You're lucky you're wearing sandals. Heat primarily escapes through your head and extremities."

Veronica handed me a glass of water, and I immediately started sucking it down.

"You look nervous," she said. "Stop it."

"It's my first time in a foreign country."

"Relax. It's not that different."

I almost choked on my water. "Yes it is."

"Whatever." Veronica took a swig of her own water and frowned. "I heard somebody at a table say that we have to take a tour after orientation. Bummer."

"That's great. It'll help us scope."

Veronica rolled her eyes. "You can't scope in a huge group with a tour guide. Maybe we can ditch the tour."

"Don't you want to learn anything about Prague?"

"I already know everything."

"That's not true."

Veronica cleared her throat. "It all started a million years ago with a hunting party. There were settlements. Wars. Religion was huge, and they built a castle and a bunch of cathedrals. A bridge went up. They put a bunch of saints on it. More wars. Puppets exploded on to the scene and stayed. Russia took over and forced everyone to be Communists. People got sick of that. There was a fight over a hyphen. The Slavs went one way. Czech people went the other. And now I'm here. There you go. History of Prague."

"I think you've skipped over some stuff."

Veronica took another drink of water. "Let's get back."

When we returned, the Short Fiction table was still disappointingly guyless, and Mrs. Knox was still chatting with Syd Covert. Contrary to what Veronica had said, she didn't seem too offended by him. In fact, it almost looked like they were flirting.

Veronica pretended to ignore them. "Your pits look way better," she said.

"Stop referring to them," I said. I fished through my bag to locate my pen and notebook. A million conversations were going on around me. My mom had told me to always be ready to write down good restaurant and sightseeing suggestions. Most of the people I saw were college-aged, but there were a few older people too. One woman at the Novel table, when she laughed, looked a lot like my mom.

"Wow," Veronica said. "You're going to take notes?"

"Someone might say something useful," I said.

"Yeah. I've been saying useful things for six years." Veronica shot me a devilish smile, and I smiled back.

"We have a small group," the older woman at our

table said to me and Veronica. She was knitting some-thing pink. It looked like a tubular-shaped hat.

"Oh, there's guys in the group too, but they got plastered last night. They'll probably stumble in late," Veronica said.

"Well, the beer here is pretty cheap," the woman said. She continued to knit. She seemed unfazed by Veronica, and I liked that.

"That's probably Annie Earl," I whispered to Veronica.

"I bet the other one is Brenda," Veronica said.

I looked at the attractive brunette with pale skin and delicate features seated next to Annie Earl. She was read-ing a book by Philip Larkin. "Probably."

Veronica didn't look too happy. "I was hoping the other girls would be potato-ugly."

"I know."

"Wow," Veronica whispered. "Do you see them?"

I did see them, and I couldn't believe Veronica was going to comment on Annie Earl's scars while she was sitting right there.

"Not now," I said.

"When I see something like that, it makes me think of my own mortality," Veronica said.

"Shh," I said.

I didn't think Annie Earl could hear us, but the idea that we were discussing her discolored arms right in front of her made me squirm.

"Maybe she escaped from a burning hotel room," Veronica said. "Maybe she was riding a train and it caught fire and she had to run through the flames and then jump off into a random field like a hobo."

"Stop," I said.

"There's a story there," Veronica said.

"Shh," I repeated.

And then somebody rang a bell.

"Welcome to Prague," Syd said from a podium. "A city of exceptional beauty."

At the word "beauty," Kite, Waller, Roger, and Frank all rushed into the room. I sat up straight. Veronica's beaming smile returned.

When the conference room door slammed behind them, Syd stopped talking, and everyone turned to watch them find their seats. Syd said, "Welcome!" He seemed sincere, and I liked how forgiving this program appeared to be. I thought it boded well for Veronica and me.

"Prague is a place wholly unlike any other. Here, I expect you to write and live. To explore and reflect." Syd lifted his arms heavenward. "Here, you will dream. Here, you will drink. Except for our two high school students."

The audience laughed.

Syd pointed to Veronica and me, and I felt myself blush. "They're seated next to Tabitha Knox. Let's do our best not to corrupt our underage colleagues."

The audience laughed again. I was mortified that he used the phrase "high school students" and "underage." I already felt scandalously self-conscious about my teen status.

"What a jerk," Veronica said. "I feel so labeled now. Just like that woman we read about in freshman English in *The Scarlet Number*."

"*Letter*," I said. "*The Scarlet Letter*."

"Are you sure?" she asked. "I thought she had to wear a number that represented all the guys she'd slept with in the forest."

"No," I said. "Her name is Hester Prynne. She gives birth after committing adultery and has to wear a scarlet *A* as a symbol of shame. But she ends up turning it into a symbol of identity."

Veronica looked at me like I was the seated embodiment of a fart. "Did you eat SparkNotes for dinner last night?"

Syd had a lot of things to say about Prague. Goulash. Kafka. The plague. He briefly recapped the fall of the Iron Curtain. He then rattled off some vague warnings about pickpockets, money changers, and prostitutes. Something he said concerning the red light district triggered a short meditation about the journey of our souls. Finally, Syd closed by announcing that two tours were getting ready to leave the dorm. One was a historical tour highlighting sights of great cultural importance. The other focused on popular local establishments: restaurants, museums, clubs, cafés, bookstores. The latter sounded like stuff that was right up Veronica's alley.

Before Syd stepped away from the podium he called all of the instructors to the front of the room. After short introductions, followed by applause, the room filled with chatter. Veronica didn't waste any time leaning over the table and waving to Kite, Waller, Roger, and Frank. Her eyes were bright and focused. Mostly on Frank. I wasn't surprised: he was the sort of guy Veronica fantasized about. Tall. Blond. Athletic. Wholesome-looking, yet, based on the events of last night, most likely considerably flawed.

"How are you feeling?" she asked him.

"Okay," he said.

But I thought he looked a little yellow.

"My name is Veronica. This is my friend Dessy. My mom is Tabitha Knox," she said.

"I'm Frank. This is Kite, Waller, and Roger," he said.

"Yeah, we've met," Veronica said. "Last night." Veronica pretended to face plant into the table. Then she popped back up. Frank looked at the floor and wiped his nose with his hand.

"Don't worry. It's cool," she said. "I've been to college parties. I've seen plenty of guys pass out before."

I felt the sweat glands on my fingertips begin to

perspire. Veronica and I had never been to a college party. It was alarming to see her so grandiosely fabricating our social history. What sort of reputation was she trying to create for us? And where was she hoping it would get us?

Out of the corner of my eye I saw Waller talking to Brenda. I tried to listen to what they were saying. I think Waller had read her story. He liked her "flow" or something. Veronica managed to keep Frank so occupied that he never had the chance to meet Brenda. Typically her strategy with cute girls was to shut them out and ignore them completely. She felt it limited their power. Veronica. She always played to win.

Finally the terribly embarrassing news that Syd had disclosed about me and Veronica got repeated.

"I didn't know you two were in high school," Kite said.

Mrs. Knox returned from the gathering at the front just in time to hear Kite's comment. "They are both definitely still in high school," she said.

"I just felt my chastity belt snap shut," Veronica whispered to me.

"Shh," I said. I didn't enjoy hearing Veronica talk about her private parts. Veronica looked at me and mouthed the word "chastity." Then to my horror, I saw Roger grin. I caught his eye for a split second, then looked away. Oh my god. He could read lips.

"Here we go," Mrs. Knox said. Her arms were filled with light blue folders. "It's everything you'll need. Maps. Schedules. Tourist cards. Restaurant recommendations."

"Sweet," Veronica said, plucking hers from the pile.

I took my folder and flipped it open. There was a lot of information in it. I mean, there was a whole section on how to avoid being cheated by cab drivers.

"And these are your travel passes," Mrs. Knox said, handing me something that looked like a driver's license.

"I love that picture of you," Veronica told me. "You have such sexy eyes."

I agreed. My eyes looked seductive and so did my lips. And in this rare instance my blond hair, flyaways and all, framed my face in a way that made me look amazingly hip. I'd turned my picture in last month, and until I was handed my travel card, I'd totally forgotten about it.

"Use this to ride everything: metro, buses, trams, funiculars," Mrs. Knox said. "And if a person approaches you with a badge, you'll need to show her your pass. Otherwise, keep it in your pants."

I slid my pass into my wallet and nodded. Then I watched Waller take his pass, walk away from Brenda, and approach his friends. Veronica noticed this too.

"Follow me," she whispered urgently. "We can't let them get away." We passed Brenda and hurried toward the guys.

"So are you going on one of the walking tours?" Veronica asked Waller.

"Yeah," he said. "We're just deciding which one."

"Too bad we have to pick just one," Veronica said.

I smiled like I agreed, but really I couldn't tell whether or not she was joking.

"We're doing the historical tour," Kite said. "Roger and Waller have roots in this country."

"Poland, actually," Roger said.

As we all drifted in the direction of the dorm's front glass doors, I looked at the guys. I don't know if it was out of loneliness or curiosity, but I wanted to study them. They seemed so different from high school guys. Taller. Thicker. More chin stubble. And in addition to feeling that I could like them, I felt that I could trust them. They were high school graduates who, when faced with life's many options, had decided to go to college. They read textbooks. And wanted to write novels. Their heads must have been filled with amazing ideas. I wanted to have conversations with them and prove to them and myself that I had interesting ideas too. I imagined talking with them about mature issues, like drug-resistant bacteria, oil prices, and soccer.

"Which tour?" I asked.

"Historic," Veronica said.

"Really?" I asked. "I thought you'd opt for the contemporary tour. I mean, restaurants, clubs. It's catered to our interests." I was curious about Prague's history, but it seemed more practical to learn about the city's immediate resources.

Veronica flipped her head in disapproval. "It doesn't matter what *our* interests are," she said. "We follow the guys. I mean, duh. They're our interest."

"Right," I said.

Then something unforeseen and terrible happened. Through the glass doors of the lobby we could see four tour guides in orange vests dividing the students into smaller groups.

"What should we do?" I asked. It was like watching an ice floe break apart and trying to decide where it was safest to stand.

Veronica and I followed the horde out to the sidewalk but stayed on the periphery.

"Historical tour number one!" yelled a guide on the far left.

"Historical tour number two!" yelled a guide in the middle.

"Contemporary tour number one!" yelled a guide on the far right, waving a batch of tour books over his head. "We stop for dumplings!"

The second contemporary tour guide didn't yell at

all. He stood with his hands clasped over his fly and rocked back and forth.

"I'll go this way," Veronica said, pointing to the far left. "I want to stay close to Frank. You go that way." She pointed toward the middle. "Track Brenda for us."

"Really?" I asked. Splitting up seemed like a random move. How and when would we reconnect?

It was too late to discuss it. Veronica had disappeared into the crowd, so I followed Brenda toward historic tour group number two.

It was a hot day for such a tour. The sun beat down on us without mercy. I looked around for the boys but didn't see them. The two contemporary groups began to drift left out of the parking loop. I watched as the last of them rounded a corner and disappeared. The other historical tour kept drifting farther and farther away from ours.

"I'm wearing way too many clothes for this." I knew this was Veronica's voice, but the crowd was too dense for me to see her.

"So you're Dessy?" Brenda asked me. "We're suitemates."

"Cool," I said, though I really had no idea whether or not this was cool. "You're Brenda?"

"Yep. So you came with Veronica?" she asked. "You're high school friends, right?"

I nodded.

"And Veronica is Tabitha's daughter?"

"Yes," I said, trying to think of a question, because I needed to turn the tables. I should be prying into Brenda's life, not the other way around.

"So you're from Maine and you eat granola?" I asked. Only after I said this did I realize that it might have sounded like an insult.

"I am from Maine. And I eat granola sometimes. I like easy snacks."

"Cool," I said again.

Unlike the other historical group, ours didn't appear to be moving anywhere.

"Have you seen much of the city yet?" Brenda asked. She swept her long hair up into a ponytail.

"No," I said. "We got in really late."

"Group! Group!" our tour leader called. He was very short, and his severe buzz cut contrasted strangely with his huge smile. "I am Jiri. Let's start moving toward the good stuff. Right now we are standing in Praha Six, fifteen minutes northwest of Praha One, the city center. This way! This way!" Jiri lifted a small wooden crate over his head and led us away from the dorm.

"I'm excited for this," Brenda said beside me. "I'm hoping he'll take us to Powder Tower and the exhibit for alchemy. And the evolution of science!"

"So, are you a science major?" I asked.

"Psychology."

I had to keep this conversation going. "I bet that's useful for your writing. Getting into your characters' heads."

Brenda looked at me with gushing enthusiasm. "Totally. I get in there so deep, I dwell."

I didn't think her psychology interest was a positive development. It meant she was armed with textbook knowledge of the male brain. I felt this gave her an advantage over Veronica and me.

"Look!" Brenda said.

I followed her finger, expecting to see either an essential Prague landmark or a crime being perpetrated.

"That suit of armor is moving!" she said.

It took a moment for me to spot the distant metal-clad figure against the backdrop of a gray building. If she hadn't pointed him out I would have missed him entirely. "Weird," I said. I watched him clank down the sidewalk and enter a liquor store.

Brenda shook her head. "No. What's weird is that last month I saw the same thing in London."

"Wow. That's completely medieval."

"Yeah, it must be some kind of traveling installation art."

"Oh." I moved closer to Jiri. I couldn't believe it. I was about to tour Prague, and instead of Veronica, I'd become partnered with Brenda, who apparently enjoyed making intimidating observations every five seconds.

As we followed behind Jiri, Brenda began debating with herself the true direction of north.

"It's got to be that way, right?" she asked, pointing behind us. "Because the sun is there and it's noon. I should know this. My father sails."

"The sun moves west," I said, hoping that was helpful. I just didn't know what to ask Brenda anymore. She and her sailing father seemed experienced and cultured in ways I wasn't used to. I tried one last question.

"I like your shoes. Are they made out of real leather?"

"I guess," Brenda said. "Are you a member of PETA or something? Because I totally respect that."

"No," I said. Veronica was going to be very disappointed when she deposed me after the tour.

Our conversation fizzled and we continued to walk. After a few blocks, the world around us began to buzz. Hotels, busy streets, and convenience stores gave way to the old city. It was nothing like Parma. Or Cleveland. Or anywhere else I'd ever been. The sidewalks weren't made out of cement anymore; they were made out of stone. But as soon as I looked up I forgot all about the ground. Because Prague's skyline was the most amazing thing I'd ever seen. The buildings soared. Their roofs were all curved or pointed or tiled or domed. And a lot of them looked orange. And there were spires everywhere. It was like a group of architects had decided that what this city needed was a bunch of buildings that looked like they were throwing lances into the sky.

"This city is so deep," said a girl somewhere in front of us.

"It's actually a thousand feet above sea level," a male voice answered. It sounded eerily like Hamilton. In fact, that was the exact kind of random fact Hamilton would know. He loved being informed about city elevations because it tied into his knowledge of birds. I stood on tiptoes to see who'd made the comment, but I wasn't tall enough.

Jiri led us through a series of small, crowded alleys. Brenda and I were too far back to hear what he was saying. But the Hamiltonlike voice continued to dispense interesting facts.

"According to legend, Prague was founded by a Bohemian princess in the seventh century. She had a vision and named the city Praha, which means *threshold.*"

"He's talking about Princess Libuse," Brenda told me. "It's a great story. Prague has a rich feminist background."

"That's really cool," I said.

Jiri had brought a wooden crate to stand on top of, but the edges weren't even, so it wobbled. Therefore, he didn't utilize the crate. I tried to push myself closer to the front.

"Look!" Brenda said again.

I began scouring the scene for something bizarre that she might have already seen in London.

"Look at her hat."

A tall blonde walked passed us wearing a fashionable white headpiece. I'd seen a lot of women wearing little netted hats. "Do you want to buy one?" I asked.

"No!" Brenda said, practically laughing. "It's an old

Czech custom that married women wear some sort of cap or scarf to signal that they're married. I think that's what those are. Also, men used to wear long feathers in their hats, and once they got married they clipped them."

"So these customs are still relevant?" I asked. Feathers in caps seemed Robin Hood ancient.

"Of course they are," Brenda said sternly. "Capitalism has destroyed most Americans' understanding of culture. That's why we're always appropriating other peoples' culture."

"True dat, yo," the Hamiltonlike voice said.

"Who said that?" Brenda asked.

"Who's asking?" the male voice called.

The tour was starting to feel like a knock-knock joke.

"I am. Brenda."

I watched as Waller wove his way out of the front of the tour, back to where Brenda and I stood. I was thrilled to see him, but not thrilled that he was seeking out Brenda.

"Hey!" I said, waving.

Waller smiled at me. "What's your name again?" he asked.

"Dessy," I said.

"Can you two hear what the guide is saying?" he asked.

"No," I said.

"He's incredibly quiet," Brenda added. "He needs a bullhorn."

"Yeah. I'm only catching every fifth word," Waller said. "Which building did he say had the golem in the attic?"

"He said *golem*?" I asked. "I thought he said *goy gum*. And I had no idea why anyone would keep that in an attic."

We turned a cobblestone corner and passed a row of yellow buildings with ornate white trim.

"For all we know, Kafka lived there," Waller said.

I looked back at the houses. "Wouldn't there be a plaque?"

Waller smiled. "Touché," he said.

But I wasn't trying to score a point. I was being serious. I smiled at him again, unable to control my mouth.

"It's hot," Waller said. "I didn't realize Prague was this close to the sun."

"The information packet says that in July temperatures can climb into the nineties," I said. "And stay there."

"Maybe they should have sent us those packets before we left the States," Brenda said.

Our group came to a stop at a corner with a puppet stand on it.

"Maybe we get to see a marionette production of *Don Giovanni*!" Brenda said.

I watched the two puppets being dangled by their handlers. One looked like a horned red devil. The other appeared to be a nun. They were big. Almost the size of kindergarteners.

"I don't think this is *Don Giovanni*," Waller said.

We watched as the nun swam through the air on her strings toward the devil. Dramatic music blared out of a boom box beside the small stage. The man handling the nun let her fists fly. She punched the devil in the head over and over while he apparently tap danced.

"We're supposed to root for the nun, right?" I asked.

"I guess," Waller said. "That devil looks like a masochist."

"I'm sure there's a subtext of religious persecution that we're missing," Brenda said.

After the nun finished punching the devil, she began kicking him.

"Ever since the Middle Ages, Prague has been a huge

puppet center," Waller said. "After the Nazis invaded, puppetry was a popular form of political dissent."

I found Waller's Prague knowledge very sexy. How he talked about stuff wasn't how Brenda talked about it. It didn't make me feel intimidated. It made me curious. Once the nun defeated the devil, she broke into a series of dancing high kicks.

"I wonder how much they cost," I said.

"Do you want me to ask?" Brenda offered. "I'm pretty good at haggling."

"No, I was just curious." I didn't want anyone to think I was some sort of puppet freak.

We left the puppet corner, and Jiri began talking about the Charles Bridge.

"Did he just say it was made out of eggs?" Brenda asked.

"Oh yeah! It's totally crazy," Waller said. "I read that when they built the Charles Bridge they mixed in egg yolk with the mortar, to strengthen it. And all the surrounding towns shipped their eggs here. But one town was worried their eggs would break in transit, so they hard-boiled them. And their town was mocked for a few centuries after that."

"That is so funny," Brenda said. "How many guidebooks did you read before you came here?"

Waller smiled so big that I saw the sun reflect off his teeth. "Maybe ten," he said. "I like history."

"I hear you. My parents took me backpacking in Morocco when I was twelve, and I brought a whole library of guidebooks. The weight of them nearly killed me. I had to unload them in Accra. I gave them to a homeless woman to sell."

"That's hilarious," Waller said. "I can totally picture you there."

I felt so out of place, like I should let Waller and

Brenda discuss the finer points of international travel while I hung back and fell out of the picture.

"You've been to Accra?" Brenda asked.

"This is actually my first trip abroad," Waller said.

And when I heard this, I felt a little less lame. I almost felt okay with the fact that neither of my parents owned a backpack. So what if the farthest anyone in my family had ever ventured was Seattle, where my father attended a parking meter conference last year.

"This is actually the first time I've left the Midwest," I said. Why I decided to be this honest, I wasn't sure.

"Wow," Brenda said. "That's rare."

Before I could think of a smart response, Waller said, "No shame in that. You're from Ohio, right?"

He was so sweet! "Yep, near Cleveland. The mistake on the lake."

He smiled. "Ah, the Great Lakes. I'm from Chicago. Lower West Side. So is Roger."

I nodded. "Did you two meet in college?" I asked.

"No," Waller said. "We knew each other long before Northwestern. Roger and I go all the way back to fourth grade. We're both from the Pilsen neighborhood."

It seemed like Brenda had tuned out. Waller had probably told her all this at Orientation.

I said, "Cool," which I immediately regretted because I didn't think it fully communicated what a good listener I was, and I wanted to maximize on our Midwestern commonalities.

"It is cool," Waller said. "I feel like I can appreciate diverse cultures because I come from an area that has a lot of variety."

"I live by the Ridgewood Golf Course. It's given me a fear of balls," I said.

Waller laughed politely. I felt myself blush. Why was I telling my hot-dude jokes about balls?

"I guess that would," he said. We were all silent for a moment.

"Golf balls," I muttered to myself. "A fear of golf balls?"

After a while, Waller said, "I love Chicago. I think I could live there forever."

"What do you like most about it?" I asked.

"Good question." Waller stopped to scratch his ankle, and I waited beside him. But Brenda kept walking. Waller and I didn't rush after her.

"Great skyline," he continued, as we resumed strolling behind the group. "Nice waterfront. Good art scene. Fantastic restaurants. Sports. The city has everything."

"Sounds like it," I said. "So what's your major?"

"Neurobiology," he said.

"Wow."

"I'm kidding. I'm an English major."

"Do you have a minor?"

He shook his head. "I'm dabbling in history, philosophy, political science, French, and religion."

I couldn't think of another question, but I needed one. Things were going so well. "You must take a lot of classes," I said.

"I'm in school, but I'm also an autodidact. I devour information."

I had never heard of autodidacts. I hoped it wasn't a mental disorder. If things were going to progress much further with Waller, I apparently needed to buy a good dictionary.

"Do you want some water?" Waller asked, pointing to a drink stand shaded by a large blue umbrella.

My clothes clung to me, and my skin felt sticky with sweat. Water sounded necessary.

"I don't have crowns yet," I told him.

"My treat," he said.

I watched Waller jog toward the stand. He jogged

nearly exactly like Hamilton. Three happy bounces followed by an almost skip.

"They have ice cream!" he yelled. "This quarter of Prague is known for its ice cream."

"Great!" I said. My mind raced through several licking strategies. Based on Veronica's advice, I now had a chance to gain considerable ground with my brand-new crush.

Waller returned with two chocolate ice creams, a cone in each hand, and two bottles of water, one shoved in each of his armpits.

I reached out to grab one of the cones, but he handed it to me at the same time. The chocolate scoop dislodged from its nest of cone and rolled down my shirtfront. Then it splattered on my sandals.

"Shit! I'm sorry," he said.

"It's okay," I said.

"It doesn't look bad," he said, which was a stupid thing to say because it implied that spilled ice cream on your shirt could somehow look good. "You can have my cone," he added.

"No," I said. "You keep it. All I want is water."

I furiously rubbed a napkin over my shirt until the paper started to disintegrate into shreds. Luckily the stainage had occurred mostly in my valley, not atop my boobs. This seemed less conspicuous.

"Maybe you could use some water and try to rinse it off," he said.

"I'm wearing a white shirt."

"Then maybe not," he said. He licked his cone and then held it out for me. He wanted me to lick the unlicked side. The situation suddenly felt like a test. I lowered my mouth to the chocolate ball of ice cream and nibbled. Waller pulled it back to his mouth and took another lick. "Mmm. *Mmm.*" The sound escaped from his mouth in a deep seductive hum. It traveled through the air and struck my body like electricity. After a couple more licks, he asked, "Hey, where's the group?"

Once we caught up to the tour I uncapped my water and took a long drink. In three blocks I'd finished the bottle.

"Are you enjoying this?" Waller asked.

"Yeah," I said. "Except I'm looking at the back of a lot of heads."

Waller laughed. "Look. We're here," he said.

It hadn't occurred to me that the tour had an ultimate destination.

"It's amazing," Waller said.

He was right. I'd never seen anything like it before. Right in front on me, on a hill, sat a castle. The tall spires reached high into the sky, piercing the low, thin clouds. The castle was dark, almost like it had been burned; it didn't resemble any of the castles I'd seen in Disney films. It was the sort of place that somebody mysterious and deranged might have once called home.

"The president of the Czech Republic has his office here."

"That so does not look like an office building," I said.

"The first incarnation of it was constructed in the ninth century. But it's been rebuilt a lot since then. It houses the crown jewels," Waller said.

"No way! I want to see those."

"We'd have to go on a tour, then."

An enormous dark river flowed at the base of the hill. Ferries and paddleboats glided under its many stone bridges. We followed Jiri until we were nearly at the river's edge. "That's the Vltava River," Waller said. He pronounced it *vul-TAH-vah*. "And that's the Charles Bridge, the one made with egg yolks. It's a cultural landmark."

He pointed across the street to a bridge that was crowded with people and street vendors. Large statues rose up all along the bridge's sides. They were saints, I knew from my guidebooks. They looked like protectors the way they hovered over the flocks of tourists.

"Do you study numerology?" Waller asked.

I did not think I could bluff my way through pretending I'd studied numerology. "No," I admitted.

"This is really fascinating. The foundation stone for the bridge was laid in 1357 on the ninth day of the seventh month at 5:31 a.m., so the date and time make a palindrome: 135797531."

"Cool," I said.

"It was done for luck. The court numerologists figured out this was the luckiest day, because that sort of palindrome won't occur again until 2468."

"Is Jiri even mentioning these things?" I asked.

"I think he's talking about Emperor Charles the Fourth," Waller said.

I didn't bother telling Waller that I'd never heard of this emperor, or that my knowledge of emperors in general was pretty scant.

"There's so much to see in Prague. Wenceslas Square. Powder Tower. Saint George. Týn Church. Saint Vitus's Cathedral," Waller said.

"You're better than a guide book."

"I don't know," he said. "Guide books have pictures."

"Touché," I said.

Waller reached up and shaded the sun with his hand. "I feel like I'm being baked," he said. "Like I'm a pot roast."

The image made me laugh. "I know," I said. "I'm sweating." Since I knew I wasn't stinking, I figured it was okay to admit that I was sweating. We leaned against a stone wall, squinting in the afternoon sun. The rest of our group had disbanded. I watched Jiri cross the street toward the bridge and disappear in the crowd.

"Did you like the tour?" Waller asked.

"Yours or Jiri's?"

He laughed again and was about to say something else when Veronica, Frank, Kite, and Roger showed up.

"We're going to grab goulash. Do you want to come?" Kite asked.

Hearing this, I realized how much I wanted goulash. Urgently. Even though I didn't know what was in goulash. Fish fins? Horse intestines? Tiger genitals? I didn't care. I couldn't imagine anything better than sitting across the table from Waller. I looked at Veronica to see what we should do. But then I looked behind Veronica because I saw Mrs. Knox approaching.

"Hi, girls," Mrs. Knox said. "I got us a taxi so we can do our grocery shopping."

"Actually, we've been talking about grabbing some goulash," Veronica said.

Mrs. Knox looked surprised. "What about your snacks?"

I knew that inside, Veronica was probably horrified to hear her mother championing snacks, but she didn't show it in front of the guys. "Let's shop later," she said.

Mrs. Knox frowned. Then things got worse. Brenda materialized out of nowhere. "Did I hear someone say goulash?" she said.

I watched her smile a very beautiful smile. She had fantastic lips and teeth. Then I heard Waller invite her to join us for lunch.

"I'm glad everyone enjoyed their tours," Mrs. Knox said. "But the taxi is charging me. Girls, we need to go."

"Wait! I want a picture. Come here!" Veronica said.

She stepped in front of Brenda, tugged on Frank, and let Roger and Waller move out of the way. Veronica tucked her chin down, smiled mischievously, and flipped her hair so that it tumbled over her shoulders. By the look on her face, I knew that these would be the pictures that she'd e-mail to Boz. She beamed as Mrs. Knox clicked the camera three times.

"Okay," Mrs. Knox said. "Beep, beep, let's go!" She slid the camera into her purse.

"Can't we get goulash too?" Veronica begged.

"Goulash sounds great," I piped in.

"Yeah!" Veronica said. "It's what Czech people eat. And it would be culturally insensitive of us not to experience it."

"Groceries first. Goulash later. That's practical."

I watched the guys and Brenda drift down the street. They hadn't even said good-bye.

"See you tomorrow in workshop!" Veronica yelled.

"You don't have to shout," Mrs. Knox said. "That was right in my ear."

I watched Waller turn around. He saw me watching him, and he waved. I thought about waving back, but I didn't. Because maybe he wasn't waving entirely at me. He could have been waving at Mrs. Knox. And Veronica. Like a big group wave. Or maybe he was saying good-bye to the street performer behind me. Okay. I was overthinking. I'd just spent an hour with him. Of course Waller was waving at me.

But what did it mean? That I wasn't too young for him? Was it fine by him that I didn't know about numerology? Did he have a universal attraction to blondes slathered in chocolate ice cream? He finally lowered his hand. But that didn't stop my analysis of this complicated gesture. Waving. Veronica read my mind.

"Don't be an idiot," she said. "Wave."

So I did.

Chapter Eight

cl woke up the next morning feeling nervous for a variety of reasons. First, I wanted to impress Waller and make him topple over in mad, disorienting, bone-burning love for me. Second, I didn't know how to do that. Third, I really wanted to hone my writing skills, and I feared that my preoccupation with worry number one and worry number two might impede that.

When I got back from my shower, Veronica had attached three new hot-dudes to her man-wall.

"Where did you meet them?" I asked. It was a little shocking to see them multiplying at this speed. Though she *was* doing a nice job of keeping their heads and legs in scale with their arms.

"The first hot-dude, I met in line at the grocery store. I accidentally touched his butt. His name is Mike. I've got his number here in town. He's from England. He's not that interesting."

"How come you drew stars on his shins?" I asked.

"Oh." Veronica tapped the paper cutout's legs. "His shins are awesome. Perfect amount of hair and bone protrusion."

I sighed. "Did you meet the other guys at the grocery store too?" I didn't exactly understand how she could meet guys in the checkout line. I mean, I had been right there with her, and I didn't remember her touching some British guy's butt or getting his phone number.

"I met the second hot-dude in the lobby last night. You'd gone to bed. I felt like roaming. His name is Chad. He's from New Jersey. He goes to a community college and has triple-pierced ears. He thinks he's a playwright, and basically his life seems pretty hopeless. But he's staying in the same hall as Frank and the guys, so he might be useful to me."

I sighed more heavily. "So between late last night and right now, how did you meet a third hot-dude?" I asked.

She pointed to the most recent hot-dude on the wall. "Peter? I met him a few minutes ago while I was randomly riding the elevator. You were in the shower. He's not part of the writing program. He's here with a group of watercolor painters from Michigan."

"You're out of control, Veronica."

"Seven hot-dudes on my man-wall isn't even close to being out of control," Veronica said. "Get ready. Let's head to the university. We've got a lot of living to do."

I put on a T-shirt and jeans.

"You're going to be so overheated that your crotch will sweat," Veronica told me.

I changed into shorts while Veronica primped in the bathroom.

I was surprised by how little we'd seen of our suite-mates. I'd heard Brenda return last night, long after we'd come back from grocery shopping. In the middle of the night, seized by hunger and curiosity, I'd inspected the minifridge and found her leftover goulash stinking it up.

"Their crap is everywhere," Veronica announced on her way back from the bathroom. "Brenda keeps her natural toothpaste on the side of the sink. Annie Earl hangs a bathrobe on the only bathroom hook. And look at the table! There's a dirty spoon on it."

"Didn't you leave that there after you ate your yogurt last night?"

"Oh, yeah." Veronica slung her bag over her shoulder. "Are you stressing about Brenda? Don't stress about Brenda."

"But I think she likes Waller."

"That chatty Mainer is a big yawn," Veronica said as we walked to the dorm lobby. "Actually, so is Annie Earl. But Corky seems at least mildly appealing."

"Why?" I asked.

"That whole business about looking for Prague's counterculture. I mean, culture usually bores me. But *counter*culture might be worth investigating."

"Yesterday you acted like you had no desire to meet Corky. You insulted her. I mean, pick an opinion and stick with it. You're totally jumping around."

Veronica commenced jumping. Down the hallway. Around the corner. Onto the stairs. She had so much energy pouring out of her that when I tried to imagine her seated for our three-hour workshop, I couldn't. And this frightened me.

When Mrs. Knox opened her door, she was still in her pajamas. "The workshop isn't for another hour," she said.

"I'm trying to be hyper-responsible," Veronica said.

"You have no idea where the university is," said Mrs. Knox. "You're not going alone. You need to cool your jets."

"I do know where Charles University is," Veronica said. "We went past it on the tour. The building is enormo."

"And I have a map!" I said, lifting up my bag. "Dejvicka to Staroměstská. We don't get off the green line."

Mrs. Knox shook her head.

"What's the worst that could happen?" Veronica asked.

"Death and dismemberment," Mrs. Knox said.

This wasn't going well at all.

"Dad let me take the metro in Rome by myself all the time," Veronica said. "And the bus."

Mrs. Knox smoothed her bed-head with one hand.

"We'll be fine," Veronica said. "There's daylight everywhere."

Mrs. Knox appeared unconvinced.

"Seriously, Mom. I found the Coliseum and the Vatican all by myself."

I was surprised that Veronica had visited the Vatican. It was the first I'd heard of it.

"Fine. I'll see you in an hour," Mrs. Knox said, then shut the door.

"To the metro!" Veronica cheered.

We walked outside into the muggy air.

"It feels like the world has been wrapped in a hot towel," Veronica said.

"At least the sky is blue," I said.

"Oh no."

"What?" I immediately began surveying the scene for Brenda and pickpockets.

"I forgot to bring snacks."

Since going back wasn't an option, we stopped at a small market along the way. The store had only three aisles, and on the counter next to the cash register was a big stack of pornographic magazines. Veronica saw them and smiled. Then she bought crackers, apples, and two candy bars, and dashed out to the street.

"Why are you running?" I asked, jogging behind her.

She glanced back over her shoulder and laughed. "We can't leave anything to chance. We've got to scope the room."

I hurried after Veronica, hoping she'd stop running when she reached the stairs that led to the metro escalator, but she didn't.

"You're getting too far ahead," I called down to her. I raced down the stairs, made a left, and got on the escalator. Riding down, I could see the machine where you purchase your tickets, in the middle of the platform. I edged past a large man and a woman with shopping bags. When I got off the escalator, I ran to the machine. But I didn't understand what I was supposed to do. It had about twenty buttons, and everything was a different color.

"What do I press?" Nobody answered me. "We're taking the green line, so do I press the green button? Why does it have a sticker of a dog on it?" I was officially panicked. Did this thing even take debit cards? How had Veronica already managed to purchase a ticket? I felt completely abandoned.

The train was coming. At the other end of the platform, Veronica positioned herself next to the yellow line. That's when I remembered my travel pass. I grabbed my wallet and ran for the approaching train. "I can't believe that you were going to leave me!"

"Nobody left anybody," Veronica said as she stepped onto the train ahead of me.

The car was crowded, and neither Veronica nor I could find an open seat.

"Commuters," Veronica said. "And tragically, no hot-dudes among them."

I scanned the car twice, and she was right. "We can't be lucky every day of our lives," I said.

She frowned at me. "Sure we can."

We both hung on to a bright orange pole near the door. The orange seats held people reading newspapers and magazines. Even the standing people were reading. And the few women who had purses were clutching them tightly in their laps, fearing pickpockets, I guessed. Following their example, I unslung my backpack and set it at my feet, where I could keep a vigilant eye on it.

At every stop the train lurched with dramatic force, sending me sideways into fellow passengers. It didn't matter how tightly I held on. The same thing happened to Veronica, though I don't think she minded, because she was positioned next to a young, dark-haired businessman wearing what looked to be a soft and expensive dark gray suit.

"Where did *he* come from?" she whispered.

"Malostranské stop."

I decided our fellow passengers didn't really look all that different from Ohioans. Their clothes and faces resembled those of people I'd expect to see walking through the mall on a Saturday. The only exception to this was their footwear. Both the young and elderly were clad in shoes that looked considerably orthopedic.

When the metro stopped at Staroměstská, Veronica was first off the train. I clumsily dashed out behind her.

We rode an escalator up into the daylight. Hurrying down the sidewalk, I realized that we were at the same place where the tour had ended yesterday.

"There's the castle," I said, pointing across the river.

"I'm not blind," Veronica huffed. "This way. The school is around the corner."

Charles University was old, stone, and impressive. I didn't remember seeing it on the tour. We climbed a set of shallow stone steps and entered through a set of heavy wooden doors. Veronica immediately began climbing the central stairs. When we got to our room on the second floor, Veronica yanked on the door and then said, "Shit."

"Is it locked?" I asked.

She pulled a credit card out of her purse and wedged it into the door near the lock.

"What are you doing?" I asked. I was shocked. Unless

you count her locker, I'd never seen her break into anything before.

The door popped open and she smiled. "Entering. Now, the reason we're here early is so we can secure our seats strategically."

"Good idea. We should sit by the door in case we need to use the bathroom."

"Yeah," Veronica said. "Because nothing turns a guy on more than a girl who's intent on emptying her bladder. Seriously, Dessy, can you try to think like a cheetah?"

"Probably not," I said.

"We want to penetrate the guys' circle," she said.

"You make it sound so sexual. Can't you just say that we want to sit next to them?"

Veronica walked to one of the chairs and smiled like a devil. "This is how it will go. Guy ass. My ass. Guy ass. Guy ass. Your ass. Guy ass." She walked down the row and slapped the back of a chair each time she said the word "ass."

"How on earth do you know where the guys are going to sit?" I asked.

"A lot of it's mental," she said.

I glanced around the classroom. Things looked dilapidated. Huge maps of Europe hung on every wall except the windowed one. There was an aquarium too, containing a keyboard and several feet of cable. Was this an omen? Veronica remained fixated on the chairs.

"And how will that work?" I asked.

"Don't you remember that time that I moved a balloon across the floor using just my mind at your birthday party two years ago? It'll be a lot like that." Veronica tapped her temple.

"Oh my god," I said. "This plan is bonkers."

"You're not going to say that after it works."

"You really think you can control the other workshop participants?"

"Yeah." She plopped down in a chair. "We need to capitalize on every moment. Every second." She snapped her fingers in quick succession to emphasize, I assumed, the dramatic passage of time. "Do you want to know what I said in my e-mail to Boz last night?"

The way she was treating Boz upset me so much that I hadn't asked her about it.

"No," I said.

"I said, 'I'm enjoying every second of this place.' And it was the truth. And I will continue to live my truth."

She climbed onto her chair and then up onto a table. She lifted her index finger and jabbed it heavenward. "My truth!" she yelled.

"Get down," I said. "You're going to freak people out."

Veronica leaped off the table. "Adventurous girls make guys horny," she said. "That's why superhero chicks give guys boners."

"Superhero chicks? Are you serious?" I asked.

"Hawkgirl, Wonder Woman, Supergirl, Zatanna, et cetera, et cetera. It's way obvious."

"Maybe it's their low-cut tops, skintight clothing, and gargantuan breasts."

"Either way, adventurous girls are turn-ons. Big time," Veronica said.

"You act like you know everything," I said.

"I know a lot," she said. "Admit it."

I didn't want to fight. Why was I picking a fight? Why not just agree with her? Veronica Knox *did* know a lot. Even her superhero-chick observation had merit.

"You're right," I said.

She ran to my side and hugged me. "Isn't it amazing how we're incapable of fighting for longer than thirty seconds?"

"Yeah," I said.

"Okay. You sit here," she said.

I sat.

"I'm going to sit here." She slid into a chair and pulled out the stories for workshop.

"Now that you've actually met these people, are you really going to make snarky comments about their work?" I asked.

Veronica looked at the ceiling and blinked several times. "Probably," she said.

"Why?"

"I want to look smart. I mean, it's a lot easier to rip something apart than to offer useful feedback. Have you ever wondered why delinquents vandalize cars and mailboxes and abandoned buildings? It's because it's so much easier to wreck something than to build it."

What she said made sense.

"Besides, the stories are a little freaky," Veronica said. "I like Kite, and I wouldn't mind hooking up with him, and going all the way to first base, or possibly second. But after reading his piece, there's no way he's going to third with me, because I think it's pretty obvious that he's a sexually injured person."

"I'm not sure I'd say that," I said.

"You're not sure of a lot of things, Dessy." Veronica looked down and started to read.

"How can you tell that he's sexually injured?" I asked. "He wrote about a goat."

Veronica groaned. "You *think* he wrote about a goat. And on the surface it may look like he wrote about a goat, because he was using the word *goat*, but trust me, the goat is a metaphor."

"It is?"

"Yeah, Kite is either talking about his last failed love or his mother. Either way, he's sexually injured. That becomes totally obvious during the milking scene."

"Wow. I completely missed that," I said.

"We're not dealing with high school material anymore, Dessy. We're tackling college issues."

I was already nervous about commenting on the stories. It was pretty clear that they had been submitted by people who were older and knew what they were doing. Would they even want my opinions?

Probably not. My anxiousness turned into nausea. I glanced at Veronica. She appeared fine. I took a deep breath and tried to appear fine too. Today we were discussing two stories: Kite's and Brenda's. Yes, I'd already scribbled comments. But after Veronica's revelation about Kite's goat, everything I'd written seemed so obvious. Why hadn't I dug a little deeper? I flipped through both stories again. Brenda's was set in Maine. It was about a woman who buys a lobster at the grocery store and then takes it to the ocean and sets it free. The story ends with her returning to the grocery store to buy a crab.

"The lobster story isn't about sex," I said.

Veronica kept her head down while she talked. "Right, it's about confronting mortality."

"Exactly," I said. "That's what I wrote. Because the lobster lives."

"We don't know if that bottom-feeder survives," she said. "She never even tells us if she took the blue rubber bands off its claws."

"We're definitely supposed to root for the lobster," I said.

"Dessy, the story isn't really about the lobster or the crab. It's about *her*. And maybe some fixation she has for an uncircumcised fisherman. Did you read that description of the fishermen she sees in the grocery store?" Veronica looked at me and waggled her eyebrows, then she licked her thumb and turned a page.

"Oh my god," I said. "I missed everything!"

I furiously began marking up both stories. I continued to make notes even as the group straggled in. Waller sat two seats away from me. So much for Veronica's powers of mental persuasion. But as he passed he brushed against my arm with his arm and its thick forest of hair. It was the hairiest arm that had ever grazed my skin. I loved it so much that I kept hoping he'd regraze me. But he didn't.

Annie Earl came in with Brenda, and they sat next to each other. Brenda glared over at us, and I didn't know why.

"I got your note about the goulash," she said.

"Cool," Veronica said.

I leaned over the empty chair between us and asked her, "What did you do?"

Veronica smiled. "I got up in the middle of the night and ate most of it."

My eyes got big.

"Calm down. We didn't miss much. I've had better."

Frank ended up sitting right next to Veronica, and Roger sat beside me. A slightly chubby girl with a lot of tattoos sat by herself. Kite sat on the other side of Veronica. Except for Waller, everybody sat exactly where Veronica had planned. I was amazed.

"Let's go ahead and get started," Mrs. Knox said.

My pulse raced. I flipped back through the stories again. Everything began to blur. I wasn't ready.

"As all of you know, I'm Tabitha Knox. My specialty is the short story, and that's what we'll be working on in this class. One of my favorite quotes on writing is, 'You can't wait for inspiration. You have to go after it with a club.' Some people think that writing is all about putting your butt in a chair. That's a wrongheaded approach. I've met plenty of writers who spend too much of their lives sitting, waiting for the magic, waiting for the spark. They wait at their desks like a shipwrecked sailor waits on the shore of a deserted island, unshowered, desperate, nutritionally compromised, and fashion challenged."

Everybody laughed at this, even Veronica, who must have heard it dozens of times before.

"As writers, we need to learn to rescue ourselves. We will work hard in this class, because writing is hard work. In addition to the stories that we'll workshop, I'll also be assigning small amounts of reading. Flannery O'Connor. Raymond Carver. Joyce Carol Oates. Stuart Dybek. Ralph Ellison. And more. Because writing isn't just about writing. It's also about reading."

"I agree," Veronica said. "I hope we get to read some vintage Hemingway."

"Probably not," Mrs. Knox said. "Hemingway isn't my favorite." She cleared her throat. "I'll also be assigning small writing exercises. Sometimes I'll collect them and sometimes I won't.

"Here's my philosophy for workshop," Mrs. Knox continued. "We start with what's good. After we've discussed what's working, we can move into more critical areas. You aren't allowed to say that you don't like something without offering a thoughtful reason. Don't discuss typos during the workshop. If you have grammatical concerns fix them on the page. We want to get to the meat. We want to give the author nine extra sets of eyes. We want to show them where their story succeeds and where it may be falling short. And one last thing, no commenting or contributing while we're discussing your story. It's your job to absorb and take notes. You can make clarifying inquisitions at the end. Questions?"

"Shouldn't we introduce ourselves?" Veronica asked.

Mrs. Knox nodded. "Yes. I was getting there. Who'd

like to start? Say your name and where you're from. And tell us something interesting about yourself."

It looked to me as if Mrs. Knox was trying to maintain a neutral position with Veronica in front of the class. And it also looked to me as if Veronica was trying to act very mature and collegey.

"I will. I'm Veronica Knox. And I'm from Ohio. I like to run, salsa dance, and bake. And I can hold my breath for six minutes and twenty-nine seconds."

I heard somebody gasp. Veronica beamed. I'd never seen her do any of the things she listed. And as for holding her breath? I had no idea why she'd told that whopper.

"Wow. That's tough to follow. But I'll go next. I'm Roger Kobe. I'm from Chicago. And I'm a Cubs fan." Roger pointed to his hat. "And don't try to talk me out of it. I'm a loyal dog. I'll be a sophomore at Northwestern where I study English and Education."

"I'm Waller Dudek. Also from Chicago. Also attending Northwestern. And I like the Cubs, but I got tired of having my heart broken annually, so I don't claim a team. Also, I want to add that I'm not a fan of Hemingway either."

He drummed his fingers on the table. This set off small vibrations that traveled through the wood and into my bones. I felt flushed. Then he glanced at me, and I took it as a sign to go.

"I'm Dessy Gherkin. I'm from Ohio. And while I'm not a Cubs fan, I do like watching big cats at the zoo."

Roger laughed.

Veronica mouthed, "What?" But I liked my answer. I thought it showed pizzazz.

"I'm Frank Adler. I'm from San Diego, and I'm a student at UCSD. And this is the first summer that I haven't spent working at SeaWorld or the San Diego Zoo since I was fifteen." Frank looked at Veronica and me and gave us a knowing grin.

Why did he grin? Did he think I was fifteen? Did Veronica and I *look* fifteen? I felt my ears grow warm. I wanted to shout, "I'm not fifteen. I'm seventeen! And a half! World of difference." But I held myself together.

"Kite Geld. I'm from Escondido. It's near San Diego. I study at UCSD too, and when I was seven I kissed Shamu."

"And what was that like?" Roger asked.

"Damp," Kite said.

People laughed. I think this meant we were beginning to bond.

"I'm Brenda Temple. I'm from Bar Harbor, Maine. I love seeing new things. Traveling. I guess I'm the kind of person who, when I encounter a closed door, I like to open it. I also enjoy watching whales and independent films."

"We've got a lot of marine life enthusiasts," Mrs. Knox said. "I wonder if any whales made it into the stories."

"I'm Annie Earl Wert. I'm originally from Omaha, but I currently live in Coral Gables, Florida. No real whale or baseball interests. I knit. And play the banjo. And I once had dinner with Ronald Reagan."

Nobody laughed. I think I heard a small gasp.

"The dead president?" Veronica asked.

"He was living at the time," Annie Earl said.

The next person jumped in before Annie Earl could elaborate.

"I'm Corky. Just Corky. I don't like using my last name because I feel it defines me in a way that is inauthentic to my ambitions. I think capturing whales and imprisoning them in fish tanks is a hostile act. But don't worry, I'm not an ecoterrorist. Bombs aren't the way I plan to change the world. What else? I like to hike. I've survived a plane crash. And I once killed a mountain lion with my shoe."

Corky looked a lot like how I pictured her after I read her sticky note. Again, nobody laughed.

"With your shoe?" Veronica asked. "Were you wearing vicious high heels?"

"Boots," Corky said. "The lion attacked my sheltie. I kicked it off of my dog and then stood on its neck until it suffocated. It was a young cat. A size I could handle. I protect what's mine."

She unscrewed the cap of her water bottle and took a sip.

"Oh my god," Veronica said. "That's amazing."

"A girl's gotta do what a girl's gotta do," Corky said.

"Okay. Thanks, Corky. Moving on. Does anybody have any questions?" Mrs. Knox asked.

Nobody had any questions.

"Kite, why don't you start. Please read from your story. Just a page or so."

"Anything?" he asked.

"Yep," Mrs. Knox said.

"I'd like to read from the milking scene."

"The barn smelled like Indiana and it made me miss California. I'd left San Diego and her crowded sidewalks and thoroughfares two weeks ago. Everything about her felt missable, even the faint stench of piss. I approached the goat slowly and offered her my hand. I expected her to lower her moist snout and sniff it the way a golden retriever would, but she turned away from me and stamped her hind legs. Like a nervous girl on prom night, she knew what I was after.

"'Come,' I said. I rubbed my hands together to warm them. No, I didn't really connect with my country cousins, but I could milk their goat. I reached down for her udder. It was warm and rubbery, and when I touched it, she released a

bleating refusal. But I didn't back down. I shoved the bucket under her with one hand, and with the other I yanked her teat. Not softly, but hard. I wanted milk."

I felt myself stand up. My knees turned to jelly. No wonder Hamilton dumped me. Things were starting to make sense. This was all about my second flaw. *Dessy, you enjoy life's surface pleasures so much that you resist looking for the deeper meaning. You have an analytical mind, but you don't use it.* Kite's metaphor was right there for me to see, and I had missed it. I hadn't applied my analytical mind!

I hurried to the door and thought about my original comments on Kite's story. "I'd enjoy more details about what the barn looked like." "How many cousins did the character have?" "What color was the goat?" All of them missed the obvious. Kite was writing about sex. SEX. I hadn't gone below the surface.

My head swam. I felt so stupid. And young. How could I have overlooked the sexual connotations of a young city boy milking his first country goat? Kite didn't stop reading. I walked out into the hall and shut the door behind me. I sat down and concentrated on breathing. I pictured my lungs taking in air and pushing the oxygen through my blood. If I didn't focus like this, I was worried I'd hyperventilate and pass out. This sort of panic had hit me once before. The wounded owl incident.

I closed my eyes. I hated to think too much about the wounded owl incident. But when that particular memory surfaced, I couldn't drive it out of my mind. I had to replay it over and over as a way to exorcise the trauma.

Hamilton and I had found the bird together. It was staggering through a crosswalk.

"*Bubo virginianus!*" Hamilton shouted. "A great horned owl!"

Hamilton parked his Volvo on the side of the road and we both sprang out of the car.

"There's a towel in my gym bag!" he yelled.

I ran back to the car for it. When I reached the owl it looked like a scientific experiment gone wrong. Its body was mangled. Burned.

"It needs a vet," he said.

He wrapped the owl like a baby. Its yellow eyes studied me, and its black beak curved into its white chin feathers like a dangerous hook. I held it while Hamilton drove. The owl grew hot on my lap. I kept looking into its eyes. They were so intelligent. And so scared. I kept saying, "You're going to be fine."

Hamilton sped into a vet's parking lot, grabbed the owl, and left me in the car. I didn't move. My heartbeat quickened. I thought of the bird and how it must have felt. The towel pinning its wings to its body. An unfamiliar pain pulsing through it. Would it ever be able to fly again? Would it want to? Would it develop an unbreakable fear of guns? Or the sound of guns? How would it handle thunderstorms? Would it be able to find a mate? I felt twisted. Like a rag. My emotions were being wrung out of me. I didn't like thinking this hard.

I sat and waited for Hamilton to come back. In retrospect, I realize that I could have gone into the vet's office, but at the time this didn't even occur to me. I'd sat and focused on the outcome that I wanted. The bird was going to survive. We'd found it. And saved it. It was going to pull through. But was this enough? I dreaded the idea that the owl would be altered. Would it still be able to hunt? Would it have to live in a caged-in area? Ugh. Probably. It was never going to be whole again. I leaned my head against the window and cried. And I didn't try to stop crying. I fogged up every window in Hamilton's car. When he came back, he didn't ask me what was wrong; he assumed that he knew.

"I know," he said. "It's terrible to see that kind of suffering. But it's going to be okay. They'll send it to a sanctuary. The people there know how to handle this exact sort of owl injury."

A sanctuary.

Hamilton rubbed my knee and smiled. Maybe this was the best thing for the owl. Maybe it didn't even know the difference between captivity and freedom. Maybe it would never know it was damaged.

"You still look sad," he said. "Why?"

I shrugged.

"Once it's better, we'll go and visit it," he said. "I promise."

The owl died that night.

When Hamilton called to tell me, he almost cried. After I hung up with him I called Veronica and told her about the unfortunate incident. But I didn't go into too many details. I emphasized the incredible adventure. And the intensity of trying to save a wounded animal. And the closeness I'd felt with Hamilton during and after the whole ordeal.

"Wow," Veronica said. "What kind of coward shoots an owl?"

"I don't know," I said.

"I do. An asshole coward."

And at the time I didn't even realize that I was trying to sanitize the sadness of the situation by leaving out certain parts. But it was a classic example of flaw number one: *I had selectively withheld important information for the sake of creating a more pleasant reality.* But was it so wrong to reshape a tragic event in order to make it less tragic?

I must have sat in the hallway for a half hour. When the class broke for a ten-minute break, Veronica hurried out to check on me.

"What's wrong?" she asked.

"I'm not even sure," I said.

"Is it gastrointestinal?" she asked. "I mean, we're in an *Eastern* European country, and you're drinking a ton of tap water."

I shook my head no. I saw somebody poke his head out of the room. It was Roger.

"Are you okay?" he asked.

I nodded. His head disappeared back into the classroom. Then I heard the clicking sound of heeled shoes. It was Mrs. Knox.

"You look a little pale," she said.

"I feel pale," I said.

"We should probably call a taxi, and I should escort her back to the dorms," Veronica said.

I shook my head. "I want to go back to class. I don't want to miss Brenda's story."

"Are you sure?" Veronica asked. "I know how to hail a taxi."

"She says she wants to go back to class," Mrs. Knox said. She held out her hand and helped me up.

"Thanks," I said.

I walked back into class feeling thirsty and light-headed. Veronica intuited this, and handed me an apple and some water. She seemed angry, but I knew she'd get over it. She moved Frank's things and made a place for me to sit. Class was important. We couldn't blow off the first workshop.

Brenda wanted to read from the middle of her story.

"Have you ever heard a lobster scream? They don't go peacefully into the boiling pot. They want to live as much as anything. I held my lobster in a box and walked past a fisherman in the parking lot. Goshdarn these fishermen and

their rubber yellow coats. Goshdarn their toggles and boots. Goshdarn their weathered faces. Goshdarn their smelly pants. Didn't they know that lobsters mattered? Furious with the world, I drove like a maniac with my lobster to the sea."

"Wow," Veronica said. "Cool scene. But I think you 'goshdarn' yourself into a corner."

Mrs. Knox gently slapped the table. "We start with what's working."

"I'll tell you what I like," Annie Earl said. "I like how she turns the rest of the world into savages. Lobsters die. We know that. But this story made me consider their point of view."

"Thanks," Brenda said. "My boyfriend is a fisherman. And I'm really conflicted about it."

"Shh," Mrs. Knox said. "No talking until after we finish responding to your piece."

I glanced at Veronica. She looked as thrilled as I felt. Our only competition for male attention in the workshop had been Brenda. And she'd admitted right in front of all of us that she had a boyfriend, and so now she was out of the game. It was a gift from the heavens.

"I liked your description of the clambake," Frank said. "I've never been to one. You're great at capturing smell images."

I had never heard of a "smell image."

"I really enjoyed this story," Roger said. "It's a great premise. The way we cook lobsters is torture, but because they're *lobsters*, the narrator's mission is, in society's eyes, borderline crazy."

Brenda smiled and nodded, like he'd gotten it.

"That's so compelling in itself," Roger continued. "And because her passion felt so sincere, I found the 'goshdarns' kind of grating. They felt loaded, like they were somehow criticizing the narrator's conservative, working-class background. For me, the language of the story began to challenge the narrative."

Brenda stopped smiling. Veronica leaned in toward me and whispered, "Meet our workshop's Derrida." I didn't know who or what a Derrida was.

"I also felt a little clobbered," Roger continued, "by the appearance of the seafood-loving priest in the second grocery store scene. He seemed a little too convenient. It felt deus ex machina, and it made the lobster feel less central."

"Maybe the lobster is Catholic," Waller joked.

Roger grimaced at that comment.

"The message hit me in the face too," Veronica said.

"The religious references did feel a bit shoehorned in," said Corky.

"I liked the priest," said Frank. "He was creepy, but so are lobsters and fishermen. Also, so is the chick buying groceries and tossing them into the sea."

"How much do lobsters cost?" Kite said. "I've seen them in the grocery stores, but never bought one. The story might be addressing, like, class."

"The fisherman did strike me as underpriviliged," Annie Earl said. "I think the protagonist feels conflicted about this. I think that's a big part of what's motivating her."

"Yeah," Roger said. "But gender is important too. All the lobsters' opposition is male."

"Even the bag boy," Waller added.

For the next twenty minutes the class discussed the price of live lobsters and then moved on to class warfare. Then we dissected the male characters and their symbolic roles. Everyone commented except for me. I just wasn't sure what to say. When I reread sections, the fisherman's untoggled rubber coat took on all kinds of new meaning. Like maybe I was supposed to imagine what was underneath that coat. Maybe the piece was a lot more carnal and sophisticated than I gave it credit for.

At the end of the criticism, Mrs. Knox gave Brenda the go-ahead to speak.

"Roger, I appreciated your comments. Mostly," she said. "I'm sorry you felt clobbered by the priest. I think he's thematically essential to the story." She looked at Mrs. Knox. "When I was a sophomore at Bowdoin, I sent an earlier version of this story as part of a collection to an editor at Knopf. It got rejected, but I got a very thoughtful letter. It really all came down to platform and market. She said that she needed a clearer way to position it. It was regional and quiet. She felt it needed more hooks. A quirky underdog. Religion, repression, sex. She said she could already see hints of these things and that I needed to tease them out. I think she was right."

Veronica leaned into me again. "Suck-up alert." I pulled away from her.

"My classmates at Bowdoin don't get it. They don't pay attention to the market. They want to play with their own minds at the expense of everything else. They write experimental, marginal, nonlinear *crap* because they like it, and frankly, it's masturbatory. I'm not saying I'm the next Lorrie Moore, but, well, maybe I am saying that."

Veronica leaned back into me. "I plan to use the word masturbatory in defense of my piece too."

Mrs. Knox nodded with a faintly amused smile. "Was the editor Kathryn Carter?" she asked.

Brenda nodded, surprised.

"She and I went to college together. Funny she'd come up. She always did have a thing for hooks." Mrs. Knox did a subtle imitation of a cat with its claws drawn. A few people laughed, but she talked over them. "Brenda has raised an interesting point. It's true. Editors, those fickle cultural gatekeepers, are usually the people who decide whether your writing makes it to the marketplace. It's important to read. And all writers I know follow the industry *somewhat*."

Brenda smiled like she was the true genius among a flock of floundering nongeniuses.

"Brenda, I admire your ambition. But I would never encourage a young writer to tailor her vision for an editor or add 'hooks' that feel inorganic to a story. I thought the voice would have been more compelling with *fewer* quirks." She smiled kindly. "Compromising sincerity is the worst injustice a talented writer can do herself."

Veronica made a gag face, which her mother thankfully didn't notice.

"I came to Prague to teach you the craft of writing—character development, inventiveness with language, paring away excess, and homing in on truth. There's absolutely nothing wrong with holding a magnifying glass over the raw, daily patterns of human life. If you know and love the human heart, you can write a heartbreaking best-seller about canning beets."

For the rest of the workshop, Mrs. Knox said amazing, insightful things about books she loved, and chatted with my classmates about their favorite and least favorite protagonists. I thought she was brilliant. Everything she said was worth writing down, so I had to start using shorthand. Veronica, though, acted like she'd heard it all before.

Mrs. Knox ended the class by giving us an assignment. "Visit one of Prague's historical synagogues and write ten descriptive sentences about it. Remember, focus on creating vivid images. The nature of image is about perception. Don't be afraid to use all five senses."

After class I handed back the stories to Kite and

Brenda. I didn't want to, but I felt obligated. I thought Veronica would pump the guys for information about where they were headed, but instead, she hooked her arm in mine and rushed me toward the stairs.

At the bottom of the stairs, Veronica veered left, past the front doors.

"Where are we going?" I asked.

"I think I saw a computer lab. I want to see if Boz wrote back." She grinned wickedly and walked toward a side door. "It'll only take a minute," she said, holding the door for me.

I followed her out into the warm afternoon. Maybe I should e-mail Hamilton and admit to him that I was beginning to understand the nature of my flaws. Maybe something like this would make a difference. I mean, it seemed possible that proper introspection could rekindle a broken bond.

"Oh my god!" Veronica said. "Look at that guy's ass. It's the most bulbous thing I've ever seen."

I didn't look. "Bulbous good or bulbous bad?" I asked.

"Bulbous fantastic," Veronica said.

I looked. "Isn't that his wallet?"

"Maybe. Let's go introduce ourselves. Do you know how to ask *What time is it?* in Czech?"

"No," I said.

"Doesn't matter. Men love foreign girls in distress. Follow my lead."

I watched Veronica jog ahead. When the guy with the bulbous butt turned around, I noticed two things. First, he had a bushy red beard. Second, he had a baby strapped to his chest. Veronica must have noticed these things too, because when she reached him, she jogged right on past. Then she ducked into the computer lab. I was relieved.

I took the bearded baby-guy as a premonition. From behind, he looked interesting. But full frontal was a different story. Therein lay the message: we shouldn't introduce ourselves to strange men. Because strange men might appear one way, but be a totally different way in reality. I mean, Veronica seemed to be forgetting that we were teenagers. Who had no business chasing after random Czech men we met on the street. I walked into the lab and scouted for Veronica's familiar head. She was beaming as she waved me over.

"He wrote me back!" she said. "Oh my god! You'll never guess what Boz said. My plan is totally working. It's like taking candy from a tween."

"You mean baby," I said.

"Tweens *are* babies," Veronica said, happily pecking the keyboard. "Haven't you ever noticed the way they dress?"

Chapter Nine

"Is somebody at our door?" I asked.

What began as polite light thudding had grown into distinct pounding.

"Sounds like a psychopath," Veronica said. "I'm not answering it."

"Veronica! It's your mother! Are you there?"

I got out of bed and answered the door. A very bedraggled-looking Mrs. Knox entered our suite and walked into our bedroom.

"This humidity is wrecking my hair," she said. "I'm headed out to buy a curling iron. I thought you two might want to come."

"That sounds cool," Veronica said, throwing on some clothes. "I need crap."

"Me too." I quickly slipped on my shorts and sneakers and followed the Knoxes out the door.

"Last time I was here my hair behaved wonderfully, the way it does in Moscow and Berlin," Mrs. Knox said as we exited the building. "But this time, atmospherically, Prague is behaving like a totally different beast. I feel like a puff ball."

"I think you look good," I told her.

"Ha," Veronica said, skipping ahead of us down the sidewalk.

"Oh, but have I ever told you how much I covet your hair?" Mrs. Knox asked me.

I was shocked to hear that anyone would covet my hair, let alone somebody blessed with thick, flowing masses of it.

"It falls around your face in a way that seems happy."

I reached up and pushed some of it behind my ear. Veronica was at least two car lengths ahead of us as she descended into the metro station.

"She has two speeds," Mrs. Knox said. "Stop, and go-like-hell."

This made me laugh. Because it was totally accurate. When we caught up with Veronica, she was studying a map of the metro and tapping her foot like an over-caffeinated rabbit.

"Will the store have thermometers?" she asked.

"Are you already anticipating a fever?" Mrs. Knox countered.

"I might have brought a thermometer," I said.

Both Veronica and her mother looked at me in total surprise.

"My mom had me pack a small first-aid kit," I said. "I think it has one."

When the train arrived, Veronica found a seat right away and plunked herself down in it. Mrs. Knox sat across the aisle and invited me to take the seat next to her. The ride was short, and Mrs. Knox was too preoccupied with her hair to chat. She touched it over and over. It wasn't until the end of the ride that she refocused her attention on me.

"Are you feeling better since yesterday?" she asked.

I didn't like thinking about my meltdown in class. And I didn't want to confess that it stemmed from feeling wholly inadequate as a commenter.

"I am," I said.

"Travel can be disorienting. There's no shame in taking naps."

"Okay," I said. But in reality I couldn't imagine informing Veronica that instead of going off and tracking down hot-dudes with her, I was opting to power nap in the dorm.

"Also I want you to know that you shouldn't feel any pressure to say things in class," Mrs. Knox said. "But you shouldn't feel intimidated either. The first time is the hardest, but after that it gets easier."

It was as if she were a mind reader.

"Okay," I said.

She looked at me with genuine concern.

"Don't worry about me," I said. "I've rallied." And I had. I'd culled over the short stories for Friday's class very thoroughly. Annie Earl's and Frank's were up next. After locating several sexual metaphors in both pieces: a missile silo, hedge clippers, and a partially deflated raft among them, I felt like a much more competent reader.

We got off the metro and walked a short distance to a steep and enormous set of fast-running escalators.

"Are they broken?" I asked.

"No," Mrs. Knox said. "In this part of town, they're just aggressive in their ascent and descent."

I climbed aboard and felt a light breeze as the metal stairs whooshed me to the street level.

"Can I pick up a few essentials too?" Veronica asked.

"Five essentials," Mrs. Knox said. "And that's it."

Normally, Mrs. Knox wasn't so firm with Veronica's shopping habits. Many times in Ohio I'd seen her hand over a credit card and let Veronica do whatever she wanted. But here she was attempting to keep Veronica's impulsive demands to a minimum. I doubted she'd be able to hold that line.

Even when the crowded sidewalk began to incline,

Mrs. Knox didn't slow her pace. We rushed past dozens of brightly lit, high-end boutiques and hordes of amazingly slim women wearing designer clothes—skirt suits, zippers the entire length of torsos, asymmetrical collars. I saw more gorgeous people in ten minutes on this boulevard than I'd ever encountered before in my life. These locals looked like they belonged on television.

"The place we're going must have awesome crap!" Veronica said.

"It's called Tesco," Mrs. Knox said. "And it's Prague's version of a Walmart."

Veronica didn't say anything, but I knew she was disappointed.

Tesco turned out to be nothing like Walmart. It wasn't big enough. And the merchandise on the shelves didn't feel endless or offer an obscene amount of variety. Plus, the shopping carts were way too tiny. Furthermore, unlike the Walmarts in Ohio, which spread *out*, Tesco had multiple stories.

Due to the store's limited selection, Mrs. Knox found a curling iron quickly, in the pea-sized appliances section.

"I want a fan," Veronica said. "Can I get five essentials plus a fan?"

"Are you sure you need a fan?" Mrs. Knox asked.

"Yes. I'm certain. By dawn I'm sweating like a pig in my bed," Veronica said. "Dessy too. We wake up glistening in our own perspiration. It's terrible. I get out of bed practically sticking to myself! It's not sanitary—"

"All right. I don't need you to catalogue your moist parts," Mrs. Knox said. "You can get a fan."

She drifted over toward the audio equipment, while Veronica zeroed in on a fan in a box as tall as a fourth-grader.

"Is this big enough?" she asked me.

"I'm not sweating that much," I said.

"Sometimes, to really sell my mom on something, I have to exaggerate the state of my suffering."

"Whatever," I said as I followed her to the register.

"Hey. The cashier is trying to tell me something," Veronica said. "WHAT–ARE–YOU–TRYING–TO–TELL–ME?"

"You don't need to shout," I said, mortified.

Mrs. Knox came back looking over the instructions for her curling iron. "They need to assemble it before you can buy it," she said. "It's their policy."

"Why?" Veronica asked.

"So they can guarantee that all the parts work."

The clerk appeared nonplussed as she dumped the parts onto the counter and commenced assembling our fan. The woman moved slowly and methodically. It took about ten minutes. Then, once it was assembled, she plugged it in.

"Yay!" Veronica said. "Let's get out of here and shop on the good floors."

"Wait. They need to disassemble it and put it back in its original box," Mrs. Knox said. She smiled at the clerk. "I'm sorry."

"You're joking," Veronica said. "I'm wasting valuable shopping time here."

"At least you know your fan will work," Mrs. Knox said. "You should be happy for the test run."

I was amazed that the clerk was able to fit every single part back inside the box. When she was finished, she handed Mrs. Knox a piece of paper to sign.

"What's that?" Veronica asked.

"I'm agreeing that the fan was assembled and works."

"How much does this thing cost, anyway?"

"Roughly twenty dollars," Mrs. Knox said.

"This country is totally prehistoric," Veronica said.

I glanced around at the other shoppers, while Mrs. Knox paid. Nobody seemed to be paying attention to us, which relieved me. Maybe they were used to foreigners behaving like this.

"I'm headed back to the dorms," Mrs. Knox said, smoothing her hair with one hand. "I need to correct this explosion."

"What about my other five things?" Veronica asked.

Mrs. Knox reached into her purse and handed Veronica a few bills.

"Will you take my fan back to the dorm for me?" Veronica asked. "Dessy and I want to explore."

"You can't stay out all day," Mrs. Knox said. "We're touring the Old Jewish Cemetery this afternoon. And I'm expecting college-level work on your writing assignment. This is not a vacation, Veronica."

"Right," Veronica said.

"Be back in two hours."

"Gotcha." Veronica saluted her mother, who turned and walked down the stairs.

"She's really getting on my last nerve," Veronica said.

"She's having a bad-hair day," I said.

"That's what I like about your mom," she said.

"Oh, my mom totally has bad-hair days. I mean, she has bangs."

"No, I'm saying that your mother would never act like *that*. She'd never create a self-indulgent writing assignment which forces us to tour a cemetery and a long list of synagogues."

"Are you insulting my mother?" I asked.

"No." Veronica tugged on my arm and led me to the stairs.

"I love your mom. She's not complicated like my mine. Your mom does mom things. Bakes. Gardens. Power walks at the mall. She's so reasonable. Loving her must be totally effortless."

I followed Veronica down the stairs without commenting on her observations. They seemed slightly offensive. Like somehow her mother was far more interesting than mine. Even if this were true, hearing Veronica say it made me uncomfortable.

"Your mom is a basic mom," Veronica said. "You're so lucky. It's like you won the mom lottery."

"I like your mom," I said.

"I like my mom too. I'm not saying that I don't like my mom. I love her."

"Great. Drama over."

Veronica paused on the stairs and turned around to glare at me. "Maybe if my dad comes back, then the drama will be over."

It stung. I felt like I should apologize, but I wasn't sure what for.

"I'm saying you're lucky. Your mom is always there for you. She thinks about *you* before she thinks about herself. I'm giving you a compliment."

I nodded, and she turned around and started moving again. Soon, we were back at the ground level of Tesco.

"I saw a ton of cool crap on this floor," Veronica said.

"What do you want?" I asked.

"Good question. I'm feeling totally greedy," she said. "I wonder what kind of lotions they have. This climate has thrown my skin for a loop. I think I'm chafing again."

I looked at her legs and arms. She was sporting a pair of white shorts and a pale yellow T-shirt. Her skin appeared totally normal.

"Veronica, you brought an entire vat of lotion," I said.

"But what if Czech lotion is creamier? I've got to find out!"

I watched her uncap and sniff tube after tube. Sometimes it felt like Veronica had a touch of OCD. Cap on. Cap off. Squeeze tube. Sniff. Sniff. Sniff. Repeat. Repeat. Repeat. She was drawn to lotion like a mosquito to exposed leg flesh.

"Another way that you're lucky is that your mom gave you great skin," Veronica said. "You don't have to doctor it with ointments like I do."

"You consider glitter lotion an ointment?" I asked.

"Totally."

I wandered behind her, entering into the distinctive stink of perfume.

"Doesn't this smell make you gag?" I asked.

"No. Why? What are you smelling?" She was holding an enormous green container of lotion.

"Rotting flowers," I said.

"I kind of like it," Veronica said.

She put the lotion in a basket and continued to shop.

"But the ingredients aren't written in English. You don't even know what's in that stuff," I said.

"Control your level of freak. Lotion is lotion. And it smells great."

"What if it's a depilatory?" I asked.

"Then why would it be in a green tube with a picture of hands on it?"

We circled the first floor six times while she continued to add to her haul. Two dozen tea candles. A half dozen greeting cards written in Czech. A hammer. Mascara. Two packages of nylons. Face wash. And gum.

"Do you want anything?" she asked.

I wanted a lot of things, but I was too worried about my current financial state to spend any money at the moment.

"Are you hungry?" Veronica asked.

"A little," I admitted.

"Go pick something out," she said.

"I think I saw some granola bars over there."

"Get them. My treat. And any other snacks you want. Seriously, why not live a little?"

I took Veronica at her word and gathered an entire basketful of munchies. I knew she'd eat most of them anyway.

"Let's go check out Wenceslas Square," she said as soon as we got back outside. "I've been studying my map and I think we're really close."

"We have to be back to the dorm in less than two hours," I said. "We promised."

"It's not like we'll be late for our own weddings."

I looked down the busy cobblestone sidewalk. I *was* craving a little more adventure. "Okay," I said.

Waller had mentioned Wenceslas Square during our walking tour, but I wasn't exactly sure what it was. A park? A shopping center? A farmers' market? Once Veronica and I were in the crosswalk, it became perfectly clear that the square was one of Prague's major hubs. Parked cars lined the traffic-crowded boulevard. Multi-storied and brightly colored buildings rose up over the wide road, shading half of the bustling crowd. There were restaurants and shops and apartments. We walked alongside the old stone buildings, and every time I had the chance, I reached out and dragged my fingers along their surfaces. They didn't build things like this in Cleveland.

At the end of the square stood a bronze statue. An enormous building rose gorgeously behind it. I figured it might be a museum, because the building itself looked like a piece of art.

"I want to look at that statue," I said. "Let's see whose it is."

Veronica rolled her eyes. "Why? It's just going to be

some dead guy we've never heard of. Probably atop a horse."

"Come on," I said. "I like statues."

"Dessy, nobody likes statues except sculptors and pigeons."

"What about art history majors?" I asked.

"Trust me. They just fake it."

Veronica reluctantly followed me to the top of the square. She was right. The figure was on a horse.

"There's nothing here written in English. For all we know, this statue is the Czech interpretation of Paul the Baptist."

"Who's Paul the Baptist?" I asked.

"You know. That guy from the Bible who loses his head."

I shaded my eyes from the sun. She was talking so loudly that I was worried other people would hear her and think she was a total bonehead.

"I think you mean John the Baptist," a man said.

Fantastic. Now some random person was going to think that Veronica and I were both bonehead tourists. I mean, we were carrying very similar bags. And with her present footwear, we were similar heights. And our clothes weren't all that dissimilar. I wanted to tell the man immediately that I knew there was no such person as Paul the Baptist. As I turned to look at him, I bit my lip. It was worse than I'd thought it would be. This guy was gorgeous. Great. He looked like a swimsuit model only he was wearing all his clothes.

"I'm Veronica Knox. This is my friend Dessy. We're here for the July Prague College Writers' Conference."

I couldn't help but notice how Veronica included the word "college."

"So you're writers?" he said, extending a hand to shake.

"Yes," Veronica said, reaching out to take it. "We're

both English majors. I'm a huge Walt Whitman fan, and Dessy loves Tolstoy."

"Really?" the man asked. "*Anna Karenina* is my favorite novel. I'm Scotty Dee."

My eyes must have been huge. Why couldn't she have made me a John Steinbeck or Sylvia Plath fan? Those were writers I'd actually read. But Tolstoy? I wasn't even sure of his first name. Theo? Leo? Ron?

"Where are you from?" Veronica asked.

His accent was obvious, I thought.

"Australia," he said.

"I LOVE Australia!" Veronica said.

The man laughed. He looked like he was in his early twenties, possibly older. He was tall and lanky. He could have been Frank's attractive older brother. They both had corkscrew blond hair. I thought this guy's jeans were a tad snug. But historically speaking, Veronica thought tight clothing on slim people was a sign of a healthy level of self-esteem. I looked at her face. I could tell she was falling for him. Big time.

Then I spotted it. The one thing a guy can have that always sent Veronica into head-over-heels obsession mode. The one thing Boz was still too chicken to get. A tattoo. And this Aussie's tattoo wasn't a small one. It was, I thought, a real uninspiring clunker. A fat red heart sat squat like an apple on his upper arm.

"Ooh, does that say *MOM*?" Veronica asked, touching his skin with her finger.

"Worse," Scotty Dee said. "It says *Smudge*. They're an Australian band you've probably never heard of. I got it after a concert. Never a good idea."

"I think tattoos are cool and can really define a person," Veronica said.

"Yeah, literally," Scotty Dee said.

"So, what are you doing in Prague?" she asked.

"Just looking around. I came here with my friend Kirk."

Veronica peeked over Scotty Dee's shoulder.

"He's not *here* here," Scotty Dee said, smiling. "He's in the country today."

"And why aren't you in the country today?" Veronica asked.

This was a total flirt fest. I felt like a complete fifth wheel. I wasn't sure if I should jump into the conversation or stand still and be quiet. Or walk off. Or detach and meditate. Or what.

"I like the city more than the country. I'm from the country."

"We're from Ohio. Have you ever heard of Ohio?" Veronica asked.

"Yeah, isn't Cleveland there?" he asked.

"Yes. Dessy and I live right outside of Cleveland," Veronica told him.

"They have a famous river there, right? It caught on fire?"

"Oh, that was a long time ago," Veronica said. "It's totally fine now."

I saw my chance to contribute, so I leapt at it.

"You're thinking of the Cuyahoga River Fire. It happened in 1969. And it only lasted thirty minutes. And it wasn't so much that the river caught fire as it was that a concentrated area of industrial pollutants ignited. In a weird way, it was a good thing, because it led to the Clean Water Act," I said.

Veronica looked at me and wrinkled her brow. She wasn't happy with my recitation of gloomy Ohio trivia.

"Oh," Scotty Dee said. "I didn't realize I'd learn so much about Ohio while on holiday in Europe."

"Forget everything Dessy just said. Ohio really is fantastic."

He nodded.

"So, whereabouts in the city are you headed?" Veronica asked.

"The museum," Scotty Dee said, pointing to the building behind the statue.

"We're heading off to the Old Jewish Cemetery today. You know, check out the graves and then tour some synagogues. Well, look at the time. It's getting late. Nice meeting you," Veronica said, lifting her hand in a wave. "Catch you later."

"Wait," Scotty Dee said, reaching out and touching Veronica's arm. "I was going to tell you about this statue. So you wouldn't go around with the impression that you'd just seen the likeness of Paul the Baptist."

Veronica smiled. Sometimes I was surprised at how well she could read guys. She could sense he was losing interest, perhaps I'd spooked him a bit with my Cuyahoga River Fire trivia. And in response to his response, she'd pulled back. She was prepared to bolt. Which was something she'd told me many times about how to keep a guy interested: "Whenever you feel his interest waning, make a bold exit. It works every time. If his gaze wanders, even for a flicker of an instant, you get the hell out of there. Trust me. He'll watch your butt as you leave." And even here in Prague, with a fully mature Australian guy, her "bolt strategy" had worked like a charm.

"All right, Scotty Dee," Veronica said, flipping her hair over her shoulder. "Tell us what we need to know."

He laughed and pulled out his guidebook.

"I don't want to get anything wrong. Wouldn't want to dispense misinformation to American college students," he said, thumbing through the book.

"We wouldn't want that either," Veronica said.

"It says here that Saint Wenceslas is the patron

saint of Bohemia. Wenceslas was murdered by his brother. The body, hacked to pieces, was buried at the place of his murder, but three years later his brother ordered its transfer to the Church of Saint Vitus in Prague."

"Holy shit," Veronica said. "Stories like that give me great relief that I'm an only child."

"I'm not finished," Scotty said.

Veronica looked like she'd heard enough about this saint.

"And legend says that an army sleeps inside a mountain and they will wake under Wenceslas's command when the motherland is in ultimate danger. And when his horse stumbles and trips over a stone, a sword will appear. And wielding this, King Wenceslas will slaughter all the enemies of the Czechs, and bring peace and good fortune back to the land."

"Is that everything?" Veronica asked.

Scotty Dee winked. "It's a shame to meet and part ways," he said.

"Shames. Life is filled with them," Veronica said.

"We should meet up again," Scotty Dee said.

"We've got classes during the day," Veronica said. "Three days a week. Workshops. They're intense."

"I wouldn't want to derail your studies," he said.

"Yeah. Our studies are very important to us," Veronica said.

"Why don't you two meet me and Kirk here Sunday? Say six o'clock? Does that work for you?"

Since today was Thursday, that meant he was suggesting we meet up again real soon.

Veronica pursed her lips like she was thinking. "That works for *moi*. What about you, Dessy?"

I nodded. I guess hanging out with hot guys with amazing accents worked for me.

"Hey, let me get your picture," Veronica said. "I'm a huge fan of photography."

"Uh-oh. I don't have my camera," I said. Because it was a cheap disposable one, I'd left it in the room on purpose. Using it in front of people, I feared, would draw attention to me and make me feel poor.

Veronica looked devastated.

"That's okay. Bring it on Sunday," Scotty said. "At six o'clock."

Veronica reached out and touched the heart on his arm again. "Okay," she said.

As we walked off I bumped her with my shoulder.

"Ouch," she said.

"You came on way too strong," I said.

"I had to do something to combat your weirdo Ohio info drop. The Cuyahoga River Fire?"

"You saw him. He's trivia minded. He knew where Ohio was and he's not even an American. He ate that river story up!"

"Yeah. Yeah. Here's something you need to know," Veronica said. She sounded very serious. "If a guy asks us both out and he has a guy friend, it's called a double invitation and that's cool. If a guy asks one of us out for a date, it's called a single invitation and that's cool too. Never try to convert a double invitation into a single or vice versa. Because men have very sensitive egos and they'll take it the wrong way."

"What if one guy asks both of us out?" I asked.

"That's called a sex party and we don't go," Veronica said. "Oh my god! It's the guys. It looks like they're eating lunch. Let's go harass them."

Veronica took off, and I followed her. Waller, Frank, Roger, and Kite were sitting at a table littered with pizza crusts on paper plates. I guess their earlier impulse to pursue authentic Czech cuisine had been a short-lived one.

"It runs counter to my nature to tease flood victims," Waller was saying, "but when I realized the guy was canoeing down Main Street in two feet of water, I couldn't resist running past him in my waders, making some waves, and yelling, 'The current has me!'" Waller put his arms out and moved them around like he was swimming. The guys sat around him laughing and drinking beer under the sun's hot glow.

"Hey," Waller said. "How's it going?"

"Sorry to interrupt," Veronica said. "That sounded like an interesting story."

"Oh, I was just telling them about when I worked a sandbag line in my grandparents' hometown."

"That's very philanthropic of you," Veronica said. Her tone was totally sincere.

"How are you feeling?" Waller asked.

"Pretty good," Veronica said. "We just checked out the Wenceslas statue. When I visit a square, I always stop by its namesake." She winked and flipped her hair.

"Okay," Waller said. "And how are you doing?"

His eyes fell on me. They looked concerned, and it made me melt a little.

"I'm feeling better," I said.

"Did you visit the plaque for Jan Palach?" Waller asked.

"Who?" Veronica responded.

"Jan Palach, the student who set himself on fire to protest the Russian occupation?"

"The Russian tanks rolled into town right there," Roger said, pointing in the direction of the statue.

"That's tragic," Veronica said.

"It really is. People tried to stop them, but really, there's no way for a group of citizens to stop an army of advancing tanks."

"Good point," Veronica said. "Hey, you seem like you're headed somewhere."

The guys exchanged glances and mischievous smiles. "Not all of us," Roger said.

"Where are the rest of you headed?" Veronica asked, twirling her hair with her pointer finger.

"Well, that's privileged information," Kite said.

"Yeah," said Frank. "We wouldn't want anybody to tell their mom." He glanced at Waller again.

"I don't tell my mom things," Veronica said.

"Frank is just teasing you," Roger said. "Don't take him seriously."

"Well, I'm being serious," Veronica said. "You should tell me. I keep secrets like you wouldn't believe."

"That's not even tempting," Kite said. "Because you come across as a gusher."

Veronica's jaw dropped. "A gusher? I'm not a gusher. What makes you think I'm a gusher?"

"It's a hunch." Kite wiped pizza crust crumbs off his lap. "Listen, how about we tell you later?"

Veronica's mood had shifted. She was practically scowling at the guys. "Cool," she said. "See you later."

And she turned on her heel and walked off. She left me standing in the wake of her pissy attitude—with four college guys—feeling like a total idiot.

"Her mother is having a bad-hair day," I said.

"I've had a few of those," Waller said. He ran his fingers through his long hair and shook it. Watching him do this made me tingle.

"What did you buy?" Roger asked, pointing to my bag.

"I'm not totally sure," I said.

"What do you mean? Do you shop with your eyes closed?" he asked. I studied his face to decipher his tone. But all I saw was brown eyes and a freckled nose and neat trimmed sideburns. I couldn't tell if he was playing with me or making fun of me.

"No. I'm pretty sure they're snack items. Everything was written in Czech."

"Dessy!" Veronica yelled. "We're going to be late for the bones."

"Bones?" Waller asked.

"The Old Jewish Cemetery," I said.

"I thought maybe you were going to Kutná Hora," Waller said.

I didn't respond. Because I thought I heard him say the word "whore," and why would Veronica and I be going to look at those?

"Have you ever heard of Kutná Hora and the Sedlec Ossuary?" Waller asked.

"Oh yeah," I said. "Veronica and I are dying to go there."

"Dessy!" Veronica yelled.

"We might drive out there later this week. You two should come," Waller said. "It's supposed to be unbelievable."

"Okay. Sure. I've got to go," I said. "We're going to take a tour. With a guide and stuff. It's rude to make tour guides wait. Because it suggests that you aren't very interested."

"Enjoy the tour. Don't forget to close your eyes sometimes and let everything sink in," Waller said.

"I won't," I said. Then I waved good-bye. And ran off.

I was hoping to hear Waller yell something after me, like, "See you later, Dessy!" or "I love talking to you!" or "Nice legs!" But that didn't happen.

As I hurried after Veronica I could hear the guys laughing. Not at me. I knew it was about their top secret plans. Seriously, though. What could be *that* funny?

Chapter Ten

"Just go ahead and cremate me," Veronica said. "I mean, the idea that somebody would be buried on top of me, let alone several people piled directly above a box containing my remains. The concept wounds me. I couldn't endure it. I just couldn't."

Veronica collapsed into the first available metro seat and stared at the floor. I sat next to her and patted her leg.

To say that Veronica had not enjoyed the tour of the Old Jewish Cemetery was an understatement. She'd found it abhorrent and, therefore, unlike me, couldn't be impressed by any of the tour facts. I mean, we had just seen the oldest Jewish cemetery in Europe. Was it spooky? Certainly. But it was also very interesting.

"Don't you think we're sort of lucky to have seen it? Because it's amazing that the place exists at all. Remember what the guide said about how the Nazis made it a policy to destroy Jewish cemeteries? How they even used the tombstones for target practice?"

"I don't feel lucky to have seen any of it. Seriously. When my time comes, go ahead and incinerate me and then scatter my ashes at the mall." She reached down and squeezed my hand.

"I didn't think it was that bad," I said. "There were parts I liked. Even loved."

Veronica made gagging noises, but I ignored her. She rested her head on my shoulder. If Veronica had been a more reasonable person I could have debated with her until she realized that our tour of the Jewish Quarter had been a meaningful experience. As it was, I was going to have to wait and talk to my mother about what I'd seen. I knew she would understand. Even though she hadn't done much of it, she thought seeing the world was important.

"Collapsing headstones aren't tour-worthy. Castles. Cathedrals. Crown jewels on display behind bulletproof glass. Those are tourist destinations," Veronica said.

I wanted to remind Veronica that we'd seen a lot more than a few graves. Before the cemetery, our tour had started off at the synagogues. And I had done exactly what Waller had said. I'd let everything sink in. I hadn't understood that it was possible to feel emotionally stirred by a building. But I was. I saw things at the Spanish Synagogue that were so amazing their beauty was now lodged inside of me forever. Walls outlined in gold. Pillars decorated with dizzying amounts of green, red, and black paint. And ceilings so high and ornate that for the first time in my life I was able to imagine the idea of heaven.

Veronica hadn't even wanted to go inside.

"We were just in a synagogue," she'd said to her mother.

"We're going into another one," Mrs. Knox said.

"Why?"

"It's part of the tour!"

There was so much tension between the two of them that I seriously thought about stepping outside.

"Life shouldn't be *this* structured. You don't leave any time for random fun crap to happen. All you do is plan, plan, plan," Veronica had said. "Living life shouldn't feel like plotting a story."

Mrs. Knox seemed to bristle at this comment. "We've

got two more synagogues to tour, Veronica. Maybe random fun crap will occur when you take the subway home."

"I thought we were going out to dinner after this," Veronica said.

"Change of plans," Mrs. Knox said in a brusque tone. "I want to investigate purchasing some art from a local painter I met."

Veronica shrugged as if she didn't care. But I knew she did. She'd been looking forward to dinner out.

After their fight, Veronica couldn't appreciate anything we saw. Even when I'd told her what Waller had said about letting everything sink in.

"If Waller were standing right here and he said that to me, I'd flip him the bird," Veronica said.

"I'm going to give you a little space," I said.

And I did. I'd breathed in the synagogue's air. Every inch of it was covered in color, even the stained-glass windows. The guide said that the Spanish Synagogue got its name because it was inspired by the Alhambra, a palace in Spain that was built by the Moors. So it was like I was touring that place too. Veronica hadn't wanted to hear anything about the Moors.

"I read *Othello*," she'd said. "When it comes to the Moors, I think I've got their number."

But I loved hearing about the Moors and how they were followers of Mohammed and the Koran. I didn't know that one of the laws of the Koran forbids any human figures or animal forms in sculpture or painting. The guide explained that this is why Moorish architecture only used geometric figures in decorating the synagogue. I fell in love with the place. Its floors, and walls, and arches, and benches. If our guide hadn't been sixty, I bet I could have fallen in love with him too.

I didn't understand everything he said, but I paid

attention because my mother had studied architecture in college. Sometimes we'd drive through neighborhoods and she'd point out what was Roman versus Victorian versus Gothic. I'd listened intently to the words the guide used: "features a low stucco arabesque," "use of stylized Islamic motifs," "carried out on the doors and gallery balustrades."

The metro jerked to an abrupt halt, and Veronica moaned.

"Are you going to throw up?" I asked.

"I should have. Right there in that awful cemetery. If she makes us go to anything else like that, it'll kill me. Seriously. I'll have an aneurism and die."

Because Veronica was visibly green, I didn't argue with her.

Our stop was next, and thankfully the train was lightly populated. It seemed unfair for other passengers to have to endure Veronica's complaining.

"My mom is obsessed with tombstones," Veronica said as we stumbled off the train and walked toward the escalators.

"Veronica, one hundred thousand people were buried there."

"That's just too many," she said. She covered her ears like she was trying to block out all dissenting arguments. "There should never be one hundred thousand of anything. Let alone dead people."

Back at the dorm, Veronica swept her card over the front door and made a beeline for our room. Then she groaned. And turned back around.

"I feel like I'm being assaulted with sticky notes," she said. She pulled one from the door and slapped it to her forehead. It stayed pasted to her skin for about a second, then it fluttered to the floor. I caught the words "kitchen duties and bathroom responsibilities."

"Is that Veronica and Dessy?" a voice called from behind a closed bedroom door.

"Yes," I said.

"We don't have to answer," Veronica whispered. "There's still time to run."

I shook my head.

Brenda and Annie Earl both emerged from their room. They looked eager to talk.

"Corky is in her room too," Brenda said. "This is perfect timing."

I looked at Corky's door and saw smoke wafting out from beneath the doorjamb.

"Is she a smoker? Should we be worried?" I asked.

"Let's knock!" Annie Earl said, barging toward Corky's presumably locked living quarters.

After three loud pounds, Corky flung open the door. She stood before us completely nude. Her body looked like a perfect pear. I tried to focus on her head.

"What are you doing in there? Do you need a towel?" Brenda asked. She stared at Corky in utter disgust.

"I'm being naked. And no, I don't need a towel. I made peace with my body eons ago," Corky said. "I don't punish it for its imperfections. I embrace it."

"I didn't realize you'd collected such a variety of piercings," Annie Earl said.

"Yeah, yeah. My mom has already given me those lectures," Corky said.

"Oh. I'm not lecturing you. It's just that usually I'm able to notice a person's nipple rings through their shirt. Yours somehow escaped me."

I aimed my gaze at the ceiling. I wasn't used to female nudity other than my own. Even in gym class.

"Um, maybe we should go over lists and duties after dinner," Brenda said.

"How about tomorrow? After workshop? I need

to get to work on my story," Corky said. "I've hit an impasse with a machete and a hot air balloon." She yawned and scratched her neck.

"All right," Brenda said. "See you tomorrow."

"Cool," Corky said. "Rock on."

I watched her turn around, revealing her bare pear ass, and return to her room.

"We need to work on our stories too," Veronica said. "I've reached an impasse with a big-tailed animal and a small-tailed animal."

Brenda looked defeated, but nodded.

"Good luck with that," Annie Earl said. "I think I'm going to go buy a marionette."

I followed Veronica into our room and shut the door behind me.

"Corky is so awesome!" Veronica said. "I mean, there she is. Chubby. Terrible haircut. Wearing an obscene amount of eyeliner. And she's a total nudity freak."

"How does that make her awesome?" I asked.

Veronica threw her hands up. "Because she looks like a disaster and she doesn't try to cover up this condition with nice clothes. She's a free woman. She doesn't plot her life. She just lives it. And that's so rare."

"Maybe," I said. But I wasn't sure. Because shouldn't life be partly planned? Isn't that why we lived in a place called "civilization," where we had freeways and mortgages and orthodontists?

Veronica lay back on her bed and took out her notebook. "Sometimes I worry that I don't know enough about foxes to write this story."

"Have you done any research?" I asked.

"Well, I watched a fox on television once."

I rolled onto my side and looked at Veronica. "I don't think that's enough."

"What about you? What kind of research have you done on Ecuador?"

"I haven't done any research on Ecuador because I'm writing about Guatemala."

"Same difference," Veronica said.

I wagged my finger at her. "That's not true. I picked Guatemala for very specific reasons."

"Please, do not start lecturing me about Guatemala."

"You think everything is a lecture," I said.

"You're acting like you're on your period. Let's declare some silent time and work."

"Fine," I said.

Sometimes Veronica drove me mad. Okay, so maybe I *had* been intending to let loose some lecturelike information. But where's the hurt in that? She definitely didn't know enough about foxes to write her story. She could have benefitted from some additional knowledge about all sorts of countries. Central and South American ones especially. To be honest, she could have used some refresher facts about North American countries as well. Even the United States.

"Don't pout," Veronica said.

"I'm not. I'm utilizing my silent time."

Veronica got up and clicked on the oscillating fan to its lowest setting. Every four seconds the air above me stirred, and it felt like a bird was flying over me. After coming to this realization, I tried not to think about Hamilton.

"Aren't you excited about our date Sunday with Scotty Dee and Kirk?" Veronica asked. "Aren't you impressed that I pulled that off?"

I sighed. "I was at first. But to be honest, upon reflection, Scotty Dee seems old," I said.

"Get over it. He's gorgeous," Veronica said. "Boz will freak when he sees pictures of me with a rock star–hot Aussie."

I hated the idea of the continued torment of Boz.

"Frank is cuter," I said.

"Oh my god! I think so too," Veronica said. She hurried across the room and plopped down on my bed. This maneuver made my whole body bounce.

"What happened to silent time?" I asked.

"Duh. Silent time ended when we started talking about guys. Okay. On a scale of one to ten, how attracted do you think Frank is to me?"

"I don't know," I said.

"Guess."

I mulled it over. "Seven," I said. "And a half."

Veronica's eyes bugged out. She looked thrilled. "Oh my god. Seven and a half is high. What about Kite?"

"Seven and a half."

Her grin intensified. "Roger?"

"I'm not sure," I said. "He's reserved. Let's just say seven."

The seven range seemed safe. It kept Veronica pleased and also put her in a place where she didn't ask for elaboration.

"What about Waller?"

"What do you mean?" I asked.

"On a scale of one to ten, how attracted do you think Waller is to me?"

I blinked at her several times. My stomach tightened. Veronica and I had never been interested in the same guy before. What was she doing? Didn't she have enough potential flings on her plate?

"Stop making that face," Veronica said. "I'm totally kidding. I know you like Waller. I'd never make a move on a guy you liked. Ever."

Veronica picked up my hand and kissed the back of it.

"That was a terrible trick," I said.

"I know. But the important thing is that I think Waller is interested in you at least at a level eight, possibly a level nine," Veronica said.

This made all my anger flow out of me.

"He's so cute," I said. "I can't wait to read his story."

"Yeah. Everybody's writing is better than I thought it would be. I mean, I didn't like Brenda's"— she stuck her finger down her throat—"but I liked Kite's. And I like Frank's and Annie Earl's stories for tomorrow."

"He knows a lot about marine animals," I said. "I had no idea that if you messed with a dolphin's blowhole it had the potential to charge you and deliver a fatal head butt."

I waited for Veronica to offer some sort of sexual interpretation of Frank's story, but she didn't. I couldn't come up with one either.

"Do you think his story is a metaphor for something else?"

Veronica sighed. "Basic postadolescent male horniness."

"Yeah," I said.

"Can you believe that Annie Earl won a pie-making contest and was given an award of five hundred thousand dollars? That's so huge. And for a cherry pie? Can you imagine?"

"That was a true story?" I asked.

"Totally. I Googled it. She won five hundred thousand smackers."

"Have you Googled anyone else?" I asked. "Maybe I'll Google Waller."

"We don't know his real first name. He's un-Googleable," Veronica said. "It's one of those sucky things you're going to have to live with. Or we could break into his room and sneak a peek at his passport." She was perfectly serious.

"No way," I said. "I think I'd rather let there be a little mystery involved."

"Your choice. The only guy I found on the Internet was Roger. He won some prize in Chicago for writing a poem about a trout."

"He fishes?" I asked.

"No. The poem isn't about catching the trout, it's about eating it. I suspect he might have a sexual hang-up. But I'd need to read more poems."

I wasn't clear how writing a poem about a trout dinner turned you into somebody with a sexual hang-up.

"He seems really normal to me. Nice, actually," I said.

"Time will tell."

Veronica flipped onto her side and narrowed her eyes at me. "I know it's probably rude to talk about this, but I think it's time we discuss it."

"What?" I asked. I was worried she was going to bring up my BO. This city made me sweat so much I couldn't help it.

"How do you think she got burned?" Veronica asked.

"Annie Earl?" I asked.

"Duh," Veronica said. "I bet it was a crazy ex-lover. I bet it was one of those, 'If I can't have you, no one can' situations."

"I don't know. She's a cook. Maybe it was a grease fire," I said.

"I don't think so. I think it was something dramatic. I know!" she gasped. "Maybe Ronald Reagan set her on fire!"

"What?" I asked.

"She said she had dinner with Ronald Reagan, and the way she said this made me think there was more to the story."

"Ronald Reagan did not set Annie Earl on fire."

"You're probably right."

"Probably?"

Veronica returned to her own bed and took out her notebook again.

"Maybe you should Google some information about foxes," I said.

"Shhh. Our walls are pretty thin. I don't want people to hear you say that."

"You don't want people to hear me say Google?" I asked.

"No, foxes," she whispered.

She'd already said the word "fox" much louder than I had, just moments ago, but I didn't point that out.

"Why?" I asked.

"Because it's a great idea and I don't want anybody to steal it," Veronica said.

"Should we develop a code word?"

"Totally. From now on call them otters," she said.

"Seriously?" I asked.

"Yeah. When you have a 'great idea' like this"—she drew scare quotes in the air—"it's important to prevent people from ripping it off."

There were many reasons to object to this argument. Not the least of which was that it was based on irrational paranoia.

"Okay. I'll call them otters," I said.

"This may surprise you, but my 'otter' story is going to turn out to be pretty great," she said.

"Why would that surprise me?" I asked.

"Because I've made it seem like I don't care very much about it," she said.

I lay down on my own bed and reached into my backpack for the first six pages of my Guatemala story. So far the two main characters had driven half-way through Mexico in a rental car they'd secured in Oklahoma, though they would only drive while the guy was sleeping, because he was afraid of being in a moving car. I heard Veronica's pen scratching against her notebook.

"I know you care about your story," I said.

She tossed her pillow at me, and it thwacked me in the head.

"Why did you do that?" I asked.

"I don't know," she said in a low monotone.

"Why do you sound so unhappy all of a sudden?" I asked.

"Writing makes me feel conflicted," she said. "It makes feel like I'm being self-centered."

"Why would it make you feel that way?"

"You'd have to live with a writer to understand." Veronica rolled onto her stomach and commenced chewing her pen cap.

"You complain a lot about your mom being selfish," I said. "But I don't see it that way."

"That's because she acts differently when you're around."

"We've been friends since seventh grade," I said. "I think I would have picked up on it by now."

"It was way worse when I was younger," Veronica said. "My mom was always typing. Or reading manuscripts for her class. Or reading other people's books. Or traveling to read from her new collection."

"It's her job," I said.

"I know that. But a lot of times things came down to a choice. Attend Veronica's gymnastics meet or be a visiting writer at Breadloaf. Celebrate Veronica's birthday with her or fly to New York to give a reading. And a lot of the time it was about her daily choices. Given the chance to spend time with her family or write, she always chose to write. Seriously. She always chose that over us. Every time."

I didn't say anything.

"If she'd been around more—I mean, really been there for us—I think things would have ended up differently. Even with my dad."

When Veronica talked about her father, I never knew what to say.

"I am the only person I know whose father left his family to live in Rome for the weather," she said.

"Your statement implies that you know of other dads who left their families to live in Rome," I said. I didn't mean it snarky. I was merely making an observation.

"This is no time to pick me apart," Veronica said. "I'm opening up."

"You're right. I'm sorry," I said.

"Clearly, you have a better relationship with your mom than I have with mine," she said.

I didn't argue.

"But who do you think has the better relationship with their dad? Now that he's gone, I see him two weeks out of the year. I fly to Rome and we bond like crazy. Then I leave and we talk on the phone twice a month. I know it's nontraditional, but I still think it's healthy. Don't you?"

Mrs. and Mr. Knox never got divorced. They lived in this sort of limbo place. It was weird to me, but I tried not to judge it.

"I think your relationship with your dad is decent," I said.

"Decent! That's a complete understatement. We're very close," Veronica said.

"You talk twice a month," I said.

"So, you don't ever really talk to your dad. He's around, but you never talk to him. It's like he's a stranger. You have a way worse relationship with your dad than I do with mine."

"Shut up," I said.

"Don't tell me to shut up. I'm trying to work through something here. Writing makes me feel miserable. And I think my egomaniac mother is to blame."

"Your mother isn't an egomaniac. You can't blame her for everything. Especially for what happened with your dad. When relationships go kaput, the blame is fifty-fifty," I said.

"You really believe that?" she asked.

My mind zoomed to Hamilton. Fifty-fifty? Did I really believe that?

"I don't know. What I'm trying to say is that maybe things would have ended up happening just the way they did no matter how much your mom wrote or didn't write. Maybe these things were supposed to happen," I said.

Veronica didn't look at me. "She could have done more."

I wasn't sure about this. But I was tired of fighting. Veronica was on the verge of tears. I didn't understand why she always had to be so mad at her mother. It made sense to me that Mrs. Knox had to work. Sometimes that means making sacrifices. For everybody. Plus, when a relationship busts up I don't think it's fair to blame the woman for everything. I'd done all I could to captivate Hamilton. It's not like I wanted to have flaws.

"I think your relationship with your dad is pretty healthy," I said.

"Thanks," Veronica said.

"And I think your mom is trying really hard now to be the mom you want her to be."

Veronica didn't respond for a moment.

"Okay. Let's say I give her a free pass for forcing my father to seek out Rome. So maybe she is trying harder now, but does that mean she gets an additional free pass on everything? Like all the years where she sucked at being a mother are swept under the mattress and forgotten?"

"You mean rug. Swept under the rug," I said.

"That's even worse," Veronica said. "Because that's where all the floor dust of the world lives. I don't want to be swept under there."

"What are you talking about? Your mother's screwups would be swept under there. Not you. That's what the metaphor means," I said.

"Are you saying that's what I should do?" she asked. "Just let her sweep all her mistakes under the rug?"

"I think you should do what makes you happy," I said. "And I don't think that being upset and disappointed by your mom for the rest of your life is the best choice."

"I wasn't planning on staying mad for the rest of my entire life," Veronica said.

"You talk about this a lot. I think blaming her for what happened with your dad actually gets in the way of your happiness."

"What an awful thing to say," Veronica said.

"I'm your friend."

"Then why are you saying such awful things to me?"

"I'm not."

"Yes you are. First, you slam me about my relationship with my father, and then you start telling me how I'm destined to be miserable because I'm a lousy daughter."

"That's not even close to what came out of my mouth. You're twisting things," I said.

"You don't get it."

"Sure I do."

"No. Your mom acts the way a mom should. She's dedicated. Her life is defined by her mother duties. You don't even get how lucky you are."

I thought about my mother. Home. Doing laundry. Calling her best friend, Collette, to exchange recipes. She had a simpler life. That's true. But to hear Veronica talk about it made it seem like my mother had made a sacrifice. Like I'd made her make a sacrifice.

"I'm going to go talk to Corky. She doesn't seem like the sort of person hell-bent on wrecking my happiness."

"I'm not trying to do that," I said.

"Sure you're not," Veronica said.

"What about our amazing ability to only fight for thirty seconds and make up?" I asked. "What about dinner?"

"It's not like we're sharing the same lung. You do your thing. I'll do mine."

Chapter Eleven

*V*eronica's man-wall had exploded with hot-dudes. There were fourteen new hot-dudes with stars drawn all over them. A star on a face. A star on a foot. A star on both kneecaps. I was stunned. While I'd sat miserable and alone in a café last night, eating an overpriced plate of fried potatoes, an order I'd placed because it was the only thing I could identify on the menu, Veronica had gone on a wild guy-meeting spree. Phone numbers were scrawled along their paper torsos. I felt like ripping Veronica's hot-dudes right off the wall and tearing them into tiny bits.

Below the man-wall, Veronica slumbered in her bed. We hadn't said anything since yesterday's fight. I hadn't even heard her come home. I slid my covers off and looked out the window. The sun was up, but it was still too early to get ready for workshop. I glanced at Veronica again. Her dark hair covered most of her face. Was she still wearing her clothes from yesterday?

I got up and stood over her so I could give her a closer inspection. Yes, she was. I tried to see if she was still wearing her shoes, but her feet were tangled in the white folds of her top sheet. I leaned in closer and spotted a bare rectangle of flesh below her calf. There was something stuck to her leg. It was an ankle bracelet. And it had an ivory pendant dangling from its delicate silver chain. A skull? And there was black ink! Was it a tattoo? No. It looked like ink from a ballpoint pen. It said, "Property of Corky." And it had a thick arrow pointing to the ankle bracelet. I pulled myself back to a standing position. Even while sleeping, Veronica Knox came across as complicated. And interesting.

"I know you're standing right there," she said. "And you're totally freaking me out."

"Oh," I said. "I just wanted to make sure you were breathing."

Veronica pushed the hair out of her face and rolled onto her back. "No you weren't," she said, opening her eyes. "You wanted to see if I'd changed clothes from yesterday."

How did she know that?

"I wanted to make sure you were okay," I said.

"Yeah, yeah." She pulled her pillow over her head. "I'm still mad at you."

I didn't offer any sort of defense. Nor did I launch into an apology. Let Veronica Knox stay mad at me. Whatever. Like she'd said the previous evening, it wasn't like we shared a lung. I got my things and walked to the shower.

After I got ready, I decided my best plan would be to walk around and find something interesting to stare at for two and a half hours. I didn't tell Veronica where I was going. I grabbed my bag and left. Let her wonder. She was the one who instigated the fight. Two could play at this game.

Upon closing the door, I spotted a new sticky note. I almost didn't read it. But the five exclamation points grabbed my attention. Uh-oh. It was for me.

Dessy, please call your mother!!!!! She called the front office and left a message for you. —Annie Earl

My mother! I'd meant to call her yesterday. I guess thinking about her so much during the Old Jewish Cemetery tour had somehow given me the impression that I'd actually talked to her. I slid the sticky note into my pocket. I'd call her after workshop. I didn't have the mental energy to sound overly upbeat. And to keep her from worrying, that was the only mood I wanted to project over the phone.

I walked down the long hallway. It felt good to put some distance between me and Veronica. I mean, I was my own person. I felt fierce. And ready to tackle something. Like my day.

But after I left the dorm, even though I was walking at a brisk pace, I realized that I didn't have a clear idea of what would be interesting to look at. I'd spent so much time following Veronica around that, left to create my own agenda, I felt a little stumped. I pulled out my tour guide and flipped through it.

There were a lot of "must sees" in this town. I picked two things right away. The Old Town Hall Astronomical Clock and the Dancing House. The clock was one of the things I'd researched before I came. Every guidebook mentioned it and the fact that its oldest parts dated back to 1410. At the top of the hour, a skeleton called Death tips his hourglass and pulls a cord. This rings a bell and a window opens. Then, out roll the Twelve Apostles and they circle around. The show ends when the rooster crows and the hour is rung. It seemed like something everybody should see at least once. The other thing, the Dancing House, my mother had mentioned while I'd packed my suitcase.

"It's not the most interesting building you'll ever see in your life," she had said. "But based on this photo, it's at least worth a walk-by if you're in the neighborhood."

My mother was sitting on my bed, straightening a

stack of underwear already loaded into my suitcase.

"Why is it called the Dancing House?" I had asked. "Who danced there?"

"No," my mother said. "The dancing doesn't take place on the inside. It's the actual building that's dancing. Look." She handed me a picture she'd printed off the Internet.

The glass building twisted at its center, making the building look cinched, like it had a waist. It was supposed to look like a man and a woman dancing. But it was also called the Drunk House.

My mother took my underwear out of the suitcase and refolded it, flattening down the fabric to reduce the stack's bulk. Then she reached into her pocket and handed me a bunch of twenty dollar bills and an ATM card.

"It's a hundred dollars," she said. "And this ATM card is connected to our checking account. You can pull money directly out of it."

My parents didn't have a lot of money for my trip. This was a huge gesture. It meant I'd be traveling to Prague with four hundred dollars and the option to pull out additional cash. Though I knew I would never do that.

"Thanks," I said.

"You're going to learn so much," my mother said. "You're so lucky to be going to Prague at your age."

And even though I knew my mother didn't want me to feel guilty, as I folded my last pair of jeans and handed them to her, I couldn't help but feel something negative. My mother had never been to Prague. She'd never been anywhere interesting at all. And the worst part about this was that she tried to pretend it didn't matter to her. But I knew different.

Once, after she'd picked me up from a fifth-grade

play practice, she'd turned to me, breathless, and asked, "Do you want to drive to Canada?" It took me a second to realize that she meant right then. She reached over and squeezed my hand, but I pulled it away. Canada? My mother had never said anything so bizarre. I felt like saying, "No way!" Because we couldn't leave the country. And it was a weekday. Dad would be home for dinner soon. We didn't have time. Plus, I was dressed like a mouse. "Maybe next week," I told her, scratching my whiskered face. And she dropped it.

And even though she'd never brought up that idea again, I knew it hadn't been a joke. Since then, in bookstores, I was always painfully aware that my mother preferred to drift right into the travel section, even though she rarely bought travel books. It didn't seem fair that somebody so curious about the world would be born *and* raised in Ohio. And it also didn't seem fair that unless her financial situation changed dramatically, like if she won the lottery or found a suitcase full of money in our driveway, she might never go anywhere worth going.

Visiting the Drunk House meant taking a metro I'd never ridden before. I traced my finger along the route to make sure that I had my bearings.

"Are you lost?"

I looked up. It was Waller. I said the first thing that came to mind.

"You look terrible."

"I know," he said. "Last night was a rough one."

"What happened?" I asked.

He ran his hands through his hair. "Dessy, I've been changed in ways that I didn't know I wanted to be changed."

He reached out and took hold of my shoulder. Our chemistry made me swoon.

"Are you going to be okay?" I asked.

"I don't feel the same way about anything anymore," he said. "Has that ever happened to you? You wake up one day and realize that everything you were aiming for in life, every rule you'd been honoring, every impulse you'd been denying yourself, is total shit?"

"Um, not really," I said.

"I am a man with new eyes," he said, opening his arms wide, like he was preparing to embrace an elephant. "I mean, do you smell that?"

"What?"

"The morning, Dessy. It's got this new clarity for me. Like somebody has thrown water over the entire world and splashed it clean for me."

A picture of a soap commercial and a man in an outdoor shower flashed through my mind.

"What exactly did you do last night?" I asked. I was beginning to suspect drugs.

"I broke down some walls," he said.

"Literally?" I asked. "You vandalized something?"

"No." He shook his head. "Hey, let's get going. We can talk on the way."

He grabbed my arm and pulled me toward the metro station.

"Do you want to see the Drunk House?" I asked.

Waller looked back at me and laughed. "That sounds perfect."

Waller's grip slid down my arm to my wrist, until finally, somehow, he held me by my hand. I let my fingers open, and his moved into mine. Then he squeezed my hand. And I looked at him like I didn't know what to expect.

I surrendered the map to Waller during the metro ride.

"So we're visiting an office building downtown?" Waller asked.

"Yeah. But it looks like two people dancing," I said.

"Drunk people?"

"It's called the Drunk House or the Dancing House. Though if it ever topples over, it probably will be called the Drunk House that Danced."

"Oh, you mean the Fred and Ginger House?" Waller asked. "It's named after Fred Astaire and Ginger Rogers, the dancers." He lifted my hand to his mouth and kissed the back of it. Things felt dreamlike. Yes, by stomping out of the dorm room I'd strained my relationship with Veronica, but everything else seemed to be on the upswing. For instance, my connection with Waller was blooming like mad! I leaned back and melted into the metro seat and listened to him talk about the importance of creativity when it came to modern architecture.

"A building is more than its bricks," he said. "I should be able to look at an edifice and hear a saxophone. I should be able to ride in its elevator and smell chocolate."

I had no idea what Waller was talking about. But I nodded and patted his knee.

"I want to eat the world, Dessy," he said.

He leaned over and bit my shoulder. His teeth left wet bite marks on my green shirt. It was the first time a guy had ever bitten me. It wasn't entirely unpleasant.

The metro stopped and Waller jumped up.

"Come on!" he said.

And I did.

We walked along the Vltava River at a quick pace. I wanted to talk to Waller about a bunch of things, to strengthen our connection. But we were hurrying so fast that I got winded.

"We're going to look back on this time and be amazed by how much freedom we had," Waller said. Then he stopped and turned around to face me. He placed both of his hands on my shoulders. "Let's promise each other right now that no matter what ties us down in life—marriage, kids, jobs—that we'll never forget this feeling." He touched his own stomach and then mine. "You feel the feeling, don't you?" he asked.

"I think so," I said.

He placed his hand back on my stomach. "No. Concentrate. You need to feel totally and completely free. Right in your gut."

His observations were beginning to feel New Age to me. And not in a way I could relate to.

"How old are you?" he asked.

"Why?" How come everybody was so hung up on my age in this city?

"Because you'll never be this age again. Here. Right now. That moment is gone. Your life is ending. My life is ending. Tick. Tock. Tick. Tock."

"I'm seventeen. And my life isn't ending, Waller," I said, breathing hard. "That's fatalistic."

He leaned in close to me, and for a second I thought he was going to kiss me. I lightly closed my lips to prepare a place for his to land. But he pressed close to my ear instead.

"You need to grab life, Dessy," he whispered. "You get one turn. One ride. One trip through this universe."

His lips sent a feeling into my ear that I'd never felt before. I lost my balance. I put my arms around his waist to steady myself. And he held me.

"You are so sweet," he said. "You even smell sweet."

"Thanks," I said. I considered mentioning that I used an almond-scented shampoo. But I wasn't sure that a college guy would care. I leaned farther into him, pressing my face against his chest. He smelled good too. Unlike Hamilton, who usually smelled like soap, Waller had a scent that was similar to my father's favorite snack— olives stuffed with pimentos. He kept his arms around me, and I nuzzled my head deeper into his chest.

"Do you know who you remind me of?" he asked.

"Who?"

"You remind me of my little sister, Allie," he said.

I ceased nuzzling. Did he say what I thought he'd said? I kept my arms around his waist, and face pressed against him, but after his revelation, holding him in this manner felt slightly weird.

"I remind you of your sister?" I asked. "How old is she?"

Maybe she was a hot twenty-two-year-old. Maybe she was adopted. Crushing on your adopted, hot sibling seemed acceptable. Kind of.

"Allie is twelve," he said. "But she's very mature. She's already devoured Kurt Vonnegut's fiction and Marianne Moore's poetry, and right now she's reading the Bible."

The Bible? Twelve? Marianne Moore? I pushed away from him. Had I misread something? I thought he was flirting with me. Veronica sensed he liked me at a level eight or nine. But if I'd sent him prepubescent sisterly vibes, clearly there was no chance he was romantically interested in me. Ugh. If Veronica were here, she could tell me what I needed to do to avoid making a complete fool of myself. And protect my heart from further bruising.

"To the Fred and Ginger House!" Waller yelled, tugging me by the hand.

Okay. Maybe I was supposed to overlook the sister comment. Everybody says something dumb in their life. It happens. *Screw it. Just screw it. So what if I have flaws? So what if I don't understand guys? So what if I put my heart out onto the sidewalk for anybody to stomp on? My heart is smooshed. I want a rebound. And I want it to be with Waller Dudek. I want it. I want it. I want it.*

It was settled. Not even logic would hold me back.

"Are you paying attention to the scenery?" Waller asked.

I nodded, then realized that he was in front of me and couldn't see my head, so I yelled, "I'm loving the scenery. It's exactly how I want to spend my life. Looking at scenery. Tick. Tock. Tick. Tock."

I'm not sure he heard me.

"Look at those pigeons!" he yelled.

A group of dirty gray birds strutted in front of us on the sidewalk. They pecked at the ground, appearing both cocky and content. When we reached them, several burst into flight and landed across the street. Waller let go of my hand and lifted his arms up from his sides. Then he began to turn in circles. His feet moved quickly, like he was dancing. Birds continued to rise around him.

"What are you doing?" I asked.

"Having a moment," he said. "Join me."

But by the time I entered the pool of pigeons, they'd nearly all fled to a less trafficked area. Waller reached out and grabbed my hand again. Then he pulled me back in the direction of the Dancing House.

Hamilton never would have allowed us to run through a group of pigeons like that. He would have made us stop and observe them from a distance, possibly even insisting that we hide behind a garbage can in order to encounter the birds' most natural behaviors.

"We only have two more hours before workshop," Waller said. "We should be going faster."

The force with which Waller pulled me this time nearly dislocated my shoulder. But I went along with it. The sooner we got to the Dancing House, the sooner we could continue our conversation. And talking to Waller made me feel like I was learning something. Not just about him and his wacky ideas concerning "special moments" and pigeons. I felt like I was gaining information about key life issues. Like happiness. And guys. And myself.

Chapter Twelve

Waller ran exactly how you'd expect a guy to run. Fast. Which was unfortunate, as I ran exactly how you'd expect a girl to run, especially in a foreign land. Daintily.

"There it is!" Waller shouted. He stopped and doubled over, gasping. "That building doesn't look like it's dancing or drunk."

The glass twisted the way it did in the picture. The building was supported by several cement pillars that looked like bending legs.

"I wish I had a camera," I said. I thought about the disposable one I'd left back in my room. I think I was forgetting it on purpose. I needed to get over the fact that I was too poor to have a nice camera. I was in Prague. And I had what I had.

Waller shook his head. "You should take the picture with your mind. You don't need a camera," he said.

"I wanted to take a picture of it for my mother," I said. "I can't show her what's in my mind."

My potential rebound was beginning to annoy me. His philosophical view on how to live life had become bossy. Waller threw his arm around me. "Yeah," he said. "It's too bad we can't peel open our heads and show people what's going on inside there."

I thought about agreeing with him, but I found

the mental image so disgusting that I just stood there instead.

"Do you want to see the Astronomical Clock?" I asked. "I think we still have time."

Waller grabbed my hand again. "Good idea!"

We started running back down the street the way we came. I didn't mind running, really. I thought it was good exercise. But even though it was morning and still cool outside, the humidity was oppressive and I didn't want to develop sweat circles around my armpits.

"Maybe we can walk," I suggested.

"Yeah," Waller said. "That way we could talk more. I really like talking to you."

This was fantastic! I felt like we'd regained substantial ground since that whole, "you remind me of my twelve-year-old sister" comment.

"How's your story coming along?" I asked.

This seemed like the perfect topic. Because it gave him the chance to talk about himself.

"I've hit a snag," he said.

"A big one?" I asked.

"Yeah," he said. "I want this thing to happen, but I don't know how to make it happen."

"Could you Google it?" I asked.

Waller stopped walking and shook his head. "I've hit an impasse at an emotional level."

Before coming to the July Prague Writers' Conference I had never heard of anybody encountering an impasse. Now it seemed like everybody I'd met had hit one.

"Do you see that?" Waller asked. He pointed to the side of a melon-colored pub.

I knew it was a pub because it had two words written on it: "Pub" and "*Hostinec*." "The pub?" I asked.

"The waterline." He left my side and walked toward the building. "It's from the flood of 2002. It was the worst natural disaster in the country's history. Look at how high the water rose."

The pub's melon color was much darker on the first story. Below the windows on the second level, you could see clearly where the water had peaked.

"Fifty thousand people were evacuated from the city."

"Wow," I said. I wanted to keep talking about personal stuff, not a natural disaster.

"There was so much damage." He turned and walked back toward me. "And the zoo sits right on the Vltava. It went through an apocalypse."

This was such a depressing tangent.

"An elephant, hippo, lion, and bear had to be euthanized. They got caught in the floodwaters and were going to drown."

"They should have evacuated them." I knew nothing about the Prague flood, but my suggestion seemed sound.

"And there were four sea lions. Three escaped, but one stayed behind."

"Did it die?"

"No. That one lived. And two of the escaped ones were caught, but the fourth one, Gaston, he wanted freedom." Waller bit his lip and stared off in the direction of the river.

"He crossed into Germany and swam down the River Elbe toward the North Sea."

"That makes sense. Sea lions are designed to swim."

"Authorities caught him in Dresden. He'd made it almost eighty miles. But he was weak and infected from the floodwaters. He died in transport on his way back to Prague."

"That's terrible."

Waller walked back and put his arm around me. "Tick. Tock. Tick. Tock."

I tried to think of a way to redirect the flood tangent.

"Speaking of running out of time, have you thought about discussing your impasse with Mrs. Knox?" I asked.

Waller let his arm fall away from me and shook his head. "I need to sit with it a bit more. It's deep." He patted his heart three times.

Then I did something very bold. In fact, until I'd done it, I couldn't believe I was brave enough to attempt it.

"Waller," I said. "If you ever want to talk to me about whatever this impasse is, just call. Any time. I'm there for you," And then I patted his heart three times.

He looked down at me, and for a second I thought he was going to share his impasse. But something else happened. And it sucked.

"Waller! Dessy!"

Even though I didn't want to, I looked away from Waller. And saw Roger running toward us. And he didn't look happy.

"Shit," Waller said. "He's the last person I want to see right now."

"Isn't he one of your best friends?" I asked.

"He *was*," Waller said.

Roger jogged up to us and stood toe to toe with Waller. "I can't believe you!"

"Dude," Waller said. "I'm giving everybody some space until things mellow."

"*Mellow*?" Roger asked. "Frank is not going to *mellow* after what you did to him."

Waller looked away in disgust. "He's being a baby."

"No," Roger said. "You need to apologize and smooth things over."

I felt very awkward. I didn't want to leave, because I liked how standing next to Waller made me feel, but there was so much tension between Waller and Roger. If Veronica were here she'd know what to say to defuse the situation. She's very good at hijacking conversations; unfortunately, I don't have that skill.

"Hi, Roger," I said, pretending everything was cool. "Waller and I are headed to the Astronomical Clock. Want to come?"

Roger shot me a confused look. "You're out sight-seeing?" he asked Waller. "I bet you're not even sober."

Waller shrugged. "Maybe I'm not."

"Sounds like you guys had a wild night," I said, trying to sound engaged and nonjudgmental.

Roger looked at me with a mildly stunned expression. Then he glanced back at Waller, then at me again. He appeared increasingly unhappy as he assessed the situation. "Actually, I worked on my story. It was the rest of the clowns that went out and had a wild time at the circus," he said finally.

"We're in Prague!" Waller said. "We're supposed to imbibe recklessly amongst the natives."

"Only alcoholics and idiots operate under that assumption," Roger said. "You need to come back and talk to Frank. He's having some kind of breakdown."

Waller folded his arms across his chest. "If I'm not sober, he's not sober. And talking to drunk Frank is like talking to a cognitively impaired chimp. We'll talk tomorrow."

"We've got workshop in an hour," Roger said. "And Frank wants to beat your ass."

"Frank can't beat my ass."

Roger exhaled a deeply frustrated breath. "You're acting like a dick."

The next thing happened in a flash. Waller reached out and pushed Roger. Hard.

"Get off my back," Waller said. Roger stumbled and caught his balance. He didn't say anything else, just walked off.

I didn't realize that Waller had such a temper. Whatever had happened between him and Frank must have been pretty serious. I wondered if it involved a girl.

"I gotta get out of here," Waller said.

"No Astronomical Clock?" I asked. "Because it's right there." I pointed in the direction of Old Town.

"I need to clear my head," Waller said. "I need to experience five new things in order to shove the last five experiences out of my consciousness."

This made me feel terrible, because wasn't his morning with me one of his last five experiences? I watched Waller storm off in the opposite direction from Roger. He ran across the uneven cobblestone path like it was a groomed track. He was a lot more athletic than I'd realized. And he didn't look drunk at all, which buoyed my spirits somewhat. Because I didn't want to believe that my entire deep conversation with Waller had occurred while he was inebriated. I watched his bobbing head until it got lost in a crowd of non-bobbing heads.

I swallowed hard and re-aimed myself toward Old Town. Let Veronica be pissed at me. Let Waller mysteriously race off. I didn't need a companion to visit this clock. It was something I wanted to see, and I knew how to get there. So I walked there by myself.

Chapter Thirteen

The astronomical clock was both memorable and forgettable. The scene played out exactly as the tour book said. Death rang a bell. The Apostles paraded around. A rooster crowed. And then the crowd dispersed. Though, to be honest, I did miss death ringing the bell because I wasn't looking right at the clock when it started. I didn't wait around another hour to watch it happen again.

Old Town was a fun place to kill time. The buildings were stunning and totally unique. The crystal shops looked like baubles more than buildings. One had a fresco painted over its entire four-tiered storefront. And across the square, the Týn Church climbed above everything, towering over the other buildings with its dark and enormous spires topped with gold balls. It was so Gothic it made me revise my definition of Gothic. I wandered aimlessly, peeking inside windows. Even in tearooms and jazz clubs. Nobody seemed to mind.

When I got to the university, Veronica and her mother were the only ones there.

"If we can't find bananas, we can't find bananas," Mrs. Knox was saying. "You're just going to have to live without them."

"But I've seen other people eating bananas," Veronica said.

"Next time try to buy one from them," Mrs. Knox said.

"When I was in Rome, bananas were everywhere," Veronica said. "Markets. Street vendors. Hotel counters. Dad's backpack."

"Veronica, I have made my last banana inquisition in this city."

"Fine. I guess there are two kinds of people in this world. Those who want something and are willing to go after it until they get it. And those who refuse to look for bananas."

"You never even eat bananas in Ohio," Mrs. Knox said. "You're on some sort of weird, ethnocentric power trip. You need to knock it off."

I waved to Mrs. Knox. I didn't even bother asking how they'd spent their morning. It seemed pretty clear.

"How was your downtime?" Mrs. Knox asked me.

"Pretty good," I said.

Veronica looked at me and smiled. This surprised me. Was she being sincere? Or was she being Veronica?

"Did you see anything interesting today?" she asked.

Mrs. Knox flipped through papers. I saw Brenda and Annie Earl walk into the room. Annie Earl was wearing a long-sleeved shirt. Considering the temperature, I couldn't help but wonder if she was trying to cover her scars. Even though she had to be used to the fact that her arms drew stares, maybe some days she didn't feel like having people gawk. Maybe some days she didn't want to see them either.

Veronica cleared her throat and repeated her question. "Did you see anything interesting?"

"I visited the Drunk House and the Astronomical Clock," I said.

"Really?" Veronica asked.

I nodded.

"I thought we'd see the clock together!"

"I'll look at it again," I said.

"Cool." Veronica patted the chair next to her, indicating that she wanted me to sit there.

I obeyed, but I was deeply suspicious. Veronica would rather sit next to me than one of the guys?

"I need to talk to you after class," she whispered in my ear.

"I thought we were having a fight," I whispered back.

"I'm over it," she said. "What about you?"

To be honest, I didn't even remember what had started the fight.

"Ditto," I said.

Veronica rested her head on my shoulder and rubbed her hair against me.

"You two look like best friends," Annie Earl said.

"We are!" said Veronica.

When Corky walked into the room, Veronica sat up straight and said, "FYI, I'm avoiding the Corkster."

"Did you have a fight?"

Veronica shook her head. "No," she said. "Worse."

"What's worse than a fight?"

"I think Corky wants to kill me," she whispered.

I laughed. But Veronica didn't. I looked at Corky, and she glowered over the table at both of us. Then she drew her finger across her throat.

"God," Veronica said. "She's so melodramatic."

"What's wrong?" I asked. "What happened?"

"I think Prague makes people go crazy," Veronica said.

"Did something happen last night?"

Veronica shook her head. "No. Everything was fine last night. Something happened this morning."

"In the last three hours something happened that led Corky to decide that she wants to kill you?" I asked.

"Well, I didn't want to tell you this way," she said,

"but I'm pretty sure Corky wants to kill both of us."

"What?" I asked. I looked back at Corky. She had one of those small plastic pencil sharpeners, and she was screwing her pencil into it with a lot of enthusiasm. "What did you do?"

"What makes you think I did something?" Veronica asked.

"Because that's the most likely explanation," I said.

"Okay, you're right. I did something. But before I tell you about it, I need to fill you in on something else."

"Is it about Waller?" I asked.

"No," Veronica said. "It's still about Corky."

"Maybe we shouldn't talk about her when she's sitting right there," I said.

The room was still pretty empty, as none of the guys had arrived yet. Annie Earl sat chatting with Brenda about a marionette she had just purchased. Veronica's mom was reading a manuscript intently. And Corky just sat across the table from us, stabbing us with her deadly glare.

"Yeah," Veronica said. "I see your point. But I think you should know this."

"Let's go into the hallway," I said. "Or the bathroom."

"Let me handle it," Veronica said. She sprang out of her chair.

Corky pushed away from the table like she was ready to go too.

"Mom!" Veronica said.

Mrs. Knox looked up from her paper.

"Corky was curious about attending a classical concert in Prague; maybe you can offer her some advice."

"You're interested in attending a concert?" Mrs. Knox asked.

Corky paused, like a deer caught in headlights. "I like Mozart," she said.

Veronica bounded toward the door, and I followed her. I could hear Mrs. Knox asking Corky what sort of venue she was looking for.

We hustled down the hallway to the bathroom and locked ourselves into an empty stall. We were both breathless. And I was peeved. My first budding romance since Hamilton, and I didn't have a chance to form a plan of attack with Veronica, because she'd inadvertently provoked a potentially homicidal maniac.

"What is it?" I asked.

"Corky has a criminal record," Veronica said.

"Is she a thief?" I asked. "Or a drug dealer?"

"I wish it was something that minor," Veronica said. "Turns out, Corky is bat-shit insane. Her crimes are vast. She keeps a blog about them. It's supposed to be anonymous, but I figured it out. Oh, Dessy, she's a very venomous person. She sugars gas tanks and blows things up. She cut the ears of her neighbor's goat and she's burned down a house. And there's so much more."

My stomach felt sick. Veronica had to have misread something. "It must be a fake blog," I said. "We're in a creative writing workshop with her. I bet it's all fiction."

Veronica's grabbed my hands and pleaded with me. "No, Dessy. The blog has pictures. I've seen the goat."

I heard myself gasp. "This is serious."

"Of course it is," she said. "Our lives are in total danger."

"We've got to tell your mother."

"No," she said. "I won't do that. We're not getting along at all. And she'll just turn this into my fault."

"Veronica, this *is* your fault."

"I am *not* telling my mom! We can deal with this."

"Do you realize how vulnerable I feel right now standing next to this toilet?" I asked.

"Yeah," Veronica said. "If I were you, I'd be a paranoid mess too."

"Veronica, you need to tell me everything," I said. "I feel completely thrown off balance."

"All right. All right," she said. "But it's a long story."

"Start at the beginning," I said.

"First, I need to tell you something else," she said.

"More important than why Corky wants to kill us?" I asked.

"Yes," Veronica said, grabbing onto both of my shoulders.

"What is it?"

"You've got bird crap in your hair."

"I do?" I touched the back of my head and felt a crusty glob of something. Then I pulled a wad of toilet paper from the dispenser. "I can't believe Waller didn't tell me this."

"Waller?" Veronica asked.

"I spent the morning with him," I huffed. The bird crap had dried and was difficult to get out.

"Why didn't you tell me this right away?" Veronica asked.

I quit wiping my hair and stared at her.

"Okay," she said. "I guess the Corky disaster trumped the Waller development. So what happened?"

"We bumped into each other outside the dorm," I said.

"Was he sober?" Veronica asked. "Corky and I came across him in an alley last night and he was totally hammered."

I blinked. "Actually, I don't know if he was sober."

"Doesn't matter. Keep going."

"Okay. So we went sightseeing. And he held my hand. He even kissed the back of it!" I said.

"Oh my god! He totally wants to hump you!"

"Whatever," I said. "But then he told me that I reminded him of his sister." I dropped the toilet paper into a small garbage can.

"His sister?" Veronica groaned. "Wait. Maybe it's not as bad as it sounds. Maybe she's adopted. Maybe she's hot."

I shook my head. "She's twelve. Her name is Allie and she's currently reading the Bible."

Veronica gasped. "Wow! People still read the Bible?"

The bathroom door squeaked open. Veronica pressed her hands against our stall's closed metal door. "I'll hold her off," she said. "You crawl on the floor into the other stall and escape. And bring back help!"

I glanced down at the tiled floor. It was filthy. "You've lost your mind," I said.

"Girls." It was Mrs. Knox. "It's time to start class. You need to wrap this up."

"Hold your horses," Veronica called back. "Dessy is still constipated."

I couldn't believe she'd said that.

"It's a very common condition when people travel," Veronica said. "It's nothing to be self-conscious about."

"But I'm not constipated," I said.

"I don't think you need to go around broadcasting that fact," Veronica said. "In my experience, people really don't enjoy hearing about the quality or frequency of your BMs. Even medical doctors."

I couldn't take it anymore. I stabbed my finger into her back two times. "My god! It's like you're trying to take every last piece of dignity that I have away from me," I whispered.

"I've got some tea that might help loosen things up," Mrs. Knox said. "Oh, hi, Corky. No, everything is fine."

Veronica flicked the bathroom lock and threw open the door. "Finished!" she said.

I hurried out behind her. Mrs. Knox gave us a puzzled look, but held the door for us without comment. As I walked past Corky, I thought I heard her growl.

Veronica leaned close and whispered, "The girl has no conscience. None."

"Great," I said. "You know, Veronica, you are a terrible friend."

"Don't be like this," she said. "So I have some flaws. Everybody makes mistakes."

She was so right about that one.

Back in the classroom, the atmosphere had gotten even stranger. No one was talking. As I panned the room I saw something that made me do a double take. Frank. He didn't have any hair!

"Oh my god!" Veronica said. "You look so bald."

I shoved her lightly to try to get her to make a different, more pleasant facial expression.

"I don't want to talk about it," Frank said.

He threw himself down in a seat across from our stuff and unzipped his bag. Kite and Roger were seated on either side of him, looking glum. Waller wasn't there.

I sat down next to Veronica and tried not to look at Frank's pale, glowing scalp. Mrs. Knox ignored the issue altogether.

"Waller called to say that he won't be with us today," she said.

"That's because he knows I'm going to kill that jackass!" Frank yelled.

We all turned to look at him. He rubbed his bald head over and over.

"Normally, I don't like to pry," Mrs. Knox said, "but it looks like we have a situation."

There were tears in Frank's eyes. This was so weird. He was almost crying. I'd never seen a guy cry before. Even in metal shop when Mr. Toliver had accidentally shaved off the tip of his pointer finger on the rotating sander.

Roger slapped Frank on the back a few times in an apparent act of consolation. "We're moving through it," he said.

Kite shook his head and looked down at his hands. "Things got a little out of control with some locals."

Frank slammed his fist on the table. "Locals?" he said, pointing to his scalp. "A local didn't do this to me."

Roger looked directly at Mrs. Knox. "We'll work it out."

"Easy for you to say. You still have hair," Frank said. "Look at me. I look like an alien. I look like I've been radiated."

"You're way too meaty to look like you've been radiated," Corky said. "And your color is all wrong. Too healthy. Trust me."

"As your instructor," Mrs. Knox cut in, "I'm not comfortable with this turn of events. Frank and Roger, I want to speak with you after class."

I thought after class might be a good time to throw the Corky issue onto the table, so I raised my hand. But Veronica reached over and pinched me, and I took that as a signal to stay silent. So I lowered it.

"Frank isn't going to hurt Waller," Roger said.

"Yeah," said Kite. "He won't do anything stupid."

"Don't speak for me!" Frank said. "Where were you last night? Huh? Where were you when I needed somebody to say, 'Hey, Waller, put down the razor'? Where were you then?"

"I was still in the alley," Kite said.

"You're telling me that Waller shaved your head?" Mrs. Knox asked.

Frank nodded. "I don't remember it. But I'm pretty sure he was the one."

"Well, I think that's an act of assault," Mrs. Knox said. "And that's something that the July Prague Writers' Workshop doesn't tolerate."

"Whoa, whoa, whoa," Roger said. "Frank asked Waller to shave his head."

"I did not!" Frank said. "I'm not an idiot. And I love my hair. It's very important to me. Or at least I did."

We sat in silence, looking at Frank. It felt like we had entered into some sort of recovery group together.

"This is freaking ridiculous," Corky muttered.

We stopped looking at Frank and repositioned our stares on Corky.

"Hair grows back," she said. "I've shaved my head bald four times. It's no big deal. It's not like he scarred your face or cut off your manhood. It's hair. What will you do when you're forty and it all falls out anyway?"

"We need to get started," Mrs. Knox said. "Frank and Annie Earl are up today."

I grabbed Frank's dolphin story and Annie Earl's pie story out of my bag.

"If you want some time to gather yourself, I'll go first," Annie Earl said to Frank.

"No," Frank said. "I actually wrote something this morning that I'd like to read instead."

I stared down at all the marks I'd made on his story. I didn't think we were allowed to swap material.

Frank took out a stack of paper and passed it around. He leaned over the table to hand Veronica and me ours, and I could smell strong booze on his breath.

"Actually," Mrs. Knox said, "we need to work on the story you submitted. You don't want feedback on fresh material. You need to give writing time to sit."

Frank didn't stop passing his papers. "I disagree," he said. "I practically bled on these pages. I gave everything I had."

Mrs. Knox seemed stuck. Should she defend her authority over the workshop, or defuse a volatile situation? She decided to let him read the new material. It was a poem.

"I want to read the whole thing," Frank said.

Mrs. Knox glanced through the poem and nodded. Frank moved his chair back and stood up. "My poem is called 'Kill the Razor.'"

Then he read it in a very powerful and, at times, choked-up voice. He also rubbed his head a lot.

"Kill the razor. Kill
the blade. Kill the hand
that held them both.
My head is what matters.
My shorn scalp.
I came to Prague a man. A man.
A man. Until he took
my hair. My hair.
My hair. I stand next
to the white toilet. I gaze
into the cold bathroom mirror.
I am so hungry for
what I've lost. No, I cannot
forgive. No, I cannot forget.
Under the moon. Under the
stars. Under the canopy
of my ruined life. My bare head
glistens in limitless pain."

"Wow," Annie Earl said. "That was very powerful."

"You're still a man," Brenda said.

"That was really great," I said.

I nudged Veronica again. She kept writing the word *BALD* and drawing frowning faces over Frank's poem.

"Good job, man," Roger said. He sounded sincere, but I could tell his patience was wearing thin.

Tears dripped down Frank's face and splattered on the floor. I felt really sympathetic toward him. Because even though Corky thought hair didn't matter, I realized it did.

"I need to get out of here," Frank said.

"Do you want company?" Veronica asked, starting to stand.

I wasn't sure if Veronica wanted to help console Frank, or if she was looking for an excuse to ditch class.

"No," he said. "I don't. I need to go back to bed."

"Frank," Mrs. Knox said, "if you leave, it's unlikely that we'll be able to workshop your dolphin story at a later date. We've got a tight schedule."

Frank didn't say anything. He took his bag, tossed it over his shoulder, and walked out the door.

"He'll be fine," Roger said. "We're all still a little hung over."

"Well," Mrs. Knox said, "I think the alcohol consumption is getting a bit out of control. Could we taper it off for the next couple of weeks to avoid some of this drama? I feel like I'm on *Dynasty*."

"Nobody even knows what *Dynasty* is, Mom," Veronica said.

Mrs. Knox blushed. "Let's just drop it. And no more substitutions. The material you submitted is the material we workshop."

I thought we all needed to take a break, but Mrs. Knox didn't give us one. "Annie Earl, shall we proceed with your story?"

Annie Earl nodded. "What I've brought for you isn't fiction. 'Baking & Heartache' is an essay I wrote about entering a baking contest and subsequently getting a divorce. I plan to write a collection of them that deal with my life and its unlikely trials and unlikelier travails."

"That last sentence would make great jacket copy," Brenda said.

"It would," Mrs. Knox agreed. "I expect some of you may have read this as a piece of fiction. If so, Annie Earl has asked that you let your comments on the page stand as they are. But for in-class feedback, let's address the story with sensitivity. Annie Earl has trusted us with something more personal than fiction, and that takes a great deal of courage."

"Thank you," Annie Earl said. Then she read from her bleached-flour scene.

"My fat was liquefying. I'd taken precautions against this, but as temperatures rise, there's always a risk. The clock on the wall ticked down the minutes. The seconds. Over my shoulder, other women worked their rolling pins with confidence. I pulled my warm hands from the dough. My own heat might be partly to blame. Things felt too sticky, but I didn't want to add more flour—I needed a flaky crust. I slipped off my long-sleeved shirt. Underneath I wore a T-shirt. Now they were going to see my arms. This would be on television. No more hiding. Let them look at my scars and wonder. I pulled my lard from the refrigerator and started over. I deserved to be here. All my life I'd been waiting to take home the prize."

After Annie Earl read, nobody spoke for a minute. Then Brenda commented. "Your narrator, I mean, *you* really allow yourself to be vulnerable. It makes me care about you. I think that's really powerful."

"Yeah," Roger said. "This is one of the most suspenseful stories I've ever read. I felt everything that was at stake for you."

Mrs. Knox cleared her throat. "When a writer takes

an emotional risk, it can be a vastly rewarding experience for the reader—but only if it's an honest risk. The controlled, frank narration of this story's opening scenes gave me that reassurance that what I was reading was a search for meaning, not a plea for sympathy or admiration. Annie Earl doesn't sensationalize *anything*, and because of that, each revelation brought me to surprising emotional places."

"I felt that," Kite said. "I like pies, but I could care less about baking. But this piece put me in the middle of a kitchen. The scene was written so well that I could feel the heat coming off the stove. And it was hot!"

Everyone seemed to like Annie Earl's essay. It made me happy because it would have been painful to hear people criticize it. The things she'd written about were moments taken from her actual life.

I glanced at Veronica, who was staring at Frank's bald poem again.

"You'll bounce back," I whispered.

"I don't want to bounce back," she whined. "I want Frank to have hair." She jabbed her pen at the poem, making holes in the paper.

"I like your cliff-hanger ending," Corky said. "Closing on the announcement that you're getting a third divorce implies there's so much more heartache around the bend. And you are a very believable wounded person."

I was still too shy to comment. I took notes while everybody else discussed what details they wanted more of in the essay. Like tactile sensations and dialogue and flashbacks.

When class finally ended, I was totally ready to go.

"Waller will either be e-mailing you his story or delivering it directly to your room. Corky, do you have yours?"

Corky nodded and passed around a stack of papers.

"And for an assignment," Mrs. Knox said, "following up on Annie Earl's piece, I want you to think about place. I want you to pick one place where you have lived, and I want you to write a page of description about that place. List everything about it. I want you to engage all five senses: sight, sound, touch, smell, and taste. I want you to picture this place and recover it to the best of your ability."

We all filed out while Mrs. Knox pulled aside Roger and Kite.

"Go! Go!" Veronica whispered to me.

I threw all my stuff into my bag and followed her out the door.

"This way!" she yelled.

I reluctantly followed Veronica into a small, ancient AV room. Clunky VCRs cluttered the room's lone worktable.

"At this point, do you really think we can continue to live with Corky?" I asked.

"Not safely," Veronica said.

"I don't know. Maybe we're overreacting."

I heard Annie Earl and Brenda walk past. They were discussing how to get rid of soap scum. Then I heard the sound of clogs.

"Corky?" I gasped.

"Shh," Veronica said.

We crouched in silence. The footsteps stopped.

"You two can run," Corky said. "You two can even hide. Temporarily. But what you can't do is escape your consequence. I will find you."

"Corky Tina Baker, you are freaking mental," Veronica said, pounding the door with her fist.

Corky didn't respond.

"You think you're so tough because you killed a mountain lion. And have a criminal record. But I think you're bluffing."

There was a light tracing sound against the door. Like Corky was writing on it.

Then I heard the sound of Corky's clogs as she walked off.

"Do you think she's really gone?" I asked.

"I do," Veronica said.

"You don't think she's tricking us?"

"I don't," she said.

I held my breath as Veronica slowly opened the door. A sliver of light fell onto the floor. She poked her head out. Then she shoved the door open in one quick motion.

"Watch it!" Kite said. "You could have given me a concussion."

"Sorry," Veronica said.

I followed her into the hallway and shut the AV door.

"What's that?" Roger asked.

Veronica and I stared at the large shape Corky had drawn. It looked like half of a Twinkie with the letters "RIP" written on it.

"It's a tombstone," Kite said.

Oh my god. It was a symbol of our fates.

"Does this mean something?" Roger asked.

"I'm not really sure," I said.

Roger took my arm and led me farther down the hallway.

"I want to apologize for this morning," he said.

"It's okay," I said. I could hear Veronica pumping Kite for details about the shaving incident. They walked together toward the stairs.

"I'm not an angry person," Roger told me. "It's just, Waller has been acting insane these last few days, and when I found him today I was really fed up." He shoved his hands in his pockets and looked down at me.

"No hard feelings," I said.

Roger was still agitated. "I don't mean to trash

Waller," he said, "but you can't come to Prague and get plastered and then shave someone's head."

"I would never do that."

"Right, because people who go through life with no impulse control are boring. I'm not saying he's boring. But he is definitely prone to bouts of unnecessary flagrant stupidity."

I loved that phrase: *unnecessary flagrant stupidity*. I stored it away in my brain to use against Veronica.

"Anyway, while sauced, he likes to flirt with things, especially disaster." Roger shook his head. "I'm sorry if I ruined your morning," he finished.

"You didn't," I said. "I had a pretty good morning. I mean, until now."

He nodded at the AV door and raised his eyebrows. "She's joking, right?"

"I hope so."

He looked back at the door and then at me. "Let me know if you need anything. I've had EMT training," he said. "So I'm good at responding to distress signals."

"That's cool," I said. We walked outside and found Veronica waiting at the bottom of the stone steps.

Roger waved good-bye to me. "Thanks for listening."

I smiled and would have said "Any time," if Veronica hadn't thrown her arms around me and semi-collapsed into my chest.

"I can't believe something this terrible happened to my main hot-dude."

"Your main hot-dude?" I said. "You're seriously worried about *Frank* right now?"

Veronica reached out and fluffed my hair. "We're fine," she said. "We just have to look out for Corky as we search for more hot-dudes. Also, I really need to find a banana."

Chapter Fourteen

$\mathcal{I}$ wasn't sure why I'd postponed calling my mother until the fifth day I was in Prague. It just seemed like so much was happening. Yesterday, after workshop, Veronica and I walked over the Charles Bridge and took a funicular to the top of Petřín hill, and then ate cheap Thai food at a restaurant that only had nine chairs. Miraculously, after that, Veronica went with me to attend a Black Light Theater show, because four hot-dudes from Spain, whom we met at the park, were going. However, when the two dudes Veronica had found hottest began to make out during the show, her enthusiasm dwindled.

In the dorm lobby I fed enough crowns into the payphone change slot to talk for seven minutes. I only had $350 of my $400. And I still had twenty-three days left in Prague. It didn't take an economist to realize that, financially, I'd soon be on the ropes.

ME: Mom! I've been so busy here. How are you?

MOM: If you hadn't called today, I was going to phone the embassy.

ME: Wow. Sorry.

MOM: Why didn't you call sooner? We said two days. That was the plan.

ME: I know. I know. It's just been crazy here.

I watched Corky enter the building. She bent her fingers into the shape of a gun and shot me.

MOM: Things are crazy? Has something happened? Your voice sounds funny. What's going on?

ME: No. Nothing is going on. I mean it's been crazy busy.

MOM: How's your money holding out? Should I deposit more into the account?

ME: No. I'm fine. I have enough.

MOM: Okay. Now that I know you aren't dead and dismembered in a ditch, why don't you tell me about Prague?

ME: It's amazing. The buildings are totally different from anything in Ohio. And I toured a few synagogues with ceilings that were so high that they must use cherry pickers to clean the cobwebs.

MOM: It sounds wonderful.

ME: It is.

MOM: Are you liking the food?

ME: We eat cereal in the cafeteria for breakfast. And Mrs. Knox bought us a bunch of regular groceries.

MOM: Don't let her do that!

ME: I know. Don't worry. The food is pretty cheap.

MOM: Do you have any roommates?

ME: Um. Yeah.

MOM: Tell me about them.

ME: There's not much to tell. I'm just getting to know them. Mainly I hang out with Veronica.

MOM: This could be a fun chance to meet new people.

ME: Yeah.

MOM: You might end up making a lifelong bond with a roommate. You never know. She could turn out to be a bridesmaid at your wedding.

ME: I'm not really thinking about my wedding.

MOM: Right. You know, I'm not sure if you want to hear this, but Hamilton called.

ME: Oh my god. Why? Did something happen to him?

MOM: No. Calm down. He wanted your mailing address in Prague.

ME: He did?

MOM: Yes. And he also asked for a phone number, but I told him that you didn't have one.

ME: This is shocking. I mean, I haven't talked to him in over a month. If he wants my phone number, he must want to talk to me, right?

MOM: I'd assume so. Dessy, I gave him your address. Is that okay?

ME: Yes! Did he mention what he wanted to mail me?

MOM: No. He didn't. But Dessy, you're in Prague. You shouldn't be thinking about Hamilton.

ME: I thought you liked Hamilton.

MOM: That's not the point. You've got so much potential. Don't saddle your heart to the first boy you fall for.

ME: But you and dad met in high school.

MOM: (Silence)

ME: Don't worry, Mom. I've hardly thought about Hamilton at all. It mostly happens when I see birds.

MOM: Life is long. You should date.

ME: Yeah. It would be a lot easier if guys weren't so weird.

MOM: You're meeting weird guys in Prague? What's your curfew there?

ME: No. I'm not talking about Prague. In general, I just mean that guys are hard to understand.

MOM: Sorry to tell you this, but it only gets worse.

ME: What?

MOM: Because of the Y chromosome.

ME: Oh, Mom.

MOM: You're both young. You might find your way back to each other. But you might not. In the meantime, date.

ME: Prague guys?

MOM: No, wait until you get home.

ME: You're making this sound like a Lifetime movie.

OPERATOR: You have one minute left.

MOM: I love you, Dessy. I think about you all the time. Wait. Your father is right here. He wants to talk to you. He picked up a book about Prague at the library. He's got a question for you. Here he is.

DAD: Dessy? Are you there?

ME: I'm here. How are you, Dad?

DAD: Well, my sciatica is acting up again. But other than that I can't complain. I've been reading about a castle—

ME: I've seen it! It's right along the river. It's by the university where I'm going to class.

DAD: Let me tell your mother. Judy, she's already seen the castle. It's by her school.

ME: Well, I haven't taken a tour. My new friend Waller and I will probably go next week.

DAD: Waller? What kind of parent names his daughter Waller?

ME: No, Waller is a guy.

DAD: What? A guy? Is that some sort of gang name?

ME: No, Dad. Waller is from Chicago.

DAD: You're trying to tell me there's not gangs in Chicago?

ME: No. I mean, I know that there's gangs in Chicago. But Waller isn't in a gang. Waller isn't his real name. It's a nickname. It's short for Walnut. He has a talent.

DAD: I warned your mother this could happen. Judy, she's met up with a gang kid named Walnut. In Europe!

ME: Dad, don't tell Mom that. You'll freak her out. Waller is totally respectable. He's in college—

DAD: College!

Click

Uh-oh. That wasn't a very reassuring phone call. For anyone. Why did my father act like that? Didn't he trust my judgment? I could tell the difference between a decent guy and a cruddy guy. Couldn't I?

I walked back to the dorm and crouched down outside the hallway window. Coast clear. I swiped my magnetic card and ran for my bedroom door. Veronica had wedged a sock in the doorjamb; the protruding cotton heel was a sign that she was safe inside the room with the window sealed shut. We didn't dare open the window anymore, unless both of us were in the room. We figured it would be harder to ambush two people at once.

I unlocked our door, raced inside, and slammed the door. Veronica stood on the other side of the room, slowly turning around in front of the full-length mirror.

"How did the conversation go?" she asked. She was dressed in a denim miniskirt that I'd never seen before. It barely covered her butt. And she was wearing a tight pink tank top. She didn't look trashy, but didn't look parent-presentable either.

"Why are you dressed like that?" I asked.

"I'm trying to decide what to wear on our date with Scotty Dee," she said. "I want him to notice my legs. But I also want him to pay attention to my shoulders."

"Why your shoulders?" I asked.

"I think they're one of my most mature features. Seriously. Look at them."

She stretched her arms out wide in front of me and leaned forward to emphasize her shoulders.

"Don't you think they make me look twenty?" she asked.

"Sure," I said. "Hey, that skirt is way too short. You should wear jeans."

"But everybody wears jeans," she said. She let her arms drop to her side and frowned.

"Can't you do something normal for once?" I asked. "What if we end up walking a long distance? Or have to jog to catch a cab? You're wearing clothes that constrain you."

"That's not true," Veronica said.

"Then lift your arms above your head."

Veronica raised her thin arms over her head, and her skirt lifted up, revealing first the top of her thighs and then her pale yellow underwear.

"Is there a problem?" she asked.

I sat down on my bed and closed my eyes.

"Hey, what's wrong?" Veronica sat down next to me and put her arm around my shoulder. "If you hate my clothes that much I'll go ahead and change."

"This isn't about your wardrobe," I said.

"I know. The thing with Corky is totally wearing on me too. I wasn't going to tell you this, but last night she stood outside our window for two hours."

"She did?" I asked. "What was she doing?"

"Arranging rocks."

I slid Veronica's arm off me and walked to the window.

Corky had taken small stones and spelled out the words "Return it."

"Holy shit," I said. "What does she want us to return?"

Veronica shrugged. "Her dignity. Her sanity. Her liberty. Who knows? In addition to being psycho, Corky is a real mystery."

"Great," I said. "But that's not even why I'm upset."

"Waller issues?" Veronica asked.

I shook my head.

"A Hamilton flare-up?"

"No. You make heartbreak sound like hemorrhoids."

"Well, it makes sense. Because they can both burn your ass."

"Can you just stop being *Veronica* and be serious for a minute?"

"Yeah, you're right. What's wrong?" she asked. "I'm here for you."

"It's about my dad. I think you're right. We don't connect."

"Did you talk to him on the phone?" she asked.

"I tried," I said, "but he brought up his sciatica. And then he got mad when I mentioned Waller."

"Wait," Veronica said. "You mentioned Waller? Why?"

"I wanted to tell him what I was doing."

"No father wants to hear *who* his daughter is *doing*."

"Hey, that's not what I meant."

"You two need therapy," she said.

"That depresses me on many levels. First, we don't have the money for it. Second, my father would never go."

"First, that's only two levels, and you said that it depressed you on many. Second, I don't know what to tell you. My best advice would be to stop bringing up your sex life with him."

"Veronica, I'm not having sex with anybody. It's like you're not even listening to my problem. You're just saying whatever is on your mind regardless of what I need to hear."

Knock. Knock. Knock.

We both looked at the door.

"Doesn't it bother you that we can no longer open our door for fear that Corky the Maniac could be waiting on the other side?" I asked.

"Of course that bothers me," Veronica said. "That's why I always ask you to open the door."

"Well, I'm not doing it this time."

"Fine," she said. "I'll get on the floor and look under the crack."

Veronica got on her stomach and pressed her face right up to the doorjamb.

"What do you see?" I asked.

"Toes," Veronica said.

"You see bare feet?" I asked. "Do they appear Corky-like in any way?"

"They have hair on them," she said.

"Gross."

"Is anybody in there?" a male voice asked.

"It still could be Corky," I said.

I didn't know if she was an expert at disguising her voice, but I wouldn't have put it past her.

"We can't live like prisoners," Veronica said. "God! Screw Corky! This is my door and I'm opening it."

I covered my ears and watched as Veronica dramatically yanked on the knob.

It was Waller! I quit holding my head and waved.

"Hey," he said, waving back. "Is everything okay in here? I thought I heard yelling."

"I was reading my story out loud," Veronica said.

"You yell 'Screw Corky' and 'This is my door' in your story?" Waller asked. Then he winked at me. Then he did a double take when he saw Veronica's man-wall.

Veronica jumped onto her bed and held up her arms, trying to conceal some of the hot-dudes.

"Is that a map?" Waller asked. "Of guys?"

"No," Veronica said. "I'm plotting something. For my story."

"Right," Waller said, giving Veronica a slight nod.

"Moving on," Veronica said, stepping down off her bed and turning Waller's body away from the man-wall. "What brings you to the girl wing of the dorm? And, more precisely, what brings you to room 106?"

My heart nearly stopped when Waller pointed to me.

"The guys and I wanted to drive up to Kutná Hora. We're leaving tomorrow morning, and we've got some extra space in the car."

"Really?" I said.

"Yeah, do you two want to come?" he asked.

"Absolutely," I said.

"Kutná what?" Veronica asked.

"They're going to this cathedral outside of town," I said.

I didn't want Waller to explain it, because if he made it sound boring, I knew Veronica wouldn't go. And we'd been given a double invitation. Both of us had been asked. And it seemed risky to try to convert it into a single invitation. That would sound like I was being way too eager to make it a date.

Veronica sat down on her bed. "How long would we be gone?"

Her date with Scotty Dee wasn't until late. We'd be back in plenty of time. I couldn't believe she was asking that.

"We'll be back by late afternoon. You two will make a good buffer," Waller said. "Things are still a little tense between me and the guys."

"Duh," Veronica said. "What did you expect when you balded Frank?"

"Frank isn't going," Waller said.

"I guess that makes sense," Veronica said.

"So we'll see you guys tomorrow?" Waller said.

"Yeah," I said.

I couldn't stop smiling, even after he left.

Veronica took her skirt off and stood in her underwear in front of the mirror.

"So you're forgoing pants entirely?" I asked.

She ignored the question and turned around to look at her butt. "I sort of don't like Waller anymore."

"Really?" I asked. This surprised me, because I was liking him more and more.

"He ruined Frank for me," she said. "Because not only is Frank bald, but he's also bitter. And I don't find that emotion attractive."

"If he wasn't bitter, do you think you could look past the baldness?"

Veronica pulled on a pair of jeans. Then she stuck out her tongue and released a puff of air, imitating the sound of a fart.

"Probably not," she said. "Looking at him before made me feel horny. Now it's like staring at my dumpy-looking Uncle Terry's head."

"That's harsh," I said. I'd met her Uncle Terry.

"I need to be honest with myself. Frank isn't a hot-dude anymore."

I watched Veronica walk to her man-wall and tear Frank off with a quick pull.

"You're taking him off the man-wall?" I asked. I hadn't realized hot-dudes were removable.

Veronica held the paper Frank in her hand and tore his head off his body. Then she slapped the newly be-headed hot-dude back on the wall.

"Frank is a compromised hot-dude now. And I think his paper depiction should reflect that."

Veronica sounded very somber. She returned to her mirror and smoothed her jeans. "In other somewhat related terrible news, I'm out of crazy-cute clothes," she said. "And I need more."

I didn't waste my time offering to let her borrow some of mine. I didn't own anything "Veronica" enough.

Veronica bent over and aggressively fluffed her hair. Several weak strands snapped and drifted to the floor.

When she finished and flipped her head back up, her hair didn't look large and exaggerated. She appeared ready to do a photo shoot for a magazine cover. She was awesome.

"I bet Corky calms down in five days," she said.

"Really?" I liked the idea of that.

"And I bet Waller kisses you in Kutná Hora."

"No!" I said.

"Yes!" Veronica answered.

I thought of Waller's lips closing in on mine in a cathedral.

"He won't kiss me in front of everyone," I said.

Veronica smiled and shook her head. "I know. He's going to say he wants to show you something. Then he's going to lead you around a corner. Then he's going to look both ways. Then he's going to lean in and say something sweet. Then he's going to move his mouth slowly toward yours. Also, after a few light presses there will probably be some tongue."

"Really?" I asked.

It had taken Hamilton a whole month of kissing before he'd slipped me any tongue. To be honest, I think I was the one who slipped it to him.

"God," she said. "You're so lucky I'm going. I'll be a diversionary tactic for you. I'll keep the other guys busy and give you the space you need to conquer your new man."

"Wow," I said. "Thanks. So you really think this is going to happen?"

"He came to our dorm room and practically asked you to be his girlfriend."

I blushed.

"I hope things can go half this good with Scotty Dee. By the way, we can't spend all afternoon at Kutná Hora. We need to be back in time so that I can get ready for our

Aussie date. He's my new number one hot-dude. And I'll need adequate time to primp."

"You'll have time." I said.

"I better. Or I'm hitchhiking back."

She slipped off her tank top and put on a tight white T-shirt. Then she fluffed her hair again, and pulled out a bottle of hairspray.

"I want to see what happens when I volumize around my roots," she said.

A pungent odor filled the room. I opened the window in an attempt to create breathable air. That's when I spotted the tops of Mrs. Knox's and Corky's heads exiting the dorm through the back door.

"It's your mother," I said. "With Corky!"

Veronica joined me at the window. Mrs. Knox and Corky were walking off.

"We have to tell your mom that Corky is crazy!" I said.

Veronica shook her head. "Corky isn't going to hurt my mom. She worships her. Haven't you noticed how she kisses her butt every class? She's a classic suck-up. They don't make them any suckier."

"Brownnosing is one thing, but going out socially is a different ballgame," I said.

"Really, unless we plan on telling my mom the whole Corky story—my wild night out, what I found on her computer, yada, yada, yada—our hands our tied."

"So we're just going to let this happen?" I asked, gesturing out the window. "Doesn't it bother you?"

Veronica kicked off her sturdy leather walking sandals and stepped into her unstable black platform sandals.

"Ever since my dad walked out, everything my mom does bothers me."

"What if Corky tells your mom horrible lies about

you and tries to really wreck your life?" I asked.

"Corky is a very temporary fixture in my life. As long as she doesn't kill me, or turn me into an amputee, she'll be out of my hair at the end of the month."

I didn't think that Veronica seemed as unhinged as she should have been. I gave her a panicked look.

"I'm seventeen," she said. "I'm not supposed to get along with my mother. There's supposed to be a ton of dissonance. It's basically required. I read all about it in that book on the plane. *Examining the Triad: Mother, Father, Daughter.*"

"You really read a book on the plane?" I asked.

"Don't sound so surprised. I learned a lot. Even about you."

"You did?" I asked.

"Yeah, you're doomed. But I'm doomed too. It's called the parent/gender triad tragedy. Simply put, guys want to marry their mothers but continue to sleep with whores. And girls want to track down younger versions of their fathers and fix them. And if you have a disinterested dad you're extra doomed."

"That seems way too simple and terrible," I said. "Did you read the whole book or just the table of contents?" Sometimes Veronica only made it that far.

"I read the whole thing. Listen, I know it's a bummer," Veronica said. "But it explains a lot. The book also gave me insight into why I can't get along with my mother until I'm out of college and mature."

I didn't challenge her any further. Again, she had a valid point. Mother-daughter relationships were notoriously fraught with tension, particularly during the teenage years. But Veronica looked so miserable about it.

"Screw the Corkster. Let's go. We've got a whole world out there to experience," she said.

She shoved some money into her pocket and pulled me toward the door. And then we were gone. Out the door. Out of the dorm. Onto the crowded sidewalk. Swallowed by Prague and her powerful heat.

Chapter Fifteen

*I*f Veronica had wanted to wear a T-shirt with Kafka's head on it, we could have scored that item, in any size or color, right away. Locating the perfect dress, however, took a bit more time.

"Why is everything in this store made out of hemp?" Veronica asked. "I mean, what sorts of people choose to wear drug plants? And what do they know that I don't?"

"It's a hemp boutique, Veronica. I think hemp is a very durable and eco-friendly material."

She took a sturdy green dress off a rack and lifted it up. A crude rope belt hung around its waist. "I might wear this," Veronica said. "If I were a refugee."

"Come on," I said, tugging her out of the store.

After three hours of searching through the Castle Quarter area of town for the perfect dress; after wading through unpractical boutique after unpractical boutique; after trying on dresses with crystals sewn into their neck-lines and hems; after trying on linen blouses so thin I could see every dotted discoloration in Veronica's skin; after slipping on beaded skirts that were so expensive they rivaled American used-car prices; after the disappointing spin through the hemp store, Veronica and I reached a hill that was too steep to climb.

"If we go any farther, I'm going to require a tram," I said.

Veronica glared at the hill and then at the sun.

"Global warming has definitely hit Eastern Europe," she said. "Why are we climbing this hill anyway?"

I puffed out air. I was out of breath. Veronica turned her back to the hill and stared at me, waiting for an answer.

"Seven blocks ago you said you thought you could smell maple bars. You suspected it was coming from this direction. So here we are," I said.

"Yeah," she said, wiping sweat off her forehead. "The sun is affecting my short-term memory. I did say that. But in all honesty, I lost the scent of the maple bars about four blocks back."

I wished the sun had been affecting my memory, both long and short term. I was plagued with issues.

What did Hamilton mail me?

When would it arrive?

Was Waller going to kiss me?

How come my father and I couldn't connect?

Would I have enough money to last me?

Would Boz be waiting for Veronica when we got back?

When should I call my mom again?

If I came across Corky alone in a public bathroom, would she really stab me?

"I think Boz just sent me an e-mail. I can feel it," Veronica said. "We need to find a café."

I opened my guidebook and located an Internet café four blocks away.

"What do you think Boz wrote to you about?" I asked.

"Well," Veronica said, slowing her pace to fall in step with me. "He's probably providing me with information about Corky."

"Boz knows Corky?"

Veronica shook her head. "Right before Corky and

I got into that big fight because I'd borrowed her computer, I e-mailed Boz about her. I told him if he had any free time he should research her online. I said that she frightened me," Veronica said.

"You got in a big fight with Corky because you borrowed her computer?" I asked.

"Sort of. That's how I came across her blog. And also read all her e-mail," Veronica said.

This information fell out of her casually, like she was refreshing my memory.

"Holy shit. You read all of Corky's e-mail?" I asked. "You totally invaded her privacy. No wonder she hates you."

"Please," Veronica said. "I did it out of self-preservation." She stopped walking. "Hey. Is it just me or are you drawn to men with rifles?"

"Like on television?" I asked.

"No," Veronica said. "Like hot Czech soldiers. Oh my god. They're the same ones I saw yesterday. Follow me."

I looked ahead. I'd seen Czech soldiers standing guard beside the castle in their crisp blue suits and hats. But I didn't think the guys we were walking toward were soldiers. I pulled on Veronica's arm to stop her. I looked in her eyes to see if she was joking or possibly had grown delusional from sunstroke.

"They're not soldiers. They look like security guards, Veronica. I think they're guarding that bank."

She stared back at me with perfectly lucid eyes. "Having a cool job only makes a hot-dude hotter," Veronica said.

There was no stopping her. She walked up to a guard with thick dark hair. Normally I thought she'd go for the blond. But the dark-haired one had amazing eyes and strong-looking lips. Had he not been armed and on duty, had be been six inches shorter, had he have been living in Parma, Ohio, I might have mistaken him for Boz.

"It's me again," Veronica said.

The hot-dude glanced down at her, but he didn't say anything. His brown eyes were sexy, awesome, and powerful.

"I know that you're on duty and that you probably can't talk to me. But I'm going to put my phone number in your pocket. We're here for the month." Veronica turned and gestured to me. "Call us."

He didn't respond at all. I was mortified. This was beyond reckless. Then we started walking away.

"I'm going to die," I said. "Right here on this Prague sidewalk. You can't give your number out to armed security people. What's wrong with you?"

"I can't help myself. Something about this area of Prague makes me crave hot-dudes with an unbearable intensity."

I frowned at her in disappointment.

Then the hot-dude responded. "What's your name?" he called out in a thick accent.

Veronica turned back around and smiled. "I'm Veronica."

I kept walking. I could not believe this.

"How old are they?" I asked when Veronica caught up with me.

"Twenty?" she said.

"Either that guy has led a really hard life, or he's thirty! Can't we locate some guys who are still in their teens?"

"Teens are babies. Seriously. Roger is the only hot-dude we've come across still in his teens. He's a boring nineteen, the rest are twenty," Veronica said. "And tragically, due to his aggressive politeness, I'm beginning to see him more as a brother figure than a hot-dude. I mean, he's no challenge at all. I could crack him like a peanut."

"Hot-dudes can't be nice?" I asked.

We stopped in front of the Internet café. "My Boy Scout years are behind me," she said.

Veronica had never dated a Boy Scout.

She skipped into the café and sat down at an open computer. I dragged a chair across the floor and joined her.

"Maybe I should check my e-mail after this," I said.

Veronica didn't respond.

"My mom said that Hamilton called. It sounds like he wants to talk to me," I said.

There was a weird pause, which I didn't know how to analyze.

"The phones here are so unreliable," Veronica said.

"Yeah. My mom gave him the dorm address. He's going to mail me something. But he might have sent me an e-mail too," I said.

I stood up when I saw a guy vacate a computer.

"No! Don't open another account. Save your money. You can use this one when I'm done," Veronica said.

I sat back down. Veronica pecked away. She was very focused. But when I tried to look over her shoulder, she hid the screen with her body.

"Did Boz write you?" I asked.

"No," she said.

"Then who did you just send an e-mail to?"

"Somebody else," Veronica said.

"What are you reading now?" I asked.

"Other e-mails," Veronica said.

I hated it went she acted ridiculously secretive.

"Yeah. I know. Whose?" I asked.

"Mine."

"Who sent them?"

She sighed. "Right now I'm reading a couple from Gloria."

I stared at the back of Veronica's brown head like I

was glimpsing the ponytail of a lunatic. "Gloria Fitz?" I asked.

"Yep."

"Why is she writing to you?"

"Because I wrote to her."

"Why are you writing to Gloria?" I asked.

"I don't remember."

This made absolutely no sense.

"Okay," Veronica said. "I remember now. I wrote to her and apologized about the mall incident."

"You did?" I was stunned. This was so un-Veronica. "Why?"

"Because I need her help. She's keeping track of Boz for me while I'm gone."

I continued to gawk at the back of Veronica's head. What was she thinking? "You can't trust Gloria Fitz. She hates you."

"I know."

"Then why bother reading her e-mails?"

"Listen, she's been giving me useful information. Men are capable of anything. Zigging instead of zagging, in particular. While I'm here and he's there, I need somebody to be a set of eyes for me."

"She's spying on Boz for you?" I asked.

Veronica turned around and looked at me. "First, keep your voice down. Second, I didn't like the judgmental tone in that last question. I'm not perfect, Dessy. You know that I have gaping imperfections. Why start calling me out on them now? And she's not spying so much as she's attempting to thwart any additional doghouse construction and Celerie encounters. The exchange student ships out in two weeks, you know?"

I felt ill. It's one thing to have gaping imperfections, but it's quite another to jeopardize the fate of your broken relationship by enlisting the help of a known enemy.

"Veronica, I'm not judging you. I just worry that you might not have thought this through. Have you ever considered that Gloria might be giving you inaccurate information in an attempt to sink your relationship with Boz?"

"I'm not brain damaged. Of course I think that," Veronica said.

"Then why trust her? Why take advice from somebody who actively wants to see you miserable?" I asked.

Veronica turned back around and commenced typing. "Listen. I didn't want to tell you this because I didn't want to involve you, but I'm blackmailing Gloria. So there's no way she's got the nerve to screw me over on this completely."

"You're joking. Please tell me you aren't really blackmailing a fellow high school student in a stupid attempt to save a relationship that you wrecked!"

Veronica turned around again, looking offended. "You don't even like Gloria."

"She doesn't deserve to be tormented," I said.

Veronica shrugged. "Sure she does."

I leaned back in the chair, and it moaned.

"Don't worry. I'll sort this out when we get back to Ohio. Once things get normal again," Veronica said.

"Normal?" I asked.

Things hadn't really been "normal" for me and Veronica for years.

"Sometimes I feel like our lives resemble a cheesy cable drama," I said.

Veronica used the mouse to emphatically click and close her account.

"And what would you rather your life felt like?" she asked. "A PBS special? A medical documentary? A sports telecast?"

I leaned back a bit more and didn't answer her.

"Our lives are pretty good," she said.

"I know," I said. "It's just that I find your whole plan with Gloria alarming."

Veronica sighed. "Maybe it is stupid. Maybe I am being unethical. But we all have things we need to work on, right?" she asked.

I'd never told Veronica about my conversation with Hamilton and my three flaws. But right now it seemed like she was somehow able to read my mind.

"One of the things that I love about you is your ability to look past my weaknesses. For me, I think a lot of my interpersonal relationships—Boz, my mother, most of my peers, et cetera—are negatively influenced by my controlling nature and inability to troubleshoot without employing various levels of manipulation. And it's like you can totally see all that and you love me anyway."

Veronica was right. I did love her. And it was oddly reassuring to hear her speak with a fair amount of accurate introspection. She stood up, and I followed her out of the café. She turned and, not surprisingly, began walking back toward the vicinity of the hot-dudes with rifles.

"Veronica, slow down. There's something about my breakup with Hamilton that I never told you," I said.

I didn't want to carry my flaws around with me anymore. If Veronica could come clean about her flaws, I should be able to air mine, to share with her the whole awful truth of everything that Hamilton had laid out against me. We walked in a hurry down the sidewalk, passing underneath the awnings of a series of outdoor cafés.

"I thought there might have been more to that story," Veronica said.

Bang! Bang! Bang!

I'd never heard the sound of gunfire before. I froze.

"Get down! Get down!" Veronica screamed, yanking

on my arm. "Don't shoot me. I'm an Australian!"

We both fell onto the hard walkway. My cheek was flat against the pavement. But everybody else kept moving. Legs and feet dodged my body. I couldn't believe that people could be this unaffected by open gunfire in the middle of the day!

"We should get up," Veronica said.

"Is it safe?" I asked.

"Yeah," she said. "Look over there."

I did. But I didn't see anything dangerous or criminal.

"It was a motorcycle," she said. "It backfired."

I quickly made it to my feet. "Oh my god. I feel like such a fool."

"I wouldn't lose any sleep over it." Veronica dusted off her jeans and motioned with her head for us to cross the street.

"Veronica!" a voice called.

I looked around. Oh my god. It was the armed hot-dude.

"Are you hurt?" he asked, walking toward us. "I saw you fall."

Veronica shook her head.

"I was hoping to see you again. Here." He handed her a small piece of paper, and the two of them stood there smiling at each other like love-struck baboons.

Veronica finally looked at the note, then refolded it. "I'll call you," she said.

"Good," he said. "It's Alexej."

I wanted to rip his note out of her hand and eat it. Alexej didn't stay long. He quickly jogged back to his post in front of the bank.

"He is way too old, Veronica."

She had a big stupid grin on her face. "He's perfect."

"And he's not very responsible. Did you see how he just abandoned that bank for no reason?"

"He was worried about me. He saw me on the ground, and like a prince, he came to my rescue."

"You were on the sidewalk for a couple of seconds. We weren't in any danger."

She turned to me and grabbed my arms. "But Alexej didn't know that."

Veronica then proceeded to skip into the crosswalk. She also began to sing.

"What is that song?" I asked. I couldn't quite place it. "Is it country?"

"It's my own song. I'm making it up as I go along. It's about my new, number one hot-dude.

"Melt me, melt me, melt me," she sang. "In the street. In the sky. In a big banana pie." The words grew crazier, and the melody more bizarre. This was so stupid. She needed to drop her hot-dudes. Relationships weren't *that* difficult. If she liked Boz, she should tell Boz. If she cared about him at all, she should stop mangling his heart. *"Melt me, melt me, melt me."* I listened in disbelief as Veronica sang her inane hot-dude song, over and over, all the way home.

Chapter Sixteen

We decided to grab breakfast in the dorm cafeteria. Since I had to turn my story in on Monday, and it was now Sunday, I carried my copy with me at all times, pulling it out and reading through it, searching for rogue typos, combing through every word of dialogue, polishing every noun, clause, and sentence until it shined. I brought the "place" assignment with me, but since I wasn't photo-copying it and dispersing it to the entire class, I didn't feel the same sense of urgency to make it perfect.

"You've become obsessed with your story," Veronica said. "I'm worried that any negative feedback might send you into a self-esteem spiral."

I shook my head and peeled open a corner of my small cardboard box of cereal. "I just want my story to be the best that it can be," I said.

"So that it can enlist in the marines?" Veronica asked. She laughed at her own lame joke. Then her eyes looked sparkly happy, and she said, "Hi, Waller! Want to join us?"

I looked up. Waller was wearing a gray T-shirt and jeans. He looked very clean and fresh and adorable. Then Veronica did the coolest thing ever.

"I'm going to go make a phone call," she said. "You can have my seat."

Veronica left, and Waller sat down. I felt my heart rupture in happiness.

It was quite fortuitous that I'd chosen a wheat square cereal for breakfast, because I could eat it one piece at a time, seductively. I broke the final three squares into halves with my spoon. Waller sighed heavily. I thought he looked exhausted, but figured he must have been working on his story or something.

"I had the most amazing dream about Uma last night. It woke me up at two and I couldn't get back to sleep." Waller began gnawing on a bagel.

"Uma?" I asked. "Is she another sister?" I almost couldn't breathe. It would crush me if Uma was his girl-friend.

"Uma was my dog. She died when I was ten. But the 'place' assignment Tabitha gave us has taken me right back to my childhood. And Uma." Waller's eyes looked soft and reflective. "That dog used to do anything for a spoonful of peanut butter."

"What kind of dog was she?" I asked. I was proud of myself for being so quick with a follow-up question, because Waller's deceased childhood dog was a conversational topic that I hadn't expected to have to field.

"Uma was a German shepherd, and even though she was smart, she used to eat everything: flies, tin cans, my ant farm."

"And peanut butter," I said.

Waller laughed. "You're so easy to talk to. I haven't thought about Uma in ages. My family had her cremated. We spread her ashes at the soccer field at my elementary school. She used to love to run there."

I had never heard of anybody cremating his dog before. Or spreading the ashes at a school. "Did you get special permission?"

Waller shook his head. "It was summer vacation.

We just showed up and spread them."

"Cool," I said. And then I worried that maybe I'd said "cool" too many times.

"I'm really looking forward to Kutná Hora. This will be my first ossuary," he said.

I didn't have a clue what an ossuary was. "It'll be my first one too," I said.

Waller's face lit up. "Have you ever seen a real skeleton before?"

I felt that this was a gross question to ask somebody who was eating. "I think the one in my science class was fake," I said.

"Kite wants to touch the skulls," Waller said. "But I don't. Just because I'm an American tourist doesn't mean I have to act like one."

"Right," I said. I didn't understand why Waller was suddenly hung up on skulls. What exactly was Kutná Hora? Whore bones? "This place has more than skulls, right?" I asked. Because I knew that if Veronica ever saw a skull she would die.

"Haven't you seen pictures?" Waller asked. "They've got every bone in the body. Femurs on the ceiling. Skulls on shelves. Thousands and thousands of bones."

This was the worst news ever. Veronica was going to see a skull and die. And Waller was going to French kiss me next to a pile of femurs. Now the big trip seemed stupid.

But then something happened that took me far away from this emotionally dreadful place and deposited me in a spot of pure bliss and romantic hope. Waller reached across the table and touched my hand. "Is that your story?" he asked.

"Yes. Actually, this one is my story and this one is my 'place' assignment." I pointed to the separate paper piles so he would know which one was which. "I'm writing about the Coneflower Trail." Tragically, I felt compelled to elaborate. "It's on a reservation outside of Cleveland. I hiked there. Once. With a friend. There were cardinals and snapping turtles and salamanders. It's a cool place. I really like turtles. That's why I chose it. I still have a long ways to go with it, though."

"I still haven't finished mine either," he said. He pulled his hand away from me, but my fingers kept tingling.

"Impasse issues?" I asked.

I loved being able to demonstrate that I was a good listener.

"Yeah," Waller said. "Stupid impasse."

"Maybe you should tell me what your story is about," I said. "Maybe I can help you."

Thus far in my life I'd never had a conversation with a guy I'd liked that had gone so well.

"Okay," he said. "But this could get weird."

After successfully transitioning out of our skull discussion, I didn't want things to get weird again. "Just tell me what it's about in one word," I said. I figured that was safe. What could he possibly say?

"Desire," he said.

Things now felt weird. "Did you write about a relationship?" I asked. "That's what my story is about."

"I guess I did write about a relationship."

"So what's the impasse?" I asked.

"It's the ending," he said. "I don't like it."

"What don't you like about your ending?"

"Well, I don't like the fact that it sucks."

"Okay," I said. "But what sucks about it?"

"I wanted the characters to really arrive somewhere. But they're both kind of stuck in this moment of not committing."

"That sounds like something you can fix," I said.

Once Waller confessed his story's shortcoming, I was a bit relieved. It wasn't like he'd created an unlikable narrator that he had to overhaul, or had a ton of plot holes to patch.

"But I have to get it to people by tonight," he said. "I don't have time."

"I think you have time," I said.

"Maybe if I knew how to fix it," he said.

"So you're *really* stuck?" I said.

Waller reached his hands across the table toward me, but I didn't want to seem too eager, so I ate another half square of wheat. I really wanted Waller to touch my hand again.

"You like to get right to the point, don't you?" he asked.

"Tick. Tock. Tick. Tock," I said.

"Okay. Here it is. Something deep needs to happen between the two main characters. It's got to be physical. But I'm just not sure how to write it."

"Oh," I said. I didn't know how to talk to Waller when he used words like "deep" and "physical." The conversation suddenly felt more advanced than I was prepared for.

"I'm having a hard time with this because the characters are loosely based on me and my ex-girlfriend."

My heart leapt at the word "ex-girlfriend." I hoped she was extremely ex. Like maybe she was a regrettable hookup he'd made during the eighth grade or something.

"It's so hard to tell a story that involves people you care about. I have this tendency to want to focus on their flaws," he said.

I didn't like hearing that Waller was so fixated on his ex's flaws. But I pressed forward.

"Just be honest," I said, though I thought the answer sounded too easy.

"It's not just her flaws. I'm stuck in other ways too.

It's hard for me to write about being physical with Lori. I mean, when I was with her it was exciting and fantastic. But writing about that stuff. . . . I don't know. When I put it down on the page it really loses something."

Oh my god. We weren't just talking about desire anymore. We were talking about sex. He was talking about his sexual history with his ex-girlfriend Lori. I had no idea what to offer or add or counsel.

"How come you aren't saying anything?" he asked.

"I didn't realize you were finished," I said.

"But I stopped talking," he said.

"Yeah," I said.

"Do you not want to talk about this with me? Is it weird? God, of course it's weird. You're still in high school. Never mind. I withdraw those last comments."

To say this remark wounded me would be an understatement. "Don't withdraw anything," I said. "I've got advice for you."

"You do?" he asked.

"Sure." I cleared my throat. "I bet if I had to write about being physical with my ex-boyfriend, Hamilton, it wouldn't be nearly as exciting as actually being physical with him."

I decided that "being physical" sounded a lot more mature than "making out."

"Right. Right," he said. "But I have this feeling that the story needs a really physical, a really sexual and complicated closing."

"That's rough," I said. Because really, what else could I say?

"But I can't write about Lori that way," he said. "And I can't write about myself that way either."

"Well," I said, "does it have to be the two of you?"

"Of course it does," he said. "We're the ones in the story."

"I know. But you didn't say that the story had to end with the two main characters doing something sexual. Maybe it could end with something else happening—sexually."

Waller sat up very straight; he seemed really intrigued by this.

"Yeah, maybe they see something really sexual happening."

"Yeah, yeah," I said.

"Maybe it's not even people," he said.

"Good idea!" I said.

"Maybe they come across two animals having sex," he said.

"Okay," I said. But I worried that it sounded a little bit like Veronica's story.

"But not big animals," he said. "I don't want anything comedic like walruses or elephants humping each other."

"Right," I said.

"And I don't want any animals that look awkward and would be difficult to capture through quick images. No giraffes. Or ostriches. Or alligators."

"Absolutely," I said.

"And no animals that might accidentally injure the other with their teeth or claws while doing it," he said. "No tigers. Or grizzly bears. Or sharks."

"I agree," I said. It surprised me how quickly Waller could categorize animals and their mating styles.

"I want something small," he said. "And clever."

I finished my last half of wheat square.

"What about otters?" I asked.

"No, I want land mammals," he said.

"Kangaroos?" I asked.

"Too comedic. And not common enough for my setting. My story takes place in Michigan."

"Oh," I said.

"I've got it!" he said. "I'll describe a couple of foxes doing it."

Uh-oh. This wasn't good.

"Foxes?" I asked. "Are you sure?"

"Yeah," he said. "I saw a couple of foxes doing it on a nature show once, and it was one of the most amazing things ever. All that fur. They were totally wild, but they were also incredibly tender."

"Foxes feel wrong," I said.

"No," he said. "The more you resist, the more certain I am that foxes are the exact right animal."

He ran his hands through his hair and smiled. "I gotta go. I gotta rewrite the ending. This is so amazing."

Waller took his tray and got up and left me. This meant we'd be reading two stories with foxes mating. Veronica would not be happy. In fact, I feared that she might even be crushed. She thought her concept was so original. And I didn't like the idea that I'd steered Waller toward the revelation that led him to write about foxes. Ugh. If Veronica knew that, she'd never talk to me again. My safest bet was to deny any knowledge of Waller's fox sex scene. Then, like the dutiful friend I was, I'd support her during her inevitable meltdown.

The cafeteria was suddenly flooded with a group of German photography students. They buzzed around me wearing brown pants and speaking an emphatic and vowel-heavy language. I didn't even bother checking out whether or not there were any hot-dudes among them. I had enough on my plate already.

Chapter Seventeen

Veronica looked gorgeous. Her long hair was pulled back, but she let a curve of bangs fall to the side of her face. Without makeup she was so natural. I understood why guys fell for her. She was special, even when crazy things flew out of her mouth.

We planned on meeting Waller and the other guys in front of the dorm at noon. Veronica had plopped down on the curb, but I was too nervous to sit. I hadn't brushed my teeth after breakfast. This worried me.

"My mouth will taste like cereal," I said. "Is that really what I want him to associate me with?"

"Don't you have any gum?" Veronica asked.

I looked in my bag. All I had were pens, baby wipes, and my story.

"God, you should always carry gum," Veronica said.

"Do you have some?"

"Yeah," she said, stretching her toned legs out in front of her.

"Can I have some?" I asked.

"Totally," she said. "The reason I didn't offer it to you right away is because I wanted you to panic a little bit. Because then maybe you'd start planning ahead. Now that you're dating again, you need to be more prepared. For example, familiarize yourself with the day's headlines so you've got some solid conversation starters. And *always* make sure you have gum. And clean underwear. And push-up bras. And condoms."

"Stop, stop, stop," I said. "When you mess with me like this you make me blush."

"I know," she said. "That's mainly why I do it."

"Do you have any other, more useful advice?" I asked.

"Well," Veronica said. "This is not about you in particular, but I've been thinking a lot about interest shifts."

"What are those?"

"When a guy really likes you and then his interest suddenly shifts. If this happens, and you haven't done anything course-changing, I think it means he's met somebody else."

"Course-changing?" I asked.

"That would be something you've done to make him lose interest. Drastic haircut. Inflated like a blimp. Peed yourself at Applebee's in front of his friends. If you haven't done anything from that category, and his interest shifts, then another woman has entered the picture and captivated him."

"Where do you come up with these ideas?" I asked.

"My brain and life experience."

A little after noon, Waller and Roger emerged from the dorm looking cute and collegey in their well-worn jeans and T-shirts.

"Where are the others?" Veronica asked them.

"Frank went paddleboating down the Vltava," Roger said. "And Kite went to rent the car."

"Frank went paddleboating by himself?" I asked.

Roger nodded. "He's still adjusting to his condition."

"Balding people is wrong," Veronica said, pointing to Waller.

"I know. I've apologized. Can we move on?" Waller said.

I was really hoping that the guys could move on, because all this tension was a real mood-killer.

Beep. Beep. Beep.

Kite rolled up in one of the smallest cars I'd ever seen in my life. It looked like a glorified shoe.

"We're all fitting inside that?" I asked.

"Relax," Waller said. "Two in front. Three in back. It'll work."

"I think small cars are good for the environment," Veronica said. "One day I hope to live in a country that only has electric ones."

"I think that place already exists. Tomorrowland at Disney World," Roger said. "Beep. Beep." He grabbed at the air like he was honking a horn.

I don't know why I thought this was so funny. Maybe because I liked seeing Roger tease Veronica, but I laughed so hard I snorted. Veronica stared at me in horror. As I climbed into the backseat after Waller, she leaned into me and whispered, "Watch the sound effects. The only fans of pig noises are actual pigs."

Kite drove. Roger sat in the passenger seat because he was clearly the tallest. And I positioned myself in the middle of the backseat between Waller and Veronica. Waller smelled yummier than he had the other night. Like an orange and some sort of spice. Veronica smelled like a banana.

As we rolled along, I felt too challenged to have a conversation with Waller. My like for him made me pull back into myself. From this introverted place I tried to think of funny things to say. But I couldn't figure out if they were funny or goofy. And everybody knows that, for guys, funny is sexy, but goofy isn't. In the front seats, Kite and Roger were talking about a story I hadn't read.

"You really didn't like it?" Roger said. "I seriously loved it."

"I was annoyed by the Miracle Whip jar," Kite said. "He's trying to foreshadow the upcoming failed miracle. It was heavy-handed. He could have just called it mayonnaise."

"No way. The irony is brilliant—the kid searching for this miraculous soup to put in a ubiquitous Kraft jar. The only miraculous thing about Miracle Whip is that food could be so cheap and disgusting. It's about our concept of miracles. Stuart Dybek is a genius. That one detail adds so much."

While interesting, the conversation was making me tense. Because I hadn't even considered trying to communicate with my reader using every tiny detail. And condiments? During my picnic scene, I think my characters ate their turkey sandwiches dry. Had I used any symbolism at all? I compulsively pulled out my story and started skimming it.

"So how did all you guys meet?" Veronica asked. "Street luging? Heli-skiing? Scuba?"

I almost answered for Waller and Roger, but then caught myself because maybe Veronica had some sort of agenda.

"Roger and I have known each other for years," Waller said. "We went through puberty together. We got into lots of trouble."

Roger turned around and looked into the backseat. "I think it's more accurate to say that I assisted you out of lots of trouble."

"A kid can encounter all sorts of melee on the streets of Chicago," Waller said.

I loved that comment. It made him seem dangerous and sexy but in a reformed and approachable way.

"It's not like we were ever held hostage," Roger said. "We had paper routes. We went to church. Your mother hired clowns for your birthday parties."

Waller lowered his mouth to my ear. "My street was a lot dicier than his."

"Oh," I said as empathically as I could.

"How did you meet Kite and Frank?" Veronica asked.

"We met them in an online writers' group," Waller said. "We send stuff out for group critique a couple of times a month."

"Wow." Veronica tucked a strand of hair behind her ear. "You guys are dedicated."

"You're not going to get where you want to go if you don't put your butt in the chair and type," Waller said.

I was a little disappointed that Veronica was monopolizing Waller. Wasn't this trip supposed to be about me and my kissable lips?

"Are you trying to write a novel?" Veronica asked.

"I'm focusing on my short stories," Waller said.

"But Frank sure is," Kite chimed in. "He's the next Dan Brown."

Waller laughed snidely.

"He wrote almost a hundred pages yesterday. He's like a madman," Kite said. "He says his energy comes from his plot."

"I want more than a loud plot to deliver my sales," Waller said.

I was glad to hear Waller say this. It reinforced my belief that he had good taste.

"You have to work hard," Waller added, "but really, when it comes down to it, it's all about who you know. Which reminds me . . . I need to give you two my story today."

"Cool," Veronica said. "I'm not even going to ask you what you wrote about, because I want it to be a complete surprise."

Waller laughed and rubbed his hands on his jeans. "Okay," he said. "I won't give anything away."

I don't know if it was my conscience or the fear of Veronica's wrath or some other powerful force, but the world around me began to turn very rubbery. It was like every solid thing had started turning flimsy on me. My legs. Veronica's body. The car seat. The windows. My pen. Waller. I didn't look at anybody. Instead, I stared at my rubbery story. The words danced. It was as if my own deep disappointment in myself had triggered a hallucination.

"When are you up?" Waller's voice only partially broke the spell.

"I turn my story in on Monday," I said. "I get critiqued on Wednesday." I sounded like a robot.

"Are you nervous?" Waller asked.

"Yes," I said.

"Don't be," he said. "You should relax about it."

"Yes," I said. "I should relax."

Veronica looked at me. Then she swiped my pen.

"Put it away and chill out," she said.

Before I knew what I was doing, I punched Veronica with my fist and grabbed my pen back.

"Ouch," she said.

"Wow," said Waller. "Here's a girl who's intent on revision."

He glanced down at my story. I felt my fist tightening again. Veronica saw this and grabbed my arm.

"I don't think she's ready to share," she said.

"What's going on back there?" Roger asked.

"Nothing," Veronica said.

"I'm trying to sneak a peek at Dessy's story," Waller told him. "The first sentence is 'Before I let him kiss me, I made him tell me a secret: His father was coming unglued, and spoke about the Rapture as though it might arrive before Arbor Day.'"

Oh my god! He was reading my story. That was my

first sentence. I hadn't told him he could read the first sentence. What was Waller doing? Were there no rules in my new rubbery world?

"Sounds good," Roger said.

"Yeah," said Kite. "I haven't thought about the Rapture in years."

In protest, I wildly waved my pen in the air. Veronica and Waller both pulled their faces away from my swinging hand.

"Don't read it now!" I said.

"Okay," Waller said. "Calm down."

"Mellow," Veronica said. "He stopped reading it."

"I'm just not ready yet," I said. "I still might change something."

Waller playfully tugged at a corner of my story. I pulled it out of his grasp.

"I like where it's going," he said.

I glanced over the four paragraphs on that page. This particular scene reeked of sexual tension. It was, in fact, my fictive couple's first attempt at a kiss. I lifted my butt off the seat and tucked my story underneath me. Then I sat back down. This maneuver made a crunching sound. Veronica stared at me.

"Do I need to get back there and sit between anybody?" Roger asked.

"Maybe," Waller said.

Roger turned around and smiled at me. "Where's your story?" he asked.

"She's sitting on it," Waller said.

I could feel myself blush. Why couldn't I have just stuck it back inside my bag? Things kept getting more and more rubbery. We traveled mile after mile without any conversation. What was I doing? I decided I had to reclaim a sense of normalcy. So I reached forward and patted Roger on the shoulder.

Veronica shot me a sideways glance.

"How are things in the front seat?" I asked.

Roger turned around and looked at me. "Decent," he said. "Backseat?"

"I haven't seen a single cow," Waller said.

"There's supposed to be cows?" I asked.

"He was kidding," Roger said. "It's an inside joke."

I wondered what it could be. I shifted my weight and heard my story crunch beneath me.

"So, do you take workshops in high school?" Roger asked.

"No," I said.

"Our school pretty much ignores the arts," Veronica said. "You know how it is. Midwestern values. Most of us have never heard of Brueghel, but our football games are freakishly well attended."

The only reason Veronica knew about Brueghel was because of her mother. Mrs. Knox had written a short story about him around the time Mr. Knox had fled to Rome. She'd also bought a goldfish and named it Brueghel. Veronica had hated that thing. She'd even refused to feed it. It only lasted two months. I wanted to shift my weight again, but I feared releasing any more sounds.

"So what kind of classes do you take?" Roger asked.

"The basics. Trigonometry. Government. Metal shop. Botany. Et cetera," Veronica said.

"What do *you* take, Dessy?" Roger asked.

"Yeah, what's your favorite high school class?" Waller added.

I hated hearing the words *high school*. Okay, so I hadn't completed my secondary education. Did it need to be brought up with every question? Things felt so awkward. Why were relationships this hard? And of all the materials on the planet, why did everything make me feel like *rubber*?

"I like English," I said.

"Nice," Waller said. "That's Allie's favorite class too."

That response totally bummed me out. And even though I felt this nagging impulse to rearrange my weight again, I didn't do that either. Veronica must have been able to sense my clumsy desperation.

"Does this car have a radio?" she asked.

Kite didn't answer, just turned it on. We listened to techno dance music as we drove to the bones.

Chapter Eighteen

$\mathcal{I}$ wasn't ready to move. I still had things to figure out. Thus, I didn't want Veronica to open her car door. But she did. As I climbed out behind her, I grabbed my story off the seat and stuck it inside my bag.

"Where is this church?" Veronica asked.

Roger pulled a map out of his pocket and studied it. "It's two blocks that way," he said, pointing down a normal-looking street.

It relieved me that the street didn't look like something out of a horror movie. Maybe the bones didn't even look like bones. Maybe they were ground up into stucco or something. I mean, could a church really be built out of bones? Weren't they prone to breakage and splintering? And what about osteoporosis?

We filed down the sidewalk past other tourists.

"My god," said a woman wearing a Miami Dolphins T-shirt. "That place was satanic."

Once the woman was out of earshot, Veronica turned and looked at Kite. "Sometimes, tourists can be so close-minded," she said.

Veronica's need to flirt and score points with every member of the male population was somewhat astounding. I watched her twirl her hair and glide giddily between Kite and Roger. She seemed to think that by standing in the proximity of guys, she was saying something important about herself.

"What's that?" Veronica asked. On top of a hill sat an enormous sand-colored church with tall windows and slender spires.

"That's Saint Barbara's Church," Roger said. With his long-legged strides, Veronica had to walk twice as fast to keep up.

"It looks like a crown," Veronica observed.

"It's supposed to," Roger said. "But that's not where we're going. Sedlec is up ahead."

"Too bad. It's totally cool!" cheered Veronica. She pulled on my arm and pressed her mouth next to my ear, but she didn't say any words. She just released kissing sounds. It tickled so much that I laughed.

"Hey, I want to hear the joke," Waller said.

Veronica pushed me toward Waller and fell back in step with Roger and Kite.

"You should tell him the joke," she said.

Waller touched me on the shoulder. "Yeah," he said. "Tell me."

I wanted to kill Veronica. Could she have stopped messing around for one afternoon, long enough for me to kiss Waller? Seriously.

"Just like our love of roadside cows, it's probably an inside joke," Roger said.

I nodded gratefully. "It is."

Soon the gates of the ossuary loomed before us. Kite was first in line, followed by Roger and then Veronica. I guess I thought that either Veronica would realize we were about to enter into a bone cathedral and refuse to go inside, or else she'd walk into the bone cathedral and the bones would be so tastefully and artistically attached to the walls that she wouldn't freak out. She might have mistaken them for synthetic bones. If I hadn't been told to expect real bones, I'd have assumed everything I saw inside was faux. Wouldn't I?

"Is it sick to want to see this?" Kite asked. "I mean, I can't wait."

"So I take it you're not religious?" Veronica asked.

"I'm Catholic," Kite said. "Lapsed."

"I'm really looking forward to this too," Roger said.

"Are you a lapsed Catholic as well?" Veronica asked.

"I'm less lapsed than Kite," Roger said.

"Good to know," Veronica said.

The fact that Veronica was so clueless as to what the guys were really talking about bothered my conscience considerably. But I just couldn't muster enough courage to bring up the skeletal remains.

"Churches can be so threatening," I said. I had *almost* convinced myself that the bones would be understated. That was not the case. Upon entering, we saw tall shelves showcasing skull after skull. Fibulas were wired to their lower jaws. And in a corner, a large coat of arms was formed from what looked to be the bones from dozens of arms and legs. A chandelier made of bones hung heavily above us.

Pelvises. Scapulas. Spines. There was no mistaking what we were seeing. They were bones. Pitiful, ugly, innumerable bones.

"Jesus," Veronica said. "They look so real." She tilted her head back, taking in the bone-decorated ceiling. They draped the tops of the high walls like an icing border on a cake.

"They *are* real," Roger said. "They're from people who died during the plague."

"Yeah," Kite said. "This place is an ossuary."

"What?" Veronica asked, covering her mouth with her hand. "These are people?"

"They used to be," Roger said.

Veronica stared at me in disbelief. I felt that rubbery sensation return. It began in my feet and traveled upward.

"You don't look shocked at all," Veronica said. "You knew! You knew!"

I blinked at her. "I'm sorry."

"Why?" she yelled. "What have I ever done to deserve this?"

I kept blinking. "Nothing," I said.

I watched her swing her arms like she was trying to propel herself outside. Behind her there was a doorway big enough for a doll that led through the bones into a small room filled with more bones.

"Get me out!" Veronica yelled.

Things started happening in slow motion. I felt my knees give way. Then I felt myself hit the floor.

"Dessy?" Waller yelled.

The next sound I heard was the noise of somebody repeatedly retching.

"We'd better get out of here," Roger said.

Waller picked me up off the floor. I wrapped my arms around his neck and let my head lean against his chest. The orange-and-spice scent of his chest region smelled manly and safe. I caved against it. Then I heard the sound of more retching.

"This is bad!" Kite said.

"You grab her feet. I'll take her arms," Roger said. "Lucky for us she's light."

I continued to hold Waller and didn't open my eyes. But I imagined Veronica being removed from the bone church the way people carry rolled-up Oriental rugs. I'd betrayed her. And I wasn't sure if she could forgive me.

It didn't take long for us to reach the car.

"We need to clean her up," Roger said. "She has puke on her face."

"And arms," Kite said.

"And shoes," Roger added.

This was very terrible news.

"I have baby wipes," I mumbled.

"What?" Waller asked.

"I have baby wipes," I repeated. "They're in my bag."

Waller set me down in the backseat and opened up my bag. He took out the box of wipes and then kissed me. Not romantically on the lips like I'd hoped and planned for. He pressed his mouth to the top of my head, then carefully shut the door.

Had I wanted to jerk myself into a state of total alertness, I probably could have, but drifting in this odd place of half-awareness felt pleasant. When Roger opened the front passenger door, the sweet powdery smell of baby wipes nearly overwhelmed me.

"Did anybody tell her what an ossuary was? She seemed genuinely surprised," he said. "You'll be okay." He gently set Veronica in the front seat. "Hopefully, it'll reduce the chance of motion sickness."

"What a god-awful place," Veronica said. "That's what hell will look like."

"I don't think so," Kite said as he strapped himself into the driver's seat.

Roger slid into the backseat beside me. "I think when we get to hell, we'll all be very surprised by what we see."

They laughed, but not in an easy, free-spirited way. They seemed nervous.

"If you need us to pull over, Veronica," Roger said, "just tell us."

"I'll be fine," she said. "Just don't parade any skeletons around in front of me."

"You got it," Roger said.

"This feels like the worst day of my life," Veronica said. "Again!"

I rested my head on Waller's shoulder. My third flaw. It had finally surfaced, even here in Prague. Hamilton had said that the worst thing about me, the thing that rendered our relationship "over," was my inability to challenge Veronica.

"You surrender to her every whim," Hamilton said. "You're a serial caver."

"I'm a what?" I'd asked him. I'd fiddled with my purse strap while I sat in his Volvo. I didn't want him to dump me in the car. I mean, I didn't want him to dump me at all. But I always thought that when people broke up they should do it in an actual place. A restaurant, living room, or post office. I wanted a place I could return to and, in a gesture toward closure, relive what had happened a few times.

"You're a serial caver," Hamilton repeated. "Veronica presents you with bad idea after bad idea, and you cave and cave again."

Hamilton was right. I didn't even need him to laminate that flaw.

From the backseat I watched Veronica nibble on her fingernails as we drove through the green Czech countryside. Kite adjusted the volume on the radio several times as it continued to pump out dance music. Crazy drumbeats. Hypnotic melodies. I guess it was an appropriate soundtrack for the day.

As we entered Prague, I leaned forward and smiled at Veronica. She chose to ignore me. I wasn't sure how my friendship with her had turned into such a struggle. Or why I'd suddenly decided to resolve our tensions by being actively dishonest.

Originally, by not telling Veronica about the bone church, by tricking her, I thought I had stood up to her. But looking at it now, I realized that I was afraid to be honest with her, so I dodged the issue altogether by being dishonest. Hamilton thought that my dependency on Veronica crippled my own identity. I tried to tell him that after Mr. Knox left, things had shifted for her. My friendship with her hadn't always been this way. But he'd looked at me and said, "Reality is reality. You've surrendered your trim tab to her."

Hamilton, whom I considered fairly deep, often spoke of trim tabs. It's the small rudder that steers ships. He felt there was a considerable amount of honor in making conscious decisions toward your life's goals. Hamilton believed that my three flaws rendered me goalless. I think that was the hardest part of his big lecture: the words, "You don't have any aim. Take away Veronica, and I have no idea which direction you'd go." It was a problem I couldn't deny that I had. Yet it was one I didn't know how to fix. I liked Veronica. Even if she did inhibit my trim tab.

Hamilton had been quiet after that. I'd absorbed what he'd said and felt miserable. And then, in an effort to make sure that I hadn't misunderstood anything, I'd asked my final question.

"So we're not just taking a break, are we?"

We'd taken a break once before. After I'd scared him by reading a bridal magazine in his allergist's waiting room during one of his monthly appointments.

Hamilton kept his sunglasses on and stared out the windshield. "I'm headed to Dartmouth in a few months. Breaking up makes the most sense."

I nodded. And then I realized that I was home. He'd steered his car into my driveway and pulled the gearshift into PARK. Then he did the cruelest thing. He turned to look at me and said, "I still think you're pretty great."

Lamer words had never been spoken. I got out of the car and walked into my house and ate dinner with my parents. Baked chicken and peas warmed from a can. There might have been a salad involved.

"Is something wrong?" my mother had asked.

"Cramps," I said.

Neither one of my parents asked me anything after that. We weren't that kind of family. I didn't tell my mom about the breakup for a week. And later that night, when I'd called Veronica from my bedroom and cried to her about it, she'd said the things I thought I wanted her to say. "What a loser. I bet he comes back. Crawling."

But I never told her about my flaws. Because that's not how I wanted others to see me. It certainly wasn't the way I wanted to see myself.

I found it hard to stay awake inside of the warm car. Sitting between Roger and Waller made things feel warmer too, like I was positioned next to radiators. I tried one more time to lean forward and have a pleasant exchange with Veronica, but she wasn't having it. So I settled back, closed my eyes, and leaned against Waller again. Except Waller smelled totally different. He smelled like leather. When I opened my eyes I was horrified to realize that I was leaning against Roger instead of Waller. I shouldn't be leaning against Roger. He wasn't my crush.

"Tired?" Roger asked me.

"Uh-huh," I said.

I sat up straight. I needed to say something right away to override this awkward feeling.

"Nice belt," I said.

"Are you talking to me?" Roger asked.

"Yes," I said. "I like your belt."

"I'm surprised you can see it when I'm sitting down," he said.

Roger made a good point. While in a seated position, his belt was hidden under his shirt.

"I noticed it while you were standing," I said. "Sometimes it takes me a while to form compliments."

Roger laughed at me. And I couldn't blame him. "Thanks," he said.

I stayed stiff and didn't lean in any direction for the rest of the ride. What was wrong with me? Every time I opened my mouth around a guy, I had the potential to sound like a freak. Who openly admits to staring at the area located just above a guy's crotch? Apparently I did.

Kite and Waller parked the shoe-car in front of the dorm. Roger escorted Veronica and me back to our room.

"Do you need anything to eat?" he asked.

"No," Veronica said. "I'm fine."

"Dessy?"

"I'm fine too," I said.

We all looked at each other as if we knew we needed to part ways, but we also felt obligated to say more.

"You two take it easy," he said finally.

He left me with Veronica in the hallway outside our room.

"Do you think Corky is in there?" I asked.

"I have no idea." Veronica swiped her card and walked directly to the bathroom. I heard her brushing her teeth. Nobody was there. Not Corky. Not Annie Earl. Not Brenda. I opened our bedroom door and lay down on my unmade bed, exhausted. Confronting the remains of the dead *and* your personal flaws was a lot to pack into one afternoon.

Veronica slammed our bedroom door shut, kicked off her sandals, and climbed into her bed.

"I'm sorry," I said. And I really was.

Veronica pulled the covers over her head. I ignored this easy grab for isolation and walked across the room to sit beside her sulking lump.

"You're not the only one with gaping imperfections," I said.

She didn't respond.

"Aren't you going to say anything?" I asked. "Don't be like this. You're acting very passive-aggressive."

Veronica threw the covers off her head, leaving several strands of hair swimming in the static air above her.

"I don't think that now is the time to be hypercritical of me," she said.

"Okay. But we were only in that church a few minutes. How many bones could you have seen?"

Veronica slapped my leg.

"Ouch," I said.

"Are you kidding me? How many bones did I see? They were everywhere, Dessy. I couldn't not see bones. It's what Disneyland would look like if Walt Disney had been a freak of nature with a bone perversion."

"I know," I said, thinking back to the chandelier. Apparently it had been composed of every bone in the human body. "It was pretty intense."

"Those images are burned into my head forever. Can you imagine what my dreams are going to be like now?"

"Listen," I said. "Don't torture me about this. I feel like rubber. My relationship with Waller has become absurd. When it comes to guys, I'm a failure."

"God, Dessy. What did you expect would happen with Waller when you began openly flirting with Roger?"

I stood up. I couldn't believe what she'd just said.

"What are you talking about?" I asked.

"Don't play dumb," Veronica said.

"But I didn't!"

"You did. You touched Roger's shoulder and complimented his belt!"

"So?" I said.

"Flirt!" she yelled at me. Then she reached out and mockingly put her hand on my shoulder.

I swatted it away. I was angry. At Veronica. At myself. At my current situation. At my years of subservience. Still, I couldn't see a solution to any of it.

Knock. Knock. Knock.

"Corky has the worst timing," Veronica said.

"Maybe it's not Corky," I said.

Knock. Knock. Knock.

"Go away!" Veronica said. "And take your deranged ass and plant it somewhere where somebody has the desire to see it. Do you hear me, Corky Tina Baker?"

"It's Waller," the voice said.

"What do you want?" Veronica asked.

"I forgot to give you my story."

Great. The last thing I needed was for Veronica to read his story. Veronica rolled away from me and stood up. She opened the door a crack and took the papers from Waller. Then she closed the door and turned to me. Her face appeared surprised.

"What?" I asked.

"I have some bad news."

"How bad?"

"Oh, it's bad," she said, exhaling dramatically.

"What?" I asked.

"You know how you like Waller?"

"Yeah."

"That might change."

"Why? Did he tell you something?"

She shook her head. "Worse."

"What is it?" I felt breathless.

"Waller doesn't have eyebrows anymore."

"Are you sure?" I realized that question sounded dumb. But he had just dropped us off a few minutes ago, and he'd totally still had eyebrows.

"Yeah. Do you want me to make any adjustments to the hot-dudes?" she asked.

I didn't say anything. I just stared at her. Then at the man-wall.

"I know it's shocking," Veronica said. "It looks like Frank shaved them off. I bet he went crazy and ambushed him."

"You're lying!" I said.

Veronica handed me a copy of Waller's story. "Nope," she said. "That's your job. I'm going to take a nap."

Chapter Nineteen

$\mathcal{W}$atching Veronica sleep did nothing to calm my nerves. Corky still wanted to kill us. I had no connection with my father. Hamilton was right about every single last one of my flaws. Plus, in addition to giving away Veronica's favorite plot point to Waller, it turned out that I was a complete liar to boot. Also, I'd inadvertently flirted with Roger, who I didn't even really like. (Did I?!) And now the guy I'd been falling in love with didn't have eyebrows. How was a seventeen-year-old supposed to cope with this?

I decided to read Corky's story because hers was up next. I dove into it optimistically, hoping the piece would show her kinder, gentler side.

> *Every fairy has a breaking point. And Lilith had definitely reached hers.*
>
> *"Are you sure he deserves to die?" Cecil asked.*
>
> *"Yes," Lilith said, drawing her blade against a whetstone. The point was so sharp, it looked like it could bisect a mosquito.*
>
> *"You mean you can't forgive him?" Cecil asked.*
>
> *Lilith held the blade under the glowing moon.*
>
> *"Maybe you could just punch him in the face and then tear off his wings," Cecil said.*

Lilith sighed, her white face burdened by her upcoming job.

"No," she said. "His heart needs to stop. I'm sure."

At fourteen, Cecil was too undeveloped to understand why one fairy needed to kill another fairy. There were rules in place. Rule one: You can't lie to another fairy. Rule two: You must honor every fairy's secret. Rule three: You can't break another fairy's heart.

Lilith had never killed a man before. She returned the knife to its sheath and licked her lips.

"I'll hack him apart before midnight."

Cecil shook her sad head. "I won't wait up."

The death scene in Corky's story gave me goose bumps. The closing paragraph approached a pornographic level of violence that made me check the lock on the door and window. In it, the fairy graphically butchers the unfaithful guy. I was stunned. The fairy had no conscience. She was methodical and quick. And Corky seemed so comfortable analyzing the torturous way the man was split apart.

Even though it didn't seem like the perfect solution, I decided to reach out to the one person you're supposed to reach out to in a dire situations like this: your mother. But before I could make my way to the lobby, I first had to successfully leave my room. I got down on my hands and knees and peeked under the door. I didn't see any feet or shadows. It was time to make my quick getaway.

I grabbed some cash out of my desk drawer; that's when I noticed Waller's story lying on Veronica's desk. I snatched it. Waller had titled it "How to Break My Heart." I held the pages to my chest; he was so introspective and romantic. But now I needed to get rid of them.

I watched Veronica's chest rise and fall. She looked so

unsuspecting. I doubted that my friendship with Veronica could survive another betrayal, so I stuffed the stories into my bag and slung it over my shoulder. After a quick mirror check, I grabbed my keys and slipped through the door.

"What's your hurry?" a voice called.

I froze. Annie Earl and Corky were eating white puffy rolls at the kitchen table.

"Did you know that Corky has traveled extensively through Turkey?" Annie Earl asked me.

I shook my head. I didn't know that Annie Earl and Corky were friends. Why would Annie Earl want to be friends with Corky?

"It's good to see the world while you're young," Annie Earl continued.

"Yeah," I said.

"Where are you going?" Corky asked.

"Out," I said.

"Do you want a roll?" Annie Earl asked. "Corky bought them at a bakery. They're still warm."

I glanced at the rolls. Here it was again. The "zoo strategy." Corky was a masterful manipulator. They looked delicious and smelled buttery. But I didn't want to be indebted to Corky for anything. Even carbs.

"Is Veronica taking a nap?" Corky asked.

I glanced at our bedroom door. At this time I didn't feel comfortable disclosing Veronica's whereabouts or sleep state.

"I'm not sure," I said. "Well, gotta go!"

"You're in a hurry," Annie Earl observed.

"I need to make a phone call."

"Are you going to the lobby?" Corky asked.

Oh my god. I'd inadvertently disclosed my plans. Corky was so treacherous.

"Maybe," I said.

"Why don't you use the phone in your room?" Annie Earl asked.

"Um," I said. "I'm dialing out."

"You can dial out on the phone in your room," Annie Earl said.

"Really?" I asked.

"I'm surprised Veronica didn't tell you that," Corky said. "I helped her figure out how to call her boyfriend in Ohio."

What? Was Corky lying?

"Well," I said. "The lobby phone is cheaper."

Annie Earl and Corky looked at each other.

"No it's not," Corky said. "It costs way more."

I felt like an idiot. "Well, I like the privacy."

Annie Earl looked at me and tilted her head in confusion. "But aren't there always a lot of people in the lobby?"

I felt like I was saying such random, stupid things. I needed to leave. "Talking in crowds doesn't bother me," I said. "I feel very hidden. Hey, I better go before it gets late. Bye!"

And I ran out of the room, tore down the hallway, and flew down the staircase toward the lobby. Once I got to the phone, I fed it my money, entered all the necessary codes, and waited for my mother to answer.

MOM: Dessy? It's late here. Is everything okay?

ME: Yes.

MOM: Why are you calling?

ME: I didn't feel like we'd finished our first conversation.

MOM: Are you sure nothing is wrong? Your father said that you met a boy?

ME: No. No. No.

MOM: You didn't meet a boy?

ME: I did meet a guy named Waller. We're just friends.

MOM: I think it's good to get out there and look at all the fish.

ME: Yeah. I'm looking.

MOM: Good.

ME: You know what I've been wondering about? What was Grandpa like?

MOM: Your Grandpa Gherkin and your Grandpa Polk are both still alive. What do you mean?

ME: I mean, what was your relationship like with Grandpa Polk?

MOM: (Sigh)

ME: Was he really involved in your life? Or was he—

MOM: I'd say your Grandpa Polk was a lot like your dad. A good, hardworking man. Why are you thinking about your grandparents? Are you homesick?

ME: Something like that.

MOM: Dessy, you sound tired.

ME: To be honest, I'm experiencing a little friction with my roommate.

MOM: I knew there was something wrong. Is it Veronica?

ME: No. It's this person named Corky.

MOM: What's the problem?

ME: She's sort of crazy.

MOM: Crazy how?

ME: She's like a maniac.

MOM: What's she done?

ME: She threatens me.

MOM: Are you sure it isn't a misunderstanding?

ME: I'm pretty sure she's threatening me.

MOM: I had a crazy roommate once. Her name was Pam. And do you know how I handled her?

ME: How?

MOM: I sat her down and talked to her.

ME: About what?

MOM: I had an honest conversation about who I was and where I was coming from. It opened up an important line of communication.

ME: Did she stop being crazy?

MOM: Most people who act crazy aren't really crazy. They're just unhappy.

ME: Well, then I think Corky must be extremely miserable.

MOM: Have you tried talking to her?

ME: No. She seems too crazy.

MOM: Dessy, it sounds like you should have a conversation with the poor girl.

ME: I'm scared. She's not like anybody I know at home. She's different.

MOM: She sounds like she needs a friend.

ME: Maybe.

MOM: Give it a try and let me know how it goes. Pam and I became good friends after our talk.

ME: I've never heard of Pam before.

MOM: I lost touch with her about ten years ago. After she moved to Saskatchewan.

ME: I wish that story had a better ending.

MOM: Is there anything else you want to talk about?

ME: No. I better go.

MOM: I'm so proud of you for not asking about Hamilton.

ME: Why? Did he call again?

MOM: No.

ME: I never got his package.

MOM: I never said he sent a package. I said he mailed you something. It's probably a letter.

ME: Oh.

MOM: Why don't you call me tomorrow? Let me know how things went.

ME: Is Dad there?

MOM: He's sleeping.

ME: Oh.

MOM: Do you want me to wake him up?

ME: No.

MOM: Good. Because it's one a.m. And you know how he

gets when he's behind on his sleep.

ME: Yeah.

MOM: (Yawning) Good luck with Corky. Conversation is the best way to bridge distance.

ME: You're probably right.

MOM: I'm so glad we had this talk.

ME: Ditto.

Click.

Standing in the lobby, staring at a garbage can, the world made sense again. I reached in my bag for Veronica's copy of Waller's story, and dropped it into the can. The conversation with my mother was so inspiring that when I came back to the dorm room I didn't even do a "Corky check." I didn't need to live in fear anymore. All I needed was to have an honest conversation. I swung open the door. And there she was. Still sitting at the kitchen table. Cutting an apple into pieces.

"I've been waiting for you," she said, pushing the butter knife through the fruit's crisp flesh.

"I'm actually glad to hear that, Corky, because I think it's time we had a conversation."

I cleared my throat. "Corky, it scares me to think that you might be lying in wait in order to jump me," I said. "I'm not a fighter. I'm a nice person. I don't know where things went wrong between us. Honestly, I think we can be friends."

"Are you joking?" Corky asked.

"No," I said.

"That's what you wanted to tell me?"

"Pretty much. This whole 'I'm a dangerous person out to get you' dynamic doesn't work for me. It's not healthy."

"Anything else?" Corky asked, slowly scratching her neck.

"I think we'd all enjoy ourselves more in this city if we could remove all these vendetta vibes from our living situation."

"Oh," Corky said.

"So . . . what do you think?"

Corky stood up and walked toward me. I realized that she was still holding the butter knife, and this made my breath quicken. She squinted her eyes. "I think the only reason you're saying this is because you know that you're screwed," she said.

I shook my head. "You're wrong."

"I'm not wrong. You are screwed. And so is your friend," Corky said. "Screwed. You can count on it. In fact, you can endorse that threat and take it all the way to your hometown credit union and cash it."

"Okay," I said. "So you're not ready to be healthy?"

"I don't know what kind of self-help trash you've chosen to indoctrinate yourself with, but I don't plan on drinking the Kool-Aid."

"You're being very unreasonable."

"Veronica started this. And she knows what she needs to do to stop it," Corky said.

"She's not capable of that. She basically has no peace-making skills. That's why I'm offering the olive branch."

"Well, I'm declining it. So continue to fear for your life. This dynamic works fine for me. I'm used to it. I have a cold heart and quick hands." I watched her karate chop the air.

"It doesn't need to be this way," I said.

"Whatever. Have fun on your date with the Aussies."

"How did you know about that?"

"Thin walls."

Which, as far as I was concerned, was the most ominous thing your next-door sociopath could say.

Corky turned on the chunky heel of her clog and walked out of the suite.

I went back to my room and sat on my bed.

"Give up on the Corkster," Veronica said.

"I thought you were napping."

Veronica sat up. "It was a beauty slumber. Now I need to do seventy-five crunches before our date." She climbed onto the floor and commenced crunching.

"Have you forgiven me yet?" I asked.

"You look like hell," Veronica said. "Take a nap. We'll deal with our trust dilemma after you wake up."

She lifted herself off the floor and puffed out breaths in a staccato rhythm. I lay down. Closed my eyes. And around crunch fifty, fell asleep.

Chapter Twenty

$\mathcal{I}$ woke up to the sound of the swiveling fan, feeling disoriented and groggy. Like maybe I should keep napping for another thirty minutes. Then I turned onto my side and spotted Veronica sitting on the edge of her bed, watching me. Her face was blank. No. I focused my gaze. It was a glare. And it seemed powered by an angry bewilderment.

"Well, it's almost time for Scotty Dee," I said, stretching my arms above my head, trying to sound enthusiastic and chipper.

Veronica didn't say anything.

"What time is it? Did I oversleep?" I asked.

Again, silence.

"Did something happen with Corky?"

My questions only seemed to intensify her anger.

"You are a liar," she finally said.

I reacted to this by offering up my standard blinking.

"Haven't we been through this already?" I asked. "I thought we mostly made up."

It looked like Veronica wasn't going to let me off the hook for my bone deception as easily as I'd hoped. "You lie to me all the time, don't you?" she asked.

Her voice was spiteful. It made me sit up.

"No," I said.

She shook her head. "You know, after my dad left, you were like a pillar to me. I thought I could count on you. You were a solid beam I could lean on."

"I'm still solid."

She lifted her right hand and casually flipped me the bird. "No. You're not."

She stood up, and I noticed that she was wearing that ridiculously short skirt.

"Hey, I thought we both agreed that wardrobe selection sent the wrong message."

"Apparently, we can disregard anything we've told each other for the last month," she said.

"What are you talking about?"

"Don't play dumb."

"I'm not playing."

"While you were asleep, I read Waller's story," she said.

I couldn't believe it. How had she found it? I'd disposed of her copy, and mine was folded and tucked deep in my orientation folder. I decided to act both clueless and innocent.

"And how does that involve me?" I asked.

"I read about the foxes, Dessy. How could you do that?" she asked.

"I don't know what you're talking about," I said.

"Right. That's why you took the other copy of his story off my desk," she said.

"Maybe Corky took it."

"You are such a liar!"

Veronica turned her back to me and began fluffing her hair.

"You're not even going to give me the benefit of the doubt?" I asked.

Veronica slowly turned back around and glared at me. "Don't you have a conscience? Not even a small one?"

"Yes," I said.

"Then why don't you just admit that to score points with Waller, you gave him my fox idea."

I kept with my original clueless-and-innocent plan. "I have no idea what you're talking about."

Veronica pointed at me. "When you lie like this to my face, it makes me question every single thing you've ever told me."

"It shouldn't."

"Oh my god!"

"I'm telling you the truth," I lied.

She folded her arms across her chest and walked toward me. "So is Waller the big liar-face in this picture?"

"Veronica, you're going to have to explain what you're talking about. Did he write something in his story that upset you? I haven't even read his story."

"You haven't read his story? Wow. That's surprising," she said. "Why don't I give you a little taste?"

She walked back to her bed and picked up the story. Then she started reading.

"I saw the foxes before Margot did. Had I realized what they were up to, maybe I wouldn't have turned her attention to them. 'There!' I said, pointing away from our picnic lunch. The foxes were nearly hidden behind a bush. 'My god!' Margot screamed. 'They're screwing.' And they were. Busily. Happily. Urgently. Rhythmically. We watched the two foxes unite, fur-balling themselves into one.

"And then the story goes on to distastefully describe the encounter further," Veronica said. "I mean, he really uses a lot of unnecessary adverbs."

"Huh," I said.

"You told him about my foxes."

"I did not tell him about your foxes." I was happy that I had come across a way to phrase this truthfully. Because I hadn't supplied the word "fox" to Waller at all. I'd only suggested that something in his story other than the two main characters might be having sex.

Veronica didn't say anything. I felt panicked. But I didn't want to have to explain all this. I didn't feel good about the minor role I had played.

"You're such a snake," she said.

"Me?" I asked, pointing to myself.

"Do you want me to read what Waller wrote on the bottom of your copy?"

"No. Not right now."

Veronica cleared her throat. "'Dessy, without your guidance and fox idea, this story would have been a much lesser version of itself. Thanks for being there. You're the best. Waller.'"

"This isn't the way it looks!"

"Save it," Veronica said. "It's like you've suddenly become pathological. Or maybe you've always been pathological, but I'm just now catching on."

"No. I didn't know he was going to use foxes. He came up with the foxes."

"Then why does he thank you for the foxes? You can't even keep your own lies straight!"

"Veronica, you're not giving me a chance to explain. You're just blowing up at me."

"Have you forgotten about earlier?" Veronica asked. "About how you misled me all the way to Kutná Hora? I mean, I puked in that place. I got vomit on me. And then I find this, and you think I'm overreacting? It's like I don't even recognize you, Dessy Gherkin. It's like you're a walking lie-bomb!"

I watched Veronica put on a scandalously low-cut blouse.

"You can't wear that top with that skirt," I said.

"Why not?"

"Because it screams *prostitute*."

"Well, that's your opinion. And by the way, your

opinion doesn't count for crap anymore. And also, you're not coming with me."

I stared at her as she bent down and fluffed her hair. When I caught a glimpse of her panties, I gasped.

"This is dangerous!" I said. "You can't go on a date with Scotty Dee without me. You don't know him."

"Yeah, well, sometimes you can know somebody for a long time and it turns out that you don't know them all that well anyway."

She slammed the door, and I sat there. Stunned. Ashamed. I had to follow her. I couldn't let her risk her safety. My god! I threw on a pair of jeans and my shirt from yesterday. I might not have been able to stop Veronica from meeting the Australians alone, but I could definitely hover over their date and come to her rescue if she needed me.

By the time I got to the metro platform, Veronica was already gone, but I didn't panic, because I knew where they were meeting: the statue at Wenceslas Square. I sat on a bench and waited for the next train. Staring at the tile wall across the station, I slowed my breathing down.

This wasn't how I imagined my trip to Prague. I wanted to get a taste of Europe. Eat cheap fresh bread. See ancient churches and walk on cobblestones that were older than America. How my vacation had turned into a solo reconnaissance mission involving Veronica and two random Australians who may or may not have been in their thirties, I wasn't quite sure. I closed my eyes.

In many ways, though I probably never would admit this to her, Veronica *was* like a cheetah. Fierce. Curious. Strong. And probably capable of fetching.

Wind blew in from the metro tunnel, signaling that the next train was fast approaching. I stood up and walked toward the protective yellow line.

"You're not planning to jump, are you?" a voice asked.

I wanted to pretend that I hadn't heard the comment. But because it sounded like Corky, and because it struck me as incredibly menacing, and because I was positioned right next to the tracks, I backed away from the yellow line and turned around.

"It's not cool to joke about suicide," I said.

Corky smiled at me and moved closer, until her stomach pressed softly against me.

"Too bad about your big fight with Veronica," she said.

"I'm not afraid of you," I said.

"Is that why you're sweating?"

I reached up and swept my hand across my damp hairline.

"I always sweat," I said. "It's genetic. Everybody in my family perspires uncontrollably in humid climates."

The metro screeched to a halt beside us, and the doors opened.

"Yeah," Corky said. "Veronica mentioned your father. She said you two don't connect."

I stepped onto the train and slid into a vacant seat. I was disappointed to see Corky come stand right in front of me. She held the overhead bar in one hand and frowned down on me.

"Don't look so glum. Lots of people don't get along with their fathers," she said. "I barely even talk to mine."

"I know what you're doing," I said.

"Oh?"

"You're trying to trick me. You're lying. You heard Veronica and me talking through the walls. I know she didn't talk about my personal life with you."

The metro doors closed, and the train sped off in the direction of the city center.

"You and Veronica have a very dysfunctional relationship."

"Maybe. But you're completely insane and I don't value your opinion."

Corky shook her head. "I have something to tell you," she said.

"I don't want to hear it. And by the way, I plan on telling Brenda and Annie Earl all about this situation. You're a total emotional bully. And I don't have to live with that."

The man seated next to me closed his newspaper and stood up. Corky didn't waste any time folding herself into the open seat.

"Brenda doesn't live with us anymore," she said.

"When did this happen?" I asked.

"Very early this morning. I guess we neglected the kitchen and bathroom duties beyond her breaking point."

"Well, then I'll talk to Annie Earl about it."

"She moved out too," Corky said. "She's been wanting a fresh start in a new room with a private shower."

"I'm sure she's willing to keep an open mind and listen to how dangerous you are," I said.

Corky leaned forward in her seat and practically hissed at me. "If you try to explain this to anybody, you're the one who's going to look crazy. You don't have any proof about anything. It's my word against yours. Besides, I haven't done anything yet."

I certainly didn't like the emphasis she put on the word "yet."

"It's not your word against mine. Because I've got Veronica. It's two people against one. And we're in high school. We look innocent."

Corky laughed in my face. "First of all, you two certainly don't look innocent. Veronica dresses like a whore."

I pointed my finger at Corky and almost stabbed her with it. "You are so rude. She's a little uninhibited, that's all."

"Uh-huh. Well, in some circles those people are called streetwalkers. Moving on. My second point is that you don't have Veronica anymore. She doesn't trust you. I'm not even sure that she likes you."

"It's just a rough patch, Corky. God. You're really blowing this out of proportion."

The metro rolled into the next station, and I contemplated getting off even though it wasn't my stop.

"Can I ask you a question?" Corky asked.

"I'd prefer that you didn't."

"Why would Veronica call Hamilton? Not once. Not twice. But three times? Why would Veronica call *your* ex-boyfriend?"

Corky was manipulative in ways that went beyond unethical. I knew I shouldn't have been surprised. But I was.

"You're lying," I said.

"Well, if I'm lying, which I'm not, why do you think Hamilton calls her back?"

I stared at Corky's cold, pale face. It was evil. "You are such a witch," I said. "Hamilton hasn't called Veronica."

Corky smiled.

"I don't want you to follow me off the metro," I said. "I think you're disgusting."

"Yeah, I'm not too concerned about what you think."

As the metro approached my stop, I stood up and moved toward the door. Corky stayed seated. This relieved me, but I still felt sick. Why would Corky say something that was so outrageously untrue? And how did she know Hamilton's name? The train jerked to a halt, and I grabbed the pole near the door for balance. When the doors opened, I raced out onto the platform, feeling anxious and disoriented.

Still, I knew what I had to do. I was a good friend.

And so I continued to stalk Veronica. Also, I made an impulsive purchase at a newsstand. I spent the equivalent of two American dollars on an umbrella, figuring I could use it as a weapon. Because the way my luck was breaking, I'd probably need one before the day was through.

Chapter Twenty-one

Veronica never showed up at the statue. I watched Scotty Dee and Kirk pace at the top of the square for over ten minutes. They each checked their watches several times. Finally, they drifted off into a nearby bar.

I tried to think like Veronica. If I got pissed off at my best friend in Prague, where would I go?

Then it hit me. I was approaching this all wrong. I needed to think like a cheetah. If I were a cheetah, what would derail me from meeting Scotty Dee and Kirk, two top hot-dudes, at our prearranged meeting place and time? Of course! I'd only abandon them for a hotter hot-dude. Alexej! I hightailed it to the quarter of Prague that made Veronica crave hot-dudes more than any other area. I ran for blocks in the dark. When I finally reached the bank, it was sealed up and absent any armed hot-dudes. People strolled down the street: couples holding hands, tourists taking pictures, vendors selling soda and water. I was so lonely. And thirsty. I bought a can of Sprite and sat down on a bench to drink it.

But I didn't have the chance to do this, because at that moment I saw Veronica Knox leaning against a streetlamp, wearing bright red pants.

My attention soon turned from her mysterious new pants to the hot-dude, Alexej. A dude I knew virtually nothing about other than that he spent his days attached to a firearm. I jumped up and ran behind a tree. I held my breath. Veronica and Alexej were holding hands. And then he let go of her hand, and I saw him touch her butt. And then they started holding hands again. I was disgusted. I couldn't believe she'd allow a hot-dude she barely knew to grab at her in public. I had no choice but to follow my horny, impulsive, ridiculous friend through the streets of Prague.

They covered a lot of ground. Golden Lane. Strahov Monastery. The obelisk. Karlova Street. Not once did I see an expression flash across Veronica's face that I could have interpreted as concern for me. As far as she knew, I was back at the dorm crying myself into a puddle. And here she was, enjoying life, seemingly unharmed by the fox theft that had so easily torpedoed our friendship.

Block after block, I trudged behind her with my umbrella, ready to interject at the first sign of seedy behavior. I found myself hoping that things would turn disastrous just so that I could feel needed. But I wasn't needed. Not at the Church of Our Lady Before Týn. Or the Old Town Hall Tower. Or St. Nicholas Church. I decided to go home and let Veronica fend for herself.

I left her and her pseudo-Boz as they entered a café. This made me think that maybe I should find my own café and e-mail Hamilton. What was I running away from? If he wanted to talk to me, maybe it was time that I talked to him too. Because didn't I want that? Yeah. I did!

The café I found was hot and dimly lit. Computer screens provided most of the room's light.

"I need ten minutes," I said to the clerk. "Badly."

The clerk was a young Czech guy with a thin nose and a beautiful complexion.

"How much?" I pulled out all the crumpled money I had in my pockets and handed it to him. He took one bill and pushed the rest back toward me. I smiled at him for being honest and having a good heart. Because wasn't it about time that I connected with somebody who had one of those? "Rough day," I told him.

He nodded and turned back to his magazine.

Okay. Maybe it was too much to expect that an honest clerk at an Internet café would also be a good confidant. I took my password and sat down at a computer to shoot off a quick e-mail.

Hi, Hamilton. I'm still in Prague. I talked to my mom the other day, and she said you'd called. She said you were sending me something. That's cool. I like getting mail. Hey. I've been thinking about what you said to me during our breakup. I want you to know that I see your point. I'm a little flimsy. But I think you were a little hard on me. I think we should talk when I get back, because I feel like we both have things to say. For instance, you aren't perfect either. Your preoccupation with birds totally got in the way of our relationship. I mean, we never went bowling. Or skiing. Or dancing. And it was hard to walk around with you because every time we came across a bird, we had to get low to the ground and freeze and observe. I think it's fair to say that we both have flaws. I think that's the difference between you and me. I saw your flaws and looked past them. And you saw mine and laminated them. Anyway. I still think about you. A lot. Even here. I miss you. Dessy

For the subject I typed "Your Globetrotting Ex Is Thinking About You." And before I could question anything I'd written, or edit out any hint of desperation, I hit SEND. And then I immediately felt like puking. Why had I e-mailed that? Why not just tell him hello and send him a virtual postcard? Oh. My. God. All the compliments

Veronica had paid me for not groveling back to him. All the restraint I'd shown in not picking up the phone before I'd left and blathering on and on about my feelings. All the heartache I'd endured in my best attempt to heal myself. It had all been for nothing. I'd just blown everything. I'd sent Hamilton Stacks the lamest e-mail ever. The only way it could have been more lame is if it had been longer.

Then the worst thing in the world happened. Hamilton sent me a response. Right as I was sitting there in the café kicking myself, it popped up on my inbox. His subject line was "Dessy, You Need to Read This." I couldn't bring myself to open it. I felt all rubbery again. What had he written back to me? Whatever it was, I could tell that it was going to break my heart. Before I could stop myself, I clicked DELETE. Then I stared at the computer screen. And when my time ran out, I didn't stop staring.

Finally, somebody waiting for an open computer tapped me on the shoulder. I knew that it was time to go home. I stumbled out of the café into the night air, too distracted to look around me. Corky could have been standing right next to me with an ice pick and I wouldn't have noticed. I'd never know what Hamilton had written to me. My life felt so over.

I walked down the sidewalk, past couples nuzzling on benches. Everyone seemed to be in pairs. Even leashed dogs.

The station was jam-packed. I got sandwiched between two couples on the escalator. The pair behind me was necking, releasing graphic squishy noises, while the two in front of me, wearing matching bandanas, kept staring longingly into each other's eyes. They blinked at each other with nauseating tenderness.

Once I reached the platform, I ended up sitting next

to the larger, more reserved bandana couple. The public affection was inescapable. I could hear the train whistling down the tracks as it approached, but I didn't stand up. I let the crowd pool near the yellow line. That's when I saw a familiar head poking out above the rest.

I watched Roger step onto one of the center cars, and I stepped on just a few passengers behind him. But I never got any closer. I felt like my karma was off, so I just hung back and observed him. He grabbed a seat by the door, but when a pregnant woman boarded the train, he quickly stood up. He didn't sit down again. At the next stop, I watched him help an elderly man with his groceries. And when a child hit him in the chest with a misfired plastic projectile, Roger laughed and handed it back.

Were people normally this polite on subways? Was it like this in Chicago? I watched an attractive Czech woman chat with him. They conversed so effortlessly. At one point she brought her delicate hand to her perfect mouth and laughed. Then Roger laughed too. He held on to an overhead pole with one hand, revealing well-defined biceps. The Czech woman kept laughing and lifting her hand, and I wondered if she was trying to get Roger to look at her mouth. Did Roger know her? Why was he being so friendly? Then I remembered the pregnant woman, the elderly man, and the boy. Roger was pathologically nice.

When we got to our stop, I didn't wait for Roger to get off the train. For all I know he stayed behind with his new friend. I hurried to the street level and began walking home. Clouds passed in front of the moon, making the world around me feel darker than dark. My skin goose pimpled against the cool night air. I wished I'd brought a jacket. I had no idea Prague could feel this cold.

Chapter Twenty-two

Veronica was avoiding me. She'd come home after I'd gone to bed, and left in the morning without even waking me.

I sat up and looked at her shoes. She'd lined up six pairs of them. They all had a sizable heel and looked ridiculously uncomfortable. There was one pair, yellow pumps, that were so pointy I was surprised Veronica was able to fit her big toe inside, let alone the other four.

I walked over and picked them up. Then I grabbed another pair. Soon I was holding all of her shoes. Maybe if I hid them, I could convince Veronica that Corky had stolen them, and then Veronica and I could bond by trying to find them. It wasn't a terrible idea, was it? A black ankle boot slipped from the pile and landed on the floor.

"What are you doing with my shoes?" Veronica asked.

I looked up. She had an apple in her hand with a big bite taken out of it.

"I'm not doing anything," I said.

"It looks like you're about to steal them or something."

"I thought you'd left."

"I went to the cafeteria."

"Oh."

"Put my shoes back," she said.

I loosened my hold and let them fall on the floor.

"So in addition to being a liar, you're also a thief. Fantastic!"

"I didn't take anything. I was just looking at them."

"I don't want to talk to you," Veronica said. "And please don't touch my stuff."

I bent down and began arranging her shoes back into a tidy row.

"Stop touching my things," Veronica said.

"Okay," I said. I stared out the window while Veronica changed clothes.

"Is your story ready for workshop?" I asked.

Veronica pointed her hair pick at me. "I am not talking to you."

She spent a few more minutes primping, and then she was gone. I got ready at my own pace. I even read through my story one more time. I was happy with it. My characters felt like real people.

When I arrived at the university, I stopped by the computer lab and printed out ten copies. I slid them into my bag while they were still warm. Climbing the stairs to class, I realized how much I needed people to like it. What if they thought it was immature, or shallow, or dull? I'd be crushed.

When I walked in, Mrs. Knox and Corky were chatting over pastries wrapped in napkins.

"So true!" Mrs. Knox said. "Death scenes shouldn't be easy to write or read. It takes a lot to extinguish life on the page."

"Yeah. And there's no real comparison between a knife scene and a sword scene," Corky said. "Because knives say 'This is *real* reality,' and swords say 'This is *exaggerated* reality.'"

I didn't want to hear any more. Seriously. Wasn't

Mrs. Knox alarmed that a student would be so hung up on death and lethal weapons? Weren't these subjects universally acknowledged as red flags? How many *realistic* knife scenes would she have to read before she notified authorities?

Waller and Roger came in a few moments later. Roger looked different to me today. Deeper. Kite and Frank walked in behind him. Frank still looked very bald. And Waller, absent eyebrows, looked perpetually surprised. Roger sat next to me and patted my already cooled stories. I sat up straight. I wasn't expecting that.

"I'm excited to see how you deal with the Rapture," he said.

"What?" I asked. Why did Roger think I was writing a story about the end times? Did I look like the kind of person who was hung up on writing a story about the end times?

"In the car, Waller read the first sentence."

I nodded, wishing Roger hadn't brought that up. "Yeah, I don't really address the Rapture head-on."

"Not many writers do," he said.

I wanted to tell him that I'd seen him on the metro last night, that I'd watched him surrender his seat and help the old man and chat up the attractive brunette. I worried he'd think I had stalker issues.

"The Rapture was a device," I said. "A way to introduce early on in the story the theme of absolute endings." I looked him in the eyes. "Theme is hard for me."

"Theme is hard for everybody," he said. "Except people who write revenge porn." He shook his head. "It's an issue I have."

"Porn?" I asked, raising an eyebrow. Did Roger have a porn issue? And was he trying to talk to me in our workshop about it?

Roger briefly glanced at Corky, then lowered his

voice. "I think some violent urban fantasy is actually just revenge porn. It's full of gratuitous torture and has one message: 'How ya like me now?'"

He bumped me with his elbow. An effort to cheer me up? Was he saying he could see through Corky? Whatever it meant, I appreciated the gesture.

"Revenge porn is an apt assessment," I said.

Annie Earl and Brenda walked in, chatting up a storm. Probably about how much they loved their new rooms. Veronica came last and set her stories on the table, then plopped down in a seat on the other side of Roger.

Mrs. Knox pulled herself away from her conversation with Corky. "Soon, we'll be finished with our stories," she said. "At that time we'll be discussing all the exercises I've assigned. Next on the docket: image and dialogue. For the next week I want you to collect bits of conversation. Roommates. Salesclerks. Strangers on the metro. If somebody says something interesting or compelling, write it down. By next Monday you should have an entire page of found dialogue.

"And for our *next* next assignment, I want you to write a scene. You're at the grocery store. You're shopping. The first line should establish that it's a normal day." Mrs. Knox lowered her voice and leaned forward. "But I want your second sentence to introduce a complicating circumstance. A man runs down your aisle without pants. A bagger sees somebody with a gun. A rabid raccoon gets into the store. Something like that. Something big. Your job is to write that scene."

Corky looked thrilled. "How many pages?"

"At least four."

"Can we set the grocery store in a parallel universe?" Corky asked.

"Sure."

"If it works for the story, are we allowed to obliterate

the grocery store in our scene?" Corky asked.

"No limits on destruction," Mrs. Knox said. "It's your scene."

"This should yield interesting results," Annie Earl said.

"Can the grocery store be a liquor store?" Kite asked.

"No," Mrs. Knox said. "But you can set your scene in the liquor aisle of the grocery store."

"Awesome," Kite said.

"All right, Corky? Do you want to go first?" Mrs. Knox asked.

"No," she said. "I'd rather Waller did."

"Sounds good," Waller said. "I want to read from the middle.

"Margot stood on the edge of the lake, frowning. 'Stop looking at my butt,' she said. 'We're not dating anymore. It's off-limits.' But I couldn't stop. When she wore a swimsuit, looking at her butt was my favorite pastime. I made myself stare up into a pack of drifting clouds instead. It didn't seem fair. Not Margot hastily dumping me. Not Margot emphatically declaring her butt off-limits. Not Chad Wilky randomly popping into her life with an amazing breaststroke and stealing her away."

I stopped listening. The genuine affection he felt for his last girlfriend oozed out of what he read. On the page it hadn't seemed all that powerful, but *hearing* him read was a very different experience. Waller loved this girl. And it didn't sound like Allie/sister love. It sounded explosive. It sounded real.

I scanned the table, overtly staring at the faces of my classmates as he read. I caught Veronica's eyes and she looked away.

There was a brief moment of silence after Waller

stopped reading, then the class started making comments.

"I thought you did a great job of capturing a breaking heart," Annie Earl told him.

"I agree," Brenda chimed in. "Dixon and Margot felt real to me—young lovebirds confused by the ambiguities and contradictions of modern relationships. I admired the message—love hurts. I mean, you delivered it. But I wanted Margot to have more depth."

"I liked your fox scene," Corky said. "It was believable and well timed. I really enjoyed the contrast between the meaninglessness of the dialogue and the real animal desire that was simmering beneath it."

I could tell Waller wasn't sure whether to take this as a compliment. To me it seemed brilliantly backhanded: signature Corky.

"You've got an eye for image," Kite said. "The way you describe the natural world makes it come to life. I've never seen lady's thumb before, but now I feel like I have. What is it?"

"It's a common Michigan weed," Roger said.

Blah, blah, blah. Everybody loved Waller's love story. Lori was so lucky to have dated a guy who was creative and talented and emotionally deep enough to write so powerfully about their relationship. Then Veronica spoke.

"I like your story, Waller," she said. "But I think you turn Margot into way too big of a villain. I mean, she's young. She stops liking your main character dude. It happens. The part where your story says unflattering things about her feet. And that other part where you comment on her visible panty line. And that huge section where you criticize her kissing style. I'm sure you're not doing this on purpose, but it sort of feels like you're using your story as a chance to trash an ex-girlfriend. And those parts really turned me off."

No one responded at first. Roger was drumming his fingers on the table, clearly trying to decide whether or not to say what he was thinking. "I, um . . ." He coughed. "I liked the story," he began. "I thought it was well paced and the setting was right on. The fox scene was a great ending because of the way it foreshadowed the next confused hookup between the narrator and his ex." Waller listened warily. "But I was concerned that Dixon doesn't really seem able to reflect on what Lori was feeling—sorry. Margot. Sorry." Both boys' faces turned red.

"Anyway, *Dixon* seemed to have a blind spot about how much his refusals to go to her flute performances might have hurt her, and as a reader I felt like my perspective was being overdirected. The one weakness Dixon admits in the story is his weakness for Margot, and that seemed inconsistent with his abundant, sometimes really insightful criticism of her—so he came across as an unreliable narrator, but I wasn't sure that was intentional."

I was astonished that he could say this right to Waller's face. Telling your best friend that his narrator was unintentionally unreliable seemed like a huge slam.

"I wouldn't go as far as Veronica," he continued, "but it did seem like the story was shaped around an earnest appraisal of Margot's character. I thought it would have been a lot more powerful if it had been about how we selectively forget our own mistakes and how that gets in the way of honest communication."

Roger tried to look Waller in the eyes, as if to say, *I meant it for the best*, but Waller stoically stared past him.

"That's an interesting point," Mrs. Knox said. "Dixon portrays Margot as a classic cipher. Inscrutable, seductive. We don't get a glimpse of her thoughts and feelings, only her surface charms, which are left open for interpretation. In a way, you could view her flight to Chad Wilky's arms as a transfer of ownership." She chewed her pen for a second, thinking. "What's your take? Was the narrator unfairly controlling our access to her perspective? Ultimately, was Dixon's jealousy meant to be sympathetic, or were his flaws central to the story's message? Was he a cautionary example?"

"I'd be cautious before I dated that guy," Veronica said. "At times I think he seemed psychotic."

I wondered if Veronica really felt this way or if she was just getting back at Waller for balding Frank.

"Interesting word choice," Annie Earl said. "Once you say psychotic, I can see psychotic."

"Yeah," I jumped in. "When your heart gets broken, you can definitely feel psychotic. Because there's your heart in pieces. It feels useless. But I wasn't really sure Dixon's heart was as broken as he kept saying. Because losing Margot didn't make him feel wrecked or question what he could have done differently; it just made him self-righteous. The story seemed to take it for granted that we'd trust Dixon, and I don't think that was quite fair." I couldn't believe I'd just said that!

"I'll say it again. I think the narrator is a normal guy," Kite said. "I don't think he's psychotic. His girlfriend just dumped him."

"I think we've brought these characterization issues to Waller's attention," Mrs. Knox said. "Let's move on to something else."

I felt pretty terrible when Corky brought up how much she liked the fox scene again.

"Its originality really stood out," she said. "Two clever foxes copulating in the woods. Pretty brilliant."

Veronica didn't visibly react to Corky's comments in any way. I thought that showed real growth, though probably not forgiveness. Frank and Kite also chimed in on the fox scene. They liked it. But it didn't surprise me that guys would like an animal-mating scene.

"I thought the foxes were a little bit too anthropomorphized," Annie Earl said. "I would have liked it more if they'd remained more foxlike."

Veronica smiled. "Totally."

"They were awfully fluffy," Brenda said.

"They were like cartoons," Veronica said. "They should have been way more animalistic."

"Really?" Waller asked.

He wasn't supposed to speak, but I guess he couldn't hold back anymore.

"I had the same problem with my lobsters," Brenda said. "And then I asked myself, 'Can you write it like you are the lobster?' And I did." She wasn't joking when she said this. She was really putting her psychology major to full use.

Veronica seconded Brenda's response.

And Corky closed out the comments. "I think this fox sex scene is pretty groundbreaking. I'll compare every fox scene I ever read to this one."

"Thanks," Waller said.

I thought Veronica might barf.

After we were finished, Waller was given a chance to speak.

"I guess I don't mind if my narrator is unreliable. I think it adds a layer of interest. I mean, who among us is completely trustworthy? Who here isn't a little flawed?"

I was so sick of hearing Waller talk about other people's flaws. I started getting frustrated with his rebuttal and decided to write down some found dialogue:

"Foxes *are* very fluffy."

"Dixon is NOT a stalker."

"Corky's comments really nailed it."

"I think this piece might be part of something longer."

Mrs. Knox turned Waller's story over to signal that

we'd finished critiquing it. "Okay. Let's push forward with Corky's story. Corky, where would you like to read from?"

Corky pulled her story from her bag and carefully flipped to the last page. "First paragraph. Page six," she said.

"Ooh," Kite said. "The gruesome part."

"You got it," Corky said.

Papers rustled until we all found the place.

"Lilith had never killed a man before. She returned the knife to its sheath and licked her lips.

'I'll hack him apart before midnight.'

Cecil shook her sad head. 'I won't wait up.'

Lilith found Decker sleeping. She lifted the dagger over her head, and then she held her breath. Now he would never wake up. She wanted to pierce his heart first. But she worried about hitting bone. It seemed unfair to cage the heart."

I stopped listening. I mean, I literally stuck my fingers in my ears. When Corky finished reading, I didn't look up. Not even at Veronica.

"Well, I really liked this piece," Annie Earl said. "At first I thought spending an entire paragraph on the dismemberment of a living being was pushing it. But he certainly had it coming. Jerk."

"I have no idea who'd publish this," Brenda said. "But I have to admit, it has something. I usually don't get into fantasy, especially violent fantasy, but I thought the fairies were kind of . . . cool."

"I don't know," Veronica said. "I wished the Lilith character would have shown some restraint. I mean, after he was dead, was it really necessary to mutilate his thighs?"

"I didn't mind it," Waller said. "I thought the whole story was a metaphor."

"You did?" Roger asked, surprised. "For what?"

"I think it could be a metaphor for almost anything," Waller said. "I think that's how this kind of fantasy works."

"Anything?" Annie Earl asked. "That's impossible."

"Okay," Waller said. "The metaphor might be flight attendants. This whole story might be about flight attendant revenge."

Corky looked up and scowled at him.

"The women have wings because they're flight attendants. And the men don't because they're passengers. And when the men violate the rules, they get torn apart and dismembered, which is what would happen if the plane crashed," Waller said. "Fantasy *is* metaphor."

We all stared at Waller. Without eyebrows, hypothesizing about metaphors, he looked a lot less intelligent than he had the first two weeks of class.

"That's not how fantasy works," Annie Earl said. "You just perpetrated a hijacking, because what you just said isn't even in the story."

"If Waller thought the fairies were flight attendants, who's to say he's wrong? It's his brain," Kite said.

"But he didn't really think the fairies were flight attendants. He was using it as an example to say that in fantasy a range of readers can see themselves in the protagonists and feel vindicated. Flight attendants were arbitrary," Brenda said.

"Right," Waller said. "Fantasy is about bringing your own sense of reality to the page."

Even Veronica mulled on it. "So who are the pilots?" she asked.

"I guess there aren't any pilots," Waller admitted.

"Okay," Mrs. Knox said. "Let's address the story we have and not the story we've imagined it to be. The fairies may or may not be metaphors. I think Corky does a nice job creating three-dimensional characters. Without believable, complex characters, the reader will turn the pages out of simple curiosity. And unless you've written a potboiler, that's a sad occurrence. But because this world and its rules are so well realized, we can even sympathize with Lilith as she exacts brutal revenge. I think that's quite an achievement. I think this is a successful piece."

There I disconnected from the discussion. I didn't think Corky's story was successful. Solving a problem with a butcher knife was the wrong way to accomplish closure. In life *and* fiction. I looked at the story until the black type began to float off the page. Voices chatted away about various scenes. It was just noise to me. And then Corky was given a chance to speak.

She cleared her throat. "Thanks for all of your wonderful comments. I wanted to write a story about consequences," she said. "So many people think that you can go through life and do whatever you want. But I wanted my death scene to demonstrate how that isn't necessarily true. I hope the other message isn't too strong."

"What message is that?" Mrs. Knox asked.

"Savage revenge can satisfy a wrongdoing," Corky said. "It can make the person who was wronged feel whole."

"Wow," Roger said. "I'll never cross Corky."

"I think that promoting a message is always a risk," Mrs. Knox said. "But I think you strike a good balance. It's a very promising piece. I understood what motivated Lilith. And the violence she committed, while grotesque, seemed logical."

"Thank you," Corky said.

"Wait," I said. I couldn't let Corky get off this easy. "Am I the only one who found the blade violence extreme?"

Silence.

"Nobody else thought, Wow, a character just got sliced apart, and, uh-oh, it took a whole page, and, jeez, it was incredibly accurate in its anatomical references to muscles and tendons, and, hmm, I feel uncomfortable now? Nobody else thought that?"

Everybody stared at me.

Roger lifted his cap to scratch his forehead. "At a certain point I have to admit that I did exit the story, and I wondered if Corky had ever worked in a meat processing plant, or as a butcher in a grocery store, or as an assassin, because I agree that she was very anatomically specific when it came to the cutting scene," he said.

Veronica nodded enthusiastically, especially when Roger used the word "assassin." "It's a story of obsessions. Daggers and death among them."

Corky's face turned a pink and unhappy color. And then nobody offered further comment. And I didn't put forward any more elaboration. If our group wanted to let a sociopath explore her mind, and celebrate the creative fruits of that labor, there wasn't a whole lot I could do.

I handed my story around. Then I looked up and saw Corky staring at me as if she wanted to stab me right there in front of everybody. "I hate you," she mouthed.

The way her mouth formed the words looked dangerous and sincere. I glanced around to see if Veronica had noticed, but she was already gone. Which was the way it was going to be. I now had full control of my trim tab. I gathered my things, stood up, and steered myself out the door.

Chapter Twenty-three

$\mathcal{I}$t was Tuesday, and things felt grim. I was standing inside the Museum of Communism staring at a brown, hooded suit that was made to be worn during a chemical attack. It hung in a corner next to a series of photos of actual soldiers running away from a cloud of dust. The museum resembled an apartment, and after two rooms I had to leave. Past the bust of Lenin. Past the statue of Stalin. Past the big red Soviet flag.

I walked down the stairs to the McDonald's located on the ground level. I considered sending an e-mail to Hamilton about this ironic juxtaposition, but I didn't. I wasn't a total idiot.

I was torn inside. Part of me wanted to go out and look at every single remaining attraction in my tour book. But another part of me wanted to go home and take a nap. It wasn't long before I found myself eating a doughnut on the metro back to the dorm.

The suite was empty when I got home. I sat on my bed and was reading a brochure for a walking tour in New Town when Veronica swung open the door, carrying three bags and a big tube container.

"Did you buy a poster?" I asked.

Veronica didn't answer.

"I know we're fighting. But I could sort of use a

friend during this difficult time," I said.

Still nothing.

"It's pretty obvious that Waller doesn't like me. It's just like you said. His interest shifted. And I haven't done anything course-changing. I think there might be another woman in the picture."

The painful silence stretched on for seconds.

"I saw him getting cozy at a bar with Brenda," Veronica said.

"What?" I said. Earnest, innocent, lobster-loving, has-a-boyfriend Brenda?

"She dumped her boyfriend last week. That's why she moved into her own room," Veronica said. "Privacy."

"Oh my god!" I grabbed my pillow and held it in disbelief. "I am miserable."

After a pause, she sighed. "Don't be. Waller is an idiot."

That felt good, but I wanted a little bit more. "An idiot how?"

"He completely flirted with you because he liked the attention, but it sounds like he had little if any sincere interest."

Little if any sincere interest. How was that possible?

"But you said that he liked me at a level eight, possibly nine!"

Veronica, now dressed, turned around to face me. "Well, I was wrong." She swept a brush through her hair, tugging out the tangles. She kept her demeanor cool. And it drove me crazy, because I needed her. I needed my best friend.

"Why would he tease me like that?" I asked.

"I don't really feel like talking about this."

I let my pillow fall to the floor. And before I knew it, I was fully sprawled out on my bed, crying. I turned toward the wall and breathed erratically, trying to push all the emotions back down. But they refused to stay submerged.

"Don't," Veronica said.

"This isn't voluntary," I said between sobs. "My heart is breaking all over again. And it's not like I stand a great chance at ever falling in real love, because, like you pointed out, my dad and I don't connect, so I'm always going to be looking for his love and acceptance in other men. I'm screwed. Yeah, it's Waller today, but it will be some other idiot tomorrow. And some other bigger idiot after that."

Veronica came and sat next to me. "I'm going to talk to you for a little bit like we're still friends, but after this session I'm going to return to my pissed state and continue to work through my anger toward you. Got it?"

"Uh-huh."

"Just being aware of the fact that you are prone to dating guys who are totally wrong for you because you don't connect with your father is totally huge in terms of being self-aware. It's not like you're blindly hooking up with jerk-guys unbeknownst to you. I mean, it's totally beknownst to you."

"Right," I said.

"And I don't think that Waller broke your heart. I think he just reminded you that your heart is still cracked from what happened with Hamilton."

I rolled over onto my other side and faced Veronica. I thought of the e-mail he'd sent me that I hadn't read. My entire life seemed at stake in that little piece of electronic mail. How could I have deleted it? How could I have been so sure that it said something that I didn't want to hear?

"Sometimes I think we might get back together," I said.

"You and Hamilton?" Veronica asked.

I nodded. Veronica looked horrified.

"I never told you this, but the reason Hamilton dumped me, I mean, what he said at the time was that I had these three big flaws that he couldn't look past. He laminated them on this card and said that I needed to change. And do you know what I think international travel has done for me? I think it's helped me change. So when I get back to Ohio, I'm pretty sure there's a good chance that we might patch things up. And, well, I wasn't going to tell you this either, because I thought you'd think I was spineless, but I e-mailed Hamilton yesterday, and he e-mailed me back, but I didn't read it because I'm sort of a coward."

Veronica pressed her lips together and looked down at me. Her eyes were filled with pity. "I don't think you should have any contact with Hamilton Stacks," she said.

"Why not?"

"No guy should laminate your flaws like that. Seriously. What an asshole. How come you never told me he did that?"

"I didn't want to ruin your opinion of him. Because maybe I wasn't ready for things to be over with him," I said.

"Are you serious?"

"I knew you'd think it was lame."

"It's beyond lame, Dessy. That's cruel. That's like saying that you were the reason you two broke up. And that wasn't the case."

"What do you mean? Of course that's the case," I said. "He couldn't take my flaws anymore."

"*Everybody* has flaws. Look at me. I'm built out of them. But what he's done isn't fair. You deserve better."

I closed my eyes and whimpered. "I thought the pain would go away."

"It will," she said. "I think part of the problem is that

you have a fairly tender heart anyway. So it gets damaged easier."

This was an awful realization to share with me.

"I don't want a tender heart," I said. "I wish I had a wood heart. Or a cobblestone heart. Or a granite heart."

Veronica shook her head. "You don't mean that. I've always thought of you as having a fluffy bunny heart. When you feel things, Dessy, you feel things deeply. And that's a gift."

"A fluffy bunny heart? It's a curse!" I said.

"I'm not going to argue with you about this. You need to start pulling yourself together."

I knew she was right, but it didn't feel possible. I couldn't figure out how to turn off my pain or disappointment. I knew I would probably meet another guy, and that I would always have flaws, and he would see them, and the idea that I would be enduring these feelings over and over for years to come made my mind spin.

"Remember," Veronica said, "it's better to have loved and died than never to have loved at all."

"Loved and *died*?" I said. "It's loved and *lost*. Because if you're dead, you can't love anymore."

"I don't know if that's true," Veronica said. "I totally believe in paranormal activity." She gently brushed my hair off my face and smoothed it behind my ear.

"Do you know what hurts most?" I asked.

Veronica's perfect face turned away from me. "I don't think it's healthy to indulge you like this. Five more minutes and then I'm going to resume the silent treatment. Okay?"

I nodded.

"It's not just that my heart feels broken. It's that my overall self feels ruined, because what are the chances that I'm ever going to meet anybody who likes me for me? I was a fool to think Waller Dudek liked me."

Veronica stood up and walked over to her mirror. Even though I still had over four minutes left before she resumed the silent treatment, she was through doling out comfort.

"He did like you," Veronica said. "He's just messed up. I think this is an important lesson for you. Just because a relationship doesn't work doesn't mean you did something wrong. It's not always about you. Sometimes it's about them. If somebody is broken, that person isn't capable of adequately accepting or returning love."

"Is that from your book?" I asked.

"No," she said. "A daytime talk show."

Veronica pulled a key out of her pocket and unlocked her desk drawer. Then she took out her wallet and travel pass.

"No offense," she said. "These days, I just feel better about keeping my valuables secure."

"No offense taken," I said, even though I was offended.

"This is why I'm looking for mature men. Because they're capable of connecting. Because when you truly connect with somebody, it's totally obvious."

I watched Veronica flip her hair back and forth. She'd fallen hard for pseudo-Boz, and for some reason she wasn't telling me about it.

"I was starting to feel better, but now I feel worse," I said.

"That's too bad," she said. "I feel spectacular."

"But I feel like you're on the verge of doing something really stupid."

"I am done talking to you."

"Okay. So when will we resume being friends?"

Veronica continued to primp. Blush on cheeks. Shadow on eyes. Gloss on lips. "Listen, I need some time to feel better about everything," she said. "I'm not trying to be a bitch, but I need to heal at my own pace. You betrayed me."

A few more tears slipped down my face. I didn't say anything else, but I was hoping that she'd come to her senses in the next few hours. And then we could make up in the next few days, while we still had time to experience Prague. Because I really didn't want to return to Ohio and spend my senior year attempting to conform to a new social group. Losing Hamilton was bad enough. But Veronica had been in my life for ages. I loved her. And I wasn't ready to have things end.

She turned to look at me before she left. She seemed like she had something to tell me. Instead, she closed the door.

Veronica was gone two minutes when I heard frantic pounding on the door. I rushed to answer it. Then, standing in my doorway, I saw the smirking face of Corky.

"All you two do is deceive each other," she said. "It's insane."

"Stand back so I can shut the door in your face," I said.

Corky pushed herself inside my room. "Things are getting pretty serious between your barfy friend and Hamilton."

"Just drop it, Corky. I don't believe you."

"Listen, I bet if you managed to be home tomorrow morning at ten thirty, you'd be surprised at who calls the phone in your room."

"I can't be in my room tomorrow at ten thirty. We've got workshop."

"Well then, I guess you'll never know why Hamilton called."

I looked over Corky's shoulder. Through the kitchen window, I saw Waller and Brenda walking past our suite. Their arms were slung around each other's waists. They looked stupid and happy. I refocused on Corky.

"Why would Hamilton call an empty room? Veronica will be in workshop too."

"Or maybe she'll leave early," Corky said. With that, she laughed in my face and left. She was lying, but it still bothered me. Veronica would never do that to me. I knew that. And neither would Hamilton. I shut the bedroom door. Corky was brilliant in a terrible way. Because even though I knew she was lying, I still wanted Veronica to prove to me that I hadn't been betrayed.

Chapter Twenty-four

𝒹 walked to workshop the next morning by myself and entered an empty room. I sat as close as I could to Mrs. Knox's chair because positioning myself next to an authority figure made me feel safe. This feeling was compromised, however, when Corky walked in and sat on the other side of me.

"Veronica wanted to sit there," I said.

"You are a dreadful liar."

It didn't take long for our entire dysfunctional family to arrive. Annie Earl came first, carrying a new marionette. It looked like a flying dragon that was possessed. And when Brenda walked in I almost had to shut my eyes. She arrived with Waller, and she was wearing a cute yellow sundress. Her shoulders, like his face, were pink from the sun.

Then came the rest of the guys. I waved at each of them. I'm not sure if this was done out of an impulse toward friendship-building or loneliness. Either way, they waved back at me, and this made me feel like part of a community again.

"This whole workshop experience is really starting to drag," Corky muttered.

Mrs. Knox walked in wearing slim jeans and a black T-shirt. Veronica came in after her, wearing all white.

Their contrasting wardrobes seemed symbolic. As soon as Veronica saw that I was seated next to Corky, she happily chose a chair on the other side of the table next to Kite.

I put my head down and closed my eyes.

"I wonder if she'll stay for the whole class," Corky said under her breath.

I scooted away from her. My chair legs rubbed against the floor and released a grotesque farting sound that made everybody turn to look. "It was my chair," I said.

"How are your grocery store scenes going?" Mrs. Knox asked.

"I'm writing mine as a poem," Frank said. "A dramatic monologue."

Mrs. Knox looked right at bald Frank. She opened her mouth, I assumed to object, but instead she asked, "Is it set in a grocery store?"

"A superstore," Frank said. "There's a place to buy tires in it."

"Only Frank is allowed to write it as a poem," Mrs. Knox said. "How is the second assignment going? Are you finding dialogue?"

"I feel like I'm invading people's privacy," Brenda said. "I've overheard some very personal things."

Mrs. Knox nodded. "You're not eavesdroppers. You're anthropologists. Think of these snippets of collected conversations as verbal artifacts. Without you, they will fade into oblivion."

"That's sort of where a lot of what I've found belongs," Brenda said.

Waller laughed.

"She is so sanctimonious," Corky muttered.

I watched Corky pull my story out of her bag. There were comments scrawled all over it. She cleared her throat. "'How *Not* to Get to Guatemala.' So your story's about Guatemala?" she asked loudly.

I nodded.

"Have you ever been to Guatemala?" she asked.

"Not yet," I said.

Everybody was looking at me. I felt myself trying to shrink away.

"Wow, I'd think it would be really difficult to write about a real place that I'd never even visited. You know what all the writing experts say: 'Write what you know,'" Corky said.

I stared down at a copy of my story. The workshop process hadn't even started yet, and I felt like a loser. Had I exceeded my reach by setting my first real attempt at writing in a Central American country that I'd only read about a couple of times in *National Geographic*?

"Actually, I don't think *all* the writing experts say that," Roger said.

"Think of Kafka and *The Metamorphosis*," said Mrs. Knox. "Imagination can be your engine." She smiled at me, and I felt comforted. "So, who would like to go first?" she asked.

"I'll go," Veronica said. She turned several pages and tore off a corner. Then she took a piece of spit-laden chewing gum and folded it into the small paper triangle. She swallowed hard and read.

"The red fox steps through the field behind the church. This is not a religious story. For no reason at all, the church just happens to be a church. Quick. Quick. The fox is hungry. It hasn't eaten in days. It hurries over the snow toward turkey feathers. Toward what it believes to be certain food. The fox doesn't know the lengths a trapper will go. The fox has never heard the sound of the terrible snap. Until now. Poor fox. Clack goes the trap! Poor, poor fox. And

no matter how clever, there's no way a fox can unclack a trap."

After Veronica finished reading, she stared at her story and scribbled things in the margin.

"Let's start," Mrs. Knox said.

"It's very lyrical," Annie Earl said. "The sounds feel foxlike, and I like that."

"I liked the perspective," Roger said. "The narrator puts you right inside that fox's head."

I thought Veronica's story was amazing. I could tell that she really cared about her foxes. They were doomed, and she was so tuned in to their misery.

"The language is very strong," Mrs. Knox said. "The narration balances very careful wording with a generous sense of play." She studied her daughter for a moment, then cleared her throat. "Some of you might think that Veronica and Dessy are attending this class out of some special privilege because I'm the instructor. Not true. They applied and were accepted without any assistance from me. I wasn't even aware that they'd sent in an application. I want Veronica to know that I find this story very promising. And I feel happy for that. Your foxes, those poor unlucky animals, are wonderfully drawn. For me they were fully alive on the page. And I think you might explore more of an adventure for them. Maybe think of some scenes that lead up to the trap. And then think of some scenes after the freed fox inevitably leaves the doomed one."

Veronica looked up at her mother and smiled. "Thanks. I'll think about that."

"I've never seen a fox," Kite said. "But this story made me feel like I understood how they think and what they want. You could write a collection just about animals."

The class went on like that for a while. It was true, there was something different about Veronica's story.

I hoped people had similar kind things to say about mine.

"I liked the sex scene," Corky said. "Though it felt a little manic to me. Even wild animals have subtle rules of selection and foreplay, but your foxes were undiscriminating. The trapped fox's pain even gets lost in the frenzy."

"Whatever," Veronica said. "You would be the one person requesting more pain. Freak."

"No talking," Mrs. Knox said. The class stared at Veronica and Corky in puzzlement.

"I'm not a freak," Corky said calmly. "I'm giving you constructive feedback."

"Superfreak," Veronica said. "And I don't need your superfreak vision to provide any suggestions."

"No talking!" Mrs. Knox repeated.

Roger shot me a questioning look.

"Don't ask," I mouthed.

"There was just something so measured in Waller's fox scene," Corky went on. "Your foxes feel hurried."

"Don't address Veronica directly, Corky," Mrs. Knox warned.

"You don't even know what you're talking about," Veronica said. "Also, in case you missed it, they're existentialist metaphors."

"Please, no talking!" Mrs. Knox repeated.

"I understand that they're metaphors," Corky said. "Nonetheless, the sex lacked subtlety. The foxes were just . . . too *easy*."

Veronica jumped up. "There is nothing easy about them."

Corky shrugged. "If you say so."

"Enough," Mrs. Knox said. "Veronica, sit down. And let's hear what the others have to say."

Veronica sat, but she was breathing heavily.

"You have a good sense of rhythm," Brenda said. "But I thought there could have been a little more variation in sentence structure, especially after the appearance of the second fox."

"I agree," Corky said. "Especially leading up to the climax."

Veronica jumped up again. "Stop it!"

"That's enough," Mrs. Knox said. "Sit."

Veronica sat. I prayed my evaluation wouldn't go this poorly. Corky had impressively kept her composure and made Veronica look insane.

"Let's take a break," Mrs. Knox said.

"Tabitha is in mother bear mode," Corky whispered to me. "The story wasn't that good."

"I have to go to the bathroom." I got up and walked out, but didn't go to the bathroom. I hid in the adjacent doorway until I saw Corky turn a corner at the other end of the hall.

"That was fast," Roger said when I returned to my seat.

"I just wanted Corky to leave me alone," I said. "Talking to her feels like my brain is being massaged with a cheese grater."

"She's pretty sharp-edged," he said, chuckling.

It was good to hear. "I wish Mrs. Knox could see that," I said.

"Maybe she does," he said.

I rolled my eyes. Apparently he was naïve when it came to manipulative and insane people.

"You seem pretty laid back about your story," he said. "In the car you were a little freaked out."

"Oh, I'm freaking out," I said. "I'm just holding it inside."

"You shouldn't freak out. It's a good story."

"Thanks." It felt awkward to have Roger complimenting me. My first impulse was to downplay his praise by mildly trashing my story. But I resisted the impulse and just kept forcing a grin. Until Corky returned and wiped it right off my face.

"Okay. Time for Dessy's story," Mrs. Knox said, silencing the chatter and drawing everyone's attention to me. She gave me a reassuring smile. "You can read from anywhere in the story you'd like."

I looked around the room. "But Veronica isn't back yet," I said.

"Oh. She wasn't feeling well," Mrs. Knox said. "She went back to the dorm."

Corky snickered. I couldn't believe this! It was almost ten o'clock. Five minutes ago it seemed impossible that Veronica would leave and go take a phone call from Hamilton. But now it seemed incredibly possible. Maybe even probable.

"Dessy?" Mrs. Knox asked. "Are you ready?" I swallowed hard and tried to put the Veronica/Hamilton issue out of my mind. I knew what I wanted to read. The Mexican border scene felt like a key moment in the story.

"Tag woke up when I turned off the car.
'Are we there?' he asked.
'We're outside of Laredo,' I said.
He was sprawled out in the backseat, his head resting against the passenger side armrest.
'I want to check the tire pressure before we cross into Mexico,' I said.
'The border? We're really doing this?'
Mexico was the first of many countries I needed to drive through. Tag's hesitation made me worry about the fate of the trip.
'It's like my girlfriend has gone insane,' he said. 'I don't think I can do this.'

I turned around to face him. 'You said you'd come with me. You promised.'

'But I was drunk.'

I hated this excuse. 'You can't use your tequila consumption to worm your way out of everything,' I said.

'When you get hostile it makes me doubt *everything,' he said. 'Even us.'*

'When you wimp out of your promises, I feel the same way.'"

When I stopped reading, there was a long moment of silence. My stomach kept getting tighter and tighter.

"I really liked Dessy's story a lot!" Annie Earl said.

But I wasn't sure I wanted to hear any more.

"Stop! Stop," I said.

"You have to wait to talk until after the critique," Mrs. Knox said.

"But I'm not ready," I said. "I feel physically unable to hear what people have to say. As well as emotionally and spiritually."

Roger turned and looked at me. "But your story is good."

I held up my hands. "Right now, at this exact moment, I am very unsure of my story's ending, and I don't think I'm ready to revise."

"That's lame," Corky said. "I've got a ton of suggestions for you."

"I don't know what else to say. I feel too fragile." I was amazed to hear myself utter these words. But at the same time, I was relieved. Because not only was I unprepared for feedback, I also had to get back to the dorm.

"You should at least read our comments," Roger said.

"This is disappointing," Mrs. Knox said. "Dessy, are you sure this is what you want?"

"Totally," I said.

Everybody passed their copies of my story to me.

I looked at the clock. It was now ten. If I didn't get back soon, I'd never know for sure.

I stood up. Corky was smiling.

"I'd like to talk about your story sometime," Mrs. Knox said. "Why don't you stay after class?"

"Thank you, but I'm so sorry, I have to go right now," I said as I raced out the door.

This couldn't really be happening. Veronica wouldn't slink out of class to go back to the dorm and talk to Hamilton behind my back. Would she?

Halfway down the metro escalator, I spotted Veronica on the platform holding a shopping bag. The train was just arriving. I ran to the bottom and boarded just in time, a few cars down from her.

When the train pulled to our stop, I carefully concealed myself behind a tall man and then behind a pillar until Veronica had passed. I followed her across the platform toward the escalators, then tailed her all the way to the dorms. Nothing about what she was doing appeared weasel-like. She walked into the building, and I waited outside to give her time to get to our room. Why didn't I want her to see me? Why not just yell out, "Hey, Veronica, what are you doing?"

I already knew the answer. If Veronica accepted a phone call from Hamilton, I needed to catch her red-handed. Otherwise, I'd never believe it.

I quickly walked down the hallway, but paused outside the door to listen. Nothing. I glanced through the kitchen window to make sure the coast was clear, then slipped through the main entrance.

Our bedroom door was closed. It looked suspicious to hang out in the kitchen, so I sneaked into Annie Earl and Brenda's recently vacated room to eavesdrop through the paper-thin walls.

From Brenda's stripped bed, I could hear Veronica fishing through her desk drawer. I thought I heard a pen scratching. With a growing sense of relief, I watched the wall clock's minute hand creep past 10:35. Corky was a liar. Hamilton wasn't calling. Because one thing I knew for certain about Hamilton Stacks was that he was an on-time guy.

All this crafty behavior had left me famished. Maybe I could talk Veronica into grabbing an early lunch. She hadn't seemed too pissed off at me in workshop. She'd probably say yes.

I left Brenda's room and opened the door to mine.

"I left workshop early. I'm not built for criticism. Do you want to grab lunch?" I asked.

Veronica looked alarmed.

"What's wrong?" I asked.

That's when our phone started to ring.

"Aren't you going to answer it?" I asked.

"No," she said.

"Why not?" I couldn't believe that Corky was right after all.

"Because it's Boz," Veronica said. "And I'm getting ready to go on a date, and talking to him before I go on a date would be a real mood-killer."

I looked at the ringing phone and back at Veronica. Her answer was so callous that I believed it.

"Doesn't it bother you that you behave like such a terrible person?" I asked.

The phone stopped ringing.

"I am not a terrible person," Veronica said. "Take it back!"

"Don't go on the date and maybe I will."

"Are you threatening me?" Veronica asked. "Have you stooped to Corky's level?"

"I can't stand by and watch you treat Boz like this anymore."

"What's your point?"

"My point is that one of us needs to move out."

"If you want to move out, be my guest. But it will be permanent. Don't think you can move back in once you start to miss me."

"Miss you? That will never happen."

"You've gone certifiably mad!" Veronica stomped out and slammed the door behind her.

I spent the next half hour hauling everything I'd brought to Prague into my new bedroom. On my third trip I bumped into Corky.

"So you caught Veronica talking to Hamilton?" she asked.

"You're so stupid," I said. "It was Boz."

Corky raised her eyebrows in amusement. "If you actually believe that, I'm not the stupid one."

I backed into my room and locked the door. When I heard Corky start the shower a moment later, I figured I ought to use the opportunity to get some fresh air. So I grabbed my bag and scampered out of the suite.

I only made it three strides before I nearly ran smack into Roger.

"I was coming by to see if you were all right," he said. "That was a pretty erratic move back there in workshop."

I had no desire to talk about workshop. "I'm fine, thanks."

"You should have stayed. It would have been a good discussion."

"No, it wouldn't have," I said. "For several reasons. Hey, I don't mean to be rude, but I'm trying to get as far away from this dorm as possible. Want to walk?"

He raised a skeptical eyebrow, but then said, "Sure." We set off toward the dorm lobby.

"So what's going on?" he asked. I glanced up at his

face. He seemed more concerned than judgmental, but still, I was wary of telling him anything. Did a college guy want to hear about roommate drama and issues related to high school infidelity? Would he care? Or even believe me?

"Given the events of the past week, would you say that my credibility has been at all compromised?" I asked.

He followed me out to the sidewalk and silently kept pace beside me. Every second he didn't answer my question felt like a blow. *Thwack. Thwack. Thwack.*

"Well," he said finally, "I'm curious about the thing with Waller's foxes. And what happened at Kutná Hora was a little weird."

I felt myself shrivel.

"But for the most part, you seem like a fairly even-keeled person to me," he added.

Even-keeled. If only he knew about my damaged trim tab. Suddenly I felt claustrophobic. And misunderstood.

"Waller is a jerk," I blurted. "And I didn't give him Veronica's fox idea. I think they just watched the same stupid nature show. And I feel bad about what happened at Kutná Hora, but that pales in comparison to what Veronica did, which was to sic a homicidal maniac on us."

"You mean Corky?"

I didn't say anything. We'd reached the metro tunnel, and I wanted to enter it and go somewhere. Alone.

"I feel really bad about what happened with you and Waller," he said, stepping out of the flow of metro traffic and pausing beside a small tree. I reluctantly joined him.

"He has a screwed-up need for attention. Combine that with the fact that he has no idea what he wants, and it's a formula for disaster. For some reason coming to

Prague has only made it worse." I didn't want to hear any more, but Roger kept going. "He's telling Brenda that he's really interested in starting something, while he's in the process of reconciling with Lori. I love him, but you're right. He's being a jerk."

"I have to go," I said. Apparently, being around people could only make me feel more and more wretched. As I dashed down the escalator, I thought I might have heard Roger call after me, but decided it was just my brain tricking itself yet again.

Chapter Twenty-five

Annie Earl found me the following evening attempting to buy a dinner of mini-pretzels from the vending machine.

"You're going to miss the big mid dinner?" she asked over my shoulder.

"Yes," I said.

I'd forgotten all about the big mid dinner, a mixer with the faculty and the guest agent, Tiki Manza.

"It's supposed to be a lot of fun," she said.

I turned around and held up my pretzels. "I'm good."

"Good? Have you been crying?" she asked.

"Some," I said.

"Is this about your fight with Veronica?"

"How do you know about that?" I asked.

"My new room is right above yours," she said. "And I keep my window open."

"I don't want to talk about it." I felt my bottom lip tremble.

"Listen," Annie Earl said, "I know something substantial has happened, or at least it feels that way right now. But you shouldn't pass up a once-in-a-lifetime opportunity in order to sit by yourself and sulk."

I looked at her and tried to swallow the lump in my throat. I needed to talk to somebody, and Annie Earl was here. So I let myself spill. "Annie Earl," I said, "my heart is broken."

"You do look rather forlorn. Is it your first one?"

I nodded. "It actually got broken a couple of months ago, but due to some recent events, it feels re-broken."

"Okay," she said. "Come to dinner with me. If things begin to feel too deep for you, you can leave early."

"Things feel pretty deep right now."

Annie Earl hugged me. She seemed experienced at dealing with emotionally bruised people. Then she led me by the elbow outside.

"It's too bad you left class early yesterday, because I had some things I wanted to say about your story."

"I'm not ready for feedback."

"Actually, I think you are."

"No!" I covered my ears.

"Dessy. What are you afraid of?"

I pulled my hands away from my ears. "Criticism, I guess. I want people to like it."

"Sounds like you're afraid of rejection. That's normal. People are going to have opinions. Learn to listen. Take what's useful and disregard the rest. Remember, you aren't your story."

What she said sounded so logical. Why didn't I talk to logical people more often?

"Now are you ready for some feedback?" Annie Earl asked.

"Hit me."

"What your story captures so effectively is that moment of sacrifice that accompanies love. The car trip to Guatemala is a great metaphor for that."

We walked along the sidewalk in the pale light of dusk.

"You've got a great sense for characters. And pacing. And relationships."

"Love sucks," I said.

Annie Earl laughed. "You'll get back on that horse."

My mind flashed to Hamilton. Then Waller. "I don't know," I said.

"I know it feels like it will never happen again. But it will. I promise. It's part of life." Annie Earl gave me another hug. It felt like she was trying to transfer some of her good mood vibes onto me.

"I think I'm stuck," I said.

"Broken hearts will do that."

"But I shouldn't want this guy back at all," I explained. "Logically, I know that. But I can't help myself."

"Give it time," Annie Earl said. "There will be another one."

"I'm not sure that I want to fall in love again," I said. "I think I might make a good nun."

"Now is not the appropriate time to make that life decision. Heal first, live through your twenties, then consider pursuing lifelong celibacy."

"I hate making life decisions," I said. "I'm so afraid that I'm going to screw it up."

"Well, the great thing about life is that it usually gives you a chance to correct your screwups," she said.

"But I don't want to have to correct anything. I want to get it right the first time."

"That life strategy will lead you straight to a nervous breakdown," she said.

"I think I'm having one right now."

Annie Earl stopped me. She forcefully turned me toward her and looked me right in the eyes. "You have your whole life ahead of you. Don't be afraid to make mistakes. A lot of times what feels like a mistake in the moment, one year, two years, ten years later, turns out not to have been a mistake at all."

I didn't like thinking about how long life was. I was

mainly worried about the dramatic condition of my present situation. Plus, did I even know Annie Earl well enough to take her advice? She loosened her grip on me and we started walking again.

"I'm going to tell you a story," she said. "It's about how I got my scars."

I almost felt guilty of something heinous because I'd been so curious about Annie Earl's arms. "Sure," I said.

"One day, while vacationing in Boca Raton, I came across a burning car. It was parked on a patch of dry grass and had just caught on fire. I saw it happen. The flames licked the undercarriage for a few seconds and then quickly burst into the car itself. I raced to it. Inside I could see a child strapped into a car seat. So I punched out the rear passenger window with my bare hands and grabbed the child and pulled it to safety."

The story took my breath away. "You saved a child?"

"No," Annie Earl said. "I didn't. It turned out that it was a doll."

"Oh my god!" I said. "Who puts a doll in a car seat?"

"I don't think the people could have anticipated the car catching fire and a passerby mistaking the doll for an actual child. I think people who have children have dolls. And it just happened," Annie Earl said.

"That's terrible," I said. "I'm so sorry."

"I don't see it the way you do," Annie Earl said. "I feel I made the right decision. Because not taking that risk would have meant I was a different kind of person."

"Oh," I said. "But still."

Annie Earl frowned. "Breaking into that car meant that I was able to think about saving some helpless child before I thought about myself. That's illuminating."

"But to be scarred for a doll seems unfair," I said.

"I was given an impossible situation. And I made my choice. And I'm happy with it."

I believed her. I looked at Annie Earl and saw a woman who was fully alive and unquestionably happy. This is not what I saw when I looked at most people. Not Veronica. Not my mother. Not me.

"I don't think I can go to the mid dinner," I said. "I feel overwhelmed." I needed time alone, to figure things out. How else would I be able to unravel the knot that had become my life?

Chapter Twenty-six

$\mathcal{I}$ sat in class, rereading Roger's ending, trying to figure out the perfect thing to say. I wanted to sound smart. And mature. And even-keeled. I read the ending a seventh time.

My father was never going to be who I wanted him to be, and I needed to let go of my hope that one day I would wake up and find a guy who had at last decided to behave admirably. He would never be that guy. Up ahead, what I thought was a poodle turned out to be a monkey. Wiry and irreverent, the monkey hurried through the alley like a small, jittery man. The sailor held the leash loosely and gave the monkey a lot more freedom than I would've given my pet monkey, if I'd happened to have one.

The animal shrieked as it passed the Dumpster. The sailor smiled at me. He looked decent enough. Once they passed, I didn't turn around. I kept moving forward, through the shadowed alley, toward the sun-splashed main street. Horns honked at a double-parked car. I kept going. I needed to set a good pace. This is how it was always going to be. No matter where I went, or how I arrived, my father was his own man and I was mine. North or south, east or west, the direction didn't matter. From this day forward, I was the one who'd be picking the street.

He had written about a trip he and his father had taken to the Jefferson Memorial in Washington, D.C. At least I think the narrator was based on Roger. The two characters drive cross-country from Chicago to D.C. Along the way, the son witnesses several bungled attempts of his dad trying to pick up women. The story ends when the main character runs off and then wanders down an alley near Dupont Circle and finds a sailor walking with a small monkey on a leash. Roger's ending spoke to me, but that wasn't a classworthy comment. His closing was hopeful, but still true. I wanted to find that same sort of way out of my own story. Because what Roger wrote was honest and heartbreaking, and made me glad that I had a father who was interested in parking technology and not carousing. I stared down at my comments. Suddenly none of them looked legible.

As people began arriving, I tried not to look at anybody. Brenda. Waller. Corky. Veronica. I didn't understand how one workshop could have so many challenging people in it.

"Why don't we jump right in?" Mrs. Knox said excitedly. "Roger, where do you want to read from?"

"The middle," he said. "The lawn-mower scene.

"I spotted the lawn from the highway before my father did. It was vast and overgrown, and the red brick house at the crest of the grounds was beginning to show signs of geriatric disrepair.

'Looks promising,' my father said. 'We'll get at least a Benjamin. Maybe a Benjamin plus a Ulysses.'

For all his flaws, he was well equipped with bargaining skills.

'Just don't go inside his house with him,' he said. 'If he wants to tip you, make him pay you in cash right out on the lawn.'

It didn't matter how much money he charged for my lawn-mowing services, because I wouldn't get to keep any of it. It would all go to Jack (Daniel), Johnnie (Walker), and Jim (Beam).

This is when the fantasies usually started. I didn't want to be who I was, so I imagined other possible outcomes for myself. My dad could get arrested in D.C. I could join up with an old sea captain and cross the Atlantic on a schooner. Sure. Why not? That was possible.

The man of the house appeared after three insistent chimes of the doorbell. I almost choked. He looked like an undead veteran of the Civil War—crazy white hair, bloodshot eyes, silver stubble like metal shavings. He stared at us through the screen door.

'My boy wants to know if you'd like to have your lawn mowed,' my dad said in a phony drawl. 'I've got to do some business in the city and could come get him in a few hours. Thought it'd be good to teach him the value of a day's hard labor.'

The man appraised us for a long moment, then said, 'How much?'

My father turned to me. 'What did that gentleman pay you back in Jenkins County? I believe it was thirty an hour, but like I said, it's more about the lesson.'

I wanted to punch him and run. I could have knocked him flat on his back. But instead I played my part and swore to myself that this was the last time. Tomorrow, I would make my escape."

After Roger finished reading, we took our traditional pause and looked back over the page.

Then Annie Earl kicked off the comments. "You could publish this. Send it out."

"Yeah," Brenda said. "It's so masculine. Southern journals love that."

"When the father flashed the housekeeper in that elevator, I was furious," Veronica said. "You made that scene feel so real."

"I love your dialogue," Brenda said. "It was spare and direct."

"It's always fun to read about maniac parents renting out their kids for petty jobs," Corky said.

I felt like I should say something too, so I dove in even before I had a fully formed thought. "I think you're good at building sympathetic characters. Because as much as I didn't like the dad, I still rooted for him. He wasn't a total villain. I kept hoping that he'd turn a corner."

Mrs. Knox agreed. "A teacher once told me that when you write a villain, you have to make sure that your villain loves his mother. While you didn't exactly address the father's bond with his mother, you did give him dimensions and the ability to love, and I appreciated that. Like Dessy said, we need to be able to root for him too."

"I really liked the monkey," said Kite. "I've seen lots of monkeys, and I thought you really nailed that monkey's demeanor."

"I second that," Frank said. "Awesome monkey."

"Thanks," Roger said.

"I agree," said Mrs. Knox. "The monkey is so striking because it's a three-dimensional character as well as a symbol. It's a monkey before it's a symbol."

At the end of the workshop, Mrs. Knox handed out a list of tourist attractions: Petřín Hill, the Mucha Museum, Lenin Wall, and Municipal House.

"Next class we'll meet here, but we'll walk to Petřín Hill. I want you to bring in three images. Make sure that it's not just a collection of adjectives and adverbs." She looked right at Waller when she said this. "I want you to really study three objects and bring in precise descriptions."

I stayed seated until everybody had left. I wanted to revel in my loneliness. And it worked. When you feel depressed and send antisocial messages, the whole world will let you abandon it.

The next week passed in a blur of pitiful solitude. Without Veronica, I grew so lonely that I bought online time in various cafés and spent hours on the Sasquatch discussion boards. Some accounts outside Yakima, Washington were so persuasive that after a few days I became convinced that Bigfoot really did exist. I pictured him lumbering through thick forests, aware of his legendary status, shunning civilization and all its gadgets.

I steered clear of the dorms. My life barely intersected with Veronica's. Or Corky's. Or Waller's. Or Roger's. Or anybody's. One day after class, trying to kill time, I decided to visit an interesting café in my guidebook. It took me a half hour to get there on foot, and when I finally swung open the door, I saw that it was filled with real locals. No tourists in shorts wearing backpacks, clutching maps. These were regular Prague people living their regular Prague lives. The paint on the walls was chipped, and the posters of alcohol brands were not meant to appeal to me. The cashier didn't even try to speak English; I pointed to the roll I wanted, and she put it in a brown sack. I paid and walked out the door.

I felt savvy and cool. I didn't need Veronica to explore the gritty side of Prague. I'd found the underbelly all on my own. When I left out the side door, I stepped onto a dirt pathway and heard an eerie sound. I saw shadows zipping around on the ground. Crap! My footsteps had sent several rats scattering. No, dozens of them, and they were huge. They skittered around my feet, emitting sounds that resembled big machinery.

I threw my sack at the vermin and ran. I lost one of my shoes, but I was too freaked out to go back and get it. As I reapproached the touristy area of Prague, with one socked foot holding me back, it was clear I needed to return to the dorm. I sat on a park bench and ate a Corny bar, which tasted like cornflakes and chocolate and marshmallows and salt. A pigeon crash-landed in front of me, trying to snag a french fry. It skidded across the sidewalk. I wasn't used to seeing pigeons skid. That's when I noticed its damaged foot. It was missing its front toes. Lacking traction, it skidded a little every time it landed.

Watching that wounded pigeon made me so sad, but I couldn't stop. When it was finished with the french fries, it found a smashed muffin. It was then that my loneliness hit an unacceptable level. It was stupid for me to stop talking to Veronica. I'd let Corky put a wedge between us. Why had I done that? What happened with Hamilton hadn't been her fault. And I had lied to her about Kutná Hora. And I had let Waller take her fox idea. I watched the wounded pigeon fly off. And that settled it: with eight days left to go in Prague, I decided to patch things up with her.

I went back to the dorm and started writing her a heartfelt note. But I kept having to start over because I couldn't finish a whole paragraph without rehashing our last fight. Halfway through my fourth attempt I heard her phone ringing. I stopped writing and instinctively pressed my ear against the wall.

"I've had it up to here with you, Hamilton," Veronica said.

My knees felt quaky and I sat down right on the floor.

"Of course I haven't told Dessy," she said. "It would kill her. And I'm not the kind of person who kills my friends."

Veronica's side of the conversation with Hamilton revealed a few key, tragic things. First, Veronica had totally betrayed me. Second, this was not the first time Hamilton had called Veronica in Prague. Third, they'd been in communication with each other for some time. Fourth, feeling screwed over by my ex-boyfriend and former best friend made my internal organs wobble painfully inside of me.

The call lasted less than five minutes.

"No, she hasn't read your letter," Veronica said. "I grabbed it out of the mail pile before it could be delivered. Sometimes you're such an idiot. What were you thinking?"

But I was the one who felt like an idiot. Never in a million years would I have thought Veronica would interfere with my first boyfriend and international mail.

"There is a lot of heat on this situation. Hamilton, this is really going to hurt her. I don't see why we should tell her. Look, don't call me again. I'll call you."

I heard a snapping sound and the obvious noise of the handset being smashed back into the cradle. Then I heard Veronica open our bedroom door and go into the bathroom. The shower squeaked on.

I stood up and opened the door. Veronica was singing. Something tuneless and happy. The soft sound of her voice drifted alongside me as I hurried down the hallway. I shook my head, trying to make the noise go away, but it was already deep inside my brain. Then I heard myself scream. It didn't last very long, but it was loud. A guy in front of me turned around and asked, "Are you okay?"

"I don't know!" I said, jogging around him.

The man's question haunted me. *Are you okay?* What a ridiculous thing to ask. I might not ever be okay again. I flew down the stairs. I needed fresh air. How could

Veronica do this? She knew that I loved Hamilton. What was she trying to prove? That she could steal him away from me? Didn't she have enough men? I reached the bottom of the staircase and stopped.

My sadness had turned into a boiling anger. Without thinking, I flipped around and climbed upward, taking the stairs two at a time. At the second-floor landing, I started running. Not a casual jog. I ran with intensity. I threw open the door and stormed into the bathroom. When I dramatically pulled back the shower curtain, Veronica unleashed a bloodcurdling scream.

"I heard everything!" I yelled. "You are such a phony! And a traitor! You are so terrible! After you die you're going straight to hell, where you'll coexist with other people who have broken moral compasses!"

"Agh!" Veronica yelled. "Don't hurt me!"

She squatted down and shielded herself with her arms. The shower instantly drenched my front with warm water. I reached out and turned the knob off.

"How could you?" I asked.

She kept her head down and didn't make eye contact.

"Are you going to say anything?" I asked. Water dripped off me and splattered on the floor.

"I'm really surprised you caught me," Veronica said.

I couldn't believe it. This was the worst thing that anybody had ever done to me, and she didn't sound sorry at all.

"How could you?" I asked again. "I mean, why would you want to?"

Veronica looked up at me with her guilty, wet face. "I think we need to go somewhere and talk about this. I know the phone call with Hamilton looks bad," she said. "But it's just the tip of the ice cube. There are things you need to know."

I pulled the shower curtain shut. "This is the worst

vacation ever," I said. "I don't think I can stomach hearing more. I feel like letting Corky just go ahead and kill me. And you!"

"You don't mean that," Veronica said. She stepped out of the shower and grabbed a towel.

"Don't tell me what I mean and don't mean!"

"If you keep yelling this loudly, you're going to attract dorm security. Come to the room while I get dressed. We can talk."

"I can't talk to you!" I said. "I hate you!"

Veronica turned and stared at me. She reached out to touch me, but I slapped her hand away.

"Dessy, there's something I need to tell you. Follow me."

I was in shock. I followed Veronica back to her room. She opened her desk drawer and handed me a slim envelope addressed to me. The return address said it was from Hamilton.

Before I even realized that I'd raised it, I felt my other hand slap across her cheek. Veronica gasped and held the side of her face. Veronica Knox was the first person I'd ever struck. A stinging sensation traveled through my hand and up my arm. It felt like I'd been shocked.

"Stop doing things you're going to regret," Veronica said.

"I would never regret that. Go suck it, Veronica!"

I was finished with her. Forever. So I walked out the door, trying to project an air of real certainty. I had no idea where I was headed. Or whether I'd read Hamilton's letter. I suspected I'd never be able to speak to either one of them again. It's as if my real world, the one where I was a high school senior living in Ohio being raised by my kind mother and disconnected father, ceased to exist. I was living in Bizarre Land now.

I walked down the sidewalk holding Hamilton's

letter and looking at all the traffic rushing down the street. I never knew that I could feel so much pain. I was entirely unprepared for it. I lifted the letter and a light breeze caught it, making it flutter against my hand. I wanted to release it. I could let it slip into the street and it would be as if it had never existed. But I couldn't do it. I had to read the letter. Maybe not right now. Or today. Or this week. But one day the curiosity would overtake the dread. I brought my hand down and folded the letter three times. Then I slid it into my pocket and kept walking.

Chapter Twenty-seven

The tail of a cheetah was much fatter than I realized. And when the big cat swished it, it didn't come across as a playful act. The tail seemed capable of delivering a deadly blow. Cheetahs. It made sense that my excursion to Prague would finally lead here.

Pacing atop their grass hillock, the spotted sprinters looked bigger and more muscular than I'd expected. According to a sign on the fence, the Prague zoo had been one of the first gardens in the world where cheetahs had been bred successfully. How ironic.

I understood it now. Veronica and Hamilton were talking behind my back because they were secretly in love with each other. It explained so much. Why Veronica had compared herself to a cheetah. Why Hamilton had dumped me without any warning and why Veronica had likewise dumped Boz. Nothing course-changing had happened, and yet they'd both exited their relationships.

I left the cheetahs in disgust and sought out the polar bears. I stood on the other side of the fence and thought about how sad it was that polar bears were going extinct. Everything was heating up. The whole planet. My mind was unraveling. I mean, Hamilton and Veronica had probably been denying this for years, and then finally their passion for each other had ignited in one big fiery burst. In retrospect, this wasn't that surprising. Because Hamilton and Veronica always disliked each other so much, even when there was no reason to dislike each other. It had to have been unacknowledged sexual tension. I'd read an article about sexual tension in a women's magazine. Apparently, desire is an emotion that can't be successfully suppressed for longer than a year. Because when you push it down, it only tries harder to escape.

I couldn't recall what advice the article offered. I only remembered the picture of the exploding volcano at the top of the page.

Everywhere I looked, there were signs providing a history of the flood. I remembered the word Waller had used to describe the situation: Apocalypse. I couldn't shake that word. It seemed so apt, now that everything in my life had become a catastrophe.

I made my way to the giant tortoises and watched one inch its ridiculously large, shelled body across a cement pond. Then I walked to the gorilla pavilion and read about the tragic death of one of them during the flood. Stupid flood. Lousy apocalypse.

I staggered through the zoo like my own version of a wounded animal. I could never trust anybody again. Even people who I loved and had already been trusting for years. I don't remember how I got home. I only know that I carried a small bird feather—I think it came from an owl—all the way there.

At the crack of dawn, somebody knocked on my door, but I ignored it. Even when the knock was accompanied by the words, "It's me, Veronica. Please open up," I didn't feel the need to respond.

"I'm going to stand outside your door until you open it and are willing to talk to me," Veronica said.

I waved to the closed door and didn't say anything.

"I think I just felt you flip me the bird." She was so smart. She was trying to trick me into denying that I'd flipped her the bird in order to trigger a conversation between us. It didn't work.

"Corky, leave me alone," Veronica said.

"Well, if it isn't Veronica Knox talking to Dessy Gherkin's door. How appropriate," Corky said.

I almost felt bad for Veronica.

"You two acted like you had such a *special* friendship. But look at you. You're just a couple of frauds," Corky said.

"You say one more unkind thing about Dessy, and I will stab you with a fork," Veronica said.

"No you won't," Corky said. "Because you know I'd stab you back so much harder."

I hoped that some sort of massive fork stabbing wasn't about to occur outside my room. Because if it did, I'd feel compelled to open my door and try to tamp it down. And the last thing I needed to encounter in my present emotional state was blood.

"Can't you both go away?" I said.

"Open the door!" Veronica said.

"Keep it closed!" Corky said. "Teach this twit a lesson."

"I'm trying to sleep," I said.

"I can talk to you while you slumber," Veronica said. "If you let me explain things, you'll be less pissed."

"Honestly, Veronica, I don't think there is anything you could say that would make me less pissed."

"Dessy, if you give me a chance, I can make sense out of all of this. You know me. I'm not a deceitful person."

"Yes you are," Corky said.

"Not when it comes to Dessy!" Veronica said.

As much as I didn't want to believe Veronica, as much as I wanted to remain angry and keep my distance,

I knew that at some point I needed to listen to what she had to say. But was right now that point? I wasn't sure. I stood up and walked toward my door, but I couldn't open it. I wasn't ready.

"What do I need to do to make you leave?" Veronica yelled to Corky. "Throw a stick?"

"You're so shallow, it compromises your intelligence," Corky shouted back.

"So what if I'm shallow," Veronica said. "You're fat!"

"I can lose weight!" Corky said.

"I can gain depth!" Veronica said.

"No you can't," Corky said. "You're a douche bag!"

"So are you!" Veronica said.

I wanted the petty arguing to stop. Eventually I would have to face the truth. Rather than waste any more energy on this situation, I decided to give Veronica what she wanted. "Veronica, I'll meet you at the bagel café in an hour."

"Don't say that with Corky right here!" Veronica said. "She'll follow us."

"Maybe I won't," Corky said.

"Stop touching me," Veronica said.

"What are you going to do if I don't?" Corky asked.

"Veronica, meet me at the place where I went without you." I knew she'd understand that I meant the Astronomical Clock.

"You went someplace without me?" she asked.

"Yeah, but you also went there with Alexej," I said.

"How do you know where I went with Alexej?" she asked.

I guess this accidental confession meant that I wouldn't make a very good spy. "I followed you a little," I said.

"Wait a minute," Veronica said. "Were you carrying an umbrella, because I totally think I saw you!"

"I'm done talking about this. Just go to that place."

"I'm not sure which place you mean," Veronica said.

"The place I went with Waller that wasn't the Drunk House that you felt I should have visited with you." I was disappointed that I had to give her another hint.

"She's talking about the Astronomical Clock," Corky said.

"Shut up, Corky!" I said.

"Okay. How about this," said Veronica. "I'll meet you at Paul the Baptist in an hour."

I heard the front door slam.

"Are you still there, Corky?" I asked.

"Yes," she said. "Don't worry. I don't plan on stalking you and Veronica."

"I wasn't worried."

"Sure you weren't."

The door slammed again. Then there was silence. And even though I really didn't feel like it, I had to get up and get ready to go out into the world and live another possibly miserable day.

As I was leaving the dorm, I walked past the pay phone and it nearly leapt into my hand. Before I could even question the impulse, I dialed my home in Ohio.

MOM: I was just thinking about you, Dessy. How are things?

ME: They could be going better.

MOM: Are you low on funds?

ME: I'm okay on funds.

MOM: Well, if you've got money in the bank, all other obstacles are a matter of attitude.

ME: That doesn't make any sense. What if I was being attacked by a bear?

MOM: Cities don't have bears. Especially in Europe. Are you still in the city?

ME: Yes. But it's getting a little challenging. International travel isn't all that it's cracked up to be.

MOM: You sound grumpy.

ME: I guess I am a little grumpy.

MOM: Is there anything I can do?

ME: I sort of want to talk to Dad.

MOM: You do?

ME: Yes. That's what I said.

MOM: He's working in the garage.

ME: Really? He never goes into the garage.

MOM: He's fixing the lawn mower.

ME: When did we get a lawn mower?

MOM: Stewart raised his price, so your father bought a lawn mower.

ME: But Dad doesn't know how to fix things. Especially not a machine with sharp rotating blades and a motor.

MOM: You're being very critical.

ME: I want to talk to him!

MOM: Maybe you should calm down and call him later.

ME: I am calm!

MOM: What's this about?

ME: I'm concerned about something.

MOM: You're concerned about your father?

ME: No. I'm concerned about me and Dad. The two of us. Have you ever noticed that we don't connect? We don't talk about anything important. Ever. It's like we're related and then we don't have a relationship beyond that.

MOM: That's not true.

ME: Of course it's true! We never talk about anything important ever.

MOM: That's just the way your father's built. Some men are like that.

ME: Dad's got to talk about important things with someone. Why not me?

MOM: You really need to stop yelling.

ME: I'm not yelling! I'm just loud when I make international calls.

MOM: Is something else going on? Is this about Hamilton's letter?

ME: I haven't even read Hamilton's stupid letter!

MOM: Why not? Hasn't it arrived yet?

ME: Oh, it arrived here all right!

MOM: Oh no!

ME: Why are you screaming? How bad can Hamilton's letter be? What's in the letter?

MOM: Blood!

ME: What? Hamilton sent me blood?

MOM: No. It's your father. Don't stand there, Walter. Come over here and bleed in the sink!

ME: Is it serious?

MOM: Your father cut off his hand!

ME: Off?

MOM: Not off. I've got to go. Wrap a towel around it, Walter!

Click.

I hung up the phone. That exchange did little to comfort me. Plus, it had done nothing to further my relationship with my father. My ears still rang from my mother's piercing cry of the word "blood." I hoped things weren't as bad as they sounded. At least my parents had health insurance. I'd call back later to check on them.

Walking down the boulevard at Wenceslas Square, I wasn't sure what Veronica could possibly say. That she actually hadn't started dating Hamilton yet, but that she wanted my permission? Was she going to make some philosophical argument about love and destiny and the fickle heart? I tried to picture Veronica with Hamilton. It made me want to vomit.

I spotted her right away, standing beside the statue

wearing a pair of cute lavender shorts and a white T-shirt. She had her dark hair pulled back into a tidy ponytail, and she was smiling.

"Thanks for coming," she said, rushing toward me.

I let her hug me, but I didn't hug back.

"I want to tell you everything," she said. She took my hand and led me to a bench. I sat down next to her and remained stiff.

"Can you not shoot daggers at me when I talk?" Veronica said. "It's going to make this harder."

"Well, considering how I feel, I really can't control what my eyes are doing," I said.

Veronica nodded. "I'm trying to figure out where to start."

I didn't try to help her.

"I mean, there's this thing that happened three months before Prague, and then something happened a few days before we left, and then there's stuff that's happened while we've been here. I mean, there's a lot of stuff to tell you."

I was stunned. Something had happened three months before Prague? What? A flirty letter? A phone call? A kiss? I grabbed my stomach.

"Why don't you just tell me how long you've been in love with Hamilton behind my back," I said.

Veronica's jaw dropped; she stared at me with the bulging eyes of a truly flabbergasted person. "I'm not in love with Hamilton!"

"I think you're lying," I said.

"Dessy, what's happening with me and Hamilton isn't romantic in any way," Veronica said. "In fact, it's the opposite of that. I've only been in contact with him because I'm worried about you."

"Why did you tell him that the situation is hot?" I asked.

"Because it is. This has turned into a freaking inferno!"

I couldn't disagree with that.

"Okay," Veronica said, "clearly you haven't read his letter."

"I haven't been able to gear myself up for that."

"After you hear what I have to say, you probably don't even need to read it. It's probably going to be very hurtful."

"His letter isn't about getting back together, is it?" I asked.

"No," she said. "He's going to admit that he was seeing somebody else."

Hearing it felt like somebody had dropped a piano on me. Followed by a series of bowling balls. And then jabbed pushpins into my already crushed heart. He wasn't in love with Veronica. That was an enormous relief. But the one thing I didn't want to believe about Hamilton Stacks turned out to be true. He was a cheater. A terrible, horrible, atrocious cheater.

"Who?" I wiped tears from my cheeks.

"He's a real, genuine asshole, Dessy. They don't make them any assier."

"Who?" I demanded.

"Gloria Fitz."

I nearly tipped off the bench. Veronica reached out and stabilized me. I assumed the person would be some sort of brilliant scholar and fellow bird lover.

"But she's not even interesting!" I said. "She just follows around those other dips. She goes to the mall all the time. She's nothing like Hamilton. I bet she doesn't even recognize birds, let alone respect them."

"Trust me, those two will be busted up before Labor Day for sure."

But Labor Day was weeks away, and I wanted their

relationship to disintegrate immediately. "When did they start dating?" I asked. "How did it happen?"

"They were lab partners in anatomy and physiology. I suspect it happened when they dissected a starfish together," she said. "It's sort of an intimate endeavor. You have to sit very close for that. And share a scalpel."

My mind kept trying to picture Hamilton and Gloria together. But it couldn't. Their features didn't match. Their personalities were too different. They didn't belong together, even in a mental image.

"Weren't you in that class?" I asked. "Didn't you see this happening?"

"No, not at all," Veronica said. "I was busy dissecting my own starfish. Plus, I slept a lot in there. But we were always watching those films on reproduction. It makes sense in retrospect that a relationship could be kick-started in that environment, but I never suspected it was happening. I would have come to you right away if I had."

Veronica squeezed my hand several times. I believed her. I trusted that what she had said so far was the truth.

"So when did you find out?" I asked.

"It happened in a weird way," Veronica said.

"Did you walk in on them?" I asked.

"Gross," Veronica said. "Witnessing something that disgusting would probably render me blind." She stuck out her tongue and let it hang there for a few seconds. "This is what happened. Back in February, I spotted Gloria zipping herself into some shapewear in the girl's bathroom. I guess that's how she fits into her jeans."

"She was standing in the middle of the girl's bathroom zipping herself into a girdle?" I asked. That did seem weird.

"Oh no," Veronica said. "She was in a stall. I saw her through the crack."

"You peeked at her while she was in the stall?"

"Yeah. After I heard this prolonged zipping sound, I had to know what was going on in there."

"Did she freak out when she saw you looking?" I asked.

"No," Veronica said. "She didn't see me. Her back was to me. So I decided to have some fun with this. I sent her an e-mail and told her that I knew her secret. And then she sent me an e-mail begging me not to tell you."

"You've known since February that Gloria and Hamilton have been involved, and I'm only finding out in July?"

"Relax," Veronica said. "I thought she wanted me not to tell you about the shapewear. I didn't know she was having a fling with your birdboy."

I hated it when Veronica referred to Hamilton as my "birdboy." Before I found out about his infidelity, the title always struck me as unflattering to him. Now, knowing his true character, I felt the title reflected poorly on birds.

"Why would I care about her shapewear?" I asked. "You never put two and two together?"

Veronica leaned into me. "I thought you were her body-image doppelgänger."

"Huh?"

"Her body-image doppelgänger. The person you know with your similar body type who you hold up as a point of constant comparison. In my defense, I think it was out of the realm of human comprehension that Hamilton would develop feelings for *Gloria*. By the way, Tonya Babbitt is my body-image doppelgänger. I'm constantly comparing my butt to her butt."

"I don't want to hear about your butt issues right now, Veronica. Just tell me. When did you know?" I asked.

"Not until right before we left. Something I saw at the mall triggered the realization."

"What was that?"

"Her earrings. Nobody buys duck earrings except for people who are trying to manipulate other people by tricking them into thinking that they like ducks. When I laid eyes on her cheap silver quackers instead of her cheap diamond studs, it all clicked. That's why I had that meltdown at the mall. And I've been blackmailing her about the shapewear ever since. She's *so shallow*."

"So why didn't you tell me?" I asked.

"I thought the best strategy would be to get you interested in a new guy," Veronica said. "Even before I knew Hamilton was a cad I thought that was the way to go. After I found out, I felt really stuck. I didn't want to spoil your first trip to Europe by telling you that your first shithead boyfriend broke up with you because he fell for a twit. I couldn't do that to you."

"So why was Hamilton calling you?" I asked.

"Oh, Dessy"—Veronica scooted closer to me—"when you told me that he was sending you something, I thought he might be trying to get back together with you. So I called him and told him to leave you alone. Then last week when you told me that Hamilton had broken up with you because of *your* flaws, and that he'd given you a laminated list of them, I thought I was going to die. I went straight down to the lobby and called him."

"What did you say?"

"I told him that he was an asshole and that I had intercepted his first letter and was throwing it away and he needed to write you a second letter and admit that he was wrong and that you were really great. And that your flaws weren't bad. And he was sorry for saying they were. And that he wanted to talk to you when you got home. And if he didn't, I threatened to spam all the Dartmouth incoming freshmen with evil lies about him that would impede his ability to have friends or function in a social setting."

"That's what's in my letter?" I asked.

"I don't know what's in that thing," Veronica said. "He mailed it between my messages. He's become completely unglued these days. I think he and Gloria are experiencing rocky times."

"Well, that's not surprising," I said. "Two cheaters can't build a solid union."

"Exactly," Veronica said. "Plus, he's been talking about how much he misses you. I was worried that he might try to patch things up with you. And because you didn't know the truth, I thought you might go for it. And I thought you should keep your options open and play the field. You know, experience Prague."

I looked into Veronica's perfect face. Ten minutes ago I'd thought she was a terrible friend. Now I knew she was a terrific friend. She cared about me. And in her own flawed way, tried to protect me from life's cruel blows.

"Should I even bother reading the letter?" I asked.

"That's your call," Veronica said.

"I think I should."

"Maybe you could read it to me," she suggested.

I looked around the crowded boulevard and back to Veronica. "I think I should do this on my own."

"Really?" she asked.

I nodded.

"Are you still mad at me?" she asked.

"No," I said. "Are you still mad at me?"

"Well," Veronica said, "what happened with Waller's story still bugs me. But I think my story is much better than his, so I'm okay with it."

"I never said the word *foxes*. He came up with that on his own," I said.

"I think we should just put a period there and move on," she said.

"Okay," I said.

We sat and watched the tourists milling around at the top of the square. Many of them had their cameras out and were viewing the city through the small viewfinder or LCD screen. I thought of my own camera—both of them—back in the dorm.

I looked down at the ground, where a line of ants streamed toward a cookie. They were dangerously close to Veronica's toes. When she saw them, she immediately began stomping the ants. Even after she'd killed most of them, she didn't stop. Her face was wrinkled in determination.

I reached out and touched her knee. "You got them."

Her face relaxed and she pulled out a small piece of paper from her back pocket. "I have a list of things I have to do this weekend."

"We'll be hanging out together again, right?" I asked.

Veronica bit her lip and squealed a little. "Do you want to go out with Alexej and his friend tomorrow? We're going to take a boat ride. I promise you it will be amazing. Picture us, drifting in the Vltava beneath the stars."

Veronica's face looked totally blissed out.

"What time?" I asked.

She didn't respond.

"Veronica," I said.

She reached out and grabbed my arm. "I've been dreaming about him." She tossed her head back. "He's really got me. He's the one hot-dude who just keeps getting hotter. Dessy. I have found my soul hot-dude!"

This news set off all kinds of alarm bells. "So now that you've found your soul hot-dude, have you stopped looking for other hot-dudes?"

"Not really. It's like they call to me." Veronica's face lit up like a porch light. "You're not going to believe this, but the man-wall is up to ninety-four hot-dudes."

She was right. I couldn't believe it. That was way too many hot-dudes.

"You're having too much fun with this," I said. "What about Boz? Can you imagine what it feels like for him every time you send him another picture of you with a hot-dude?"

Veronica's smile fell away. "Oh, I stopped sending him pictures of me with hot-dudes eons ago. I just sent the first couple. You were right. He got way too hurt by it, so I stopped. His second e-mail to me was a real flamer."

I couldn't believe that Veronica was surprised by Boz's response. She was lucky he'd responded to her at all. "If you really love Boz, you should probably focus on fixing your relationship and not pursuing Alexej or any other hot-dude."

"Yeah," she said. "But you've got to remember, he hurt me too."

"Maybe," I said.

Veronica looked past me like she was contemplating something. "After my date with Alexej, I'll call Boz and mend things."

"If he still *wants* to mend things," I said.

"Of course he will. He loves me."

"It just seems dangerous to play with somebody's heart like this," I persisted.

"Dessy, I'm not saying this to be mean, I'm saying this to be honest. All you ever do is choose the smart and safe option, and look at where it's gotten you."

Her words stung, mostly because they were accurate. "I think you like being mean," I said.

Veronica didn't object.

"Also, sometimes you're selfish," I said.

Veronica bumped me with her shoulder. "That's not true. I'm a giver."

"You didn't stay for my workshop."

Suddenly, it bothered me all over again that Veronica had left at such an important moment of my life.

"Listen, I'm sorry I missed it. My mom said you refused feedback."

"I only refused the verbal kind. I took the written ones home."

Veronica put her arm around me. "But your story was really good. It's funny. But it's also super sad."

This wasn't the response I'd been expecting. "You think my story is super sad?"

That seemed like a weird thing to say, because nobody dies. And by the end, the main character ends up getting back together with her boyfriend.

"They should have stayed broken up," Veronica said. "They were a terrible fit for each other. I thought it was sad that she couldn't realize that."

"She loves him," I said. "She's not ready to break up with him. She wants to get to Guatemala."

"Yeah, but by page three it's obvious that she should give up on him and Guatemala. You can tell that she's going to have a hard life. That she's not strong enough to be happy without Tag."

"You're overanalyzing it," I said. "It's a story about first love. She's supposed to be a little blind."

"That's why blind people shouldn't drive to Guatemala," Veronica said.

"Do you mean that metaphorically?" I asked.

"Maybe," she said.

"I thought your story was perfect," I said.

"Really?"

"Yeah, because the fox in the trap was suffering so much. Because he wants freedom and love. And while he gets love sort of when the other fox stops by to hump, he never gets freedom. And he knows this."

"Actually, the fox stuck in the trap is the girl," Veronica said.

I felt bad that I'd gotten that wrong.

"When I started, I thought my story was sort of a joke. Two foxes screwing each other. Ha-ha. But when I really focused on the foxes and described them and understood what motivated them, I realized that my story was really about determination."

"Determination to screw?"

"No, determination to connect with something other than yourself. Also, determination to experience joy. That's what motivated my foxes, especially the one in the trap that's going to die."

"Sounds intense."

"Well, it is intense. Because at the end of the day, our experiences matter. What we've allowed ourselves to risk and to feel, those things are important."

I thought about this idea. It made sense. Then I heard sniffling. Veronica was crying.

"Hey, what's wrong?" I asked.

"This is why my father left."

I had no idea what she meant, so I waited for her to continue.

"He wanted to experience more joy in life. And living in Ohio with me and my mom didn't bring him enough joy. So now he's screwing a twenty-four-year-old named Maria in Rome."

"What?" I was shocked. "Are you sure?"

"I walked in on them."

"Oh my god!"

"Not as it was happening. I walked in after it had happened. Both of them were in bed under the sheets. They thought I was at the Pantheon, but I'd forgotten my purse, so I came back."

"What did your dad say?"

"At first he yelled to get out because they weren't decent. Then he begged me not to tell my mom."

"I'm so sorry," I said. "Why didn't you tell me?"

"Because I didn't want to make it any more true than it already was. I'd hoped the whole ordeal could somehow be reversed."

"Are you ever going to tell your mom?"

"I think I have to. I'm just not sure when. I don't think she suspects anything like this."

"This is awful," I said. "For everyone."

Tears continued to slip down her cheeks. "Yeah. I used to think that my mom could have done something more. I still think she should have tried. But she probably knew that in the end, he was going to leave regardless of anything she did."

"That's probably right," I said. "Are you still going to visit your dad after Prague?"

"I'll visit him. He's my dad. I can't just cut him loose because he behaves like an idiot. That's not how life works. I'm sure we'll both keep at it until one of us dies."

I hated thinking that life was filled with so much work.

"I tried to call my dad today," I said. "My mom answered, but I said I wanted to speak to him. I've never done that before."

"What did he say?"

"I didn't get to talk to him," I said. "He had an accident with the lawn mower."

"What happened to Stewart?"

"He raised his prices."

"That's too bad. Stewart has a nice ass."

I thought about my father, sitting on the couch watching television. There was so much distance between us.

"Veronica, what you said about that *Triad* book really scares me."

"Don't be scared. I'm beginning to think that author

is kind of an idiot. I mean, lots of people don't even have dads. Plus, she really can't write. And I don't even think she has a degree in anything."

"Wow. So you think I still might have a chance at connecting with a decent guy?"

"Absolutely. You just need to be really self-aware. And I think you're totally getting there."

I let out a deep breath. "I'm going to read Hamilton's letter now."

Veronica turned to me. "Okay, Dessy, but afterward we need to go out. Seriously. No more wasting valuable Prague time. I mean it. Let's dance till we die."

"I don't know."

"You have to. I insist. Go ahead and read Hamilton's stinky letter. Then come back to the dorm. I'll help you get ready. You can't sulk forever."

"I'm not sulking. This is pretty significant news that really alters my recent heartbreak status."

Veronica touched her heart. "Heartbreak. It's unavoidable and it sucks worse than the power of a billion vacuums. But read the letter and then throw it away. I mean it. Then come out with me." She winked and flashed a devilish grin. "It's time to recycle that heart."

Veronica hugged me with one arm and then she got up and left. I watched her until the speck of her lavender shorts faded into a crowd of happy people. Hamilton's letter was in my back pocket. I pulled it out and unfolded it. What had Hamilton written to me? How much had he chosen to confess? What if he'd sent me this powerfully worded apology. Could I forgive that kind of betrayal? I didn't think so. But I needed to read the letter before I made any big decisions.

I carefully tore open the envelope and fished out the letter. It wasn't anything fancy. Hamilton had typed a few short sentences.

> Dessy, I need to tell you something, but I don't know how. Veronica knows what it is. Ask her.

At the bottom, he'd written something in pen.

> I'm sorry I was so hard on you. One day I hope we can be friends. You were always made of awesome.

I almost puked on the letter. Not only was my first boyfriend an asshole, but he was also an absolute coward. He wanted my best friend to make his vile confession for him. I crumpled the letter into a ball and became obsessed with finding a trash can. I ran along a row of outdoor cafés. People sat drinking coffee. Chatting. Reading. Living. Outside of myself, the world was functioning normally. But inside of myself, something had exploded.

When I caught a glimpse of the first available trash can, I nearly knocked over a toddler to get to it. Tossing the letter into a random overflowing garbage container made me feel amazingly good. It helped me arrive at a certain level of acceptance.

Let Hamilton date Gloria. Let them fail at love together. And then let them fail with the next person after that. In their hearts they would always know they were cheaters. They'd both crossed that line. Given the choice between honesty and dishonesty, they'd allowed themselves to select the most selfish option. And given the opportunity, would they do it again? They probably didn't even know. I hoped that question haunted them. I hoped that it hovered over all their romantic entanglements, making future relationships feel jeopardized and unstable. Hamilton Stacks. Gloria Fitz. I had nothing more to say.

Chapter Twenty-eight

𝒹 came back to the dorm at six o'clock. Veronica already had my clothes laid out for me: her black shirt, decorated with round, crystal buttons; my best pair of jeans; a silver belt I'd never seen before; and sandals.

"Once I make your eyes dramatic, the outfit will look even more spectacular."

"Whose belt?"

"Yours. I bought it for you. Consider it a souvenir from Prague."

So in an act of total trust I surrendered my face to Veronica. For thirty minutes she used specialized brushes to apply various powders and creams. When she was finished she asked me to close my eyes, and then she blew on my face.

"Here's a mirror," she said.

I took it and opened my eyes and saw the result of her labor. My eyes looked smoky and my lips were frosty plum. But the makeover wasn't so dramatic that I didn't look like myself. I still looked like Dessy Gherkin, just really, really hot.

"What about my hair?" I asked.

"Bend over and fluff it and I'll hit it with some medium-hold spray."

I did what she told me, and the smell and taste

of the aerosol made me cough.

"Close your mouth," Veronica said.

When I flipped my head back up, my hair resettled itself around my face.

"And the heartbroken has officially become a heart-breaker." She touched my shoulder and made sizzle sounds. "Are you ready?" she asked, grabbing a wad of cash.

"Totally."

When we boarded the metro I didn't even bother looking for a seat. I stood next to a pole and held on, just like the people in the movies. When the train lurched at stops, my body didn't jerk forward like it usually did. I had a newfound fluidity.

"You look like a rock star," Veronica said as we stepped off the metro.

I could feel eyes on me. Normally, this would have freaked me out. But I didn't let it tonight. When men glanced at me, sometimes I glanced back at them, and sometimes I looked over their heads. I felt tall. I walked through the city center with my head held unusually high.

"You look cocky," Veronica said. "I love it!"

At the dance club I got nervous when I saw the snaking line out front. There were girls in amazing skirts. Guys in leather pants. A lot of them had movie-star hair and flashy accessories. One guy looked like he was wearing a python around his shoulders. I stopped.

"That's Radek. Relax. His snake is a fake," Veronica said.

The music pulsed out of the club's open black door. "We're not old enough. They'll never let us in," I said.

Veronica gave me some money for the cover charge. "You look like a hot grad student. Seriously. You're so hot you're surreal. And they've already let me in nine times."

"Nine?"

"Dancing really mellows me out." Veronica began bobbing her head and swinging her arms.

"Wait till we get inside," I said.

"Why?" She swayed and circled her hips.

It was my turn to approach the bouncer. I tried to hand him my money. "For you, free tonight," he said.

"Thanks!" Veronica said as she passed me and pulled me into the club.

The music was loud and powerful. The techno beat pounded us as we stomped rhythmically on the hard, scuffed floor. Laser lights shot through the air. Green. Red. Blue. And rotating mirror balls splashed rainbow flashes of light around the room. My body grew hot and sticky. I found myself making bolder moves, just to try to catch some breeze. I was glad I had short hair. Veronica must have felt like she was wearing a blanket on her head. She grinned viciously at me.

"Your legs are as long as a camel's!"

I pointed to my legs and then spun my body around. Veronica began to laugh so hard that she stopped dancing. I didn't think that things could get any better. But they did. A group of guys was making their way over to Veronica and me. Soon I was dancing with a cute dark-haired guy with smooth, tan skin and amazing brown eyes.

"I'm Dessy!" I yelled over the music.

"Ronaldo!" he yelled back. He really owned his dance style. He wiggled his butt to the bass line and swung his head dramatically.

"Where are you from?"

"Spain! You?"

"I'm from Ohio! It's in the U.S."

We danced until Ronaldo had to leave with his friends. He wrote his number for me on a napkin. Then Caine showed up. He was from New York. He was skinny and had blue eyes. And he danced so hard that I thought he might rip his pants, especially when he dropped in semi-splits down to the floor. After Caine there was Telfer. After Telfer, I just felt like dancing with my friend.

The music didn't have lyrics, but that didn't stop Veronica.

"Melt me! Melt me! Melt me!" she chanted.

"Are you singing about Alexej?" I asked, frowning.

Veronica executed an energetic hopping maneuver that left her breathless. "One more date," she puffed. "Just let me see Alexej one more time. For the memories. Boz is my anchor. I know that."

Melt me. Melt me. Melt me.

I was having such a good time that I decided to agree. "Okay. One more time. For the memories."

Veronica threw her arms up over her head and danced like that for a while. I danced until I forgot about everything. I spun and shook and swayed until my whole body hummed. By the night's end, I was so tired that I wanted to hire somebody to drag me home. We walked out of the club and I sat down on the curb.

"We did it!" Veronica said. "We danced till we died!"

"I. Need. Bed."

Veronica stood over me. "Does this mean that you're done?"

I looked up at her and closed my eyes.

"Okay, okay." Veronica reached down and patted my head. "Taxi!" She stuck her fingers in her mouth and whistled like a drill sergeant.

A small yellow cab pulled up, and we climbed inside. Stars and street lights blazed above us in the inky sky. Out my window I watched the city stand still as we zoomed through its boulevards of monstrous and spectacular buildings. I was in Prague. I had just had one of the best nights of my life.

Back at the dorm, Veronica insisted that we at least take a detour to our room.

"We look too hot to just go to bed," she said. "It would be unfair to the guys."

That's when I spotted him. The one hot-dude I most wanted to see and least wanted to see, and had sort of been thinking about all evening. Roger.

He was sitting in the back lounge, reading *White Teeth* by Zadie Smith.

"Night, night." Veronica shoved me through the lounge doorway and disappeared.

"Dessy," Roger said, sitting up straight. "Wow, what time is it?"

"I have no idea," I said. It was around 2:30, but I wanted him to stay. "Let's talk."

"Sure. So, how are things going?"

"Things are great." I took a seat beside him and leaned forward to let him know that I was very interested in everything he had to say.

"Have you resolved everything with Corky?"

"Basically, she's still threatening me with bodily harm, but I'm not going to let that ruin my last week in Prague."

"Dessy, are you serious? I can't tell."

"As a heart attack. I'll be relying on you to save me once I've shown you the distress symbol."

"Which is?" Roger laughed and set down his book, which made me feel like I was making considerable progress.

"Good point," I said. "We need to pick a symbol."

I took hold of his hand and drew a circle with a dot in it.

It seemed basic enough. And it gave me a legitimate reason to slide my fingers across his skin.

"And if you don't get there in time to save me, I'll make sure to draw the symbol next to my body so that you'll know Corky was responsible for my demise." Then I pulled my hands back, because not letting go of his hand felt a little forward.

"That's pretty morbid," Roger said, still smiling.

"That's a good word for Corky."

"So what did you guys do tonight? You look like you just came from a dance club."

I smiled. "I did. And it was awesome. Do you like jungle music?"

"I don't know what jungle music is."

I tried to imitate the sounds from the club. *"Bom. Bom. Ta. Ta. Naha. Naha. Bom. Bom."*

"I didn't know you drank."

"I haven't been drinking! I've been living. Tick. Tock. Tick. Tock."

Roger put his head in his hands. "Waller says that all the time. It drives me nuts. We're not even twenty, Dessy."

This wasn't going as well as I'd hoped. I decided to change gears. "Wanna go for a walk? I'll show you a pub that still has a watermark from the big flood. Have you heard about Gaston the sea lion?"

"It's kinda late to head out to Malá Strana. We'd probably get mugged."

"Okay, okay. But at least let me tell you about Gaston the sea lion." I scooted over closer to him. "I'm pretty sure it was 1980. And it wouldn't stop raining in Prague."

Roger shook his head. "Gaston died in the flood of 2002. Did Waller tell you this story? Because I'm the one who told it to him."

I licked my lips. "Then tell me the story. I'm sure he got the whole thing wrong."

"Dessy, it's late. I think I'm ready for bed."

"Oh, don't be like that." I reached over and took his book away from him. "Let's stay and talk."

"You're acting weird."

"Weird, how?"

"You're acting like Veronica."

I got the feeling that he was insulting me, so I handed him his book back. He stood up and started walking toward the door. I crumbled into my chair.

"Aren't you going to go back to your room?" he asked.

I nodded. I felt like I'd blown everything. I'd had a great opportunity to bond with my hot-dude, and now he was leaving and we hadn't bonded at all.

Roger lingered in the doorway. "Hey, Dessy?"

I looked up at his cute, honest face.

"You don't need to act like this to get attention," he said.

I wasn't sure what he meant, but it certainly wasn't an invitation. So I stood up to leave. He held the lounge door open, and I passed through it. Then I started to drift toward my staircase and he started to drift toward his.

"Good night, Roger," I called after him.

He turned around. "Good night, Dessy."

I reluctantly headed toward my room, and then I heard Roger say something else. "I like your belt."

I flipped around to look at him again, but he'd already turned the corner and was gone.

Chapter Twenty-nine

I slept extremely late the next day. When I woke up, well after noon, Veronica was long gone. But I was thrilled to see that the man-wall had been stripped of all its hot-dudes. Finally, Veronica had come to her senses.

As six approached, I did my final primping and high-tailed it to the statue like the loyal friend I was. My excitement level dropped considerably when I saw that Veronica was wearing a black dress and strappy sandals. I was in my traditional jeans and T-shirt.

"You look great!" she said.

"I look like I'm about to go on a hike, and you look like you're ready to go to the governor's ball. I thought we were going on a boat ride."

Veronica nodded, making her voluminous and overly coifed hair slide into her face. "Yeah, but I think it's the kind of boat ride where they serve champagne and little sandwiches."

"I'm not dressed for that!" I said. "I thought we were going to go out in paddleboats."

Veronica grimaced. "Why would I want to subject myself to a paddleboat? Who wants to get *that* close to an Eastern European river? Gross. Isn't that what started the big plague?"

"No," I said. "Paddleboats didn't start the plague."

"You're so funny," she said. "I meant the river."

I rolled my eyes like that was a stupid comment, but stopped midroll when I realized that I wasn't sure whether or not the river had assisted in the dissemination of the plague.

Veronica walked up and gave me a big hug. "I'm so glad we patched things up. I hate it when we don't get along."

"Yeah," I said. "But don't you think it feels like we've still got some patching left to do?"

"No."

We found our bench from yesterday and sat down so we could watch the new horde of tourists that had flocked to the square. Veronica's bare shoulders looked incredibly creamy and petite in her black dress.

"Your shoulders do make you look older," I said.

"I know. I've somehow managed to develop the shoulders of a twenty- or possibly twenty-five-year-old. It's great."

I continued to search the crowd. There were so many people walking around on a Tuesday evening. It made me curious about their lives. What were their jobs? Were they all tourists? Why had they chosen to come to Prague?

"Do you want to know one of my favorite things about this city?" Veronica asked.

"What?" I asked.

"The smell of bread."

I inhaled deeply, but I couldn't detect the aroma of anything freshly baked in the air.

"I just smell city stuff," I said.

"Yeah, but when you walk past a bakery you smell bread."

"That's true for Ohio too," I said.

"But in Ohio I never walk anywhere. I always

drive. And when you walk, it's easier to smell stuff. Because you're going so much slower."

"I guess that's one liability of traveling at cheetah speed," I said. "You miss the smell of bread."

"Are you making fun of me?" Veronica asked.

"No," I said. "I mean, I might be making fun of cheetahs."

"Maybe we should talk about something else."

"Fine."

Neither one of us said anything for a minute.

"Jesus. Alexej and his friend are really late. What time is it?"

I hoped they didn't show up at all.

That's when I saw a shadowy figure approaching us. Oh god. It was Corky.

"What are you two kids waiting for?" she asked.

"None of your business," I said.

"We're just hanging out," said Veronica.

"I should probably tell you the reason I'm here," Corky said.

"Or you could just leave," Veronica said.

"First, I have something for you, Veronica." Corky handed her a Baggie filled with pieces of torn paper. "It might not look familiar to you, but it's something very precious," Corky said.

"Did you break into my room?" Veronica asked.

"That's beside the point," Corky said. "It's a picture of you. I paid one of the German photography students two bucks to take it. I actually bought two pictures."

"You're a pervert," Veronica said.

"Aren't you curious to know what you're doing in the picture?" Corky asked.

Veronica dumped the pieces onto her lap. I could see her face and Alexej's face. She rearranged the pieces until she unpuzzled the picture. Veronica and Alexej were kissing.

"The one I mailed to Boz isn't torn up," Corky said.

I inched closer to Veronica and put my arm around her. "Don't do anything. This will work itself out."

"But it really won't," Corky said. "Also, I'm sure you'll never hear from Alexej again. I told him how old you really are. Plus, it was obvious that he was just trying to get in your pants anyway."

By the look on Veronica's face, I knew she felt the consequences of what she'd done.

"And now I've got something else to tell you, and this is related to your hot-dudes," Corky said.

"It doesn't even matter anymore," I said. "Veronica took the man-wall down. The hot-dudes are behind us."

"What are you talking about?" Veronica asked. "I didn't take the man-wall down."

Corky laughed. "You idiots. I took the man-wall down. I collected all the hot-dudes in an envelope and mailed them to Boz along with a letter explaining that every single paper cutout of a guy represented one of your hookups."

"But that's not even true!" Veronica said. "I wasn't hooking up with them. I was flirting!"

"But with the picture I sent of Alexej, it doesn't look like that," Corky said. "And by the way, I feel like I've gotten everything I need out of this workshop, so I'm leaving for Slovenia, where I'll be taking part in another writers' program."

Veronica stared at the torn photo on her lap and then at Corky. Her hand shook with anger. "I'm going to hurt you," she said. Her voice was quiet, but believable.

"I doubt it," Corky said. "Oh, and I almost forgot. I e-mailed Boz about the stuff that's coming, so basically your relationship ended four hours ago."

Veronica narrowed her eyes and glared right at Corky. "I *will* hurt you."

"Then you will get sent home," Corky said.

"I don't care," Veronica said.

"Sure you do," Corky said.

I kept my arm tight around Veronica.

"Here's the thing, Veronica Knox. You are playing out of your league. You screwed with me and now I'm screwing you back. You shouldn't have looked at my e-mail. You shouldn't have read my blog. And you should have given me back my ankle bracelet when I asked for it."

"I am never giving you anything!" Veronica said.

"Which is precisely why I had to jack up your life," Corky said. "Because you think you're so ruthless. But really, you're just another pathetic, mean-spirited American teenager."

Corky laughed and waved. "I think this exchange has been illuminating for everyone involved. Even your sidekick. Bye, Dessy!"

She walked off in a very normal manner. At one point she even skipped a little, but not in a way that revealed her psychopathic tendencies.

"Why didn't you just give her back her ankle bracelet?" I asked.

"I couldn't," she said. "I'd already mailed it to Boz."

"Why would you do that?"

"I wanted him to think I was living on the edge," Veronica said. "I wanted to occupy every moment of his waking mind."

"Well, it looks like he gets to keep it."

"I can't believe she did this to me," Veronica said.

"What's done is done," I said, trying to sound reassuring. "Maybe you can fix it." But I wasn't sure if that was possible.

"But how can anyone be that messed up?" Veronica asked.

"Let's just leave her alone," I said. "She's dangerous."

Veronica sucked in a breath so deep that I could see her chest expand. "I won't let her leave Prague without feeling my math."

"Math?" I asked. "Do you mean wrath?"

"Maybe," Veronica said. "Either way, I'm going to teach her a lesson. I plan on bringing that head case to her ugly, chubby knees."

Chapter Thirty

 We arrived at the Church of Our Lady Victorious on Monday before the rest of the class.

"Today I hate my life," Veronica said.

I saw no point in trying to cheer Veronica out of her desperate and depressive state. Because if I were her, I would have felt the same. Veronica hadn't been able to rouse Boz in any way. He wouldn't answer his phone or return her e-mails. His mother even politely admonished Veronica to stop calling until things cooled off. By all accounts their relationship looked over.

"I'm nervous about seeing Roger." I glanced down the street to see if he was coming.

"I thought you said that things went good the other night. You told me he complimented your belt."

When pressed, rather than share with Veronica exactly what had happened, I'd once again opted for selectively withholding important information for the sake of creating a more pleasant reality.

"Relax. Roger wants to kiss your face off."

Because Veronica had been so off the mark with her Waller assessment, I didn't put much stock in her Roger one.

"You aren't going to do anything to Corky during class, right?" I asked. "Because that would be stupid."

"When the opportunity presents itself, I'll take it."

"Not in front of your mother!"

"You yell a lot more in Prague than you do in Ohio," Veronica said.

"That's because you frustrate me beyond belief a lot more in Prague than you do in Ohio."

I pulled out my notebook to look over my images. I'd described three somewhat Prague-related objects: a wounded pigeon eating french fries, a gorilla from the zoo, and my new belt. Veronica had gone hardcore Prague with hers: a broken headstone at the Old Jewish Cemetery, an ornate doorknocker, her bare foot on the bank of the Vltava River.

Veronica looked up at the towering church behind us. "I can't believe Mom is making the whole class gawk at a doll," Veronica said.

"It's a famous statue of infant Jesus," I said. "It's supposed to make miracles happen."

"But it's so hot out," she whined.

"Maybe it's air-conditioned inside."

"Dessy, this country doesn't understand the concept of air conditioning. They only understand pig-sweat heat."

We sat on the church steps and continued to bake.

"Corky is planning on leaving before anybody can find out that she's certifiably insane. It's not fair!"

"I say we let her go without incident. I, for one, want to see Corky slip out of my life and never return."

"If I see her at the church, I'm going to take her down."

"Veronica. You can't attack her during the Infant of Prague tour."

"I was thinking I'd do it afterward."

"You can't! I won't allow it!"

"Fine. Fine. I knew that would be your reaction."

"Let's just stay with the group."

Veronica smiled. "Okay."

This was very much unlike Veronica. She never surrendered this easily.

"What have you done?" I asked.

Veronica's smile intensified until she was baring her teeth.

"Let's just say that Corky's days of anonymously pestering people online are over."

"What did you do?"

"I hijacked her blog and posted her name. She's out. She's Corky Tina Baker."

"Veronica, why couldn't you wait until she'd left town? If she finds out, she'll kill you."

"I don't know. She seems pretty hung up on both of us."

"Veronica, it's gestures like these that make me question my ability to remain your best friend."

"I understand where you're coming from. But I had to do something. I couldn't let her win."

"Maybe the most important thing in life isn't winning! Maybe it's staying alive!"

"I'd rather be eating a doughnut," Veronica said.

I liked that idea.

There was a small sea of people streaming up the stone stairs to the church. They looked like tourists. Shorts. Cameras. Folded maps in hand.

"Do you think we look less like tourists?" I asked.

She looked at the crowd of people and then back at me.

"We look like cool tourists," she said. "You know, like we're happy to be here and we'll see what we see, but we're not running around like tightly wound freaks on a schedule."

I never heard her coming. One moment I was watching birds milling around some sidewalk crumbs, and the next thing I knew they had burst into flight and Corky was standing right in front of me, screaming.

"You idiots!"

"Go away!" Veronica said.

"In my world, squealers pay consequences!" Corky said. "Squealers get scars."

She was holding something silver in her hand. Was it a knife? A razor blade? Oh my god. How crazy was our crazy roommate?

"Run!" Veronica yelled. "Run!"

I leapt to my feet and shoved Corky. Then I followed Veronica. At first I was only a few yards behind her. But she quickly pulled ahead. I was stunned when I realized that she was an entire block ahead of me. I hadn't known Veronica was so good at sprinting. Soon I could hear Corky behind me, but I couldn't see Veronica in front of me at all. She'd left me. She'd infuriated a lunatic and then left me in that lunatic's path. It was unfathomable.

As I passed an alleyway, my arm nearly got ripped from its socket. I tried to scream, but a hand flew over my mouth. It was Veronica.

"Follow me this way," she said. "Even if she's realized that we've turned off, she won't be able to catch us. She's too fat."

And so I let Veronica lead me through back alleys that I hadn't even known existed, until suddenly we were back at the dorm.

We ran into the building and raced up the stairs to our room.

"She would never expect that we'd come back here," Veronica said.

As soon as she said that, the suite's front door slammed.

"I know you're in there!" Corky screamed.

"What should we do?" I whispered. "Should we call somebody?"

Veronica lunged for the phone, then whimpered, "It's been cut! It's dead!" She held up the sliced phone line. Corky!

I sat down and tried to mentally prepare myself for hand-to-hand combat.

But Veronica took a different tack. I watched her dramatically throw open our window.

"Are you going to jump?" I asked. I was sure leaping from this height would break both of her legs.

"When you flip into survival mode, you ask the stupidest questions," Veronica said.

She gathered our bedsheets and tied them together. As she tossed them out the window I thought maybe she had gone insane. Did she think we were going to climb out the window? I had no climbing abilities whatsoever. At seventeen, I'd never even managed to make it up a tree.

"Come help me tie it to the desk," Veronica hissed.

She looped her bedsheet around one of her desk's wooden legs. Her desk was the sturdiest item in the room. Unlike mine, hers was actually bolted to the floor.

"When she comes inside to attack us," Veronica whispered, "she'll see this and think we fled out the window."

"How will she think that when she sees us standing right here?"

"She won't see us. Because we'll be inside our suitcases."

She was either brilliant or suicidally dumb. Either way, I couldn't think of a better plan. So I zipped Veronica into her bag. But before I climbed inside I thought of something.

"Where's your lipstick?" I whispered.

"Everywhere."

I pawed over the desk looking for a tube, until I found one: Maneater Red. I snatched the sheets and pulled them back into the room. Then I attempted to draw a circle with a dot in it by smearing the lip color as fast as I could over the cotton surface. It only took seconds. I tossed the sheets out the window again.

"Is that some sort of weird tribal ritual?" Veronica asked, peeking out the corner of her bag.

I didn't I have time to explain. "I did it for luck," I whispered as I ran to my suitcase and climbed in. With my thumbnail I was able to guide the zipper all the way around to the top.

"Are you okay?"

I didn't answer. Was she being serious? My life was chaos, manwise and otherwise, and Corky wanted to permanently mark me as squealer with some weird scar. And I now was inside of my roller luggage.

"My bag smells like crayons."

I still didn't answer.

"You know I'm sorry. I didn't mean for things to get to this point. And I'm not just talking about Corky. I'm talking about Hamilton too."

"I don't want to talk about Hamilton."

"I know. He's a total jerk."

I didn't argue. But dating one jerk doesn't make all guys jerks. If I lived through this Corky crisis, I didn't need to let my heart stay broken. Like Roger. He was kind and smart and spicy-smelling and genuine. There had to be other boys like him in the world. I couldn't let Hamilton's actions spoil my entire future.

"How much longer do we have to stay in our suit-cases?" I asked.

"Until we know Corky's gone."

"I'm going to get my master key!" Corky yelled. "And then I'll be back."

"Don't move," Veronica said quietly. "She might be trying to flush us out."

"Do you really think she'll hurt us? Don't you think she's just trying to scare us?"

Suddenly I began to doubt all the threats. It seemed very plausible that Corky was invested in traumatizing us to the point where we'd hide and cower, but not actually intending to leave visible signs of an assault.

"Maybe she's bluffing. How come you're so quiet?" Veronica asked me.

"I'm thinking," I said.

"About what?"

"Annie Earl."

"Hey," Veronica said. "She told a bunch of us at the mid dinner how she got her scars. She broke into a burning car."

"She told me too," I said.

"When I first heard her story I couldn't stop thinking about it," Veronica said. "It made me feel terrible about the entire world. For, like, twenty minutes."

"It altered her life."

"It's good you missed the dinner. Because there were a ton of stories like that. It's too bad that everyone has to go through such giant traumas," Veronica said.

"You know what?"

"What?"

"I think that's life."

"Screw that," Veronica said. "I'm trying to avoid crap like that. I mean, I think that's part of the reason I'm slightly dishonest and, at times, mean to people. I'm protecting myself."

I ignored this statement because it seemed pretty clear to me that our current trauma was the direct result of her actions.

"I have a feeling that I'm going to experience four life traumas," I said.

"Four!" Veronica whisper-yelled.

"Yeah. I have this feeling that I'm getting more than three, but less than five."

"Well, that's four."

"But I'll deal with them, you know?"

"What if you lose both your legs?" Veronica asked.

"I'm not going to lose both my legs. Don't be stupid." I gently punched the inside of my bag to imitate the gesture of punching her in the arm.

"I don't know," she mused. "I'm sure people who lose both their legs always thought it would never happen to them either."

"What are you trying to say?" I wasn't in the mood to listen to Veronica joke around. I was thinking about serious life issues.

"Let's just say you did lose both your legs. Would you use prosthetic limbs or would you just use a wheelchair or how would you handle it?"

Only Veronica Knox would ask me that question. And even though it annoyed me on several levels, I also sort of liked it.

"I'd probably use prosthetic limbs," I said.

"Yeah. Me too," she said.

"What I'm getting at here is that I'm going to make the choices that determine what's going to happen and what's not going to happen to me. As much as Hamilton was a jerk for cheating on me and then laminating my flaws, there was some truth in what he said."

"If Boz ever tried to hand me my flaws like that, I'd either gouge his eyes out or force his mouth open and make him eat my flaws."

"I can't let other people make important choices for me. I want to stand on my own."

"Hey. Are you saying we can't be friends anymore? Because I totally love you, Dessy Gherkin."

"We can still be friends," I said. "But I'm going to have to make more decisions. And I can't let you pay for stuff."

"Wow. That's going to completely overhaul our dynamic."

"I think it will be good for both of us."

"Maybe."

"You need some free time to straighten things out with Boz," I said.

"I don't know, Dessy. I think I really screwed up. You were right. I really hurt him."

"You need to fix it."

"How do you unhurt somebody?" Veronica asked.

"Just start being a decent human being again. You've got it in you. No more lying. Or manipulating. Or blackmailing."

"You make it sound like I have to become a whole different person."

The sound of knocking halted our conversation once again.

"Dessy?" a male voice asked. "Are you in there?"

I stayed very quiet. It was a familiar voice.

"You've got a bedsheet with a circle and a dot drawn on it hanging out your window," Roger said. "And your front door is wide open. What's going on? Are you okay?"

"No!" Veronica yelled. "We're not okay. Corky is trying to cut us!"

"Open the door!" he said.

"Veronica," I said. "My zipper is stuck."

"Mine too!"

"We're coming," I called to Roger.

"I can't budge it," Veronica said.

"Open it now!" Roger said. "Or I'll break it down."

"Oh my god," Veronica said. "This is so romantic."

Stuffed inside my suitcase, I felt sweat dripping

down my back, and I could smell my own feet.

"No," I said. "It really isn't."

I heard the sound of a body slamming against the door. Then I heard the sound of the door breaking open. I finally got my zipper to move.

"Dessy?"

"In here!" I yelled.

I felt Roger tip me onto the floor. With the zipper now unstuck, he peeled open the case quickly, and I crawled out of the bag.

"Get me out of here!" Veronica yelled.

Roger unzipped her bag, and she spilled out onto the floor in a sweaty mess.

That's when I heard the distinct sound of grunting. I couldn't believe my eyes. It was Corky. She was climbing up the bedsheet. She was almost to the top.

All three of us watched as Corky's fingers grabbed on to the ledge and she pulled herself up to our small balcony.

"Oh god. Is that a straight razor between her teeth?" Roger asked.

"Yes," Veronica said. "Run!"

But Roger stayed put. He had his eyes locked on Corky, who seemed to be weighing the situation. To me, it looked like she was losing strength.

She let the blade fall from her mouth and screamed, "This isn't over, Veronica!" Then she disappeared.

"I never guessed she had that kind of upper-body strength," Veronica said. She reached over and picked up the blade. "It's real! She was going to cut our ears off or something, just like that poor goat."

"What?" Roger asked. "Corky maimed a goat?"

By this time I could hear other people racing down the hallway.

Two security guards stormed into the room and

began yelling at Veronica. "Drop it! Drop it!"

Veronica tossed the blade onto the floor. "I'm not the criminal. She just left. She's short and chubby and homicidal and wearing outdated clogs."

"That's right," Roger said.

The guards seemed more persuaded by Roger than Veronica. They yelled into their walkie-talkies and hurried down the hall.

"Do you think they'll catch her?" I asked.

Veronica rolled her eyes. "I have no faith in that duo to apprehend anyone, let alone somebody as crafty as Corky Tina Baker."

"She's been terrorizing you this whole time?" Roger asked me with wide eyes.

I nodded.

"I have a feeling there's a lot more to this story," he said.

"Best told at a later date," Veronica said.

"I agree," I said. "I'm just happy that she's gone."

"Totally. And we owe some serious thanks to you, Roger."

Veronica moved toward him, and for a second I thought she was going to shake his hand. "Your brave act of breaking into the room and assisting us out of our bags has almost made me a believer in miracles."

"Even after this you don't believe in miracles?" Roger asked.

"Oh no," Veronica said. "I barely started believing in Jesus four years ago."

Roger laughed and looked at me. The panic that had overtaken the room moments ago was turning into something else. I realized that I'd been staring at him. I quickly glanced around the room, and as I did, everything took on a heightened importance. The desks. The beds. The suitcases. Roger. Roger's blinking brown eyes.

Wait. Were they hazel? Wait. I shouldn't start staring at Roger again. Wait. Was Roger *still* looking at me? I felt warm.

Veronica walked to the window and yanked the bed sheets back into the room. She inspected the giant lipstick smear. "Why did you draw the flag of Japan on here?"

Roger cleared his throat. "It's not the flag of Japan. It's a distress signal."

Veronica rubbed at the red stain with her thumb. "We'll need to buy some bleach. It's the only way to get this shade out of fabric. Trust me." Roger smiled at me, then looked away. He kept wrinkling and relaxing his forehead. He seemed nervous.

"Well, it looks like we've missed class," he said.

"Are you guys hungry? Maybe we could grab lunch."

"Maybe," I said. Why did I say 'maybe'? Why didn't I say 'definitely'? Because that was how I felt.

"I found a good Italian place. Are you guys missing pasta?"

"Pasta sounds great," I said.

"Maybe you two should go together," Veronica said. "I'm going to go back to the church to look at that doll with my mom. Plus, I can fill her in on the fact that, following a violent outburst, one of our class members has fled the program and is currently being sought after by authorities."

"I'm sure that will be a fun conversation." I stood up and grabbed my wallet. Excitement tumbled through me.

"Have fun," Veronica told us.

"You don't need to tell me twice," Roger said.

"Take some pictures."

"Of the pasta?" I asked.

"Of your day. Maybe you two should visit the castle afterward."

"Good idea," Roger said. He was smiling at me again, and I knew it meant something real.

"Maybe we will," I said.

Roger opened the door for me. I picked up my camera and put it in my bag. I liked the idea of having some photographic evidence of my day with Roger. Maybe when I got back to Ohio I could make him a funny collage and send it to him. Who knew, maybe after this vacation we could stay in each other's lives. There were so many good colleges in Chicago. Maybe this didn't have to end in a week. As we walked down the stairs, Roger's hand swept past mine. I wanted him to take it, so I moved it closer to him until it brushed against his leg. He reached down and threaded his fingers through mine. My heart pumped so fast that it began to flutter. *Thup. Thup. Thup. Thup.* It made me feel wild and happy, like at any moment my heart might fly right out of my chest, down the hallway, into the streets, all the way to the castle.

At last it felt new and ready.